ANCESTRAL SHADOWS

ANCESTRAL SHADOWS

An Anthology of Ghostly Tales

RUSSELL KIRK

Edited with an introduction by
VIGEN GUROIAN

WILLIAM B. EERDMANS PUBLISHING COMPANY
GRAND RAPIDS, MICHIGAN / CAMBRIDGE, U.K.

Wm. B. Eerdmans Publishing Co.
255 Jefferson Ave. S.E., Grand Rapids, Michigan 49503 /
P.O. Box 163, Cambridge CB3 9PU U.K.

Printed in the United States of America

09 08 07 06 05 04   7 6 5 4 3 2 1

Library of Congress Cataloging-in-Publication Data

Kirk, Russell
Ancestral shadows: an anthology of ghostly tales/ Russell Kirk.
p.   cm.
ISBN 0-8028-3938-X
1. Ghost stories, American.   I. Title.

PS3521.I665A83   2004
813'.54 — dc22
2004047235

www.eerdmans.com

Contents

CONTENTS

Introduction

Russell Kirk is known best for his major contributions to the modern conservative movement. His seminal work, *The Conservative Mind*, remains, after more than half a century, the authoritative study of the lineage of Anglo-American conservatism from Edmund Burke to T. S. Eliot. Over a period of forty years, until his death in 1994, Kirk published a prodigious number of books and essays in the fields of intellectual history, politics, and literature, including *Beyond the Dreams of Avarice* (1956), *Enemies of the Permanent Things* (1969), *Eliot and His Age* (1971), *Roots of American Order* (1974), and, posthumously, *Redeeming the Time* (1995).

Many readers familiar with Kirk's scholarly writings are often surprised to discover that he was an accomplished fiction writer who gained a wide and enthusiastic audience among devotees of gothic and fantasy literature. Not often did these two public worlds of Russell Kirk meet — political and literary essayist and author of gothic fiction — except perhaps at Piety Hill, Kirk's ancestral home in Mecosta, Michigan, where the Wizard of Mecosta frequently regaled guests with a succession of ghostly tales.

For a comprehensive understanding of Kirk's conservative vision, a familiarity with his fiction is necessary, for it is here that Kirk's rich imaginative mind vividly casts the drama of the soul's struggle with good and evil in relation to a transcendent realm of meaning and purpose. It is in his fiction that Kirk puts to the test his principles. Eschewing didacticism, Kirk infuses into his stories his most deeply held religious, moral, and political convictions — especially belief in divine providence, a higher moral law, eternal life, and the dual nature of the human being as body and spirit.

Furthermore, his stories evoke T. S. Eliot's "permanent things," which Kirk believes are under assault in our day from political rationalism, big government, commercialism, and secularism.

Most of the stories here appeared originally in genre magazines and anthologies; but over the course of two decades, Kirk collected them in three volumes: *The Surly Sullen Bell* (1962), *The Princess of All Lands* (1979), and *Watchers at the Strait Gate* (1984). He also penned three full-length novels: *Old House of Fear* (1961), *A Creature of the Twilight* (1966), and *Lord of the Hollow Dark* (1980).

Reviewers have commented extensively on the relationship of Kirk's fiction to the gothic genre in general. Most conclude that Kirk is no mere imitator of the masters but develops a unique style, distinguished by strong ethical, metaphysical, and theological insights. Through his stories, Kirk portrays a world in which genuinely retributive and redemptive deeds are performed. This action is cast within a Christian vision of life, death, and resurrection and of time and eternity.

In a review of *Watchers at the Strait Gate*, the late Southern essayist, literary critic, and writer of fiction Andrew Lytle observes, "The subject of most contemporary ghost stories is profane. The supernatural is spurious. At best it is magic, the effort to force nature to act beyond its properties. The illusion so provoked is sentimental. It depends upon the victim's acceptance of fantasy instead of the profound meaning of symbol," as sign, revelation, and source of participation in a divine and eternal reality. Not so with Kirk.

Lytle's criticism of most contemporary supernatural fiction is surely just; typically, the spirits in these ghost stories are the gothic equivalent of science-fiction aliens from outer space, not avengers or messengers of God. The "supernatural," if it indeed is named such, is not truly *super natural*, but rather the magical, the occult, or the parapsychological. Unsurprisingly, therefore, the ghosts and the persons whom they "haunt" are not moved by any discernible belief in or fear of God. Nor is the reader invited to consider seriously the claims of religion. Although it might be said that many protagonists of these stories live a kind of "purgatorial" existence, inasmuch as they are "tested," their trials do not ordinarily involve the prospect of an eternal hereafter. These stories are constricted within the narrow borders of a worldview that is entirely naturalist. There are no eternal rewards or punishments.

In "A Cautionary Note on the Ghostly Tale," Kirk wonders whether indeed it is possible any longer for "fiction of the supernatural or preternatural, with . . . roots in myth and transcendent perception . . . [to] succeed in being anything better than playful or absurd?" That, I suspect, is a contributing reason as to why Kirk speaks of his stories as "experiments in the moral imagination." In his fiction, Kirk deliberately employs "elements of parable and fable." He aims to evoke in his reader's imagination intimations of divine presence, eternity, and immortality. "Gerald Heard [Kirk writes] said to me once that the good ghost story must have for its kernel some clear premise about the character of human existence — some theological premise, if you will."

Kirk's early stories, written during the 1950s and 1960s, are noteworthy for their acerbic criticism of political rationalism and government-sponsored social engineering projects of the day. He offers up petty bureaucrats and government agents who, with an unflinching and sometimes maniacal faith in technology and progress, threaten grave harm to the complex ecology of human life. Without the slightest regret, they are intent upon ripping up the precious fabric of traditional community and old habits of life. The story "Ex Tenebris" portrays S. G. W. Barner, Planning Officer, an arrogant and willful official who "had made up his mind that not one stone was to be left upon another at Low Wentford. With satisfaction he had seen the last of the farm-laborers of that hamlet transferred to the new council-houses at Gorst, where there was no lack of communal facilities, including six cinemas." As with other characters in Kirk's stories, Barner runs up against a ghostly agent of divine wrath.

Kirk's later stories, particularly those written in the 1970s and 1980s, are increasingly metaphysical and theological. Kirk embraces the Christian vision of life and death, fall and redemption. He does not dogmatize, however. Rather, he experiments imaginatively with possibilities of how we are eternally judged, what the nature of the "otherworldly" journey is, and what heaven and hell are like. The purpose is not to "nail down" what life after death is, but rather to help us see how our earthly lives might be improved and how we can more effectively care for our souls and the souls of others.

Kirk is a student of the great poets who have offered their own imaginative interpretations of these soteriological mysteries: Homer, Virgil, Dante, Milton, and Eliot. If his stories are "scary," it is not just because the house is haunted; the eternal destinies of human souls hang in the balance. Kirk especially employs T. S. Eliot's images of the Wasteland and poetic evocations of the experience of eternity within temporal existence. In "There's a Long, Long Trail A-Winding," recipient of a World Fantasy Award in 1977, hobo-sojourner Frank Sarsfield cuts his way through a savage blizzard into a desolate town where he takes temporary shelter in a grand old home that is no longer inhabited. Here Frank performs, by sheer willing or actual deed — it matters not, says Father O'Malley, because "what God counts is the intention" — that "Signal Act of contrition" which releases Frank from his peregrine purgatorial existence here on earth and allows him to enter heaven through the strait gate.

Kirk commences this story with a memorable description of the dying rural village of Anthonyville. It is interesting to note that a remote village — not just New York, London, or some other major metropolis — symbolizes for Kirk the spirit of the modern Wasteland. Anthonyville has been made inhospitable to genuine human community and spiritual journeying by a new, thoroughly utilitarian superhighway that bisects the village. In addition, the forests that once surrounded it have been cut down by a defunct lumber industry, leaving behind a hellish landscape of stovepipe stumps. In the midst of this desolation a "skeletal church" remains; however, its windows are blown out, and the door flaps aimlessly in the wind and admits no worshippers. The village hall is a "wreck"; no one meets in it any longer. And empty "decrepit cottages" line Main Street. Into this derelict scene enters the vagabond pilgrim Frank Sarsfield, heading toward the definitive moment of his life:

> Along the vast empty six-lane highway, the blizzard swept as if it meant to swallow all the sensual world. Frank Sarsfield, massive though he was, scudded like a heavy kite before that overwhelming wind. . . . He had walked more than thirty miles that day. . . . This was depopulated country, its forests gone to the sawmills long before, its mines worked out. The freeway ran through the abomination of desolation. . . . Main Street ended at [a] grove or park of old maples. . . . Had the trees not been leafless, he might not have discerned the big stone house among the trees. . . . Had he visited this house before?

In other stories, water, fire, iconography, hieratic gestures, and dream-like encounters with spirits convey sacramental meaning. "Saviourgate," "The Peculiar Demesne of Archvicar Gerontion," and "An

Encounter by Mortstone Pond" are noteworthy examples. In "The Peculiar Demesne," hero Manfred Arcane recounts to a small audience of guests his tale of a preternatural "dream" experience in which he is pursued by an "abominable corpse-candle," specter of one Archvicar Gerontion. The name and apparition are literary allusions: Gerontion is the sterile and despairing old man of T. S. Eliot's poem; the "corpse candle" is an image drawn from Canto XXVI of Dante's *Inferno*. In the Eighth Bolgia of the Eighth Circle, sinners who counseled fraud wander for eternity wrapped in a tall flame. The Archvicar is of the same character, having led a heretical "Church of the Divine Mystery" whose creed was the inverse of the Christian confession and through which he defrauded his followers. The Archvicar has "lived" several consecutive "lives" by seizing and "wearing" the bodies of his victims, prompted by his demonic thirst for immortality. Arcane struggles against and finally escapes the Archvicar's attempts to "use" him in the same manner by taking refuge in a church:

> "I dashed into the immensity of that church. Where might I possibly conceal myself from the faceless hunter? I blundered into a side-chapel. . . . Over its battered altar, an icon of Christ the King still was fixed, though lance-thrusts had mutilated the face. I clambered upon the altar and clasped the picture. . . .
>
> "The tall glow of corruption had got so far as that doorway, and now lingered upon the threshold. For a moment, as if by a final frantic effort, it shone brightly. Then the corpse-candle went out as if an extinguisher had been clapped over it. The damaged icon broke loose from the wall, and with it in my arms I fell from the altar. . . .
>
> "[Later] they had found that the Archvicar had fallen out of his wheelchair and was stretched very dead on the floor. After a short search, they discovered me in this little room where we sit now. I was not conscious, and had suffered some cuts and bruises. Apparently I had crawled here in a daze, grasped the feet of Our Lord there" — nodding toward the Spanish Christ upon the wall — "and the crucifix had fallen upon me, as the icon had fallen in that desecrated church. These correspondences!"

Good and evil have transcendent beginnings. Both are mysteries. Both also are active powers in this world. Yet on the cross, Jesus Christ perfected human belief and the struggle *(askesis)* for purity. He won the final victory of Good over Evil. In "The Peculiar Demesne of Archvicar Gerontion," crucifix and icon of the Pantocrator symbolize this victory. Like Satan, the Archvicar is doomed. Nevertheless, not all of Arcane's guests are convinced. "How do we know that he [the Archvicar] failed?" asks one. Could it be that the demon Archvicar even now inhabits Arcane's body and that the "real" Manfred Arcane no longer exists? Arcane invites his listeners to consider that possibility. Am I "Evil Incarnate?" he taunts. His answer, when it comes, is expressed not in words but by symbolic gesture: "Yet before leading us out of that little room and back to the Christmas waltzers, Arcane genuflected beneath the crucified figure on the wall."

Kirk's ghostly tales challenge the secular belief that man is the measure of all things and that nature constitutes the whole of reality. Some conclude that man's measure is purely a "subjective" judgment, based on emotion and desire; others maintain that this measure is "objective," that it stands on science's account of human origins and humanity's place in the natural order. Both of these views uncritically embrace naturalism and, implicitly if not explicitly, reject supernaturalism.

Kirk invites us to reconsider what historic biblical faith affirms: that a transcendent and divine reality intersects, and intervenes in, nature and time. His stories beckon us once more to imagine that not only is God the source of our existence and its sustainer, but also that our human freedom and morality do not stand on their own. Rather, they issue from God and point us back to him. Kirk is fully aware that vast numbers of people resist these conclusions. In his autobiography, *The Sword of Imagination* (1995), he observes that if the Resurrection were found to be literally true, it would be a "horrid" prospect for "many twentieth-century folk," because "if the Resurrection should be conceivable, might not a Last Judgment be conceivable? And who could put up with that?"

Judgment is the central theological and moral theme of Kirk's stories. Judgment may be retributive and punitive, but it also can be atoning and salvific. A comprehensive Christian vision holds these apparently contradictory or competing meanings together. It looks at these qualities as facets of one indivisible divine judgment. God's judgment is the final declaration of the truth about each of our lives. If we hear and receive that truth honestly and with an open heart, we will repent and happily acknowledge our dependence upon God's mercy. Thus, paradoxically, judgment also opens our lives to God's love and forgiveness, which transform us from sinful beings into righteous and holy ones.

Kirk dramatizes these several aspects of judgment in his stories. In some, avenging and retributive ghosts bring mortal terror upon a principal character (the ghost of vicar Abner Hargreaves in "Ex Tenebris," and the grotesque specter of Lord Balgrummo in "Balgrummo's Hell"). In other stories, ghosts of mercy lead characters to penance (as, for example, the spirit of Fork Causland in "The Invasion of the Church of the Holy Ghost," and Frank Sarsfield in "Watchers at the Strait Gate"). Elsewhere, Kirk contrives to bring together all of these elements of judgment, such as in "The Reflex-Man in Whinnymuir Close."

Kirk believes that divine judgment is a sign and symbol of God's love. Behind this veil of suffering and tears, God, who *is* love, desires our salvation. Thus, Kirk's stories are never merely dark and dreadful; each is pierced by shafts of light and hope. In a sinful and broken world, however, the price of hope invariably is attended with suffering and pain. Nevertheless, hope — hope even in resurrection and eternal life — has substance because it is the gift of a loving and forgiving God.

In "The Reflex-Man in Whinnymuir Close," an aged Janet Kenly, forty years after the death of her one true earthly love, does not despair over her past transgressions. Instead, she repents and waits with hope for her own release from this world of sorrows and entry into the joys of the heavenly kingdom: "I have sinned, O Lord, but let my cry come unto thee. Let me with Ian be forever not semblance, but substance. I have survived the hero these forty years: now let thy faithless servant depart in peace, awaiting the Last Trump. I have put away my vanity: let him who reads this do likewise."

Sometimes the kingdom of God comes by force. This can be in one of two ways, however. It may be through the exhaustion of a person's energy, the complete, unselfish sacrifice of self for the sake of another or others. Frank Sarsfield in "There's a Long, Long Trail A-Winding" and Ralph Bain in "Sorworth Place" are called to such sacrifice. In other instances, an individual's soul must be laid bare completely: the force or violence is not something that the person expends but rather something that is expended on him. It shakes one's entire being, and yet one survives and is made whole by the event. Father Raymond Thomas Montrose in one of Kirk's best stories, "The Invasion of the Church of the Holy Ghost," undergoes just such a transformation.

Additionally, Kirk holds that judgment is not merely individual but also social and even cosmic in scope. The whole of the modern world is under judgment, having drifted away from divine truth and righteousness and become impious and often fiercely anti-human. The terrain that Kirk's characters inhabit is T. S. Eliot's Wasteland, a landscape strewn with broken objects and images from the past, ideas and beliefs, hopes and dreams that once constituted a uniform culture informed by a vital Christian faith. The Wasteland is our modern cities and suburbs; but it reaches farther, even into the smallest country village. The decay and despair, the violence and destruction of life in the modern world are not merely external to the self, however. The Wasteland is within us also. We are porous to it. We breathe it in and out like the noxious gas fumes of cars. It is our total environment, deadly not only to our bodies but, more importantly, to our souls. Only if we recognize the truth of this assertion is there hope that the time may be redeemed. But how can people so blind to the deformation of modern society be brought to this recognition?

Flannery O'Connor, who needs no introduction as a master of the short story, writes the following in her essay "Some Aspects of the Grotesque in Southern Fiction":

> If the writer . . . looks upon us as beings existing in a created order to whose laws we freely respond, then what he sees on the surface will be of interest to him only as he can go through it into an experience of mystery itself. His kind of fiction will always be pushing its own limits outward toward the limits of mystery, because for this kind of writer, the meaning of a story does not begin except at a depth where the adequate motivation and the adequate psychology and the various determinations have been exhausted. Such a writer will be interested in . . . possibility rather than probability. He will be interested in characters who are forced out to meet evil and grace and who act on a trust beyond themselves — whether they know very clearly what it is they act upon or not.

What O'Connor says here undoubtedly applies to Kirk's gothic tales. In order to challenge effectively modern man's unbelief, his resistance to grace, and his blindness to mystery, Kirk creates stories that aim to penetrate the thick wall of naturalism and secularism that shuts people off from mystery and grace. This similarity with O'Connor is not entirely accidental. Kirk and O'Connor learned from the same masters of the gothic tale, and Kirk read and deeply admired O'Connor's own work. In his autobiography he reminisces about the time he met Flannery and how she later described him in one of her letters as looking like "Humpty Dumpty (intact) with constant cigar and (outside) porkpie hat." Kirk writes that he wholly understood "her fantastic and depraved characters, their twisted faith and all," because he had met the same sort of people in Mecosta County, who "emerged repeatedly" in his own stories. With palpable affection, Kirk adds, "She must have surmised, with her quick charitable insights, that the taciturn Humpty Dumpty esteemed her. Beyond time, we two, who met but once, may be enfolded in the community of souls."

In order to evoke the mysterious successfully, the writer must not disparage concrete life, for mystery reveals itself in and through the everyday. "Fiction begins where human knowledge begins — with the senses," writes O'Connor, "and every fiction writer is bound by this fundamental aspect of the medium. I do believe, however, that this kind of writer ... will use the concrete in a more drastic way." Thus, O'Connor presses the ordinary out to the extreme, where a drowning becomes a scene of baptismal death and rebirth, and a water stain on a bedroom ceiling becomes a predatory bird that swoops down upon a young man with Pentecostal grace.

The inhabitants of the modern Wasteland, starved of the moral and religious imagination, cannot perceive that life transcends the bounds of the physical senses. Kirk is persuaded that much of his audience is also deaf to what T. S. Eliot calls the "communication of the dead." Thus, we moderns grow increasingly lonely, despite ever more instantaneous forms of "communication" that technology makes available; and loneliness is far more dangerous to the soul than bodily violence. Many of Kirk's stories include characters who experience loneliness and find relief from it only when at last they dare to give themselves up to the mystery represented in love, the human other, and God. This self-release comes often in the face of not only violence but also death. Frank Sarsfield, Ralph Bain, and Frank Loring, three of Kirk's most memorable characters, do dare and are rewarded with an experience of a communion of the living and the dead that stretches across time and eternity.

The final story of this collection, "An Encounter by Mortstone Pond," is Kirk's little masterpiece, a haunting evocation of how time and eternity meet in the human soul and consciousness, wherein also God is present and speaks to the person. Here Kirk probes the deep transcendental relation of the self to itself and to God, which Saint Augustine brings to our attention in his *Confessions*:

> How can I call unto my God? . . . For in calling unto Him, I am calling Him to me; and what room is there in me for my God, the God who made heaven and earth? . . . Yet, since nothing that is could exist without You, You must in some way be in all that is: [therefore also in me, since I am]. . . . Thus, O God, I should be nothing, utterly nothing, unless You were in me — or rather unless I were in You . . .

As with so many of his stories, "Mortstone Pond" is based on people and places known to Kirk. In *The Sword of Imagination*, he writes,

> While little Russell was a baby, the family of three tenanted what had been the miller's house above the millpond, a very handsome Greek Revival dwelling, with a gaggle of rat-infested woodsheds to its rear, and spreading lawns. It still stands today, well maintained — the last of Plymouth's fine old houses. House and pond, six decades later, would supply the setting for Kirk's mystical tale "An Encounter by Mortstone Pond." Close by lay the Plymouth Village Cemetery [also in the story], disused and neglected since 1871. . . . With his grandfather Pierce, the boy Russell often would poke about that graveyard. There entered his head, early, something like T. S. Eliot's awareness that the communication of the dead is tongued with fire.

The Eliot passage about "the communication of the dead . . . tongued with fire" is the epitaph on the gravestone of the mother of Kirk's chief character in "Mortstone Pond," Gerard Pierce. Kirk chooses another closely related passage from Eliot's poem "Little Gidding" to head the story:

> We die with the dying:
> See, they depart, and we go with them.
> We are born with the dead:
> See, they return, and bring us with them.
> The moment of the rose and the moment of the yew-tree
> Are of equal duration.

These passages bind and enfold "An Encounter by Mortstone Pond": they are its spine and covers. In poetic speech they express the mystery that the story symbolizes: in God's vision our beginning and our end are a single "moment" within eternity. ("The moment of the rose and the moment of the yew-tree are of equal duration.") But Kirk instills another message into his story. God from eternity pronounces words of grace that possess redemptive power through revelatory "timeless moments" in our lives. The encounter by Mortstone Pond is such a "timeless moment." In twin crises of youth and old age, when loneliness and despair are about to overcome him, Gerard Pierce experiences a "timeless moment" that redeems his life. From this "single" moment of communication and communion, "twice" experienced, Gerard gains a sense of unity and meaning in his life — assurance that his parents continue to love him, and confidence that "a tender 'Other'" embraces them in His infinite love.

ANCESTRAL SHADOWS

Ex Tenebris

Then shall it be too late to knock when the door shall be shut; and too late to cry for mercy when it is the time of justice. O terrible voice of the most just judgment which shall be pronounced upon them, when shall it be said unto them, Go ye cursed into the fire everlasting, which is prepared for the devil and his angels.

A Commination, or Denouncing of
God's Anger and Judgments against Sinners.

Only one roof at Low Wentford is sound today. On either side of the lane, a row of stone cottages stands empty. Twenty years ago there were three times as many; but now the rest are rubble. A gutted shell of Victorian masonry is the ruin of the schoolhouse. Close by the brook, the church of All Saints stares drearily into its desolate graveyard; a good fifteenth century building, All Saints, but the glass smashed in its windows and the slates slipping one after another from the roof. It has been deconsecrated all this century. Beside it, the vicarage — after the soldiers quartered there had finished with it — was demolished for the sake of what its woodwork and fittings would bring.

In the last sound cottage lives Mrs. Oliver, an ancient little woman with a nose that very nearly meets her chin. She wears a countrywoman's cloak of the old pattern, and weeds her garden, and sometimes walks as far as the high-arched bridge which, built long before the cottages, has survived them. Mrs. Oliver has no neighbors nearer than the Oghams of

Wentford House, a mile down a bedraggled avenue of limes and beeches twisting through the neglected park to the stables of that Queen Anne mansion.

Nearly three years ago, Sir Gerald Ogham sold the cottage to Mrs. Oliver, who had come back from Madras to the village where she was born. In all the parish, no one remained who remembered Mrs. Oliver. She had gone out to India with her husband, the Major; no one knew how long ago that had been — not even Mrs. Oliver, perhaps — with any precision, for she had known Sir Gerald's father, but had grown vague about decades and such trifles. Sir Gerald himself, though he was past sixty, could recollect of her only that her name had been an old one in the village.

Village? Like the money of the Oghams, it had faded quite away: the Ogham fortunes and Low Wentford now were close to extinction. The wealth of the Oghams was gone to the wars and the Exchequer; the last of the villagers had been drained away to the mills at Gorst, when tractors had supplanted horses upon the farms which Sir Gerald had sold to a potato syndicate. Behind the shutters of the sixty rooms of Wentford House, a solitary daily woman did what she could to supply the place of twenty servants. Lady Ogham and the gardener and the gardener's boy grew flowers and vegetables in the walled garden, to be sold in Gorst; Sir Gerald, with a feckless bailiff and a half-dozen laborers, struggled to wrest a few hundred pounds' income from the home farm and the few fields he had left besides. The family name still meaning something roundabout, Sir Gerald sat in the county council, where he sided with a forlorn minority overborne by the councillors from sprawling Gorst.

Sir Gerald had tried to sell the other habitable cottages in Low Wentford; but the planning officer, backed by the sanitary officer, had put obstacles in the way. And it was only because they had been unable at the time to provide a council-flat for old Mrs. Oliver that they had permitted her to repair the cottage near the church. The windows were too small, the sanitary officer and the planning officer had said; but Mrs. Oliver had murmured that in Madras she had seen enough of the sun to last her all her days. The ceilings were lower than regulations specified; but Mrs. Oliver had replied that the coal ration would go the further for that. It must be damp, the sanitary officer felt sure; but he was unable to prove it. There were no communal amenities, said the planning officer; but Mrs. Oliver, deaf as well as dim of sight, told him she disliked Communists. The authorities yielding, Mrs. Oliver had moved in with her Indian keepsakes and her few sticks of furniture, proceeding to train rosebushes against the old walls and to spade her own little garden; for, despite her great age, she was not feeble of body or of will.

Mr. S. G. W. Barner, Planning Officer, had a will of his own, nevertheless, and he had made up his mind that not one stone was to be left upon another at Low Wentford. With satisfaction he had seen the last of the farm-laborers of that hamlet transferred to the new council houses at Gorst, where there was no lack of communal facilities, including six cinemas. Thus were they integrated with the progressive aspirations of planned industrial society, he told the county council. Privately, he was convinced that the agricultural laborer ought to be liquidated altogether. And why not? Advanced planning, within a few years, surely would liberate progressive societies from dependence upon old-fashioned farming. He disliked the whole notion of agriculture, with its rude earthiness, its reactionary views of life and labor, its subservience to tradition. The agricultural classes would be absorbed into the centers of population, or otherwise disposed of; the land thus placed at public command would be converted into garden cities, or state holiday-camps, or proving grounds for industrial and military experiment.

With a positive passion of social indignation then, S. G. W. Barner — a thick-chested, hairy man, forever carrying a dispatch case, stooping and heavy of tread, rather like a large, earnest ape (as Sir Gerald had observed to Lady Ogham, after an unpleasant encounter at a county-council meeting) — objected against Mrs. Oliver's tenancy of the little red-tiled cottage. His consolation had been that she had not long to live, being wrinkled and gnarled amazingly. To his chagrin, however, she seemed to thrive in the loneliness of Low Wentford, her cheeks growing rosier, her step more sure. She must be got out of that cottage by compulsory purchase, if nothing else would serve. On Mr. Barner's maps of the Rural District of Low Wentford as it would be in the future, there remained no vexatious dots to represent cottages by the old bridge; nor was there any little cross to represent the derelict church. (No church had yet been erected in the newest housing scheme at Gorst: Cultural Amenities must yield pride of place to material requirements, Barner had declared.)

Yes, that wreck of a church must come down, with what remained of Low Wentford. Ruins are reminiscent of the past; and the Past is a dead hand impeding progressive planning. Besides, Low Wentford had been a hamlet immediately dependent upon Wentford House and its baronets, and therefore ought to be effaced as an obsolete fragment of a repudiated social order. It was disconcerting that even a doddering old creature like the obdurate Mrs. Oliver should prefer living in this unhealthy rurality; and now a council-flat could be made available to her. She would be served a compulsory purchase order before long, if the Planning Officer had his way — which he was accustomed to have — and would be moved to Gorst where she belonged. The surviving cottages might be condemned to demolition as a public nuisance, Sir Gerald's obscurantism notwithstanding. What should be done with the cleared site of Low Wentford? Why, it might be utilized as a dump for earth excavated in the Gorst housing schemes. That obsolete bridge, incidentally, ought to be replaced by a level concrete one.

'Let a decent old woman keep her roses,' Sir Gerald had said to the Planning Officer when last they met in Gorst. 'Why do you whirl her off to your jerry-built desolation of concrete roadways that you've designed, so far as I can see, to make it difficult for people to get about on foot? Why do you have to make her live under the glare of mercury vapor lamps and listen to other people's wireless sets when she wants quiet? Sometimes I think a devil's got inside you, Barner.'

With dignity, S. G. W. Barner felt, he had replied to this tirade. 'I am very much afraid, Sir Gerald, that you don't understand the wants of common human beings. Elderly members of the community need to be kept under the supervision of social workers and local authorities, for their own welfare; indeed, I trust the time is not far distant when residence in eventide homes will be compulsory upon all aged persons, regardless of fancied social distinctions. Mrs. Oliver requires relief from her self-imposed isolation.'

'You're no better than a walking bluebook, Barner,' Sir Gerald Ogham had answered — red as a beet, the Planning Officer recollected with relish — and had stamped away. Opposition from such a quarter was sufficient evidence of the need for taking Mrs. Oliver and Low Wentford in hand so soon as the Council could be wheeled into action. He must find time to draw up a persuasive report on the redundancy of Low Wentford.

*   *

In truth, Low Wentford *was* a lonely place, as Mrs. Oliver confessed to herself, though she knew it never would do to tell Mr. Barner so. Some things she seemed to forget, nowadays, but she knew whom she could trust and whom she could not. Lady Ogham came to visit her occasionally, bringing a present of fruit or flowers; otherwise, Mrs. Oliver was quite alone. Despite being deaf and nearsighted and English, she had enjoyed more company in Madras. How long was it since the Major had gone? She had little notion. Sometimes children, straggling down from the potato-syndicate farm, ran from her in fright, here in the village where she had been born; children never dreaded her in Madras.

But she wanted no more visits from the Planning Officer. She knew what he was about. He had come last week — or was it last month? — and she had made him shout properly, saying she was sorry to be deaf, though really she had understood him well enough when he spoke in a lower key. She had shaken her head again and again and again. She had bought this cottage, and it was hers, and she loved her roses, and she did not want to be cared for. He had turned from her quite disagreeable. It was something about maps. And communal amenities. He would not stay for tea, although she had told him that she still baked her own bread. Mr. Barner was a cheerless man, and he frightened her. Had he said something about an old witch when he banged the door after him?

Certainly he had said he was out of patience. Almost nothing in India had frightened her: the riots would not have made her come home; it was only that she had longed to see the country round Low Wentford, even though all the old neighbors were gone. But she was afraid of Mr. Barner, because he seemed more unchristian than any Indian, worshipping his maps. And he might do something about her cottage. Sir Gerald, if she had understood him properly, had said as much. She would not go to Gorst; it was not a nice place, not nice at all, even when she was young. And naughty children in such places pointed at her nose, and at her stick. If only there were a neighbor or two . . . Sir Gerald and Lady Ogham were busy people; and, too, she needed someone less grand. Why was it that the vicar never came to call? Though she had been reared a Methodist, she could recollect the plump old vicar of All Saints, Low Wentford. Was it he who had married her to the Major? She thought so. But she supposed that he, like the Major, was gone. Perhaps the vicar could have helped her against Mr. S. G. W. Barner. Really, she had come to hate Mr. Barner. She had been reasonably good most of her life, and so felt entitled to hate a man or two, at her age. Parsons knew how to manage such people. Did the vicar know she was living in Low Wentford again? Had anyone told him?

He must have more than one parish, surely, and have been too busy to call upon her as yet. For the church was locked always. She had tried the door a number of times, especially on Sundays, but it never yielded. She supposed the vicar must come late Sunday evening, after she had gone to bed; indeed, she thought — though she could not be sure — that she had seen lights, like little candles, moving within the church, once or twice when she had risen in the middle of the night to shut a window against the rain. Doubtless he would call eventually, this poor harried vicar, and she would give him tea and her own scones. Meanwhile, she had her cat to talk with; and a fine great cat he was, named Bentinck, and she could tell Bentinck of the iniquities of Mr. Barner. The milkman came in the morning, and the grocer's van in the afternoon — that was company. But the vanmen were ever so shy: you would have thought them afraid of her. Should she fall ill, now, the vicar would be duty bound to call on her. Her health invariably was good, however — more's the pity — better than ever it had been in Madras. Lady Ogham told her, laughing a little, that she was so hale and rosy she seemed more than human. 'My flowers and my oven keep me brisk, Lady Ogham,' she had said, stroking Bentinck.

Though it had been disused for years before she came, the cottage oven was a good one. She baked little sweet cakes of all shapes and dimensions. Being very ill-tempered the day after Mr. Barner had visited her, she had made of dough one cake that looked quite like the Planning Officer, and deliberately left it too long in the oven so that it burnt black, and Bentinck would not touch it even when it was soaked in milk. But that had been spiteful. She wished she did not have to think about Mr. Barner. Perhaps if she went out of the cottage more often, he would not come creeping into her mind. She ought to cross to the churchyard every evening, to forget the poor menaced cottage for a while; and there she might look at the tombstones, if she should take a little broom with her to brush the leaves away. She knew many of the folk that lay by the church, and it would be pleasant to sit among them in the sunset.

When had she decided this? Had it been last autumn? Or had it been only a fortnight ago? Nowadays she came daily, before sunset, to the churchyard and swept the gravestones. It being March, often rain came while she was there; then she sat in the south porch of the church, wrapped in her cloak and hood, and took no harm. Always the church door was locked, but that did not much matter, for everyone whose name she could remember was buried to the south of the church, not inside. She brushed with her little broom, and found Aunt Polly and Grandfather Thomas, and Ann with whom she had played in the schoolyard, and even the plump old vicar, who, she recalled now, had been the Reverend Henry Williams. But they were not altogether satisfactory as neighbors, for of course she could see them only in memory, and they could not answer. They did not succeed in keeping Mr. S. G. W. Barner from creeping into the back of her mind. He was detestable.

Except for the fallen limbs of old rowans and the high, damp grass, the south side of the churchyard was a cheerful place, far better than the north side. The graves were few on that latter cold and windy slope, and the weeds were thicker, and everything seemed squalid. She would have liked to tell the vicar so. A small porch clung to that side of the church, too, but she dared not sit there, for even she could perceive that the heavy porch roof threatened to collapse. Probably Sir Gerald Ogham was not able to maintain All Saints as his father had done. A little low archway — she supposed it was the Normans' work — led from the porch into the tower. Sometimes it seemed to her that the door in the archway was ajar; but she could not make certain, for when she approached once, a slate fell right at her feet, and she feared she might bring the whole porch down upon her head. If this was the way the vicar entered the church, he must be rather a heedless man. She could not remember this door ever having been opened when she was a girl.

No, she did not like the north side. Having swept all the gravestones to the south, however, she felt that really she ought to treat the folk on the north equally well. One evening, then, she found herself brushing the thick wet leaves from a slab close by the north porch. Was there a name upon it? She put on her spectacles and, leaning on her stick, bent as close as she could. Then a shadow fell across the slab.

Mrs. Oliver turned sharp round, thinking that perhaps Mr. Barner had come again. But it was someone else: a parson, a tall man with a long, long face, hatched lines crossing on forehead and cheeks. She could see him more plainly than she could see most people. He must have come from the little doorway under the tower. He was nothing like the old vicar, Mr. Williams. This would be his successor, and it was good that he had come. Drops of moisture ran from his long black hair down the furrows in his sad face, so he must have walked a great way in the rain.

'I am Mrs. Oliver,' she said. Why did she have trouble getting the words out?

Though clear, his voice was harsh and grating; he did not seem to be speaking loudly, unlike everybody else, who shouted at her. 'I am Abner Hargreaves,' he said, 'your vicar.'

*   *

'Something curious happened today,' Sir Gerald Ogham remarked to his wife, at dinner. He stared at a place on the high ceiling where the faded Chinese paper was peeling, and paused, as if he regretted having spoken.

'Well?' said Lady Ogham. 'You know, this room is falling to bits. What was strange?'

'Mrs. Oliver was odd,' Sir Gerald told her. 'You'd best say nothing of this to anyone, Alice: if Barner knew, it might improve his case.'

'Odd? I always have thought her a sensible old dear, aside from her way of talking to that monstrous cat as though he were a viceroy.'

'Perhaps it was only some person passing on his way to Gorst,' Sir Gerald went on. 'But she said the vicar came to call, yesterday evening, and took tea with her.'

'Vicar? Whom could she have meant, Gerald? Mr. Harris, of Holy Trinity, in Gorst?'

'Harris has nothing to do with this parish; besides, he scarcely bothers to call anywhere in Gorst. He knows he has emoluments to receive, but forgets he has duties to perform. He never would have been poking about a deconsecrated church. And you know what a frail reed Harris is, while this fellow seems to have been a strapping parson of the old breed. Mrs. Oliver was quite overawed by him; I had thought nothing could make such a distinct impression on her — though she did forget his name while she was talking with me. I wish I had seen him. It never would do for word to get about that Mrs. Oliver talks with shadows: in no time, Barner would have her off to some insufferable eventide home. Yet I do believe — if I understood her — that she fancies the church still is in use.'

'Oh, no, Gerald, really she can't! It must have been shut when she was a girl here.'

'No, All Saints has not been derelict that long. I was a half-grown boy before they locked it. Even then, it was in a bad way; almost no one but our family used to attend. There were few parishioners left about Low Wentford, and the vicar offended most of those few. He was remarkably harsh, fond of nothing but the cursing psalms and Jeremiah. I recollect a commination, on Ash Wednesday — which, by the way, is nearly upon us again, Alice — that gave me nightmares. Then the scandal put an end to things, and they took the furniture and the bells away to Gorst. One of these days the whole roof will fall through.'

'You never told me of a scandal.'

'A nasty story, Alice. The village schoolmaster was the village atheist — Rally was his name, or Reddy. The vicar loathed this schoolmaster, who, he said, was corrupting the parish. It was against Reddy the vicar preached that commination I remember. How he cursed him! When Reddy heard what had been said, he came round to face the vicar out. Both of them had beastly tempers.

'During the first week of Lent, Reddy was found in the brook by the bridge, his neck broken. Like most convinced atheists, he drank, however, and he might have fallen from the bridge to the stones, in the night.'

'Do you mean the poor vicar was slandered merely on that coincidence?'

'No. Of itself, Reddy's death might have been passed over. Even the vicar's death might have been passed over; for he was found drowned in our quarry six months later. He might have been bathing. It was a clause in his will that caused the talk — that, and his sermons and the look on his face for months before. He left instructions that he should be buried on the north side of the church, "with other murderers and perjurers and suicides, that burn forever." The vicar was eloquent, as if inspired by angels; but what sort of angels, people wondered. How he talked of sinners in the hands of an angry God! Whatever he was, he thundered like the agent of Omnipotence. Yet Satan, for that matter . . . I believe his name was Harbound, or Harcourt, or Harbottle; but it doesn't signify any longer, except conceivably to the vicar himself, poor damned soul.'

*   *

Nearly every evening, now, Mr. Hargreaves came to call and Mrs. Oliver was comforted. Though he was in no sense a cheerful being, she was convinced that he possessed immense powers of sympathy. He sat moodily in his corner away from the fire, always dripping, somehow, even when Mrs. Oliver had thought the evening fair; and Mrs. Oliver told him her tribulations. He would eat nothing, yet he drank her tea with a prodigious thirst; and he seemed to need it, for his voice was fearfully dry and harsh; and to judge by his eyes, he suffered from malaria. She wished that she might hear him preach: he held a command of language she never before had encountered in a parson. But when she asked him about the hours of service, he did not seem to hear her. Bentinck, temperamental, wailed whenever Mr. Hargreaves entered, fleeing to the top of the cupboard, whence he spat at the vicar; but the Reverend Abner Hargreaves took no notice of the cat. Now and again he spoke at length, with wonderful passion, as clearly as he had spoken when they first met in the churchyard; and he seemed to anticipate her every thought. Mr. Barner, she told the vicar, was a wicked man.

'Cursed is he that perverteth the judgment of the stranger, the fatherless and widow,' said Mr. Hargreaves.

'I wish you would speak to him,' said Mrs. Oliver.

'All thine enemies shall feel thy hand; thy right hand shall find them out that hate thee,' continued Mr. Hargreaves, almost chanting. 'Thou shalt make them like a fiery oven in the time of thy wrath; the Lord shall destroy them in his displeasure, and the fire shall consume them.'

'I don't wish him any harm,' said Mrs. Oliver, 'but he *is* wicked.'

At that, Mr. Hargreaves rose abruptly, and went out of the cottage into the night. Mrs. Oliver hoped that she had not somehow offended him. But at all times he came and went unceremoniously. No doubt Mr. Hargreaves was zealous; yet he was not quite a cheering vicar.

*   *

Mr. S. G. W. Barner sat in his study, amusing himself by drawing up plans for a model collective agricultural unit adapted to British agronomy — something he did not intend to show to the county council, nevertheless, or at least not to a council of its present complexion — when a bell rang, and rang again, faintly.

'Susan, *will* you answer that?' he called to his wife, in annoyance.

'Answer what, dear?' his wife inquired, from the corridor.

'The doorbell, of course,' Barner told her, fidgeting with his ruler.

She was back in a moment. 'No one . . .' Then he heard the faint bell again.

'The telephone, Susan,' said Barner. 'Must I manage every trifling detail in this household?' She bit her lip and hurried out.

'No one telephoned either,' she called, in a moment. 'And I never heard it ring, dear.'

Flinging down his ruler, Barner strode into the hall, and snatched the receiver from her. 'Nonsense! Of course it rang!' And someone was speaking, as he had expected. Barner nodded contemptuously to his wife, who shrank into the kitchen.

The voice was deep, afflicted with a parched hoarseness. For some seconds, Barner thought he had the receiver the wrong end to, or that something was amiss with the instrument; but then the voice sounded more distinctly. '. . . without delay,' it was saying. 'I have spoken with Mrs. Oliver. The thing must be done with.'

Barner gathered that the agent, whoever he was, desired a meeting. 'Where?' asked Barner. This might be an opportunity to clear away the Low Wentford annoyance. 'When?'

'At All Saints,' said the voice, with something like a gasp, and then paused, almost as if the idea of Time (Barner wondered why this foolish fancy passed through his brain) were alien to the speaker. 'We meet,' said the parched voice, 'at once.'

'In the dark?' protested Barner. 'You've called far too late. Tuesday, possibly.'

'This night, at All Saints, Low Wentford.' The voice, imperious, startled Barner.

'Whoever are you?' he asked.

'Hargreaves, the vicar. I am waiting.' Then there was silence. Barner put down the telephone after an attempt to remonstrate to the void.

Well, the hour would do well enough, after all; but he would be short with this cantankerous vicar. Vicar of what? Barner knew no Hargreaves. Some relative, conceivably, of Mrs. Oliver. He was tempted to let the silly parson, with his bad manners, wait all night in the churchyard. Then, though, he might lose his chance to finish with Low Wentford. Telling his wife that he would return in an hour or two, Barner got into his automobile and drove out of the villadom that hems in Gorst toward Low Wentford.

*   *

As Barner switched off his ignition, it occurred to him that the churchyard of All Saints was a cheerless place to meet this fellow. The mist from the brook drifted upwards toward the church. Could they not have talked in that old woman's confounded cottage? It was wet here, and hard to tell haar from stone. With proper employment of scientific methodology, one day society would plan its weather, perhaps eliminating altogether the seasons. But for the stupidity of entrenched interests, the thing would have been accomplished already. Superstition! Today, for instance, was some irrational relic of superstitious rubbish — Ash Wednesday, that was it. Barner walked through the tangled grass toward the south porch. He saw no one. Would this vicar have a key to let them in, or must they parley in the drizzle?

No one stood in this porch. Barner thought he caught a glimmer of light within the church; but the door was bolted. He blundered round to the north side. As he approached the small porch by the tower, someone stalked out to meet him.

The vicar was a man of great stature; it was too dark for Barner to perceive much more of him, though he recognized at once the parched and rasping voice. 'I ask you, sir, for charity,' said the vicar, out of the fog.

'If you mean that old woman down the lane, Mr. Hargreaves,' Barner interrupted, 'the most charitable thing we can do is to re-house her where amenities and social intercourse are available.' Though the vicar had come up close to him, Barner could not see his face well enough, through the mist, to make out his cast of countenance. It would be the face of a sentimental fool, Barner knew. They stood in the lee of the north porch, the grass up to their knees, some slippery slab underfoot; and a wind had risen, damply cutting.

'Who are you, sir,' the vicar went on — his throat seemingly dry as an oven — 'and what am I, to meddle with an old woman's longing? She called me from a great way to do her this service; and I must have your charity, or else you must seek mine; and now I have none to give. "Cursed is he that perverteth the judgment of the stranger, the fatherless and widow." Do you know the verse which stands next to that, man? It is this: "Cursed is he that smiteth his neighbor secretly." In the universe are vicars of more sorts than one, but I am bound by special ordinances; and therefore I do entreat you, sir, to call it to mind that this woman's house is as the breath of life to her. The breath of life, man. Think what that means!'

Well, reflected Barner, here's the old-world Bible-thumper with a vengeance. 'Individual preferences often must be subordinated to communal efficiency,' was what he said.

'I speak not simply of whim and inclination,' the vicar caught him up, 'but of the memories of childhood and girlhood, the pieties that cling to our hearth, however desolated.'

'That's rot you're talking, you know,' Barner objected, exasperated. Did the vicar step closer to him? Barner shifted backward through the grass, so that he stood just within the porch. 'Candidly, I consider parsons just so many impediments to social unity. Leave sociology to trained minds, Mr. Hargreaves. I see you have not the faintest conception of the essentials of planning. I have an Act of Parliament at my back. Who authorized you to meddle with official programs? Perhaps some people desire your services: old Mrs. Oliver, for instance, possibly extracts some solace from your Bible stories. I do not.'

The vicar laughed. Barner never had heard a laugh like it — a sound nearer the braying of a mule than anything from a man's throat. It was indescribably dismal. 'Blind, blind,' the vicar declared. 'His fan is in his hand, and he will purge his floor, and gather his wheat into the barn, but he will burn the chaff with unquenchable fire. For the sake of a void upon a map, man, would you cast away your hope of salvation?'

'Salvation?' asked Barner, with a shrug. 'Salvation? I came to you for a practical settlement, not a sermon. I want that woman out of her cottage.'

'I have said all that it was required I should say,' the vicar answered, 'and have done all that it was required I should do.' His voice was exhortatory no longer; now a quality of devouring eagerness was in it. He took another step toward Barner, who at last saw his face distinctly.

A sentimental parson? Not this man. The jaw, long and rock-like; the cheeks, seamed and hollow; the pallid, pallid skin; the high-bridged nose, with distended nostrils; the red and staring eyes, with the look of a beast in torment — these were thrust close up to Barner's face in the gloom of the porch. Enormous beads of water or sweat ran down the vicar's cheeks.

'But I do ask you, this last time,' said the vicar, 'for charity.'

Or did he say it? His lips had not moved. And abruptly it came to Barner that the vicar's lips had not stirred before; that rigid face was a mask; and the words Barner had thought he heard had sounded only in his own brain, not in his ears. Even on the telephone . . . Barner clutched a stone bench-end within the porch. What tricks the dark and the mist played! Of course the vicar's lips must have moved; no one would play ventriloquist in this place. 'No,' insisted Barner, scowling, his assurance partially recovered, 'I never grant exceptions to any scheduled scheme.' How loathsome that parson's features were! 'I say, vicar, if you must talk of this longer, sha'n't we shift out of this wind and wet into the church?' For Barner wanted mightily to put some interval between himself and that waxy face.

'Safe in the church? You and I? Never!' cried the parson, in a voice at once exultant and agonized. He smiled frightfully. 'For now is the ax put to the root of the trees, so that every tree that bringeth forth not good fruit, is hewn down and cast into the fire.' Then he took Barner by the throat.

*   *

For more than a week, the curious death of S. G. W. Barner was a subject of conversation even beyond Gorst; the *Review of Collective Planning* observed that in Barner, pragmatic social reconstruction had lost one of its more promising younger advocates. Apparently Barner had been making a brief inspection of the derelict church of All Saints, which he intended to persuade the ecclesiastical authorities to demolish, when the roof of the north porch, weakened by incompetent restorers near the end of the eighteenth century and further imperilled by neglect, fell upon him. His body was not discovered until the following afternoon.

Two or three of Barner's acquaintances remarked that he would have been vexed by a cultural lag connected with his cremation. The suffragan bishop of Wandersley, within whose cure Gorst lies, recently had spoken with vigor against the 'barbarous practice' of scattering the ashes, after cremation, at random over unconsecrated ground; while the Reverend John Harris, vicar of Holy Trinity, Old Gorst, protested against the strewing of ashes within his churchyard, as offensive to the sensibilities of his parishioners and his wife. The undertaker and Mrs. Barner, therefore, were in some perplexity, until Mr. Harris suggested that the churchyard of Low Wentford might be suitable, there being no clergyman in residence, and the only person who might possibly object being Sir Gerald Ogham. Consulted, Sir Gerald said that, the Ogham tombs lying to the south of All Saints, these ashes ought to be strewn on the north side of the churchyard. This was done; and Sir Gerald, though not present on the occasion, told the county sanitary officer that he thought no ceremony could have been more fitting.

The county council has relinquished the scheme for clearing the site of Low Wentford; indeed, there appears to be some possibility that six or seven of the cottages near the bridge may be restored, with the aid of grants from local authorities, as part of a plan of deconcentration recommended by the new planning officer. Mrs. Oliver's cottage, in any event, seems secure. She weeds her garden, and bakes her scones, and often sweeps the gravestones clean; thus she continues surprisingly vigorous for a woman of her years. Though the vicar no longer calls, as she told Lady Ogham one day, instead she has a new confidant — a Mr. Reddy, highly opinionated, given to denying the existence of Heaven, and suffering dreadfully from some old injury to his neck.

Behind the Stumps

And Satan stood up against Israel,
and provoked David to number Israel.

1 Chronicles 21:1

ottawattomie County, shorn of its protecting forest seventy years
ago, ever since has sprawled like Samson undone by Delilah, naked,
impotent, grudgingly servile. Amid the fields of rotted stumps, potatoes
and beans grow, and half the inhabited houses still are log cabins thrown
up by the lumbermen who followed the trappers into this land. In
Pottawattomie there has been no money worth mentioning since the timber was cut: but here and there people cling to the straggling farms, or
make shift in the crumbling villages.

An elusive beauty drifts over this country sprinkled with little lakes,
stretches of second-growth woods and cedar swamps, gravelly upland
ridges that are gnawed by every rain, now that their cover is gone. As if a
curse had been pronounced upon these folk and their houses and their
crops in reprisal for their violation of nature, everything in Pottawattomie
is melting away.

Of the people who stick obstinately to this stump-country, some are
grandchildren and great-grandchildren of the men who swept off the forest; others are flotsam cast upon these sandy miles from the torrent of
modern life, thrown out of the eddy upon the soggy bank to lie inert and
ignored. Worn farmers of a conservative cast of mind, pinched, tenacious,

inured to monotony, fond of the bottle on Saturday nights, eccentrics of several sorts; a silent half-breed crew of Negro-and-Indian, dispersed in cabins and sun-stricken tar-paper shanties along the back roads, remote from the county seat and the lesser hamlets that conduct the languid commerce of Pottawattomie — these are the Pottawattomie people. Decent roads have come only lately; even television is too costly for many of these folk; the very hand of government is nerveless in this poverty of soil and spirit.

Yet not wholly palsied, the grip of the State, for all that. Tax assessments necessarily are modest in Pottawattomie, but there are roads to be maintained, poaching of deer and trout to be repressed, public relief to be doled out. There exists a sheriff, intimate with the local tone, at the county seat; also a judge of probate; and the county supervisors are farmers and tradesmen without inclination to alter the nature of things in Pottawattomie. So far, government is a shadow of a shade. But now and again the State administration and the Federal administration gingerly poke about in the mud and brush of the stump-land.

A special rural census had to be compiled. Down in the capital, a plan had been drawn up concerning commodity price-levels and potential crop yields and tabulated prices. Acres of corn were to be counted, and pigs and people. Enumerators went out to every spreading wheat farm, to every five-acre tomato patch; and Pottawattomie County was not forgotten.

Always against the government, Pottawattomie; against the administration that ordained this special census, most vehemently. This new survey, Pottawattomie declared, meant more blank forms, more trips to the county seat, higher taxation, and intolerable prying into every man's household — which last none resent more than do the rural poor.

So the Regional Office of the Special Census began to encounter difficulties in Pottawattomie. Doors were shut in the faces of certified enumerators, despite threats of warrants and writs; the evasive response was common, violent reaction not inconceivable. Reports particularly unsettling were received from the district of Bear City, a decayed village of two hundred inhabitants. Despite his pressing need for the stipend attached to the office, the temporary agent there resigned in distress at a growing unpopularity. A woman who took his place was ignored by half the farmers she endeavored to interview.

Put out, the Regional Office dispatched to Bear City a Special Interviewer: Cribben. They let him have a car and a stack of forms and rather a stiff letter of introduction to the postmaster in that town, and off he drove northward.

Being that sort of man, Cribben took his revolver with him. Once he had been a bank messenger, and he often told his associates, 'The other messengers carried their guns at the bottom of their briefcases, so there'd be no chance of having to pull them if there was a stickup. But I kept my .38 handy. I was willing to have it out with the boys.'

Tall, forty, stiff as a stick, this Cribben — walking with chin up, chest out, joints rigid, in a sort of nervous defiance of humanity. He looked insufferable. He was insufferable. Next to a jocular man, an insufferable man is best suited for the responsibilities that are a Special Interviewer's. Close-clipped black hair set off a strong head, well proportioned; but the mouth was petulant, and the eyes were ignorantly challenging, and the chin was set in lines of pomposity. In conversation, Cribben had a way of sucking in his cheeks with an affectation of whimsical deliberation, for Cribben had long told himself that he was admirably funny when he chose to be, especially with women. Years before, his wife had divorced him — in Reno, since (somewhat to her bewilderment) she had been able to think of no precise ground which would admit of obtaining a divorce in their own state. He lived chastely, honestly, soberly, quite solitary. He laughed dutifully at other men's jokes; he would go out of his way to write a friendly letter of recommendation; but somehow no one ever asked him out or looked him up. A failure in everything was Cribben — ex-engineer, ex-chief clerk, ex-artillery captain, ex-foundry partner. He told himself he had been completely reliable in every little particular, which was true; and he told himself he had failed because of his immaculate honesty in a mob of rogues, which was false. He had failed because he was precise.

'Corporal, about the morning report: I see you used eraser to clean up this ink blot, instead of correction fluid. Watch that, Corporal. We'll use correction fluid. Understand?' This is the sort of thing the precise Cribben would say — if with a smile, then the wrong kind of smile; and he would compliment himself on his urbanity.

Cribben did not spare himself; no man ever was more methodical, more painstaking. Reliable in every little particular, yes; but so devoted to these particulars that generalities went to pot. Subordinates resigned and read the 'help wanted' columns rather than submit to another week of such accuracy; superiors found him hopelessly behind in his work, aus-

terely plodding through tidy inconsequentialities. Truly, Cribben was intolerable. He knew the mass of men to be consistently inaccurate and often dishonest. Quite right, of course. Sensible men nod and shrug;
Cribben nagged. His foundry went to pieces because he fretted about
missing wrenches and screwdrivers. He thought his workmen stole them.
They did; but Cribben never would confess that moderate pilferage was an
item of fixed overhead. In Cribben's pertinacity there would have been
something noble, had he loved precision for the sake of truth. But he regarded truth only as an attribute of precision.

So down to that sink of broken men, petty governmental service,
spun Cribben in the vortex of failure. Having arrived at the abyss, which in
this instance was a temporary junior clerkship, Cribben commenced to
rise in a small way. In this humorless precisian the assistant chief of the
Regional Office discerned the very incarnation of the second-best type of
public functionary, and so set him to compelling the reluctant to complete
interminable forms. Cribben became a Special Investigator, with every in-
crease of salary authorized by statute. To entrust him with supervisory
duties proved inadvisable; yet within his sphere, Cribben was incompara-
ble. It was Cribben's apotheosis. Never had he liked work so well, and only
a passion to reorganize the Regional Office upon a more precise model
clouded his contentment. With the majesty of Government at his back,
the hauteur of a censor in his mien as he queried the subject of a survey or
interrogated the petitioner for a grant — a man like Cribben never
dreamed of more than this. For Cribben was quite devoid of imagination.

And Cribben drove north to Bear City.

False-fronted dry-goods shops and grocery stores and saloons, built
lavishly of second-grade white pine when pine was cheap and seemingly
inexhaustible, are strung along a broad gravelled road: this is Bear City.
They are like discolored teeth in an old man's mouth, these buildings, for
they stand between grass-grown gaps where casual flames have had their
way with abandoned structures. One of these shops, with the usual high,
old-fashioned windows and siding a watery white, is also the post office.
On Saturday afternoons in little places like this, post offices generally
close. But on this Saturday afternoon, in Bear City — so Cribben noted as
he parked his automobile — not only the dry-goods half of the shop, but
the post office too was open for business. This was tidy and efficient,
Cribben reflected, striding through the door. It predisposed him to amiability.

'Afternoon,' said Cribben to the postmaster. 'I'm J. K. Cribben, from the Regional Office. Read this, please.' He presented his letter of introduction.

Mr. Matt Heddle, Postmaster, Bear City, was behind the wrought-iron grille of the old post-office counter, a relic of earlier days and more southerly towns; and his shy wife Jessie was opposite, at the shop counter. They were not lacking in the dignity that comes from honorable posts long held in small places. Mr. Heddle, with his crown of thick white hair and his august slouch, his good black suit, and his deep slow voice, made a rural postmaster for one to be proud of.

'Why, I wish you luck, Mr. Cribben,' Matt Heddle said with concern, reading the letter of introduction. Mr. Heddle desired to be postmaster for the rest of his life. 'I'll do anything I can. I'm sorry about the fuss the other census man had.'

'His own damned fault,' Cribben said, largely. 'Don't give a grouch a chance to make a fuss — that's my way. Take none of their lip. I've handled people quite awhile. Shoot out your questions, stare 'em down. I won't have much trouble here.'

He didn't. Whatever Cribben's shortcomings, he was neither coward nor laggard. Only six or seven hours a day he spent in the tourist room he had rented; and by the time six days had passed, he had seen and conquered almost all the obdurate farmers around Bear City. Their sheds and their silos, their sheep and their steers, their hired men and their bashful daughters, the rooms in their houses and the privies behind them — all were properly observed and recorded in forms and check-sheets. What Cribben could not see with his own eyes he bullied out adequately enough from the uneasy men he cornered and glowered upon. He was big, he was gruff, he was pedantically insistent. He was worth what salary the Regional Office paid. He never took 'no' for an answer — or 'don't know,' either. He made himself detested in Bear City more quickly than ever had man before; and he paid back his contemners in a condescending scorn.

His success was the product, in part, of his comparative restraint: for he seemed to those he confronted to be holding himself precariously in check, on the verge of tumbling into some tremendous passion, like a dizzy man teetering on a log across a stream in spate. He was cruelly cold, always — never fierce, and yet hanging by a worn rope. What brute would have had the callousness, or the temerity, to thrust this man over the brink? It was safer to answer his questions and endure his prying.

Over the rutted trails of Pottawattomie County in muddy spring he drove his official automobile, finding out every shack and hut, every Indian squatter, every forlorn old couple back in the cedar thickets, every widow who boasted a cow and a chicken run. They were numbered, all numbered. This spring the birds were thick in Pottawattomie and some of the lilacs bloomed early, but Cribben never looked at them, for they were not to be enumerated. He had not an ounce of fancy in him. Six days of this and he had done the job except for the Barrens. Of all Pottawattomie, Bear City district was the toughest nut for the Special Census, and the Barrens were the hard kernel of Bear City's hinterland.

Who lives in the Barrens, that sterile and gullied and scrub-veiled upland? Why, it's hard to say. A half-dozen scrawny families, perhaps more — folk seldom seen, more seldom heard, even in Bear City. They have no money for the dissipations of a town, the Barrens people — none of them, at least, except the Gholsons; and no one ever knew a Gholson to take a dollar out of his greasy old purse for anything but a sack of sugar or a bottle of rot-gut whisky. The Gholsons must have money, as money goes in Pottawattomie, but it sticks to them.

On Saturday afternoon, a week after his arrival in town, Cribben entered the post office, self-satisfied and muddy. Matt Heddle was there, and Love the garage-man — Love already lively from morning libations. 'Started on the Barrens this morning, Heddle,' Cribben said ponderously. 'Easy as falling off a log. Covered the Robinson place, and Hendry's. Eight kids at the Robinsons', dirty as worms.' He looked at his map. 'Tomorrow, now, I begin with this place called Barrens Mill. Not much of a road into it. It's right on Owens Creek. What d'you know about Barrens Mill, Heddle?' He pointed, his heavy forefinger stiff, at a spot on his map.

Mr. Matt Heddle was a good-natured old man, but he did not like Cribben. Pottawattomie people said that Mr. Heddle was well read, which in Pottawattomie County means that a man has three reprints of Marie Corelli's novels and two of Hall Caine's, but they were not far wrong in Heddle's case. The appetite for knowledge clutched at him as it sometimes does at pathetic men past their prime, and his devotion to the better nineteenth century novelists, combining with some natural penetration, had made him shrewd enough. His good nature being unquenchable, he looked at grim Cribben and thought he read in that intolerant face a waste of loneliness and doubt that Cribben never could confess to himself, for terror of the desolation.

He looked at Cribben, and told him: 'Let it go, Mr. Cribben. They're an ignorant bunch, the Gholsons; they own Barrens Mill. Let it go. It'll be knee-deep in mud up there. Look up the acreage in the county office, and the assessment, and let it go at that. You've done all the work anybody could ask.'

'We don't let things go in the Regional Office,' Cribben said, with austerity. 'I've already looked in the county book: five hundred and twenty acres the Gholsons own. But I want to know *what* Gholson.'

Matt Heddle started to speak, hesitated, looked speculatively at Cribben, and then said, 'It's Will Gholson that pays the taxes.'

Love, who had been leaning against the counter, a wise grin on his face, gave a whisky chuckle and remarked, abruptly: 'She was a witch and a bitch, a bitch and a witch. Ha! Goin' to put *her* in the census?'

'Dave Love, this isn't The Elite; it's the post office,' Mr. Heddle said, civilly. 'Let's keep it decent in here.'

'Yes, Will Gholson pays the taxes,' Cribben nodded, 'but the land's not in his name. The tax-roll reads "Mrs. Gholson" — just that. No Christian name. How do you people choose your county clerk?'

'Mrs. Gholson, old Bitch Gholson, old Witch Gholson,' chanted Love. 'You goin' to put *her* in the census? She's dead as a dodo.'

'Will Gholson's mother, maybe, or his grandmother — that's who's meant,' Heddle murmured. 'Nobody really knows the Gholsons. They aren't folks you get to know. They're an ignorant bunch, good to keep clear of. She was old, old. I saw her laid out. Some of us went up there for the funeral — only time we ever went inside the house. It was only decent to go up.'

'Decent, hell!' said Love. 'We was scared not to go, that's the truth of it. Nobody with any brains rubs the Gholsons the wrong way.'

'Scared?' Cribben sneered down at Love.

'God, yes, man. She was a damned witch, and the whole family's bats in the belfry. Old Mrs. Gholson have a Christian name? Hell, whoever heard of a witch with a Christian name?'

'You start your drinking too early in the day,' Cribben said. Love snorted, grinned, and fiddled with a post-office pen. 'What kind of a county clerk do you have, Heddle, that doesn't take a dead woman's name off the books?'

'Why, I suppose maybe the Gholsons wanted it left on,' Heddle sighed, placatingly. 'And there was talk. Nobody wants to fuss with the Gholsons. Sleeping dogs, Mr. Cribben.'

'If you really want to know,' Love growled, 'she cursed the cows, for one thing. The cows of the people she didn't care for, and the neighbors that were too close. The Gholsons don't like close neighbors.'

'What are you giving me?' Cribben went menacingly red at the idea of being made the butt of a joke: this was the one thing his humorless valor feared.

'You don't have to believe it, man, but the cows went dry, all the same. And sometimes they died. And if that wasn't enough, the Gholsons moved the fences, and the boundary-markers. They took over. They got land now that used to be four or five farms.'

Mrs. Heddle, having been listening, now came across the shop to say in her shy voice, 'They did move the posts, Mr. Cribben — the Gholsons. And the neighbors didn't move them back. They were frightened silly.'

'It'll take more than a sick cow to scare me, Mrs. Heddle,' Cribben told her, the flush fading from his cheeks. 'You people don't have any system up here. What's wrong with your schools, that people swallow this stuff? How do you hire your teachers?'

'Barrens Mill is a place to put a chill into a preacher, Mr. Cribben,' said Matt Heddle, meditatively. 'There's a look to it . . . the mill itself is gone, but the big old house is there, seedy now, and the rest of the buildings. John Wendover, the lumberman, built it when this country was opened up, but the Gholsons bought it after the timber went. Some people say the Gholsons came from Missouri. I don't know. There's stories . . . Nobody knows the Gholsons. They've another farm down the creek. There's five Gholson men, nowadays, but I don't know how many women. Will Gholson does the talking for them, and he talks as much as a clam.'

'He'll talk to me,' Cribben declared.

Over Matt Heddle came a sensation of pity. Leaning across the counter, he put his hand on Cribben's. Few ever had done this, and Cribben, startled, stepped back. 'Now, listen, Mr. Cribben, friend. You're a man with spunk, and you know your business; but I'm old, and I've been hereabouts a while. There are people that don't fit in anywhere, Mr. Cribben. Did you ever think about that? I mean, they won't live by your ways and mine. Some of them are too good, and some are too bad. Everybody's growing pretty much alike — nearly everybody — in this age, and the ones that don't fit in are scarce; but they're still around. Some are queer, very queer. We can't just count them like so many fifteen-cent stamps. We can't change them, not soon. But they're shy, most of them: let them alone, and

25

they're likely to crawl into holes, out of the sun. Let them be; they don't signify, if you don't stir them up. The Gholsons are like that.'

'They come under the law, same as anybody else,' Cribben put in.

'Oh, the law was made for you and me and the folks we know — not for them, any more than it was made for snakes. So long as they let the law alone, don't meddle, Mr. Cribben, don't meddle. They don't signify any more than a wasps' nest at the back of the orchard, if you don't poke them.' Old Heddle was very earnest.

'A witch of a bitch and a bitch of a witch,' sang Love, mordantly. 'O Lord, how she hexed 'em!'

'Why, there's Will Gholson now, coming out of The Elite,' Mrs. Heddle whispered from the window. A greasy, burly man with tremendous eyebrows that had tufted points was walking from the bar with a bottle in either hip-pocket. He was neither bearded nor shaven, and he was filthy. He turned toward a wagon hitched close by the post office.

'Handsome specimen,' observed Cribben, chafing under all this admonition, the defiance in his lonely nature coming to a boil. 'We'll have a talk.' He strode into the street, Matt Heddle anxiously behind him and Love sauntering in the rear. Gholson, sensing them, swung round from tightening his horse's harness. Unquestionably he was a rough customer; but that roused Cribben's spirit.

'Will Gholson,' called out Cribben in his artillery-captain voice, 'I've got a few questions to ask you.'

A stare; and then Gholson spat into the road. His words were labored, a heavy blur of speech, like a man wrestling with a tongue uncongenial to him. 'You the counter?'

'That's right,' Cribben told him. 'Who owns your farm, Gholson?'

Another stare, longer, and a kind of slow, dismal grimace. 'Go to hell,' said Gholson. 'Leave us be.'

Something about this earth-stained, sweat-reeking figure, skulking on the frontier of humanity, sent a stir of revulsion through Cribben; and the consciousness of his inward shrinking set fire to his conceit, and he shot out one powerful arm to catch Gholson by the front of his tattered overalls. 'By God, Gholson, I'm coming out to your place tomorrow; and I'm going through it; I'll have a warrant; and I'll do my duty; so watch yourself. I hear you've got a queer place at Barrens Mill, Gholson. Look out I don't get it condemned for you.' Cribben was white, from fury, and shouting like a sailor, and shaking in his emotion. Even the dull lump of

Gholson's face lost its apathy before this rage, and Gholson stood quiescent in the tall man's grip.

'Mr. Cribben, friend,' Heddle was saying. Cribben remembered where he was, and what; he let go of Gholson's clothes; but he put his drawn face into Gholson's and repeated, 'Tomorrow. I'll be out tomorrow.'

'Tomorrow's Sunday,' was all Gholson answered.

'I'll be there tomorrow.'

'Sunday's no day for it,' said Gholson, almost plaintively. It was as if Cribben had stabbed through this hulk of flesh and rasped upon a moral sensibility.

'I'll be there,' Cribben told him, in grim triumph.

Deliberately Gholson got into his wagon, took up the reins, and paused as if collecting his wits for a weighty effort. 'Don't, Mister.' It was a grunt. 'A man that — a man that fusses on Sunday — well, he deserves what he gets.' And Gholson drove off.

'What's wrong, Mr. Cribben?' asked Heddle, startled: for Cribben had slipped down upon the bench outside the post office and was sucking in his breath convulsively. 'Here, a nip,' said Love, in concern, thrusting a bottle at him. Cribben took a swallow of whisky, sighed, and relaxed. He drew an envelope out of a pocket and swallowed a capsule, with another mouthful of whisky.

'Heart?' asked Heddle.

'Yes,' Cribben answered, as humbly as was in him. 'It never was dandy. I'm not supposed to get riled.'

'With that heart, you don't want to go up to Barrens Mill — no, you don't,' said the postmaster, gravely.

'She's a witch, Cribben.' Love was leaning over him. 'Hear me, eh? I say, she *is* a witch.'

'Quiet, Love,' the postmaster told him. 'Or if you do go to the Barrens, Mr. Cribben, you'll take a couple of the sheriff's boys with you.'

Cribben had quite intended to ask for a deputy, but he'd be damned now if he wouldn't go alone. 'I'm driving to the judge for a search warrant,' he answered, his chin up. 'That's all I'll take.'

Heddle walked with him to the boardinghouse where Cribben kept his automobile. He said nothing all the way, but when Cribben had got behind the wheel, he leaned in the window, his big, smooth, friendly old face intent: 'There's a lot of old-fashioned prejudice in Pottawattomie, Mr. Cribben. But, you know, most men run their lives on prejudice. We've got to; we're not smart enough to do anything else. There's sure to be something behind a prejudice. I don't know all about the Gholsons, but there's fact behind prejudice. Some things are best left alone.'

Here Cribben rolled up his window and shook his head and started the motor and rolled off.

After all, there was no more he could have said, Matt Heddle reflected. Cribben would go to Barrens Mill, probably count everything in sight, and bullyrag Will Gholson, and come back puffed up like a turkey. Misty notions. . . . He almost wished someone would put the fear of hell-fire into the Special Interviewer. But this was only an oldfangled backwater, and Cribben was a newfangled man.

*   *

On Sunday morning, Cribben drove alone up the road toward the Barrens. In his pockets were a set of forms, and a warrant in case of need; Cribben left his gun at home, thinking the devil of a temper within him a greater hazard than any he was liable to encounter from the Gholsons. Past abandoned cabins and frame houses with their roofs fallen in, past a sluggish stream clogged with ancient logs, past mile on mile of straggling second-growth woodland, Cribben rode. It was empty country, not one-third so populous as it had been fifty years before, and he passed no one at this hour.

Here in the region of the Barrens, fence wire was unknown: enormous stumps, uprooted from the fields and dragged to the roadside, are crowded one against another to keep the cows out, their truncated roots pointing toward the empty sky. Most symbolic of the stump-country, jagged and dead, these fences; but Cribben had no time for myth. By ten o'clock he was nursing his car over the remnant of a corduroy road which twists through Long Swamp; the stagnant water was a foot deep upon it, this spring. But he went through without mishap, only to find himself a little later snared in the wet ground between two treacherous sand hills. There was no traction for his rear wheels; maddened, he made them spin until he had sunk his car to the axle; and then, cooling, he went forward on foot. Love's Garage could pull out the automobile later; he would have to walk back to town, or find a telephone somewhere, when he was through with this business. He had promised to be at Barrens Mill that morning, and he would be there. Already he was within a mile of the farm.

The damp track that once had been a lumber road could have led him, albeit circuitously, to the Gholsons. But, consulting his map, Cribben saw that by walking through a stretch of hardwoods he could — with luck — save fifteen minutes' tramping. So up a gradual ascent he went, passing on his right the wreck of a little farmhouse with high gables, not many years derelict. 'The Gholsons don't like close neighbors.' Oaks and maples and beeches, this wood, with soggy leaves of many autumns underfoot and sponge-mushrooms springing up from them, clammily white. Water from the trees dripped upon Cribben, streaking his short coat. It was a quiet wood, most quiet; the dying vestige of a path led through it.

Terminating upon the crest of a ridge, the path took him to a stump fence of grand proportions. Beyond was pasture, cleared with a thoroughness exceptional in this country; and beyond the pasture, the ground fell away to a swift creek, and then rose again to a sharp knoll, of which the shoulder faced him; and upon the knoll was the house of Barrens Mill, a quarter of a mile distant.

All round the house stretched the Gholsons' fields, the work of years of fantastic labor. What power had driven these dull men to such feats of agricultural vainglory? For it was a beautiful farm: every dangerous slope affectionately buttressed and contoured to guard it from the rains, every boulder hauled away to a pile at the bend of the stream, every potential weed-jungle rooted out. The great square house — always severely simple, now gaunt in its blackened boards from which paint had scaled away long since — surveyed the whole rolling farm. A low wing, doubtless containing kitchen and woodshed, was joined to the northern face of the old building, which seemed indefinably mutilated. Then Cribben realized how the house had been injured: it was nearly blind. Every window above the ground floor had been neatly boarded up — not covered over merely, but the frames taken out and planks fitted to fill the apertures. It was as if the house had fallen prisoner to the Gholsons, and sat Samson-like in bound and blindfolded shame.

All this was apprehended at a single glance; a second look disclosed nothing living in all the prospect — not even a dog, not even a cow. But one of the pallid stumps stirred.

Cribben started. No, not a stump: someone crouching by the stump fence, leaning upon a broken root, and watching, not him, but the house. It was a girl, barefoot, a few yards away, dressed in printed meal-sacks, fifteen or sixteen years old, and thoroughly ugly, her hair a rat's-nest; this was no country where a wild rose might bloom. She had not heard him.

For all his ungainly ways, Cribben had spent a good deal of time in the open, and could be meticulously quiet. He stole close up to the girl and said, in a tone he meant to be affable, 'Well, now?'

Ah, what a scream out of her! She had been watching the blind façade of Barrens Mill house with such a degree of intensity, a kind of cringing smirk on her lips, that Cribben's words must have come like the voice from the burning bush; and she whirled, and shrieked, all sense gone out of her face, until she began to understand that it was only a stranger by her. Though Cribben was not a feeling man, this extremity of fright touched him almost with compassion, and he took the girl gently by the shoulder, saying, 'It's all right. Will you take me to the house?' He made as if to lead her down the slope.

At that, the tide of fright poured back into her heavy Gholson face, and she fought in his grasp and swore at him. Cribben — a vein of prudery ran through his nature — was badly shocked: it was hysterically vile cursing, nearly inarticulate, but compounded of every ancient rural obscenity. And she was very young. She pulled away and dodged into the dense wood.

Nothing moved in these broad fields. No smoke rose from the kitchen, no chicken cackled in the yard. Overhead a crow flapped, as much an alien as Cribben himself, nothing more seemed to live about Barrens Mill. Were Will Gholson crazy enough to be peering from one of the windows with a shotgun beside him, Cribben would make a target impossible to miss, and Cribben knew this. But no movement came from behind the blinds, and Cribben went round unscathed to the kitchen door.

A pause and a glance told Cribben that the animals were gone, every one of them, to the last hen and the last cat. Driven down to the lower farm to vex and delay him? And it looked as if every Gholson had gone with them. He knocked at the scarred back door: only echoes. It was not locked; and, having his warrant in his pocket, he entered. If Will Gholson were keeping mum inside, he'd rout him out.

Four low rooms — kitchen, rough parlor, a couple of topsy-turvy bedrooms — this was the wing of the house, showing every sign of a hasty flight. A massive paneled door shut off the parlor from the square bulk of the older house, and its big key was in the lock. Well, it was worth a try. Cribben, unlocking the door, looked in: black, frayed blinds drawn down over the windows — and the windows upstairs boarded, of course. Returning to the kitchen, he got a kerosene lamp, lit it, and went back to the darkened rooms.

Fourteen-foot ceilings in these cold chambers; and the remnants of Victorian prosperity in mildewed love seats and peeling gilt mirrors; and dust, dust. A damp place, wholly still. Cribben, telling his nerves to behave, plodded up the fine sweep of the solid stairs, the white plaster of the wall gleaming from his lamp. Dust, dust.

A broad corridor, and three rooms of moderate size, their doors ajar, a naked bedstead in each; and at the head of the corridor, a door that stuck. The stillness infecting him, Cribben pressed his weight cautiously upon the knob, so that the squeak of the hinges was faint when the door yielded. Holding the lamp above his head, he was in.

Marble-topped commode, washbowl holding a powder of grime, fantastic oaken wardrobe — and a tremendous Victorian rosewood bed, carved and scrolled, its towering head casting a shadow upon the sheets that covered the mattress. There *were* sheets; and they were humped with the shape of someone snuggled under them.

'Come on out,' said Cribben, his throat dry. No one answered, and he ripped the covers back. He had a half-second to stare before he dropped the lamp to its ruin.

Old, old — how old? She had been immensely fat, he could tell in that frozen moment, but now the malign wrinkles hung in horrid empty folds. How evil! And even yet, that drooping lip of command, that projecting jaw — he knew at last from what source had come the power that terraced and tended Barrens Mill. The eyelids were drawn down. For this only was there time before the lamp smashed. Ah, why hadn't they buried her? For she was dead, long dead, many a season dead.

All light gone, Cribben stood rigid, his fingers pressed distractedly against his thighs. To his brain, absurdly, came a forgotten picture out of his childhood, a colored print in his *King Arthur*: 'Launcelot in the Chapel of the Dead Wizard,' with the knight lifting the corner of a shroud. This picture dropping away, Cribben told his unmoving self, silently but again and again, 'Old Mrs. Gholson, old witch, old bitch,' as if it were an incantation. Then he groped for the vanished door, but stumbled upon the wire guard of the broken lamp.

In blackness one's equilibrium trickles away, and Cribben felt his balance going, and knew to his horror that he was falling straight across that bed. He struck the sheets heavily and paused there in a paralysis of revulsion. Then it came to him that no one lay beneath him.

Revulsion was swallowed in a compelling urgency, and Cribben slid his hands sweepingly along the covers, in desperate hope of a mistake. But no. There was no form in the bed but his own. Crouching like a great clumsy dog, he hunched against the headboard, while he blinked for any filtered drop of light, show him what it would.

He had left the door ajar, and through the doorway wavered the very dimmest of dim glows, the forlorn hope of the bright sun without. Now that Cribben's eyes had been a little time in the room, he could discern whatever was silhouetted against the doorway — the back of a chair, the edge of the door itself, the knob. And something *moved* into silhouette: imperious nose, pendulous lip, great jaw. So much, before Cribben's heart made its last leaping protest.

Uncle Isaiah

*And behold, at evening-tide trouble; and before the morning he is not. This
is the portion of them that spoil us, and the lot of them that rob us.*

Isaiah 17:14

One dusty evening, as the newsboys began to shout 'Racing Final!' just
before the shop's closing time, a squat man pushed into Kinnaird's
Cleaners and demanded twenty dollars a week. Daniel Kinnaird blinked
his mild eyes and looked at the card the squat man gave him, and shook
his head. 'You'll come across,' said the squat man, in a gin voice. 'Costa's
out. They all come through.' He grinned savagely. 'I'll be back tomorrow,
collecting.' Before Daniel Kinnaird could think of anything to reply, the
squat man had waddled back into the crowd in the street and had been
swept away.

'North End Cleaners Prudential Association,' the card read. It was a
neat white card, but Daniel Kinnaird caught a whiff of the stench-bombs
for which it was ambassador: the splintering plate-glass, the explosion,
the greasy smoke, the intolerable stench.

Kinnaird's Cleaners, Dyers and Tailors, Unusual Service, occupied a
square stone building with a quoined doorway that once had been handsome. Like most other business fronts in this street of the North End, it
had been a gentleman's house, and Daniel Kinnaird could remember
when half a dozen of these graceful mansions had remained as homes of
old families. Now only one such was a home, and that, the building next

door: the Kinnaird house. Everywhere else, slum children pounded up and down the stairs, or the old parlors were decorated with chromium and converted into hamburger-joints, or the ground-floor façades were knocked away to make room for car-wash garages. Fashionable suburbs, the automobile, and industrialization had turned the North End into a boneyard of defaced and degraded old houses.

But the Kinnairds remained. They had been among the first to come; they would be the last to go. Indeed, the Kinnairds *could* not go any longer, because their money had trickled away: the North End manacled them. Twenty years before, what remained of the Kinnaird capital had been invested in the dry-cleaning business, and at first this had been an enterprise modestly prospering. Today it was strangling. The pickup trucks of flashy, shoddy, cut-rate cleaners carried away half their custom; what trade survived came from the Italians and Poles and Negroes and nondescripts who packed their houses along this bleary ancient street — people who did their own pressing, brought cleaning only when they must, and required a tailor merely for patches.

After supper, Daniel Kinnaird blinked nightly over his ledgers. Kinnaird's Cleaners no longer could afford a book-keeper; the help consisted of a girl at the counter, two pressers, a cleaner, and the old Russian Jew who had been their tailor ever since the business had been established. Kinnaird and his wife did all they could, yet every month receipts crept down just a trifle further. Though poor, Daniel Kinnaird was not cheap: his establishment cleaned clothes carefully, and when — at long intervals — some customer wanted a suit, that suit was tailored decently. So Kinnaird's Cleaners had become a depressed undertaking in a market where cheapness was the sole factor in competition. Kinnaird could not afford paying twenty dollars a week to the North End Cleaners Prudential Association. In any event it would have been wrong to pay. Old-fangled folk, the Kinnairds still judged in terms of right and wrong.

'Costa's out.' Though Kinnaird did not read the newspapers thoroughly, he understood that. 'Costa's out' — this was *finis* for Kinnaird's Cleaners, he supposed. Last week the governor had pardoned Bruno Costa, who had been serving concurrent sentences for extortion and assault with intent to do great bodily harm; but the governor had pardoned him after less than two years in the penitentiary. An election had been won, a new chief magistrate and new judges had been sworn into office, certain pre-election pledges had to be fulfilled. To the representatives of the Press, the governor had spoken in humanitarian fashion about modern concepts of penology, and had liberated six eminent thugs. Of these fortunate six, Costa was the least; but he was big enough to run the North End.

Kinnaird went into the tailor's room. Cross-legged on his broad bench sat the old Jew, and Kinnaird handed him the card. 'Oi, Mr. Kinnaird,' said the tailor, raising his eyebrows in sympathy, 'how much?'

'They want twenty dollars a week, Sol.'

'Could be worse,' the Jew told him, spreading his palms in resignation. 'Could be worse, Mr. Kinnaird. You pay, yes? Always better to pay.'

'No,' said Daniel Kinnaird. 'They never dared come near me before. What shall I do, Sol? Why do they come now?'

In a gesture of futility, the tailor protruded his lower lip. 'Costa already got everybody else, Mr. Kinnaird. Kowalski's Drugs, on the corner, he pays. Jim's Garage, he pays. Every kind business, Costa got some association. I'm telling you, Mr. Kinnaird, better to pay. Costa's boys, they throw bombs, stink up the place; maybe they beat you, maybe me. To pay is better.'

'I'll call the police,' Daniel Kinnaird murmured, his inflection rising.

The Jew cackled joylessly. 'Maybe Costa fix the police, maybe not. Maybe not; but anyhow, the police ain't got time for watching your front window day and night, Mr. Kinnaird.'

'The Kinnairds don't pay people like Costa,' Daniel Kinnaird said, mostly to himself.

'I'm telling you, it's bad times all over.' The tailor shrugged; and then, rising suddenly, put on his coat. 'At supper, you think it over. To pay is cheaper. Good night.' He went softly out of the back door; and Kinnaird, watching him through the window, observed that Sol glanced around the corner before he stepped into the darkening alley.

Closing time past, the rest of the help had gone home; so Kinnaird locked the doors with deliberation, took all the money from the till and tucked it inside his coat, and left the shop by the door in the wall which led into his house. This he locked and bolted, once he was in his hall, and put a chair against the knob. Picking up the telephone, he dialed the number of Hanchett, the bookseller, a laconic old man of some astuteness.

'Charles?' Kinnaird said. 'A man came today from Costa. They want twenty dollars every week. What can I do?'

'Pay,' came Hanchett's rasping voice.

'It wouldn't be right to pay. What else, Charles?'

'Do you know anybody in the rackets, anybody big?'

'No.'

'No, you wouldn't.' Hanchett coughed. 'Well, if you did, you might persuade somebody to make Costa call it off. Do you know anybody in the City Hall?'

'No, and I don't want to.'

'There fades your second chance, Daniel. I'll make it short and sour: you've got to know somebody *tough*. If you don't, you'll have to pay. If you need cash, I'll lend you some tomorrow.' Hanchett hung up.

Daniel Kinnaird lingered by the telephone stand, staring at the cover of the directory. 'For an emergency call to the police, dial 0,' said a big black line of print. He shook his head and went into the kitchen, where his wife was at the stove. 'Alma,' he sighed, 'please sit down a moment.'

Having glanced at his face, tall Alma obeyed. 'What is it?' He told her.

'Do we know anyone *tough*, Alma?' he asked, after they had sat some time in silence, his wife with her hands against her temples.

'We might see Simmonds, the alderman,' she ventured.

'He knows we voted the wrong way,' was all Kinnaird answered. She nodded, and for some minutes they listened to the clock's ticking.

'We'll have to manage to pay, that's all,' Mrs. Kinnaird remarked then, as if she were angry with her husband.

'It's wrong to pay a man like Costa.' He stared her down. 'There's someone we might turn to, you know, Alma — '

Her thin lips parted, as if to ask 'Who?' But she shut them tight before the word came out; and watching her husband's expression, she shook her gray head vigorously.

'I'm not ashamed of my uncle, Alma,' he told her.

'No! Don't you dare bring him into this!' She clasped her hands convulsively. 'It would be better to pay. Besides, you never could find him in time. We've not seen him for more than nine years.'

'In some ways, Uncle Isaiah is a remarkable man, Alma.'

'Remarkable! That's putting it gently. Oh, whatever possessed Costa's gang to come after us?' She wanted no more talk of Uncle Isaiah, it was clear. 'They used to let decent people alone; or, anyway, they only plagued the foreigners and the colored folks.'

'Costa's rising in society,' Kinnaird observed with a wry little smile, 'and we're not exempt any longer. Decent people don't count nowadays. Is the chief of police decent? Is the mayor decent? Costa, or Costa's friends, delivered the vote of this ward. Costa stands for democracy in action, *à la* North End.'

'Then there's nowhere to appeal,' she muttered, rising from her chair. 'We'll pay.'

Kinnaird motioned her back. 'We'll appeal to Uncle Isaiah.'

She gritted her teeth. 'Appeal to a lunatic?'

'Isaiah was in the asylum for only two months — you know that.'

'Yes, and I know that he escaped, and after he came out of hiding, his lawyers got him declared sane again. "Homicide by reason of temporary insanity" — and so he never paid for the thing he had done that time, or for anything else of the sort. Oh, I know every old family has its nasty uncles, old men that play the fiddle and get drunk and never repay loans; I wouldn't much mind a man like that. But your famous Uncle Isaiah! Ugh, he's cold, cold, like a moccasin, and he's always watching. Whenever he came into a room, I shivered.'

'Why, I thought he always was polite to you, Alma.'

'Of course he was. His manners were exquisite, with everyone, and he dressed beautifully' — here she glanced caustically at her husband — 'and he was clean as a scrubbed baby, and as rosy. "But O! he was perfectly lovely to see, the pirate Dowdirk of Dundee." You Kinnairds! I could see that Isaiah standing behind the stakes, watching witches burn — only he was born too late for that fun. You Scotch Kinnairds, with your cruel Old Testament names and your brimstone souls! You're scary enough, most of you; but Isaiah scared the wits out of his own family. You were frightened to death of him yourself, Daniel — you know you were.'

Daniel winced, and then chuckled slightly. 'Remember, Alma, how when he was in good humor he'd act Giant Despair? You lived just down the block, and you'd be over to play . . .'

'Do you think I'd forget? I lost five years' growth from that game. We'd be Christian and Faithful; then that dreadful Isaiah would come stealing up, in some sort of enormous black sack, and all of a sudden he'd pounce, and have us, and throw us in a closet. Oh, his cold hands, his long nails! I used to cry at night, after a day of that game; but I never dared refuse to play, because then perhaps Isaiah might have lost his good humor. How I hated him! I thought he was like a pet snake, that had to be fed on milk, and stroked, or he'd choke you.'

'Really, Alma, you exaggerate. Uncle Isaiah wasn't warmhearted; but sometimes I loved him, and he knew it. He was charitable, too, and he never was in serious trouble with the city police, except for that affair before he went to the asylum.'

'No,' Alma interrupted, 'usually it was the League of Nations that wanted to put him behind bars. I'll admit he had commercial talents. Smuggled guns, illegal immigrants and emigrants, opium . . .'

'After all, the opium was only for his own use, or perhaps for those Chinese and Indian friends of his, the mystics one used to find him with. Many times I was proud of him. He was eccentric in the grand manner, when all's said. Oh, there was an anarchic streak in him. But you've no cause to despise him so; and if anyone can help us now, it's Uncle Isaiah. Whatever he was or wasn't, he took a great pride in family, Alma. He'd send help or bring it, if he knew.'

'Despise Isaiah? No, not that — I loathe him. Twice you and I saw him in those trances, huddled in his chair like a dead man; you could have pushed a pin into him, and he'd not have stirred till his appointed time. That's what those opium-smoking "mystic" freaks he patronized got him into. "Out of the body," he told us afterward. Out of his *mind* he was, really. But there's no danger of his meddling in this trouble: Isaiah Kinnaird would be a dead pigeon if he set foot in this country, let alone this city. He's in Omsk, Tomsk, or Tobolsk — or, for all anybody knows, in Hell. And you'll not find one soul in town who could or would give you his address, Daniel; so we may as well pay Costa.'

Her husband leaned upon the kitchen table, his chin between his hands.

'I don't know that,' he said, slowly and somewhat maliciously. 'I don't know. How about the Greek?'

* *

In Water Street, a little way from the ferry docks, stands the Ares Café, its back to the sluggish river, its face to that sullen and nocturnally silent road of warehouses, even the green and red neon of its sign suffocated by river fog. Flanked by two valetudinarian potted ferns, a large simulated ham on a platter took pride of place in the front window; and upon the plate-glass was lettered boldly, 'Woodrow Wilson Argyropoulous, Prop. Tables for Ladies.' Above the café, two grimy windows looked down from what might be a loft or an office, with a separate entrance leading upstairs from the street to this floor.

Only a man with high talent for observing small details would have made out a device just above this entrance: a diminutive mirror fixed upon a steel bracket, tilted at such an angle that anyone looking from the window above could see who was at his door. Mr. Isaiah Kinnaird had fastened that mirror in place, for his office had been over the Ares Café. It had mattered to Uncle Isaiah, Daniel Kinnaird reflected, that he should have a glimpse of his queer visitors before they got in. Now Daniel Kinnaird stood here by the Ares Café, looking through the plate-glass into the restaurant.

It being half-past nine in the evening, the Greek had only one patron, finishing a cup of coffee, and the Greek was engaged in his old pastime of demonstrating his private solution of the riddle of the business cycle. Pencil in hand, sheets of paper on the counter by the coffee urn, he drew interminable circles and curves and triangles, gesticulating with his left arm, his voice drifting through the open doorway to Kinnaird.

'O.K., Mr. Bronkowski? You with me so far? O.K. Now the bank give me seventeen thousand more . . .'

A tiny boy emerged from behind the coffee urn and tugged masterfully at Argyropoulous: 'Pencil, Papa, pencil.'

'Go 'way, boy,' sighed the Greek, benevolently. 'Now, Mr. Bronkowski, this straight?' The customer agreed. Outside the window, Daniel Kinnaird shifted impatiently; he must get the Greek alone.

'Pencil, Papa, pencil!' the tiny boy demanded. In despair, the Greek surrendered his pencil. And at that moment, while still watching the scene within the café, Daniel Kinnaird came to feel that he himself was watched.

He turned in alarm. But no man was in the street, not Costa nor the squat man nor anyone else. Then his eyes caught the surface of the mirror above his head: reflected in it was a face, peering downward from the lightless window above the mirror. Though dim in what light came from the café sign, this face could be made out tolerably well. A small, square countenance, with deep lines at either side of the mouth, and topped by thick white hair. A civil, if somewhat sardonic, expression was on the firm lips; the large eyes were shadowed by tufted eyebrows. It was Mr. Isaiah Kinnaird. Next, this reflection was gone.

In astounded urgency, Daniel Kinnaird tugged at the door leading to the office above, but it was locked. To have cried out Uncle Isaiah's name would not have been prudent, he reminded himself, even in this frantic moment. Regardless of the solitary customer, Kinnaird burst into the café and said to the Greek, panting, 'Woodie, I have to talk with you.'

'Play with the pencil, boy,' the Greek told his son, patting his head. Woodie's black eyes ran over Kinnaird's pale face. 'You come in the kitchen, Mr. Kinnaird?' They went behind the swinging door, back by the sink. 'You got troubles, Mr. Kinnaird?'

'My Uncle Isaiah's upstairs,' said Daniel Kinnaird. 'Take me up, Woodie.'

The Greek scowled, blinked, and then laughed. 'Ho! You joking, Mr. Kinnaird? Ho! You know I ain't seen your uncle for nine, ten years. Nobody seen him. Cuba, Mexico — who knows? Not here, never. Ho, ho! Not healthy in Water Street, not now.'

'I saw him in the mirror, Woodie. He'll want to talk with me. Take me up.'

The Greek's grin faded. 'Christ A'mighty, Mr. Kinnaird, you don't joke? You feel good? No, Mr. Kinnaird, by Christ A'mighty, your uncle ain't up there, nobody up there. Listen.' He raised his hand. A screen slammed — it was the customer going out — and then they heard only the sound of the little boy scribbling in the café. From the office above, not the faintest rustle. Lowering his hand, 'Nobody up there, not for years.'

'Show me the way up, Woodie,' Daniel Kinnaird insisted. 'I've got to see my uncle. Costa's on my track.'

'God damn to hell!' The Greek shrugged in vexation. 'The truth, that's what I tell. O.K., come up, Mr. Kinnaird, if you got to.' He took two keys from the knife drawer and led the way through the café to the outer door. 'Costa,' he added, very low. 'Oh, bad. You pay, Mr. Kinnaird. *I* pay.' They went outside, and the Greek unlocked the separate door opening upon the stairs, and they ascended some steep black steps. Then another door stopped them; the Greek had some trouble with the lock of this one. After fumbling, he got it open, and they were in a big dark loft of a place.

'No electric lights, Mr. Kinnaird,' said the Greek — or rather, he whispered it. Dim shapes of furniture loomed up: a desk, some sort of long counter, a safe, a table, three or four elderly chairs, a filing cabinet. The shadows at the far end were extremely thick.

'How about a flashlight, Woodie?' Shaking his head, the Greek felt along the counter, and presently had a candle in his hand; he lit it. No, those shadows were shadows only. Beyond the place where they had been, two more windows looked upon the river, a door between them. 'Show me what's on the other side of that door, Woodie.' The Greek fitted a key to it, and when it creaked open they looked upon the oily river. They stood high above the water; a rickety flight of steps, supported by piers, twisted down to the quay and the mouth of an alley. With now and then a gurgle or hiss, the tide was slipping languidly out. 'All right, Woodie,' said Daniel Kinnaird, 'I apologize to you. Fancies, fancies.'

Closing the river door, they stood in the middle of the disused office. 'What the hell,' the Greek said, 'I know. Me, I want him back, too, Mr. Kinnaird. You think about him coming, maybe, and think, and after while you hear steps outside, and you say, "Christ A'mighty, that's Isaiah Kinnaird!" Ho! Nothing there. Your uncle, he's too smart to come back, ever. Mexico, Cuba, Brazil, who knows? But not here. If he was, then no Costa, hey? No Costa? Your uncle, he don't spit on Costa, hey?'

'Why didn't you rent this place afterward, Woodie?'

The Greek ran his hand through his scanty hair. 'I get no money for this dump, Mr. Kinnaird. And your uncle, he lend me money. And he take me up here sometimes, me and my first boy, and we talk. Oh, how your uncle talk, Mr. Kinnaird! What a friend, so good! What he don't know, Christ A'mighty, it don't matter a damn. And he make funny poems to tickle my first boy, like this:

'"Woodrow Wilson Argyropoulous,
Born to rule this grand metropolis . . ."

'No, I leave things like he had 'em. If your uncle crazy, Mr. Kinnaird, I like every guy in Water Street crazy. Smart! No, I leave things like he had 'em. "Woodrow," your uncle say, "Woodrow, I put my trust in you." Kind! Oh, Christ A'mighty, a good man. I leave things like you see.'

'Woodie,' Kinnaird asked, 'isn't there a chance *someone* knows where to reach my uncle?'

'All right,' the Greek said. 'All right. One guy you try. What the hell, you try him. The lawyer, Simmich. Your uncle, Simmich did stuff for him.' Woodie led the way back down the stairs and into the café, and there scribbled an address on the back of an old menu. 'He don't know; but you try him.' Opening the door, the Greek started to speak again, hesitated as if doubting his discretion, and then muttered, 'You know your uncle, he usta pray?'

'I never thought of him as pious.'

41

'Oh, Mr. Kinnaird, sure. Pray? Christ A'mighty, he talk low when he talk with you; but when he pray — maybe I wash dishes down here, and I hear him pray loud, loud, hear him through the ceiling. Your uncle, he pray to God to choke his enemies. And it come true, Mr. Kinnaird, it come true every time. Oh, a good man. But me and you, we got to deal with Costa. Best to pay. Sorry, Mr. Kinnaird. So long.'

As he left, Kinnaird took a surreptitious glance at the mirror overhead, but of course it was blank. Simmich lived within walking distance; and though the hour was past eleven, Kinnaird couldn't wait until morning. He came to an old brick flat-building on the edge of a slum-clearance project, took the automatic elevator up four flights, found a door with a plate engraved 'D. L. Simmich, Attorney,' and rang the bell. After two more rings, a thin fellow with nasty little eyes, in slippers and shirtsleeves, opened the door. 'Well?'

'My name is Kinnaird.'

Simmich's manner altered; he peered into the hall, either way. 'Come in, please, Mr. Kinnaird.' They sat in a living-room with walls of a dirty cream, and Simmich said, 'Related to *him?*'

'I need to get in touch with my uncle immediately. What can you do about it?'

The nasty eyes roved calculatingly over Kinnaird's mild face and shabby suit. 'I play my hand straight, Mr. Kinnaird. I haven't had word of Isaiah Kinnaird for three years. But it might be possible to inquire among some — among certain foreign associates of Mr. Kinnaird's. Just possible, understand. Of course, there'd be cablegrams, and registry fees, and my ordinary charges . . .'

'Go ahead,' Kinnaird told him. 'I take it that my uncle's transactions with you turned out satisfactorily, Mr. Simmich.'

'Oh, yes; prompt and agreeable, your uncle, even though fixed in his opinions.' The nasty eyes seemed to recalculate possible extortion against possible retribution. Simmich sighed slightly. 'The costs won't be prohibitive, Mr. Kinnaird. I'll commence first thing in the morning.'

'Begin by cable, please, tonight.' With some inner reluctance, Daniel Kinnaird shook hands with Simmich, and went down to the foggy road, and turned into Water Street, as good a way home as any. Even cables could hardly be expeditious enough. Uncle Isaiah left his brand on people.

*　　　　*

Well past midnight, alone in Water Street with his worries, Kinnaird again approached the Ares Café. Now the café was unlighted, the Greek having closed when Kinnaird left and gone down the block to his four rooms and seven dependents. Daniel Kinnaird could recall, fragmentarily, having spent hours when he was on vacation from school, in that dusty office above the café — hours of a fearful joy spent on a stool beside his impenetrable Uncle Isaiah, shuffling bundles of old invoices, and now and then daring to tease Uncle Isaiah into some game. Small and straight and impeccably neat, his uncle never had been out of temper, never had seemed in the least busy; and his skin had been tight and smooth as a very young man's. But you did not take liberties. His mother, Daniel Kinnaird realized later, had not much liked his hours in that office; but she never had ventured to put her objections into words. If you knew Uncle Isaiah, you rarely risked talking about him, no matter how many walls separated you from him; for he knew, he *knew*.

Amidst these recollected images, Daniel Kinnaird walked slowly past the Ares Café, when a sensation made him stop short. For the past two or three seconds, an odor had drifted faintly about his nose; and now that odor found its cubby in his memory. It was the scent of a soap; it was the odor of the delicate and costly soap that Uncle Isaiah had used, the smell which always emanated from Uncle Isaiah's white shirts and square small self, the aroma of an old-fashioned man's soap. And an odor it was, no mere memory.

Daniel Kinnaird, swinging about, leaped toward the doorway of the café. No one was in that doorway nor in the adjacent recess of the door to the office; but someone must have been there not more than half a minute before. For the second time that night, Kinnaird tugged at the door which led upstairs, and now it yielded. In he went, up the steps, treading on his toes so as to hear any sound above him.

And before he had gone up six treads, a sound did come from somewhere at the stairhead: a whistle, infinitely soft, but a whistled tune, 'Dixie.' After a few more seconds, during which Kinnaird felt the hair rising along the back of his neck, the whistle gave way to a low humming, and then distinct words, sung in a melodious deep voice, though muffled:

'There'll be buckwheat cakes and Injun batter,
Make you fat or a little fatter,
Look away, look away, look away, Dixie land.'

'Uncle Isaiah!' called Kinnaird. How well he knew voice and tune! 'Isaiah Kinnaird!' In three bounds, Daniel Kinnaird was at the top of the staircase and shoving against the door. But it would not budge.

Now the chant had ceased. Kinnaird rattled the knob, tried to force the bolt. 'Uncle Isaiah!' For he felt something stirring on the other side of the door. 'It's been nine years, Uncle Isaiah!' To his mind's eye came a vision of the man behind that warped door: Mr. Isaiah Kinnaird, ageless, with his peculiar jaunty dignity, his aloof whistling, his stiff collars, his faint scent of soap, his good dark clothes, his stout thorn walking-stick, his square, genteel, old-young face with the tufted eyebrows and the restless eyes of a light blue. 'Uncle Isaiah!'

After this last cry, silence fell for a whole minute; then a quiet voice said, somewhere inside the loft, 'Good evening to you, Daniel, from your bad mad old uncle.'

'Let me in, Uncle Isaiah.' No reply, but some noise like the scratching of a stick upon the floor. 'Uncle, are you ill?'

Now Isaiah Kinnaird's voice rang clearer and stronger, full of his old whimsical deliberation. 'In me, Daniel, decades of celibacy and sobriety are rewarded. I'm as hearty as I was when we last met. But if you will pardon my recurrent eccentricity, we will keep this door shut.'

'I've got something urgent to discuss with you, Uncle, and it's been nine years since we were together, you know.'

'I'm aware of both facts, Daniel, my nephew; yet you will understand that I am here on sufferance; my tenure is precarious; and my present arrangements require that our intercourse take place wholly *per vox*, however undignified this may seem to you.' There was a deep chuckle.

'Uncle,' said Daniel Kinnaird, his heart warming, 'come home with me. It's dark, and you won't be seen. I need your help. Incidentally, your landlord, Mr. Argyropoulous, is a consummate liar.'

'We Kinnairds shouldn't sit in judgment so summarily, Daniel. Although Woodrow bears some affection for me, I think my presence might embarrass him just now, and he has no notion I am here.

'Thus sang the jolly miller, upon the banks of Dee:
I care for nobody, no not I, and nobody cares for me.

'Whenever I have deviated from this principle, Daniel, I have suffered. You recall, too, the injunction of our Stoic preceptor, "Live as if upon a

44

mountain." This affair of yours which I'm to settle requires especial privacy.'

'What am I to do, Uncle?' Daniel Kinnaird was resigned now to conducting this extraordinary interview through a locked door: it never had been of any avail to oppose the whims of Uncle Isaiah.

'As for coming home with you,' Uncle Isaiah went on, 'why, candidly — I fear Alma wouldn't survive the shock without some preparation, eh? Besides, my scheme requires you to keep all this from Alma — which shouldn't be really difficult for you, given our family's congenital proclivity to secrecy. Well, now, to business, I understand that you are in difficulty with a certain Bruno Costa.'

'People like that never dared trouble us before, Uncle.'

'Right, and therefore our dismissal of him should be rather curt, eh? Mr. Costa scarcely understands our family, Daniel. But in any case, I suspect Costa's necessities force him to seek revenue from sources normally left unmolested. Formerly, I understand, Costa confined his exactions to persons who could not speak three consecutive sentences of proper English, and so were bubbles in this great melting pot of ours. But he must have spent a peck of money to get his pardon in company so august, and he's endeavoring to recoup his losses — indeed, to fulfill certain promises. Well, we must rebuff him, Daniel, my nephew.'

'And how?'

'Listen to me: offer Costa's agent a lump-sum settlement, rather than weekly payments; and insist upon a personal interview with Mr. Costa.'

'But could we trust Costa to keep away, after he'd got his lump sum?'

'Naturally not. Our offer is bait, Daniel, to bring him to the interview. That meeting will be conducted right here, tomorrow night, at half-past eleven; and I'm the one who'll clean Mr. Costa's clock for him. Tell his man that Mr. Kinnaird wants to talk with Costa. You needn't mention which Kinnaird.'

'What can you arrange, Uncle Isaiah?' Mr. Isaiah Kinnaird, his nephew reflected, was a gentleman remarkably versatile; but he was Lord knows how old, and Daniel Kinnaird did not quite relish the idea of leaving him alone with a hoodlum like Costa.

'Daniel, I ought not to have to tell you that I don't tolerate inquiries into my business procedures. I'll solve your problem for you: that's enough. And since I am sedulous not to attract attention from Woodrow or anyone else, will you leave me to my lucubrations? Costa's to come here at eleven-thirty tomorrow, remember.' There was some relish in the voice.

'When shall we meet, Uncle?' Daniel Kinnaird felt a thorough fool, separated from his nearest kinsman, after nine years, by an inch of pine.

'That, Daniel boy, is the dispensation of a merciful Providence, and hangs also upon the issue of our business tomorrow night. Goodbye, Daniel.' Perfect silence followed on the other side of the panel. And Kinnaird, knowing the futility of crossing his uncle, went reluctantly down the stairs and across the street.

No light showed at the upper windows: elusive as a bat or a nightbird, Isaiah Kinnaird. His nephew shivered for a moment, and then hurried home, half dazed, but reassured.

*   *

To his wife, at breakfast, Kinnaird said nothing but that he had no intention of paying Costa, and would therefore 'make other arrangements.' He ignored her frightened exasperation. All day he was fairly cheerful; and at closing time, again, the squat man entered Kinnaird's Cleaners.

'Cough up the dues, brother,' said the squat man, from the corner of his mouth.

'I'd rather make a final settlement with Mr. Costa,' Kinnaird told him.

Speculatively the squat man chewed a cigar. 'That's up to the boss.'

'Then I'll meet him at eleven-thirty tonight, over the Ares Café, Water Street.' Kinnaird was firm about it; the squat man looked taken aback.

'The boss makes the dates, see,' he said.

'If Costa wants a cash settlement, he'll be there, my friend.'

'O.K., O.K.,' the squat man agreed, almost plaintive; 'but if you get the boss riled, it's your funeral. Say, you ain't plannin' any cute stuff?' He stared again at Kinnaird's mild face. 'No, I guess you wouldn't.' And he went away.

Kinnaird locked the shop and ate a hearty supper. 'You Kinnairds!' Alma said to him. 'What have you done? Sometimes you're as clammy as your uncle.'

Selecting a book, Daniel Kinnaird settled himself in a corner by the grandfather clock.

*   *

About half-past eleven that night, a tall and swarthy man emerged from an alley on the north side of Water Street and crossed toward the Ares Café. He wore an expensive suit of loud check, and he walked with a swagger, throwing his shoulders back, glancing challengingly from under the brim of his low-crowned hat. There was no one to challenge. He tried the door to the office above the café, found it unlocked, and felt for a light switch: none could be discovered. So he mounted the stairs in darkness, and knocked at the upper door. No one answered. With a curse, he pushed it open and slipped inside.

Upon a naked table in the middle of the long, dusty room, a single candle was burning. Shadows half hid the farther end of the loft, but he could make out a door there, and he could see no one waiting for him. 'Kinnaird?' he grunted.

Then — did it come from behind that old safe? — Costa heard a soft humming, as if someone were trying variations on a sea-chanty. In a deep voice, someone was crooning:

'I'd a Bible in my hand when I sailed, when I sailed;
I'd a Bible in my hand when I sailed.
I'd a Bible in my hand by my father's great command,
But I sunk it in the sand when I sailed.'

'Kinnaird, that you?' Rather than replying, the deep voice repeated the chorus, placidly, drawling out 'by my father's great command,' and then ending with abrupt speed, 'But I sunk it in the sand when I sailed.'

Still no one appeared. 'Kinnaird!' Costa demanded. He closed the door behind him. When it went shut, there occurred a distinct click. Costa started. Keeping his face to the room, he felt at the back of him with his left hand, seeking the knob, while he slid his right hand cautiously into a coat pocket. There was no knob; there was no internal lock; the door, so far as he could tell, was secured by some hidden spring. 'Kinnaird!' Costa called, furious.

Did something shift, over there by the other door, out from behind the safe? Now a voice said, in a mere murmur, 'Mr. Bruno Costa, I see.' Costa crouched instinctively.

'You playin' games, Kinnaird? Come on out!' In Costa's voice was a nervous shrillness.

Then someone did come from the shadows, moving into the dim aura of light on the far side of the candle. It was a self-assured old man, small but squarely built, dressed with care; he played with a good walking stick; his head was bare, and in the flicker of the candle Costa could see that he had thick white hair, a fresh pink skin, and great eyebrows that made his eyes circles of shadow. 'What the hell!' cried Costa. 'Who're you?'

'I represent Mr. Daniel Kinnaird,' said the old gentleman, composedly. 'My name is Isaiah Kinnaird. We haven't met previously, Mr. Costa. I'm here to arrange a final settlement with you.' He smiled courteously.

'Yeah?' Costa hesitated, and knew that the old man perceived his incertitude; so he strode defiantly to the middle of the room, where he stared across the table at the old man. Costa kept his hand in his pocket. 'Yeah? No, we ain't met, but I heard about you, you crazy old bastard. What's up?'

'I look upon you, sir,' said Isaiah Kinnaird, 'as an interesting phenomenon of social disintegration, a representative specimen of these depraved days. Your reference to my origin is inaccurate; for only one instance of illegitimacy has been recorded among the Kinnairds in more than a century; while you, Mr. Costa — if you will forgive my saying so — manifestly are the end-product of many generations of unbridled lubricity.'

'Cut the comedy,' Costa snarled, grimacing in a way that should have been alarming. 'Are you and that pants-presser going to ante?'

Now old Kinnaird came still closer to the table, so that the candle showed him very plain, and Costa could see his eyes. They were blue, and would have been innocent, had they not slid and rolled so wildly. 'Jesus!' Costa gasped, a lump in his throat, 'I don't do business with nobody that's bughouse.'

'Costa,' Mr. Kinnaird resumed, politely smiling, 'I believe we shall make our final settlement now. You were imprudent this night. Surely you noticed how that door locked behind you?'

'Keep away,' Costa spat out, shifting his hand in his pocket. 'You going to ante?'

'Are you in tolerable health, Mr. Costa?' Having said this, the old man rapidly slipped one of his slender hands (in this instant, Costa saw how terribly long the nails were) across the dusty table, and touched Costa upon the wrist. Yelling, Costa sprang to one side.

'Oh God! Keep them hands off me!' Isaiah Kinnaird was sidling round the table. 'Keep away, you old bastard!' And now Costa pulled his automatic; but Kinnaird's white hand was quicker; and as its fingers touched Costa's, the tall man screamed again, and the gun fell under the table.

What followed might have been ludicrous to anyone that witnessed it.

A powerful man, in the prime of life, dodged and ducked about the room, vaulting the table, scampering past the desk, for an instant seeking sanctuary behind the safe, trying always to gain the back door. Now and again he shrieked as his pursuer nearly grasped him. Always in his way, intercepting, snatching, chuckling, darted a small elderly man, his white hair disordered, his eyes alight, his veined hands extended, one gripping a stick.

Then Costa saw an opening: he doubled back, rolled under the table, and ran straight for the door to the river. But just before he could reach it, his foot touched the rung of a chair, and he went to his knees. Almost in the same moment he rose; yet as he caught his balance, Isaiah Kinnaird protruded his stick, tripped Costa, and was upon him.

*   *

When the clock struck midnight, Daniel Kinnaird put down his book. By now, the conference in Water Street should be concluded; and his uncle would have warned Costa off. At the last stroke of the clock, however, an engulfing conviction burst upon Daniel Kinnaird — something that devastated the marches of ordinary perception. He thought he heard a man's shriek and a chuckle anciently familiar, associated in his memory with a great black sack. All this invaded his consciousness as if someone had tumbled him into a freezing pool.

Who knows the whole power of passionate entreaty, or what a desperate longing may conjure from the depths? Into Kinnaird's bewildered mind flashed a dozen curious sensations of the past evening: the scent of soap, the tune of 'Dixie'; and without snatching up hat or coat, he ran out of his door into the road, and through the paper-littered ways of the North End toward Water Street. Some things even a Costa ought not to face.

From the pavement, he could see an insufficient light flicker behind the drawn shades of the office above the Ares Café. His flesh creeping, Daniel Kinnaird climbed the stairs and pulled open the door at the top. A candle, almost wholly guttered, allowed him to inspect an empty loft. One chair had been overturned; something had brushed dust from the table top. That back door to the river stairs stood ajar, creaking intermittently in the breeze.

Daniel Kinnaird went upon the crazy platform, and heard the tide sucking at ooze, and saw some bird of night flap over the water toward the soiled and decrepit streets of the North End. But of Isaiah Kinnaird, or of Bruno Costa, no trace — not that night, nor the next day, nor ever.

The Surly Sullen Bell

And when they shall say unto you, Seek unto them that have familiar spirits, and unto wizards that peep, and that mutter: should not a people seek unto their God? for the living to the dead?

Isaiah 8:19

Having stared at the river for half an hour, Loring walked back across the great steel bridge and turned to the left. A little past eight he would have to be knocking at the Schumachers'.

In St. Louis they have pounded the Old Town into dust. All along the Mississippi, where the little city of the French and their American successors used to lie, now is a brick-strewn desolation — no building standing but the stiff old cathedral, grudgingly spared in the fiat that destined this belt of land for a memorial park. To the modern politician and planner, men are the flies of a summer, oblivious of their past, reckless of their future. Governmental contracts and newspaper publicity are concrete; the Old Town had been only a shabby slum to the politicians and planners of St. Louis, men not given to long views or to theory.

So Frank Loring thought as he strolled down one of those forlorn streets of condemned houses that cling to a brief reprieve on the edge of the bulldozed wilderness that once was an historic community. Loring was not progressive. Candidly, Loring told himself, he was a reactionary. Ecclesiastes was Bible enough for him. Though not yet forty, he had beheld nearly all things under the sun, he thought; and yesterday's sun had been warmer than today's. St. Louis being a progressive town, in which the air stank from the breweries and the government stank from other fermentation, Loring stopped there only when God and Mammon called him.

As traveler for a publishing firm, he could not keep away altogether from dingy St. Louis, with its vast stupid 'civic center' and its decaying heart; but until this evening he had held the Gomorrah of a city at arm's length, sticking chiefly to his hotel room in the grandiose late-Victorian railway station. Tonight, though, the past had claimed him.

For Professor Schumacher had found Loring. Professor Schumacher was Godfrey Schumacher, the husband of Mrs. Nancy Schumacher; and Nancy had been Nancy Birrell; and all this past decade Loring had not seen her, praise be. She was very lovable; and being no Stoic, Frank Loring had chosen not to look upon her since she married. Ten years, all the same — some healing power, surely, in such a quarantine by time. Well, he would see her tonight beside her husband and talk of little things, and then plod back into apathy.

He had been sitting at a soda fountain with an instructor in literature when there came up Godfrey Schumacher, professor of Spanish, with whom he hadn't spoken for ten years either; and Schumacher had shaken his hand and smiled his old lordly smile and asked him to come round for an evening with Nancy and himself. Loring must have shown his surprise. 'Nancy hoped I'd be able to persuade you,' Schumacher said. 'She speaks of you often.' And Schumacher had put a large patronizing hand on Loring's shoulder. 'They told me in the dean's office you were expected in town this week, Frank.'

Nancy hoped? Why? That was what Loring wanted to ask; but instead he had smiled and agreed and lamented the day's heat, and complimented Schumacher on the gray suit he wore. Schumacher cut nearly as handsome a figure as he had a decade gone, and much of his past-president-of-fraternity air had survived, too. Mingled with it was a hint of something newer and perhaps deeper — a kind of frowning dignity, even an intensity. Again Loring was a trifle surprised, Schumacher not having been the sort of man one expects to ripen with the years. And somehow Loring relished these recent developments of Schumacher's nature no more than he had liked the old Schumacher.

Schumacher wasn't the man he'd spend an evening with if he hadn't been cornered and almost bluffed into it. As for Nancy . . . What could she and Loring have to say now that wouldn't hurt? Every smile must be a reflection of past folly, every civility a humiliation. And natty, broad-shouldered, merry-dog Schumacher there between them, now and to the end of time. Well, what did Nancy mean to say to him? For she must have been at the back of Schumacher's invitation. They'd hardly known each other, Schumacher and he, back in those days before the Great Fact; and when they had met — a half-dozen times, perhaps — there'd been no love lost. Twice a year, for five years now, Loring had been coming round to St. Louis, but Schumacher never once had sought him out.

Ah, that was Nancy's doing, that impulsive little girl's doing. Little girl? She must be thirty-five, nearly. Yet to his mind she was the windblown romp beside the lake in the pine woods, calling out, 'Frank! Frank! Do I look like Carmen?' And so she would stay for him always.

A scent brought back Loring from the lake in the woods, a dozen years lost, to the pavements of St. Louis and the present. To be detected through the air of downtown St. Louis, this scent must be a stench. Such it was, and it came from the doorways of the condemned houses past which Loring was sauntering. Their windows broken, their doors gone, their steps rotted, their chimneys fallen away, still these houses were inhabited in a sparse and furtive way. To this slum of slums crawled down the most pitiful and foul sweepings of the white populace of a great city: old men with no legs who played harmonicas outside the picture-houses at night; women wrecked by liquor; grown imbeciles subsisting on restaurant garbage; the torpid, the loathsome, the soddenly vicious. They lit fires on sheet-iron scrap in the bare rooms, and slept wrapped in newspapers or filthy old coats; they got water the devil knew where — from the river, perhaps. The stench of them and their litter, the remnants of their greasy suppers and their carpet of dust, swept sourly into the street.

Without plumbing, without heating, without lighting, they lived on in these wrecks of houses, while the plaster flaked away with damp and the rats gnawed the timbers. For condemned houses that were the last stand of the Old Town had this surpassing advantage: no one collected rent. Their site was the state's, their walls were the wreckers', and the police of St. Louis left the squatters in possession as creatures too unclean and too futile for touching.

These old houses were flush with the street, and alleys, courts, dead-end lanes, opened from the sidewalk into the back recesses of the few doomed blocks — bad warrens to enter if you looked a bit under the weather and ripe for rolling. Loring quickened his pace, it being nearly dark now and the Schumachers' address five or six blocks farther. He stepped over the legs of a burly man who slouched immobile upon the steps of a tenement; and he noticed that though the fellow wore no shirt this summer evening, a thick woollen undershirt covered him from neck to wrists, and that the man's head, nearly bald, had a great nasty protuberance, almost conical, on one side. Pleasant neighbors for the Schumachers, these squatters of the condemned streets.

A little further along he met an old, or at least haggard, man and woman lurching toward him, bleary and raucous. As they scurried past, the woman threw up a grimy hand like a witch's right in his face, screeching out, 'Ah there, lover!' And now Loring had found the house number Schumacher had given him: a square, bracketed house, decently kept, with a brick wall round it — the beginning of the mid-Victorian girdle that marched with the fringe of the older town.

In his diffident way, Loring went up the walk, raised his hand to knock, and then lowered it. Who would answer? Would Nancy be face to face with him the second the door opened? But he did not have to knock, after all. Heavy footfalls came from somewhere inside, and a night-lock was turned; and there stood Schumacher with his vast confident smile.

'I heard you on the step, Frank.'

The incarnation of certitude, Schumacher, as in his younger days; but now he looked at you longer and more closely, absorbing rather than dismissing you. He took Loring's hat as if confiscating it. 'Nancy's lying down in the living-room,' Schumacher said. 'This seems to be one of her bad evenings.'

'Bad evenings?' Loring hardly ever had known that little romp to be ill.

'Oh, your coming will help to bring her round,' Schumacher went on. 'Yes, Frank, she's not been well for some time. The doctor hasn't a notion of the cause. But then, between you and me, what do M.D.'s know, eh? Not half of what certain people I could name have got hold of — not a tenth!'

Yet Schumacher, when Loring had known him formerly, had been a complacent positivist. Changes in the fellow, yes — but the complacency remained. 'You sound as if you'd been reading those Rosicrucian advertisements, Schumacher,' Loring commented, meaning to be jocular. But the jocosity was punctured by a long heavy look from Schumacher. Schumacher condescending to be resentful?

'I don't mean quackery,' Schumacher said. 'Well, we'll go in to Nancy.' He rapped perfunctorily at a door and pushed it open.

Nancy — ah, Nancy. The girl by the lake was in her yet. She had lain on a chaise longue, her little feet bare, as had been her fashion; and in her light green summer frock, supple and poised, she was for the moment Madame Récamier. But she rose quickly, gliding into neat slippers, and reached out both hands: 'Oh, Frank!'

Loring flushed, almost giddy, as he took her hands. His shy smile, which Nancy and a few others could evoke, betrayed, he supposed, the interminable dreary story of his past ten years. And Nancy apprehended at once, he could tell — how observant she always was, and how quick they both had been to grasp each other's moods, back there before the Great Fact — yes, apprehended that he was not cured and had no hope of cure. She gave him a glance, quick and compassionate (was there something more than compassion in it?), and then swept her look on to her husband.

'We'll pull up by the bay window, eh?' said Schumacher, easily. When Nancy turned toward a big armchair, Schumacher gave her his hand, and Loring understood with a sudden pain that she needed it. Below her blue eyes were faint circles, and she was slim, all too slim, though youthful and fine-skinned still. Her eyes glowed tonight; but, despite that, she was pale, weak and pale. She put Loring upon a plump stool at one side of her — 'You always used to choose the stool, Frank, at every party, and I've been saving this one for you' — and Schumacher in a chair on her other side. Thus they sat and talked, Frank and Nancy, and natty, broad-shouldered, merry-dog Schumacher.

And every smile that Loring gave Nancy was a reflection of past folly; and every civility from her was an humiliation; and there was nothing they could say to each other that did not hurt. They talked of fripperies, college gossip, and sweltering summers and new books and tolerable restaurants. It was torment. Schumacher dominated — patronizing, self-satisfied, full of talk. Schumacher was no bore: he talked much better than Loring had expected, and he listened to you when you had something to say — at least, he watched you, meeting your eyes with an absorbed and absorbing stare. No longer content with a physical triumph, did Schumacher want to dominate your mind? Even his efforts to put you at ease were disconcerting. Or had the sight and sound of Nancy shaken Loring's nerves?

To nerves, indeed, Schumacher presently led the conversation. Certainly no positivism remained in Schumacher. A startling blend of psychiatry and quasi-Yoga, spiced with something near to necromancy and perhaps a dash of Madame Blavatsky — this Schumacher's new system appeared to be. And this emitted by a swaggering professor of Spanish, late a disciple of the mechanists! Well, the line of demarcation between the two cults perhaps was no more difficult to cross than the boundary between Fascism and Communism, Loring reflected — but kept the observation private. How was Schumacher fetching Nancy into all this?

She had been leaning back in her chair with the polite air of a woman who has heard her husband too often on certain themes; but as Schumacher introduced her name, she sat up briskly, tucking her feet beneath her, and she listened with a fixity that set Loring wondering.

'. . . waves of mind,' Schumacher was saying. 'Take Nancy: I'm sure no one suffers from a more subtle neurosis. It has to be the work of influences, waves of impulse, from origins and purposes we can only guess at — and not many of us are qualified to guess. *Neurosis* is an abused and misleading word, you understand, Frank. But there's almost no physical cause for Nancy's trouble — only physical effects. What's the source, the impulse, eh? Where does it come from? What *wills* it?'

'The only trouble with me is, I'm sick,' declared Nancy with that humorous defiance Loring had known so long ago. 'Something just ails my insides, that's all, Godfrey. I'm not the sort of girl that has the jitters, am I, Frank? I never was, was I?'

Swallowing, Loring said, 'You were cool as the center seed of a cucumber, Nancy.' Did she want to make him cry?

'You'd best take the doctors' word on that, hadn't you, dear?' Schumacher interrupted. 'Three doctors we've called in, Frank. And what did they say, Nancy?'

Nancy crossed her arms pertly:

'They cried in accents drear,
"There's nothing wrong with her!"'

'Well, not precisely that, dear,' Schumacher admonished her, 'now was it? As a matter of fact, Frank, they had to admit they simply didn't *know*. Loss of weight, loss of vitality, but no ascribable physical cause.' Schumacher seemed positively to relish their bafflement. '"Waves of mind," I told them. They couldn't follow me, of course — only M.D.'s. And they couldn't account for Nancy's dreams, either: a neurotic product quite outside their sphere, Loring — or Frank, that is. Tell Frank about your dreams, Nancy.'

'Oh, other people's dreams are boring, aren't they, Frank?' She waved a little red-nailed hand. 'And these are boring even to me, in a way, after so many nights of them. I'd better let sleeping mares lie.'

'You can understand Nancy's not going into detail, Frank,' said Schumacher, earnestly. 'Dreadful sights, some of those visions of hers; glimpses that . . .'

Nancy cut him short, her full lips compressed in the imperious spirit Loring remembered too well: 'My dreams, anyway, are my own, Godfrey. I hope you never have to share them. If you want an idea, a faint suggestion, of what they amount to, look at the pictures, Frank.'

Loring had been vaguely conscious of a series of medium-sized colored prints, handsomely framed — four hung on each wall of the room — but until now his eyes had been all for Nancy. He rose and glanced at them. They were good prints: Breughel and Bosch and Teniers and Botticelli and a pair that Loring did not recognize. They were paintings of hell, every one, prints of those exquisitely horrid Flemish and German and Italian medieval-renaissance hells, their multitudinous tiny insect-devils flaying their innumerable little damned souls, their miniature burghs belching fire, their allegories of sin and unending torment expressed in sixteen ingenious diableries.

'Deus misereatur,' murmured Loring, passing slowly from one picture to the next.

'Well, do you think my nerves have weakened with the years, Frank? Just how many wives could lie nearly all day in a room like this and not mind a bit?' She still had that naïve conceit of her courage. 'I asked Godfrey why he couldn't let us have a touch of paradise, too; but no, he's set on his red devils.'

'I didn't know you cared for this period,' Loring observed to Schumacher.

Schumacher looked at him affably. 'A man needs always to be growing, finding new interests, new fields, you know. Art of this sort is one of my new ones. Cooking's another, by the way. What about it, dear?'

'I'm proud of Godfrey as a chef, since getting dinner became too much for me. He's done splendidly.' Nancy spoke with a smiling seriousness. 'Yes, you have, Godfrey.'

'Apropos of that, it's time for coffee,' Schumacher announced. 'Coffee is one thing that Nancy can take and like, Frank. Eh, Nancy? It puts life into her; even gives her some appetite. A good nervous tonic, coffee. I'll have it ready in five minutes.' And he went down the long corridor toward the kitchen, closing the doors behind him.

They looked at each other almost without expression, Nancy and Loring, alone for the first time since the Great Fact. Then Nancy said, 'Give me your hand, Frank, and I'll show you something.' He took her fragile hand, and she rose, and they went to a door on the nearer side of the room, and Nancy led him in. In a little bedroom, a boy of five or six was sleeping with a smile. 'I can't remember when I slept like that,' said Nancy, impassively. The boy was like Nancy, even to the long lashes. After an intent look, Loring turned back to the living-room, averting his face from Nancy.

'Frank, what's wrong?' she asked, with a tenderness that Loring had hoped to forget. He faced her, in an anger of sorts.

'You know, you know,' Loring said. 'He might have been mine.'

She threw up her chin and looked him in the eyes, just the hint of tears above her lower lashes. 'Yes' — defiantly — 'and why not? Because you never really fought.'

'What should I have done?' he asked, with his slow, sad smile. 'Kicked you downstairs or locked you in a closet? You were willful then.'

'Oh, I suppose there was nothing you could have done, Frank.' She spoke now without resentment. 'You simply weren't meant to win battles.'

'I don't think I'm a coward, Nancy.'

'No, no — I mean that you're too just and too slow. I like you for it, Frank; I love you for it; but it won't do in this world. You never truly fought for me.'

'I'd fight now.'

'Yes, when the victor's carried off the spoils. Frank, I'm glad you came, ever so glad; but what possessed you to come here?'

He was surprised. 'Your husband said you wanted me.'

'Frank, I didn't know you were coming until you knocked at this door; Godfrey never said he had asked you. I didn't know whether you were alive.'

'I suppose he asked me to be polite,' Loring reflected, 'or perhaps because he thought I might perk you up.'

'We always did make each other laugh, didn't we, Frank? No, Godfrey's thoughtful of me, but not in just that way; and he's not a polite man. What got into him, Frank?'

'He said you spoke of me often.'

'Oh, I do, Frank! I've thought of you more as the years have slipped by, not less. I suppose I've spoken of you *too* often. Because Godfrey wouldn't understand what you and I were to each other. He's not made that way. He's lucky not to have sensibilities of that sort, probably. He's resented you, poor Godfrey. Now what's at the back of his head? Does he want to see what you're made of?'

'There's no cause for him to be jealous of me, Nancy, if he's thinking of the past. You never loved me as I hoped you might. But is he very jealous — in general?'

'Possessive is the better word for it. Oh, I shouldn't tell you this, Frank, but I always used to tell you everything. Yes, possessive. We don't see many people; he says he needs only me. Do you know, he doesn't much like my little boy, though he pretends to, because Johnny owns part of me. Godfrey wants all my time now, and all my future. I guess I ought to be grateful that anyone cares so much for me. And Godfrey wants my past — that, too, Frank. He's forever trying to assimilate my past, to take it away from me and make it his own. And I don't intend him to succeed. You're in my past, for one thing. He wants to know every little bit of it — when I had my first date, what boy was the first to kiss me. Poor Godfrey! He's longing to know more about you, and he won't believe there isn't any more to tell except what he couldn't understand. But he's been patient, ever so patient, since I've been sick. He waits on me, he reads to me. He watches me all the time. He calls in different doctors. He asks everybody's opinion of what ought to be done about me. Godfrey's a perfect nuisance, but a woman wants her husband to be that.'

Loring shut his eyes and said, 'There's more to Godfrey than I'd expected.'

'Meaning — '

'Meaning, for instance, these pictures on the wall.'

'Yes — don't they give you the creeps, Frank? That's not all: he reads me the most curious things, like the Kabbala, and *Satan's Wonderful World Unveiled,* and pamphlets on Cagliostro.'

'Are you afraid of him, Nancy?'

'Afraid? You know I'm not afraid of any man born of woman.' She reached out from her chair and gave Loring a playful push. 'But men in dreams, now . . .'

'Still harping on dreams, you people?' Schumacher pushed through the doorway with a tray, and on it an Oriental coffeepot of copper and little triangular sandwiches. 'Dreams are manifestations of will. The dreamer's will, or another's. And if the will's strong enough, who knows where substance begins and ends? Eh, Frank?'

'I never had enough strength of will to bother.'

'Is that really so?' Schumacher asked, with his stare of absorption. 'You ought to exercise what will is in you, Frank, for you never can tell when it may have to put up a fight. Now here's your coffee, dear, and there's more where it came from. And yours, Lor — Frank. And mine with the cream in it.'

Strong, strong, that coffee, sweetish and thick, almost Turkish. 'An interesting blend,' Loring remarked. 'I think I like it. Your secret brew, Godfrey?'

'All in the grinding,' Schumacher told him, with a satisfied little smile. 'We have our own little mill here; and like the gods', it grinds slow and exceeding fine. Here, I'll fill your cup again, Nancy. What, no more for you, Frank? Come on, old man — one more cup. I'll be offended. That's better. Nancy can drink this stuff all night; it seems to rouse her.'

So it did. With some of her old liveliness, Nancy stirred in her chair; her color heightened; she seemed the only cool thing in the hot night air. 'I want to play matching lines,' she told them. 'Remember how we used to play it when we made lemonade, Frank, and sat on the porch? But it's always coffee for us now, even on nights like this: Godfrey's so proud of his coffee. It *is* good, Godfrey. Well, let's play. You won't be so good at this as Frank and I, Godfrey, because you went to a progressive school and didn't have to memorize. But you start, anyway.'

Schumacher did not hesitate long. With a kind of sneer at the whole affair:

'"No longer mourn for me when I am dead . . ."'

'Oh, a Shakespearean sonnet!' — this from Nancy.
Loring remembered:

'"Than you shall hear the surly sullen bell
Give warning to the world that I fled
From this vile world, with vilest worms to dwell."'

'Ugh!' cried Nancy. 'I like the next better:

'"Nay, if you read this line, remember not
The hand that writ it; for I love you so
That I in your sweet thoughts would be forgot
If thinking on me then should make you woe."'

'The surly sullen bell,' Schumacher repeated, relishingly. 'Not badly put — no, not bad. More coffee, Nancy, dear? Oh, yes — you need it.'

With her clever little head, Nancy won the match. 'She laughs as she always laughed,' Loring thought, 'no silly giggle.' And this night he must go from her, back to that narrow hotel room with its silence. That girl! Well, he'd best go now. 'It's been a good evening,' he said to Schumacher, rising. Despite everything, he had no need to tell Nancy so.

At the door, Nancy took his hands again. 'How long will it be before you come round, Frank?'

'February.'

'You'll come here every night you're in town that week, won't you?' She meant it.

'If you'll have me.'

'That's the old spirit!' Schumacher put in, loudly. He gripped Loring's hand. 'Don't get lost on your way home, Frank. Sleep tight.'

When Loring turned the corner, they still were watching him from their lighted doorway — a high, arrogant head, a little dear one. Ah, Nancy. 'I never fought,' Loring said, half-aloud.

*   *

Now that the intoxication of Nancy's company ebbed away, Loring felt himself fallen into a solitude more oppressive than any grief he had known those past ten years. Quite literally the mood weighed upon him: his steps seemed weighted and painful, his eyes dim, his hearing dulled. He was aware of the fitful, warm night breeze only vaguely. And in this state Loring made his way through the district of ruined and ruinous old houses. Although he liked walking, tonight he would have whistled to a taxi, if any cab had passed; but it was late, and drivers knew they would have few fares in this slum.

Passing a building with its façade half-battered in, so that broken plaster and lath were scattered over the ground by the slum children, Loring made out, a few yards ahead, another walker in this silent night, or rather

60

morning. No third person appeared in the whole length of the street. A hulking figure, the other traveller's, and yet elusive, slipping now and again into deep shadow. For the better part of a block the other man preceded Loring — and then was gone.

Loring blinked sleepily. Gone where? He came up to the spot where he had lost sight of the other walker, and observed a filthy little alley leading to the right. Acting upon some subtle impulse, Loring turned into the alley, and in a moment found himself at the entrance to a decrepit court, strewn with old tin cans and heaped cinders, and faced by the grim backs of four or five condemned houses. There was no one to be seen. And whatever was he doing here? Why had he left the road? Loring went back to the street, and a quarter of an hour later was unlocking the door of his hotel room.

Dreams came to him that night, a series of hopeless longings and dissolving frights impossible to recollect long after waking, but sufficient to rouse him, crying out, three times in the dark. And when he got out of bed in the morning, something was wrong: a complaint like acute rheumatism combined with extreme lethargy. Loring had to eat breakfast in his room, and the elevator boy saved him from slipping as he got heavily out upon the ground floor to go about his business. All day he was in some strong discomfort, and the next day, too, and in diminishing measure for three weeks after; but then he drifted back into his old careless good health. Ah, Nancy, Loring thought — what you do to me even now.

*   *

In February, St. Louis covers its snow with grime and dust, bad as tar and feathers. Underneath, that snow was nearly two feet deep when Loring went to make his call upon the Schumachers, for the seething heat of his last visit had given way to the rigor of a continental winter. Loring stamped his feet and pulled off his galoshes on Schumacher's steps, and this brought Schumacher to the door without Loring's having to knock.

'Nancy's dozing,' said Schumacher, quietly. 'We'll sit in the living-room — she's there — and she'll wake gradually. This is the only sort of sleep she gets now. Far gone, Frank, far gone: the doctors haven't the ghost of a notion of what to do. Now and then her appetite returns, though. I watch her every moment I'm at home.' He stared at Loring as if challenging the sincerity of Loring's condolences.

That bewitched and bewitching girl! Madame Récamier as before, she opened her eyes to Loring, smiled, and whispered, 'Six months? I thought you had been away six centuries, Frank.' She did not attempt to rise, and she was pale, pale as paper and nearly as thin, though the loveliness had not gone out from her.

'I love you more than ever, Nancy,' was what Loring wished to say. Instead, he had to sit and talk follies with this shadow of the girl by the lake and with this elegant bull of a man. After a time, their conversation shifted somehow to Ends. Nancy was responsible for it, probably, and she said in her faint, piquant voice that she was inclined to believe the End was in another world altogether, this one being only a means of purging.

'Another world? Why, there's your other world for almost everybody,' Schumacher broke in, gesturing toward the holy terrors on the wall. 'Right there you can see both this life and the next. Only spiritual power can snatch you out of that trap. Not one man in a hundred thousand has that kind of power.'

'If you were right, then I'd see if I couldn't leave behind me something decent to be remembered by, anyhow,' Loring retorted. 'A name for honesty, or honest children.'

Schumacher was vehemently contemptuous. 'What's the significance of a name when there's no one to pat you on the back?'

Then what was Schumacher's End? Loring inquired.

'Spiritual triumph.' Schumacher leaned forward with a glare of conviction that made Loring shift uneasily. 'I don't subscribe in the least to the Hebrew-Christian myth, you understand: I mean actuality, the exultation of battles won in the most dangerous of fields, the spirit plane. In the spirit realm there's no time; the fight goes on forever; you must be always on guard; and you trample down the beaten. That's what all this' — sweeping a hand toward St. Louis, outside in the dark — 'is for, and all that,' motioning toward the Breughels and Bosches. 'They're both veils for the real plane of being. And in that hard reality you survive and progress by conquest. Oh, you can't comprehend my meaning till you've reached that plane. You need to dominate, to crush . . .' Abruptly Schumacher became casual again. 'Which reminds me, I'd better grind the coffee.' He went into the kitchen.

Nancy glanced up at Loring with a small smile, half-quizzical, half-appealing. 'What do you make of Godfrey, Frank?'

An awkward question to answer. 'I'd never have suspected him, in the old days, of a mystical turn.'

'It's because he's a disappointed man, Frank. He's turned to these ideas since he realized he's not going far in this world.' So faint, her voice, and yet so calm.

'Godfrey's done well enough.'

'Frank, you don't know him! He thought he was meant to be Alexander, and instead he's a professor of languages. Godfrey's ever so vain, or was. And yet he can't even contrive to become a dean; and *that's* no lofty triumph in these days, Lord knows. He's big, he's clever, he's handsome, he works hard; but there's not enough in him. He simply doesn't get ahead; and in spite of all his efforts, not many people like him. He knows these things now. So he's stopped trying in everyday life, Frank — "in this plane," he'd say — and he's seeing what *will* can do. He never loved anyone but himself, and now he detests the whole world because people won't permit him to own them.'

'Does he hate you, Nancy?' It was all Loring could manage to force that question out.

'Yes; but more than ever he wants to possess me, absorb me, lose me in himself. He married the wrong sort of wife for that. He should have chosen a meek girl, submissive and infinitely loving, shouldn't he? I've the love, perhaps, but not one ounce of meekness. I'd lose myself in him if I could, but it's not my way: I'm too *alive*, Frank. Even now, a bag of bones, there's too much life in me to be assimilated to Godfrey. He detests me because he can't swallow me whole. I loved him ten years ago because he wanted to swallow me; while you hardly dared say "Boo!" to Nancy. In a way, I love him now.'

Loring pulled his chair closer to the chaise longue. She always had been slim; and tonight it seemed as if the faintest breeze would sweep her up. 'What are we going to do about you, Nancy?' Now that he saw her pale face so close, he bit his lip.

'Frank, you're *good*. Don't think I'm a shadow because I want to end everything: I've matters to live for. I don't know what's wrong and I suppose I never will know. The sun doesn't help, or change of diet, or sleep — when I manage to sleep. Godfrey doesn't spare money in trying to help me, you understand. He never was mean about anything, least of all his wife. It just seems to be destined, Frank. The end might come this hour, or it might be next year. I'm not afraid, either.'

'I'd be afraid, darling,' Loring told her. 'Don't speak to me of death.'

'Whom else am I to speak to? Whom did I always trust? I try to talk with Godfrey about — about my prospects; but he only laughs, to turn such talk away. Laughs at a dying woman! It's hard to forgive him that opinion of my intelligence, for I know he tells everyone else about the dreadful shape I'm in. Gossip drifts back. I'm telling you, Frank, because this may be our last minute to ourselves. I want to say that I'm sorry I never was more to you. I'm sorry you see me like this, and not the way I used to be; but oh, I'm glad you came.'

Loring's breath came hard. In the kitchen a cup fell and smashed; they could hear Schumacher rearranging the coffee-tray.

'And there's one thing I ask you, Frank, though I have no right: look out for my little boy.'

'He has a father, Nancy girl.'

'I asked you to look out for my little boy, Frank.' She reached for his hand. 'Johnny's like me.'

'You know I will.' Then Loring bent and kissed her, and went in a daze to the window, with his back toward Nancy — and only just in time, if that, for Schumacher was entering with the coffee.

'There you are, Nancy dear — thick, the way you like it. Not too hot for you, is it, Frank? Don't let it cool long: heat's half the secret of flavor. There's more as soon as you've drunk that.'

If conceivable, stronger and more like a syrup than it had been six months before, Schumacher's coffee. 'I prefer your coffee to your philosophy,' said Loring, huskily.

'What's your objection?' Schumacher turned upon him that zealot's stare.

'For one thing, your doctrine of "spiritual triumph" is the rejection of morality.'

'Morality?' Schumacher waved a big hand. 'Well, if we must bring the subject up, you've heard what William James said about morality: "So long as one poor cockroach feels the pangs of unrequited love, this world is not a moral world." Morality is the satisfaction of desire.'

'So the more successful the thief, the better man he is?' Loring asked.

Nancy, roused somewhat by the coffee, smiled her approval of Loring's bluntness. 'Morality's restraint,' she said.

'No, restraint is for spiritual weaklings,' Schumacher insisted. 'Strength is everything upon the physical plane, and that's just as true, really, upon the spiritual — the moral — plane. Strength and appetite are the only tests. You'll admit that soon enough, Loring.' He refilled Loring's cup.

Loring hung on that night until he could not postpone, in decency, saying goodbye. When there was nothing else left to do, he took Nancy's hand, and they two exchanged a long look. 'Frank, remember me,' said pallid Nancy. Loring kept a grip upon himself.

She could not go with him to the door, but Schumacher did. They shook hands upon the steps. 'You've seen her, Frank, so you know she hasn't long.' Schumacher grimaced. 'She might go tomorrow, or next week, for all we can tell. It's best you came tonight.'

'I'll come by tomorrow evening, too, if I may,' Loring answered.

'Tomorrow? Oh, yes — try to stop by, if you can.'

Loring walked to the gate in the brick wall, opened it, began to turn into the street. At that instant he glimpsed Schumacher still watching him from the steps, staring intently, as if with his whole soul. His look was so fixed that Loring glared back. Then Schumacher, starting, jerked up his right hand in an awkward wave: 'Well, goodbye . . . !' The words were bleated out in a high drawl. Loring left that big queer figure and went into the dark.

*　　　*

Lead was in Loring's soles. What had come over him? He felt a touch of vertigo. Every step had become a distinct effort, every swing of his body an ache. The snow crunched beneath his galoshes. As he approached the broken tenements of the Old Town, fresh snow commenced to fall heavily; and the wind came up, wailing through the empty windows, obscuring the other side of the street with white scurries swept from loose drifts. His eyes were heavy, his pulse was distressing, his breathing difficult; and he was alone in the cold.

Alone except for the one who walked there ahead of him. Loring felt a dull necessity, in his oppressive state, to seek company; and yet something made him reluctant to overtake the fellow ahead. Anyway, the other walker seemed to be slowing his pace. Now Loring was close to him, though the other remained indistinct amid the snowflakes. They both were passing the house of the smashed façade; the other walked a mere dozen steps in the lead. A minute later, Loring came abreast of the other.

Loring glanced into his face: a large face, smiling. But after some fashion the face did not live. And it was Schumacher's face.

Crying out, Loring leaped away from that face and blundered in an agony of confusion down the alley on the right. Slipping and reeling, he got through the drifts into the stinking little court of the condemned houses. He still had courage enough to look back, and there was nothing behind him. Recovered a bit, he crept up to the shelter of a house wall. But a face was peering from a window in the wall. It was Schumacher's face.

At that, Loring fell forward in the snow, and for some time experienced nothing.

But though he lay with his face in the drift, oblivious of the court around him and of the conscious world, soon the horrors came to him. Dreams compounded of the vilest frights, visions of torment unceasing, ecstasies of revulsion, went round and round and round. And out of the chinks and corners of these arabesques peered the eyes of Schumacher. Lie still, said whatever was left of Loring: lie still, hiding yourself in blackness. Slowly the merciful blackness crept through Loring's nerves. Through the grotesque terrors of his trance, some old Scottish epitaph pounded with lunatic insistency within his twilight consciousness:

> When the last trump shall sound,
>   And the dead shall rise,
> Lie still, Red Rab,
>   If ye be wise.

And still Loring would have lain. But presently other eyes emerged from behind the arabesques of damnation. And these other eyes were Nancy's. 'You never really fought, you never really fought.' The sentence flitted without meaning among the arabesques, and Schumacher's eyes peeked out once more. Ah, to hide with Red Rab in the blackness! Yet something held him. With an immense effort, he compelled the arabesques to halt in their dance for a moment. In their place came a glimpse of Nancy, lying upon her couch. 'My little boy . . .' The terrors thrust themselves back upon Loring; but a thought, a fragment of consciousness, had intruded among them. Some wild struggle of will, or wills, was fought out then, lasting only seconds, perhaps, but seeming aeons. And abruptly Frank Loring sat up in the snow.

He opened his eyes, the bravest act of his life. The shattered window of the tenement confronted him, and the face of Schumacher was in it still, and Loring wailed shrilly. Yet Loring stared on, and in time Schumacher's face seemed to dissolve into its constituent atoms, and Loring was looking merely into an empty ruin.

Then Loring got up from the drift. He got up with strong pain and difficulty, for the sake of Nancy's memory. 'You never really fought.' He rose, his will awake, and groped along the brick walls to the street. 'My little boy . . .' He had lain a long time in the snow, and seemed frozen.

And though he was weak as water, and giddy beyond belief, and incapable of speech, he lurched and crept four blocks to a police station. The few people he passed took him for a stumble-bum. He pushed his way into the station; and there, in the over-heated room, lounged four of the tough, weary policemen of St. Louis. One of these started to say, 'Get the hell —' Then, looking at Loring, he came forward to take his arm, and asked uncertainly, 'What's up fellow?'

'I've been poisoned,' said Loring. He gave Schumacher's name and address, and then fell, deadweight, into a sergeant's arms.

*   *

When the police came to his door, Godfrey Schumacher went upstairs and shot himself, so that no questions ever were asked of him. Downstairs at the time was a doctor, certifying that heart failure had been the cause of the death, that night, of Nancy Schumacher. Presently this verdict was altered to 'poisoning from a strychnic preparation, administered in increasing quantities over a considerable period of time' — after Loring had talked with the coroner. But neither Loring nor the doctors ever knew more, and Loring suspected that their 'strychnic' was little better than approximation.

'Frank, remember me.' Aye, thou pale ghost, while memory holds a seat. And looking upon the little boy, Loring saw the bones, the mouth, the impish eyes of her for whom he had not fought until the last second of her life.

Balgrummo's Hell

Hell hath no limits, nor is circumscrib'd
In one self place; for where we are is hell,
And where hell is, there we must ever be.

The moment that Horgan had slipped through the pend, Jock Jamieson had glanced up, grunted, and run for his shotgun at the gate-cottage. But Horgan, having long legs, had contrived to cosh Jock right on the threshold. Now Horgan had most of the night to lift the pictures out of Balgrummo Lodging.

Before Jock could close those rusty iron gates, Nan Stennis — in her improbable role of new night nurse to Lord Balgrummo — had stalled her car in the pend. In the rain, Jock couldn't possibly have made out Nan's face, and now Horgan pulled off the silk stocking of Nan's that he had worn over his own head. With Nan's help, he trussed and gagged Jock, the tough old nut breathing convulsively, and dragged him into a kitchen cupboard of the gate-cottage and turned the key on him. Jock's morning mate, and the morning nurse, wouldn't come to relieve him until seven o'clock. That left no one between Horgan and those paintings except Alexander Fillan Inchburn, tenth Baron Balgrummo, incredibly old, incredibly depraved, and incredibly decayed in Balgrummo Lodging, which he had not left for half a century.

In that nocturnal February drizzle, Nan shivered; perhaps she shuddered. Though there could have been no one within a quarter of a mile to

hear them, she was whispering. 'Rafe, can you really get through it without me? I hate to think of you going into that place all alone, darling.'

Competent Rafe Horgan kissed her competently. She had left her husband for him, and she had been quite useful. He honestly meant to meet
her at the Mayfair, by the end of the month, and take her to the Canaries;
by that time, he should have disposed of the Romney portrait for a fat
sum, to an assured Swiss collector with a Leeds agent, enabling Horgan to
take his time in disposing of the other Balgrummo pictures. Nan could
have lent him a hand inside Balgrummo Lodging, but it was important for
her to establish an alibi; she would change automobiles with him now,
drive into Edinburgh and show herself at a restaurant, and then take the
midnight train to King's Cross. The principal trouble with operations like
this was simply that too many people became involved, and some of them
were given to bragging. But Nan was a close one, and Horgan had spent
months planning.

The only real risk was that someone might discover his name wasn't
Horgan. For that, however, a thorough investigation would be required.
And who would think of investigating the past of Rafe Horgan, Esq., a
South African gentleman of private means who now lived in a pleasant
flat near Charlotte Square? Not Dr. Euphemia Inchburn, gray spinster who
liked his smile and his talk; not T. M. Gillespie, Writer to the Signet, chair-
man of the trustees of Lord Balgrummo's Trust. With them, he had been
patient and prudent, asking questions about Balgrummo Lodging only casually, in an antiquarian way. Besides, did he look as if he would carry the
cosh? No, the police would be after every gang in Fossie housing estate,
which sprawled almost to the policies of Balgrummo Lodging. Horgan's
expenditure of charm, and even of money, would be repaid five thousand
times over. The big obstacle had been Jock's shotgun, and that was overcome now.

'His high and mighty lordship's bedridden,' Horgan told Nan, kissing
her again, 'and blind, too, they say. I'll finish here by three o'clock, girl.
Ring me about teatime tomorrow, if you feel you must; but simply talk
about the weather, Nan, when you do. You'll love Las Palmas.'

He stood at the forgotten gate, watching Nan get into the car in which
he had come and had parked in the shadow of the derelict linoleum works
that ran cheek by jowl with the north dyke of Balgrummo Lodging. When
she had gone, he started up Nan's own inconspicuous black Ford, moving
it far enough for him to shut the gates. He locked those gates with the big

brass padlock that Jock had removed to admit 'Nurse' Nan. Then, slowly and with only his dims showing, he drove up the avenue — rhododendron jungle pressing in from either side — that led to the seventeenth century façade of Balgrummo Lodging.

'Uncle Alec and his house have everything,' Dr. Effie Inchburn had said once: 'Dry rot, wet rot, woodworm, deathwatch beetle.' Also, among those few who remembered Lord Balgrummo and Balgrummo Lodging, the twain had a most nasty repute. It was a positive duty to take the pictures out of that foul house and convey them into the possession of collectors who, if they would keep them no less private, certainly would care for them better.

Sliding out of the car with his dispatch case of tools, Rafe Horgan stood at the dark door of Balgrummo Lodging. The front was the work of Sir William Bruce, they said, although part of the house was older. It all looked solid enough by night, however rotten the timbers and the man within. Horgan had taken Jamieson's big ring of keys from the gate-cottage, but the heavy main door stood slightly ajar, anyway. No light showed anywhere. Before entering, Horgan took a brief complacent survey of the tall ashlar face of what T. M. Gillespie, that mordant stick of a solicitor, called 'Balgrummo's Hell.'

*   *

Living well enough by his wits, Horgan had come upon Balgrummo Lodging by good fortune, less than a month after he had found it convenient to roost in Edinburgh. In a car with false license plates, he had driven out to Fossie housing estate in search of a certain rough customer who might do a job for him. Fossie, only seven years old but already a slum, was the usual complex of crescents and terraces of drab council houses. Horgan had taken a wrong turning and had found himself driving down a neglected and uninhabited old lane; behind the nasty brick wall on his right had been a derelict marshaling yard for goods wagons, declared redundant by Dr. Beeching of British Railways. On his left, he had passed the immense hulk of a disused linoleum works, empty for several years, its every windowpane smashed by the lively bairns of Fossie.

Beyond the linoleum factory, he had come upon a remarkably high old stone dyke, unpleasant shards of broken glass set thick in cement all along its top. Behind the wall he had made out the limbs and trunks of limes and beeches, a forest amidst suburbia. Abruptly, a formal ancient pend or vaulted gateway had loomed up. On either side, a seventeenth century stone beast-effigy kept guard, life-size almost: a lion and a griffin, but so hacked and battered by young vandals as to be almost unrecognizable. The griffin's whole head was lacking.

So much Horgan had seen at a glance, taking it that these were the vacant policies of some demolished or ruined mansion house. He had driven on to the end of the street, hoping to circle back to the housing estate, but had found himself in a cul-de-sac, the Fettinch burn flowing through bogs beyond the brick wall at the end. This triangle of wooded policies, hemmed in by goods yards, wrecked factory, and polluted streams, must be the last scrap of some laird's estate of yesteryear, swallowed but not yet digested by the city's fringe. Probably the squalor and unhealthiness of the low site had deterred Edinburgh or Midlothian — he wasn't sure within which boundary it lay — from building on it another clutch of council houses for the Fossie scheme.

Swinging round the lane's teminal wall, Horgan had gone slowly back past the massive pend, where the harling was dropping from the rubble. To his surprise, he had noticed a gate-lodge, apparently habitable, just within the iron grille of the gates; and a little woodsmoke had been spiralling up from the chimney. Could there be anything worth liberating beyond those gates? He had stopped, and had found an iron bell pull that functioned. When he had rung, a tall fellow, with the look of a retired constable, had emerged from the gate-cottage and had conversed with him, taciturnly, in broad Scots, through the locked grille.

Horgan had asked for directions to a certain crescent in the housing scheme, and had got them. Then he had inquired the name of this place. 'Balgrummo Lodgin', sir' — with a half-defensive frown. On impulse, Horgan had suggested that he would like to see the house (which, he gathered, must be standing, for he could make out beyond the trees some high dormers and roofs).

'Na, na; Himself's no receivin', ye ken.' This had been uttered with a kind of incredulity at the question being put.

Growing interested, Horgan had professed himself to be something of a connoisseur of seventeenth century domestic architecture. Where might he apply for permission to view the exterior, at any rate? He had been given to understand, surlily, that it would do no good: but everything was in the hands of Lord Balgrummo's Trust. The Trust's solicitor and chairman was a Mr. T. M. Gillespie, of Reid, Gillespie, and MacIlwraith, Hanover Street.

Thus Balgrummo Lodging had been added to Rafe Horgan's list of divers projects. A few days later, he had scraped acquaintance with Gillespie, a dehydrated bachelor. Initially, he had not mentioned Balgrummo Lodging, but had talked in Gillespie's chambers about a hypothetical Miss Horgan in Glasgow, allegedly an aunt of his, a spinster of large means, who was thinking of a family trust. Mr. Gillespie, he had heard it said, was experienced in the devising and management of such trusts. As venture capital, a cheque from Horgan had even been made out to Mr. Gillespie, in payment for general advice upon getting up a conceivable Janet Horgan Estates, Ltd.

Gillespie, he had discovered, was a lonely solicitor who could be cultivated, and who had a dry relish for dry sherry. After a bottle, Gillespie might talk more freely than a solicitor ought to talk. They came to dine together fairly frequently — after Horgan had learnt, from a chance remark which he affected to receive casually, that some good pictures remained at the Lodging. As the weeks elapsed, they were joined for a meal, once and again, by Gillespie's old friend Dr. Euphemia Inchburn, Lord Balgrummo's niece, a superannuated gynecologist. Horgan had turned on all his charm, and Dr. Inchburn had slipped into garrulity.

Perceiving that he really might be on to a good thing, Horgan had poked into old gazetteers which might mention Balgrummo Lodging; and, as he obtained from his new friends some hint of the iniquities of the tenth Baron Balgrummo, he looked into old newspaper files. He knew a little about pictures, as he did about a number of things; and by consulting the right books and catalogues, he ascertained that on the rotting walls of Balgrummo Lodging there still must hang some highly valuable family portraits — though not family portraits only — none of them exhibited anywhere since 1913. Gillespie was interested only in Scottish portrait painters, and not passionately in them; Horgan judged it imprudent to question Dr. Effie Inchburn overmuch on the subject, lest his inquisitiveness be fixed in her memory. But he became reasonably well satisfied that Lord Balgrummo, senescent monster, must possess an Opie; a Raeburn; a Ramsay or two; perhaps even three Wilkies; a good Reynolds, possibly, and a Constable; a very good Romney; a Gainsborough, it appeared, and (happy prospect) a Hogarth; two small canvasses by William Etty; a whole row of reputed Knellers; once, and just conceivably still, a Cranach and a

Holbein were to be seen at the Lodging. The tenth baron's especial acquisition, about 1911, had been an enormous Fuseli, perhaps unknown to compilers of catalogues, and (judging from one of Dr. Inchburn's grimaces) probably obscene. There were more pictures — the devil knew what.

Perhaps some rare books might be found in the library, but Horgan was too little of a bibliophile to pick them out in a hurry. The silver and that sort of thing presumably were in a bank — it would have been risky to inquire. Anyone but a glutton would be content with those pictures, for one night's work.

Lethargy, and the consequences of permanent confinement to his house, naturally had made Lord Balgrummo neglect his inheritance. As the decades had slipped by, he had permitted his trustees to sell nearly everything he owned, except Balgrummo Lodging — once a residence of convenience, near Edinburgh, for the Inchburns, later a dower house — and those pictures. 'After all, never going out, Alec has to look at *something*,' Dr. Inchburn had murmured.

Sufficient intelligence obtained, still Horgan faced the difficulty of entering the house without the peril and expense of a gang-raid, and of getting out undetected with those pictures. An attempt had been made several years before. On that occasion, Jock Jamieson, the night porter — 'warden' would have been a better style — had shot to death one burglar and wounded another while they were on a ladder. Jamieson and his day mates (one of them the constable-type with whom Horgan had talked at the gate) were hard, vigilant men — and, like Lord Balgrummo's nurses, excellently paid. Time had been when it seemed at least as important to keep Lord Balgrummo in (though he had given his word never to leave the policies) as to keep predators out. Gillespie had implied that the police indulged in the peculiar porters of Balgrummo Lodging a certain readiness in the use of firearms. So Horgan's expedition had been most painstakingly plotted, and it had been necessary to wait months for the coincidence of favorable circumstances, all things being held in readiness.

The presence of a nurse in the house all round the clock was a further vexation; Horgan had not relished the prospect of pursuing a frantic nurse through that crumbling warren of a place. Should she escape through some back door . . . So when, only yesterday, Gillespie had mentioned that the night nurse had quit ('Nerves, as usual, in that house — and his lordship a disagreeable patient'), and that they had not yet found a replacement, Horgan knew his moment had arrived.

For one night, Jamieson had been required to do double duty, watching the policies and looking in on Lord Balgrummo every hour. Jock Jamieson, for all his toughness, probably liked being inside the place at night no more than did the nurses. So doubtless Jock had rejoiced when a la-di-dah feminine voice (Nan Stennis's, of course) had informed him late that evening that she was calling on behalf of Mr. Gillespie, and that a new night nurse would make her appearance, in an hour or so, in her own car.

It had gone smoothly enough. Jock had opened the gate at Nan's honk, and then it had been up to Horgan, in the shadows. Had Jock been ten years younger, and less given to beer, he might have got his hands on the shotgun before Horgan could have reached him. But though disliking unnecessary roughness, Horgan had coshed men before, and he coshed Jock swiftly and well. No one came down that obscure lane after dark — few, indeed, in daylight. Therefore the investment in drinks and dinners for Gillespie and the Inchburn old maid, and the expenditure of Horgan's hours, now would be compensated for at an hourly rate of return beyond the dreams of avarice. Swinging his handsome dispatch case, Horgan entered Balgrummo Lodging.

* *

Within the chilly entrance hall, the first thing Horgan noticed was the pervasive odor of dry rot. With this stench of doom, what wonder they had to pay triple wages to any nurse! Condemned to solitude, neglectful of business, and latterly penurious, Lord Balgrummo had postponed repairs until the cost of restoring the Lodging would have been gigantic. Even could he have found the money without selling some of his pictures, old Balgrummo probably would not have saved the house; he had no heirs of his body, the entail had been broken long before, and his heir presumptive — Dr. Effie — never would choose to live in this desolation screened by the tumbledown linoleum works. There remained only the question as to which would first tumble into atoms — Lord Balgrummo or his prison mansion.

Horgan sent the beam of his big electric torch round the hall. It flashed across the surface of what appeared to be a vast Canaletto — a prospect of Ravenna, perhaps. Was it the real article, or only from Canaletto's school? Horgan wished he knew whether it were worth the difficulty of taking and concealing, its size considered. Well, he would leave it to the last, securing the certified goods first.

He had known there was no electric light in Balgrummo Lodging; nothing had been improved there — or much repaired — since 1913. He found, however, elaborate bronze gas brackets. After fumbling, he found also that he did not know how to light them; or perhaps the gas was turned off, here in the hall. No matter: the torch would suffice, even if the black caverns beyond its ray were distressing.

Before he went to work, he must have a glance at old Balgrummo, to be quite sure that the crazy old creature couldn't totter out to do some feeble mischief. (In this house, more than fifty years before, he had done great mischief indeed.) Where would his bedroom be? On the second storey, at the front, just above the library, likely enough, judging from the plan of the Lodging, at which Horgan had once managed a hasty glance in Gillespie's chambers. Hanging the torch about his neck, Horgan made his way up the broad oak staircase, at first leaning on the balustrade — but presently touching that rail only gingerly, since here and there, even though he wore gloves, it felt spongy to the touch, and trembled in its rottenness when put too much weight upon it.

At the first-floor turning of the stairs, Horgan paused. Had anything scraped or shuffled down there below, down in the black well of the ground floor? Of course it couldn't have, unless it were a rat. (Balgrummo kept no dogs: 'The brutes don't live long at the Lodging,' Gillespie had murmured in an obscure aside.) How had those night nurses endured this situation, at whatever wages? One reason why Balgrummo Lodging hadn't been pillaged before this, Horgan ruminated, was the ghastly reputation of the place, lingering over five decades. Few enterprising lads, even from Fossie housing estate, would be inclined to venture into the auld bogle nobleman's precincts. Well, that ghostly wind had blown him good. No one could be more effectively rational than Rafe Horgan, who wouldn't fret about blood spilt before the First World War. Still, indubitably this was an oppressive house — stagnant, stagnant.

'Haunted?' Dr. Effie had replied hesitantly to Horgan's jocular inquiry. 'If you mean haunted by dead ancestors, Major Horgan — why, no more than most old houses here in Scotland, I suppose. Who would be troubled, after so many generations, by old General Sir Angus Inchburn in his Covenanting jackboots? Ghostly phenomena, or so I've read, seldom linger long after a man's or a woman's death and burial. But if you ask whether there's something fey at work in the house — oh, I certainly suppose so.'

Having paused to polish her spectacles, Dr. Effie continued calmly enough: 'That's Uncle Alec's fault. He's not present merely in one room, you know; he fills the house, every room, every hour. Presumably I seem silly to you, Major Horgan, but my impulses won't let me visit Balgrummo more than I must, even if Alec does mean to leave everything to me. Balgrummo Lodging is like a saturated sponge, dripping with the shame and the longing of Alexander Fillan Inchburn. Can you understand that my uncle loathes what he did, and yet might do it again — even the worst of it — if there were opportunity? The horror of Balgrummo Lodging isn't Lord Balgrummo nine-tenths dead; it's Balgrummo one-tenth alive, but in torment.'

The tedious old girl-doctor was nearly as cracked as her noble uncle, Horgan thought. Actually he had learned from some interesting research the general character of Lord Balgrummo's offenses so long ago — acts which would have produced the hanging of anyone but a peer, in those days. Horgan nevertheless had amused himself by endeavoring, slyly and politely, to force Dr. Effie to tell him just why Balgrummo had been given the choice of standing trial for his life (by the Lords, of course, as a peer, which might have damaged the repute of that body) or of being kept in a kind of perpetual house-arrest, without sentence being passed by anyone. The latter choice would not have been offered — and accepted — even so, but for the general belief that he must be a maniac.

As he had anticipated, Dr. Euphemia had turned prude. 'Poor Alec was very naughty when he was young. There were others as bad as himself, but he took the whole blame on his shoulders. He was told that if he would swear never to go out, all his life, and to receive no visitors except members of his family or his solicitors, no formal charges would be pressed against him. They required him to put everything he owned into trust; and the trustees were to engage the men to watch the policies of Balgrummo Lodging, and the servants. All the original set of trustees are dead and buried; Mr. Gillespie and I weren't much more than babies when Uncle Alec had his Trouble.'

From Gillespie, later, Rafe Horgan had learned more about that Trouble. But what was he doing, pausing in the darkness of the second-floor corridor to reminisce? A hasty inspection by the torch showed him that the Knellers, all great noses, velvets, and bosoms, were hung on this floor. And there was the Gainsborough, a good one, though it badly needed cleaning: Margaret, Lady Ross, second daughter of the fifth Lord Balgrummo. The worm had got into the picture frame, but the canvas seemed to be in decent condition, he made out on closer examination. Well, Horgan meant to cut his pictures out of their frames, to save time and space. First, though, he must look in upon Himself.

The corridor was all dust and mildew. A single charwoman, Gillespie had mentioned, came a few hours daily, Monday through Friday, to keep Balgrummo's bedroom and small parlor neat, to clean the stairs and to wash dishes in the kitchen. Otherwise, the many rooms and passages of the Lodging were unceasingly shuttered against sun and moon, and the damask might fall in tatters from the walls, the ceiling drip with cobwebs, for all old Balgrummo cared. Nearly every room was left locked, though the keys, all but a few, were in the bunch (each with its metal tag) that Horgan had taken from unconscious Jock. Even Gillespie, who waited on his client four or five times a year, never had contrived to see the chapel. Balgrummo kept the chapel key in his own pocket, Gillespie fancied — and, over coffee and brandy, had mentioned this, together with other trivia, to Horgan. 'It was in the chapel, you see, Rafe, that the worst of the Trouble happened.'

Acquiring that chapel key was an additional reason why Horgan must pay his respects to Lord Balgrummo — though he relished that necessity less, somehow, with every minute that elapsed. Henry Fuseli's most indecorous painting might be in that chapel; for the tenth baron's liturgy and ritual, fifty years before, had been a synthesis of Benin witch-rites with memories of Scots diabolism, and whatever might excite the frantic fancy had been employed — all gross images. So, at least, Horgan had surmised from what he had garnered from the old newspaper files, and what Gillespie had let drop.

Uncertain of quite where he was in the house, Horgan tried the knobs of three doors in that corridor. The first two were locked; and it was improbable that the trustees had gone so far, even when Balgrummo was stronger, as to have him locked into his rooms at night. But the third door opened creakingly. Flashing round his light, Horgan entered an old-fashioned parlor, with what appeared to be two bona fide Wilkie landscapes on opposite walls. Across the parlor, which was scarcely bigger than a dressing-room, a mahogany door stood half-open. How silent! Yet something scraped or ticked faintly — a morose deathwatch beetle in the paneling, probably. Despite irrational misgivings, Horgan compelled himself to pass through the inner doorway.

The beam of his torch swept to a Queen Anne bed. In it lay, motionless and with eyes shut, an extremely old man, skin and bone under a single sheet and a single blanket. A coal fire smoldered in the grate, so the room was not altogether dark. Horgan's flesh crept perceptibly — but that would be the old rumors, and the old truths, about this enfeebled thing in the bed. 'In his prime, we called him Ozymandias,' Gillespie had put it. But Lord Balgrummo was past obscenities and atrocities now.

'Hello, Alec!' Horgan was loud and jocular. His right hand rested on the cosh in his coat pocket. 'Alec, you old toad, I've come for your pictures.' But Alexander Fillan Inchburn, the last of a line that went back to a bastard of William the Lion, did not stir or speak.

*   *

T. M. Gillespie was proud of Lord Balgrummo, as the most remarkable person whose business ever had come his way. 'Our Scots Gilles de Rais,' Gillespie had chuckled aridly while enjoying a Jamaican cigar from Horgan's case, 'probably would not be found insane by a board of medical examiners — not even after fifty years of restriction to his own private Hell. I don't think it was from malice that the procurator-fiscal of that day recommended Balgrummo Lodging — where the capital offenses had been committed — as the place of isolated residence: it merely happened that this particular house of Lord Balgrummo's was secluded enough to keep his lordship out of the public eye (for he might have been stoned), and yet near enough to the city for police surveillance, during the earlier decades. I take it that the police have forgotten his existence, or almost forgotten, by this time: for the past three or four years, he wouldn't have been able to walk unaided so far as the gate-cottage.'

It was something of a relief to Horgan, finding that Lord Balgrummo was past giving coherent evidence in a court of law — and therefore need not be given the quietus. Even though they no longer hanged anybody for anything, and even though Balgrummo could have been eliminated in thirty seconds by a pillow over his face, the police pursued a homicide much more energetically than they did a picture-fancier.

But was this penny-dreadful monster of fifty years ago, with his white beard now making him sham-venerable in this four-poster, still among the living? Horgan almost could see the bones through his skin; Balgrummo might have come to his end during the hour or so since Jamieson had made his rounds. To be sure, Horgan took a mirror from the dressing-table and held it close to the pallid sunken face. Setting his torch on its base, he inspected the mirror's surface; yes, there was a faint moist film, so the tenth baron still breathed.

Balgrummo must be stone-deaf, or in a coma. Dr. Effie had said he had gone almost blind recently. Was it true? Horgan nearly yielded to a loathsome impulse to roll back those withered eyelids, but he reminded himself that somehow he wouldn't be able to endure seeing his own image in this dying man's malign pupils.

The coshing of Jock, the nervous partial exploration of this dismal house, the sight of loathsome old Balgrummo on the edge of dissolution — these trials had told on Horgan, old hand though he was at predatory ventures. With all the hours left to him, it would do no harm to sit for a few minutes in this easy chair, almost as if he were Balgrummo's nurse — keeping watch on the bed, surely, to make certain that Balgrummo wasn't (in reason's spite) shamming in some way — and to review in his brain the pictures he ought to secure first, and the rooms in which he was likely to find them.

But it would be heartening to have more light than his torch. Never turning his back on the bed, Horgan contrived to light a gas-bracket near the door; either these gas-fittings were simpler than those belowstairs, or he had got the trick of the operation. The interior shutters of this bedroom being closed, there wasn't the faintest danger of a glimmer of light being perceived by chance passersby — not that anybody conceivably could pass by Balgrummo Lodging on a rainy midnight.

Lord Balgrummo seemed no less grisly in the flood of gaslight. However much exhausted by strain, you couldn't think of going to sleep, for the briefest nap, in a chair only six feet distant from this unspeaking and unspeakable thing in the bed; not when you knew just how 'very naughty,' in Dr. Euphemia's phrase, Balgrummo had been. The Trouble for which he had paid had been only the culmination of a series of arcane episodes, progressing from hocus-pocus to the ultimate horror.

'No, not lunatic, in any ordinary definition of the term,' Gillespie had declared. 'Balgrummo recognized the moral character of his acts — aye, more fully than does the average sensual man. Also he was, and is, quite rational, in the sense that he can transact some ordinary business of life when pressed. He fell into a devil of a temper when we proposed to sell some of his pictures to pay for putting the house and the policies in order;

he knows his rights, and that the trustees can't dispose of his plenishings against his explicit disapproval. He's civil enough, in his mocking way, to his niece, Effie, when she calls — and to me, when I have to see him. He still reads a good deal — or did, until his sight began to fail — though only books in his own library; half the ceiling has fallen in the library, but he shuffles through the broken plaster on the shaky floor.'

On the right of the bed-head there hung an indubitable Constable; on the left, a probable Etty. The two were fairly small, and Horgan could take them whenever he wished. But his throat was dry, this house being so damned dusty. A decanter stood on the dressing-table, a silver brandy label round its neck, and by it two cut-glass tumblers. 'Not a drop for you, Alec?' inquired Horgan, grinning defiantly at the silent man on the bed. He seated himself in the velvet-upholstered armchair again and drank the brandy neat.

'No, one can't say,' Gillespie had continued (in that last conversation which now seemed so far away and long ago), 'that his lordship is wholly incompetent to take a hand in the management of his affairs. It's rather that he's *distant* — preoccupied, in more senses than one. He has to exert his will to bring his consciousness back from wherever it drifts — and one can see that the effort isn't easy for him.'

'He's in a brown study, you mean, Tom?' Horgan had inquired, not much interested at that time.

'It's not the phrase I would choose, Rafe. Dr. Effie talks about the "astral body" and such rubbish, as if she half believed in it — you've heard her. That silliness was a principal subject of Balgrummo's "researches" for two years before the Trouble, you understand; his Trouble was the culmination of those experiments. But of course . . .'

'Of course he's only living in the past,' Horgan had put in.

'*Living?* Who really knows what that word means?' T. M. Gillespie, W. S., devoted to the memory of David Hume, professed a contempt for rationalism as profound as his contempt for superstition. 'And why say *past?* Did you never think that a man might be ossified in time? What you call Balgrummo's past, Rafe, may be Balgrummo's own present, as much as this table-talk of ours is the present for you and me. The Trouble is his lordship's obsessive reality. Attaining to genuine evil requires strict application to the discipline, eh? Balgrummo is not merely remembering the events of what you and I call 1913, or even "reliving" those events. No, I suspect it's this: he's embedded in those events, like a beetle in amber.

For Balgrummo, one certain night in Balgrummo Lodging continues forever.

'When Dr. Effie and I distract him by raising the trivia of current business, he has to depart from *his* reality, and gropes briefly through a vexatious little dreamworld in which his niece and his solicitor are insubstantial shadows. In Alexander Inchburn's consciousness, I mean, there is no remembrance and no anticipation. He's not "living in the past," not engaging in an exercise of retrospection; for him, Time is restricted to one certain night, and space is restricted to one certain house, or perhaps one certain room. Passionate experience has chained him to a fixed point in Time, so to speak. But Time, as so many have said, is a human convention, not an objective reality. Can you prove that your Time is more substantial than his?'

Horgan hadn't quite followed Gillespie, and said so.

'I put it this way, Rafe,' Gillespie had gone on, didactically. 'What's the time of day in Hell? Why, Hell is timeless — or so my grandfather told me, and he was minister at the Tron. Hell knows no future and no past, but only the everlasting moment of damnation. Also Hell is spaceless; or, conceivably, it's a locked box, damnably confining. Here we have Lord Balgrummo shut up perpetually in his box called Balgrummo Lodging, where the fire is not quenched and the worm never dieth. One bloody and atrocious act, committed in that very box, literally is his enduring *reality*. He's not recollecting; he's experiencing, here and (for him) now. All the frightful excitement of that Trouble, the very act of profanation and terror, lifts him out of what we call Time. Between Dr. Effie and me on the one side, and distant Balgrummo on the other, a great gulf is fixed.

'If you like, you can call that gulf Time. For that gulf, I praise whatever gods there be. For if any man's or woman's consciousness should penetrate to Balgrummo's consciousness, to his time-scheme, to his world beyond the world — or if, through some vortex of mind and soul, anyone were sucked into that narrow place of torment — then the intruder would end like *this*.' Gillespie, tapping his cigar upon an ashtray, knocked into powder a long projection of gray ash. 'Consumed, Rafe.'

Scratch the canny Scot, Horgan had thought then, even the pedant of law, and you find the bogle-dreading Pict. 'I suppose you mean, really, Tom, that he's out of his head,' Horgan had commented, bored with tipsy and unprofitable speculation.

'I mean precisely the contrary, Rafe. I mean that anyone who encounters Lord Balgrummo ought to be on his guard against being drawn into Balgrummo's head. In what you and I designate as 1913 (though, as I said, dates have no significance for Balgrummo), his lordship was a being of immense moral power, magnetic and seductive. I'm not being facetious. Moral power is a catalyst, and can work for good or evil. Even now, I'm acutely uneasy when I sit with Balgrummo, aware that this old man might absorb me. I shouldn't wish to stir those sleeping fires by touching his passions. That's why Balgrummo had to be confined five decades ago — but not simply because he might be *physically* dangerous. Yet I can't explain to you; you've not watched Balgrummo in what you call his "brown study," and you never will, happy man.' Their conversation then had shifted to Miss Janet Horgan's hypothetical trust.

Yet Gillespie had been a bad prophet. Here he was, clever Rafe Horgan, man of supple talents and slippery fingers, leisurely watching Lord Balgrummo in his brown study — or in his coma, more precisely — and finishing his lordship's decanter of praiseworthy brandy. You had to remember to keep watching that cadaverous face above the sheet, though; if you let your eyes close even for a second, *his* might open, for all you could tell. After all, you were only a guest in Balgrummo's very own little Hell. The host mustn't be permitted to forget his manners.

Now where would the expiring monster keep his privy effects — the key to that chapel on the floor above, for instance? Steady, Rafe, boy: keep your eyes on his face as you open his bedside drawer. Right you are, Rafe, you always were lucky; the nurse had put old Alec's three keys on a chain, along with watch and pocket-comb and such effects, into this very drawer. One of these keys should let you into the chapel, Rafe. Get on with you; you've drunk all the brandy a reasonable man needs.

'Don't you mean to give me a guided tour, Alec? Stately homes of Scotia, and all that? Won't you show me your chapel, where you and your young chums played your dirty little games, and got your fingers burned? Cheerio, then; don't blame me if you can't be bothered to keep an eye on your goods and chattels.'

Back away from him, toward the door, Rafe. Let him lie. How had Dr. Effie put it? 'He fills the house, every room, every hour.' Cheerless thought, that, fit for a scrawny old maid. The talkative Euphemia must have nearly as many screws loose as had her uncle; probably she envied him his revels.

'I really believe the others led Uncle Alec into the whole business, gradually,' Dr. Effie had droned on, the last time he had seen her. 'But once in, he took command, as natural to him. He was out in Nigeria before people called it Nigeria, you know, and in Guinea, and all up and down that coast. He began collecting materials for a monograph on African magic — raising the dead, and summoning devils, and more. Presently he was dabbling in the spells, not merely collecting them — so my father told me, forty years ago. After Uncle Alec came home, he didn't stop dabbling. Some very reputable people dabbled when I was a girl. But the ones around Uncle Alec weren't in the least reputable.

'Charlatans? Not quite; I wish they had been. They fed Balgrummo's appetite. Yet he was after knowledge, at least in the beginning; and though he may have boggled, more than once, at the steps he had to descend toward the source of that knowledge, he grew more eager as he pressed down into the dark. Or so father guessed; father became one of Uncle Alec's original trustees, and felt it his duty to collect some evidence of what had happened — though it sickened father, the more he uncovered of his brother's queerness.

'Toward the end, Balgrummo may have forgotten about knowledge and have leaped into passion and power. One didn't *learn* what one had sought to apprehend; one *became* the mystery, possessing it and possessed by it.

'No, not charlatans — not altogether. They took a fortune out of Uncle Alec, one way or another; and he had to pay even more to keep people quiet in those years. They had told Balgrummo, in effect, that they could raise the Devil — though they didn't put it in quite that crude way. Yet they must have been astounded by their success, when it came at last. Balgrummo had paid before, and he has paid ever since. Those others paid, too — especially the man and the woman who died. They had thought they were raising the Devil *for* Lord Balgrummo. But as it turned out, they raised the Devil *through* Balgrummo and *in* Balgrummo. After that, everything fell to pieces.'

But to hell with recollections of Euphemia Inchburn, Rafe. Dry rot, wet rot, woodworm, deathwatch beetle: the Devil take them all, and Balgrummo Lodging besides. One thing the Devil shouldn't have — these pictures. Get on to the chapel, Rafe, and then give Nan the glad news. Thanks for the brandy, Alec: I mightn't have got through the business without it.

*   *

83

Yet one dram too many, possibly? Horgan was aware of a certain giddiness, but not fully aware of how he had got up those Stygian stairs, or of what he had done with his torch. Had he turned the key in the lock of the chapel door? He couldn't recall having done so. Still, here he was in the chapel.

No need for the torch; the room, a long gallery, was lit by all those candle-flames in the many-branched candlesticks. Who kept Lord Balgrummo's candles alight? The stench of decay was even stronger here than it had been down below. Underfoot, the floorboards were almost oozing, and mushroom rot squashed beneath his shoes. Some of the paneling had fallen away altogether. High up in the shifting shadows, the moulded-plaster ceiling sagged and bulged as if the lightest touch would bring it all down in slimy little particles.

Back of the altar — the altar of the catastrophic act of Balgrummo's Trouble — hung the unknown Fuseli. It was no painting, but an immense cartoon, and the most uninhibited museum-director never would dare show it to the most broad-minded critics of art. Those naked and contorted forms, the instruments of torment fixed upon their flesh, were the inversion of the Agony. Even Horgan could not bear to look at them long.

Look at them? All those candles were guttering. Two winked out simultaneously; others failed. As the little flames sank toward extinction, Rafe Horgan became aware that he was not alone.

It was as if the presences skulked in corners or behind the broken furniture. And there could be no retreat toward the door; for something approached from that end of the gallery. As if Horgan's extremity of terror fed it, the shape took on increasing clarity of outline, substance, strength.

Tall, arrogant, implacable, mindless, it drifted toward him. The face was Balgrummo's, or what Balgrummo's must have been fifty years before, but possessed: eager, eager, eager; all appetite, passion, yearning after the abyss. In one hand glittered a long knife.

Horgan bleated and ran. He fell against the cobwebby altar. And in the final act of destruction, something strode across the great gulf of Time.

Lex Talionis

So ye shall not pollute the land wherein ye are: for blood it defileth the land: and the land cannot be cleansed of the blood that is shed therein, but by the blood of him that shed it.

Numbers 35:33

As twilight sank upon the wrack and glitter of the old city, Eddie Mahaffy walked beneath the great bridge and through the empty streets that ran parallel with the levee. Despite all the mercury-vapor streetlights, the old people and the drunken and the drugged and the desperately poor who still were compelled to inhabit these fallen streets did not venture out after six o'clock. The vacant lots, a legacy of urban 'renewal,' were abandoned to two-footed predators, who had slim pickings.

But Eddie Mahaffy — or Eddie Cain, as he had called himself since leaving the prison — sauntered on, immune, the mercury-vapor glare ghastly on his face. He had come to know who he was and what he was, a rare endowment, a gift of grace; and he walked with shoulders back, chest out, unassailable in his shabby black suit with the black sweater beneath it and the stained black hat slanted over his eyes. Few saw him; none touched him. 'I don't worry, 'cause it makes no difference now.' The lyric ran round and round in his head, and he whistled it softly.

Then a big black glossy car purred alongside him; drew slightly ahead of him; paused, the motor idling. Two men were in the front seat: expensively and flashily dressed, heavy-lidded, with the look of corruption about them. The man nearer Eddie beckoned. 'Say . . .'

Eddie walked over to the car, an act imprudent in these streets, and put his hand upon the door where the glass had been drawn down. Eddie did not recognize the man: yet the one, or perhaps the brace of them, might recollect Eddie from prison; he could not be sure. Although as time is reckoned it could not have been a great while since he had left the prison, Eddie's memories of those captive years were vague enough: he swaying between death and life in the prison infirmary, there had descended upon him something like grace, and he had been changed. Those years behind the wall had faded like dreams.

'Say, don't I know you?' The man peering at Eddie from the car would be somebody big in a troll-realm, some grand pusher or procurer, thinking he might make use of a fellow with Eddie's scarred face and Eddie's way of walking; oh, he may have had a glimpse or two of Eddie in the prison, like enough, but couldn't quite place him.

'Yes,' said Eddie, clearly and almost cordially, 'I'm Sergeant Cain, Vice Squad.'

The driver shifted and stepped on the gas with wonderful celerity; the car rushed away from Eddie so abruptly that he spun round on the pavement, chuckling as he regained his balance. The offense of impersonating a police office had its rewards.

Eddie strolled on, darkness settling about him. The sudden appearance and vanishing of that pair of hoody crows — did it signify something rough? Was it the presentiment of some event dashing fast upon him? Since he had been made an instrument, waiting upon the Lord's will, he had come to understand that 'coincidences' never occur; that all is design infinitely complex, rather; that what was intended for him, must happen, not his to question why. This was the first time since his liberation that a *revenant* from the prison had whirred past Eddie, like a spent bullet past a soldier's ear. Was he to encounter some other fragment from a vanished life, and soon? Then he had best pray.

His casual sauntering had brought him near to the old cathedral, isolated now amidst parking-lots empty at this hour. With reason, churches locked their doors at nightfall, nowadays; but there were lights visible behind the painted glass of those tall windows. Eddie went briskly up the stone steps and pushed open the heavy door. The handsome venerable restored interior, with its high ceiling of blue, called Eddie in. He removed his hat, touched his forehead with consecrated water, genuflected. 'Christ came to save sinners, of whom I am the chief.'

A dozen people, with a priest talking to them, were gathered near the high altar — perhaps a wedding-rehearsal party. Nobody noticed Eddie Mahaffy, Eddie Cain. He made his soundless way from little side-chapel to little side-chapel, kneeling at every *prie-dieu*, praying in turn to each saint: John Bosco; Gregory the Great; Rose of Lima; Augustine of Hippo; Francis de Sales; Mary, Mother of God. 'Pray for us sinners now and at the hour of our death. . . .' In the chapel shadows, indiscernible, beyond time and space and circumstance, he implored these saints' intercession.

He prayed for the off-duty policeman who had been shot, without malice aforethought, outside O'Leary's Bar; for Uncle Chris, who had thought himself invulnerable, gunned down some months later in an act of bravado; for Joseph, the L'Anse Indian, crippled for life in that same silly shoot-out; for all the inmates of the prison, and for the souls in Purgatory. He prayed earnestly before the images of Joseph the Worker, of Thomas of Canterbury, of (a new one!) Elizabeth Seton.

Last of all, with self-contempt and gratitude and even hope, he prayed for himself. 'Faith is the substance of things hoped for, the evidence of things not seen.' The Lord, who out of His unfathomable judgment had made the shrew, kept a place for such a one as the believing crucified thief, perhaps even for such a one as Eddie Cain. 'I believe, O Lord; help Thou my unbelief.'

During those weeks of agony in the prison infirmary, he had learnt to meditate and to pray. What a gift to the unworthy! During his two years as a novice, in that Pennsylvania monastery, before he had gone to sea — early years that he recalled far better than the later prison years — he had not mastered the art of meditation. All the novices had been required to meditate, as a body, for an hour a day, within the chapel. Eddie had sat there one afternoon, desperately struggling to restrain vagrant thoughts. Near him had sat another novice, his eyelids lowered, his young face beatific, sunk in contemplation, perhaps adrift on the blessed *via negativa*. How Eddie had envied him, that foul vice rising even in the chapel! But at the end of the meditation-hour, all novices except one had risen and filed out, Eddie among them. The single exception had been the novice with the beatific face — who had remained there kneeling, sound asleep.

We sleep away our sensual existence, Eddie thought; we forget the end. Yet upon some, in their agony of tribulation, the Dove descends; and those are taught how to contemplate and how to pray. Only this was left to Eddie now, and it sufficed.

He prayed that if his encounter with the two men in the big car had been a presage — why, that the cup might pass from him; and yet, 'Thy will be done, O Lord, not mine.' He prayed that the punishment might be lifted from him at last, after much expiation. 'But Thy will be done.'

Beyond time, he knelt in a deep but dazzling dark, all cloaked and dim. From this he was roused by a quavering voice.

'Anybody here? Anybody still in the church?'

Eddie glanced round him, rising from his knees. A little distance away, a custodian or a sacristan — they used to call them that, but they had discarded vestments now — had begun to lock up; the old man must have caught some doubtful glimpse of Eddie in the shadows.

'Pardon me,' said Eddie. 'I was out of myself.'

'Oh!' The custodian started sharply, peering in the direction of Eddie's voice. Eddie passed down a side aisle, not very close to the old man, who stammered uneasily, 'Well, we're closing up now, brother.' The custodian craned his neck, trying to make out this stranger more clearly.

'Thanks for calling me "brother,"' Eddie murmured, 'but I'm in no order.' He passed through the great portal, the locker-up shuffling hesitantly after him. What with the black suit and sweater, it had been natural enough that he should be mistaken for a monk — and especially with his hat off, for Eddie was nearly bald, and the red hair remaining to him ran tonsurelike over his ears and round the back of his skull. 'Mea culpa, mea maxima culpa,' Eddie murmured as he passed into the night; but the man locking the door did not seem altogether reassured. Doubtless sacred vessels had been taken from this church, in recent years, by vessels for dishonor.

'Pax,' said Eddie to nobody in particular, strolling on. Presently he heard himself whistling again: 'I don't worry, 'cause it makes no difference now.'

Having made his way, seemingly aimless, along many silent blocks, he found himself approaching a lighted old-fashioned restaurant-front: Old Town Bar and Grill. All about the place lay dereliction, in part the gnawing of time's tooth, in part the deliberate achievement of civic 'renewers.' Some nearby houses with steep-pitched roofs were 'mothballed,' like naval vessels left over from a war, as if restoration were intended — surprising, in this city. Right out to the suburbs of the thirties, within three decades, the city had rotted; it had been as if some diabolic impulse of destruction had conquered everyone and everything.

Eddie liked the look of the oldfangled eating-house, a staunch lonely survivor of a healthier time in this city. Somehow he never had happened upon the place before. Should he go in and sit down?

Now why had this notion come into his head? Was it bound up with the presage of an hour or more earlier? Would something come upon him in the Old Town Bar and Grill? 'Your sins will find you out'? Yet the impulse was strong in him, as if communicated; and with foreboding, he entered.

*   *

It was a big cheerful room, with promise of other rooms beyond it; it conveyed a general impression of faded elegance. There was a long walnut bar, positively venerable, that Eddie would have fancied mightily in his drinking days. The polished dark wainscoting was old, and the tables and chairs seemed old, too. Some enterprising imaginative souls must keep this restaurant together despite the ruin of the streets all round about; perhaps they were a youngish couple who did a tolerable lunch-hour trade. Eddie would have liked to congratulate them upon their fortitude.

An immense baroque mirror was fixed to the wall behind the bar, and Eddie saw himself shadowed therein: his pale face with the tonsure of flaming hair, his thin lips, his wiry gaunt body, his deep-set eyes. What wonder that he had given a turn to the old custodian dimly perceiving him in the cathedral?

Eddie sat down at a little table. There were few customers this midnight, and some of those customers were fashionable, and some of them scruffy. The former relished the atmosphere, no doubt; the latter must be locals from the mansions now divided into apartments. Nobody, not even the waitress clearing tables, noticed Eddie. He felt at ease.

But only for a moment. For suddenly he observed a big man on a stool at the bar, his profile turned toward Eddie. This was an exceedingly rough customer, and Eddie had seen him before; but never had expected or desired to encounter him again.

The man wore jeans, a blue short-sleeved shirt, and a disreputable cap; his coat was flung over the next stool. He was muscular almost beyond belief — the sort of man who exercises in gyms most of the day —

and his massive arms were covered with tattoos. This Hercules had the face of a satyr. The man was scowling — he must always have been scowling, which often is a mark that lust has cast out love forever — and his tawny eyes were tigerish. Lounging predatory there, he looked as nasty and as formidable a character as any connoisseur of brutal types could hope to encounter. In many years at sea and in the prison, Eddie had not set eyes upon a better specimen of tough depravity; why, the man was the perfection of his type. What was his name? 'Butte' — that was it; everybody in the prison had called him Butte, because once he had been a Montana miner.

Then the man saw Eddie, and Eddie felt a revulsion immerse him. Why had this been put upon him? An incredulous ugly grin spread over Butte's sullen face, and he swaggered across the floor and sat down at the table. Eddie rose.

'Where you goin'?' asked Butte, indignant.

'Wherever you aren't.' Eddie moved toward the next table.

'Here, wait a minute! Hold on, pal! Don't be choosy — you're jest like me, Monk.'

It had been 'Butte' — though he was no beauty — in the prison, and 'Monk' in the prison. Butte had had plenty of pals there: a big man behind the walls, one of the inmates who had been the real authorities in that caricature of society, a master of the inverted high justice, the middle, and the low. Butte had done well for himself in the prison. To everybody else there — even his toadies — he had done ill.

'You're just like me, buster!' Butte repeated.

'Too true,' said Eddie Cain. He sat down opposite Butte, resigned, an instrument. To himself, silently, 'Pray for us sinners now and at the hour of our death.'

'That's more like it, good buddy. Thirsty?' Butte signalled a tall waitress with an admirable figure. 'Hey, babe, bring me another boilermaker an' his helper, an' give the Monk anythin' in the world — jest anythin' he wants, get it, kid?'

'What monk, where?' the tall girl asked. 'You kidding, mister?'

'I don't drink,' Eddie murmured to Butte.

'You puttin' me on, buster?' Butte cackled. 'Well, make it a double boilermaker for me, luscious.' He reached out to pat the waitress, but she shied and returned to the bar.

'Cute kid there, hey, Monk? She ain't too bright, but she really struts her stuff, don't she? Stuck-up, though. I been askin' 'bout her: name's Mary. She's married but separated. Reckon some lazy dark night I'll foller her home an' teach her a few facts o' life — slap her around a little for a start, you know, Monk.'

'I don't know,' said Eddie.

'Oh, yeah? Stop tryin' to put me on, pal. You was in for homicide an' armed robbery; you ain't no saint. But if you're on the wagon, that's all right tonight. One of us has got to be cold sober, and it sure ain't gonna be me.'

'Now, listen,' said Eddie. 'I didn't come in here looking for you; I didn't know you were within a thousand miles of this place. What you did to me is nothing now, and you're nothing. We're told to forgive our enemies: I forgive you. All you have to do is get up and walk out of this bar: I won't come after you. You go your way, I go mine: if I call it quits, why shouldn't you? I'm giving you a chance you never gave anybody. I'm letting this cup pass from me.'

Butte leaned forward across the table, trying to look confidentially ge-nial. 'I don't get your line, good buddy, but I need you. I need you real bad, coupla hours from now.'

The world is full of men like this nowadays, Eddie thought: men like ghouls, subsisting on the flesh of a civilization that has forgotten its own ends, protected by the laws that once were made to restrain them. It would be pleasant to think that such men eventually are hoisted by their own pe-tard, in some narrow corner; but one can't be sure of that — not sure at all. Some bishop had said that though Heaven isn't necessary to the scheme of salvation, Hell is necessary; divine love made Hell. A man like this Butte could swagger through life, enjoying all the vices, his very occasional pun-ishments so many more opportunities for fraud, concupiscence, violence, atrocious acts; and nothing much might be done to him here below. But hereafter? If it weren't for that 'hereafter,' there'd be no justice in the na-ture of things. Old Pelagius, with his soft doctrine of universal salvation through universal human goodness, had been the worst of all heretics.

What Eddie said aloud was, 'Get lost. I don't need you, and you don't need me. Now mark me: for you, I'm a dangerous character.'

Butte shook with harsh laughter, slapping his powerful thigh, so that the few customers at the bar or the tables turned to stare at him, and the bartender whispered something to the openmouthed fine-figured wait-ress.

'Ain't we both?' Butte demanded. 'Ain't we both dangerous characters, Monk?'

'Quiet down,' said Eddie. 'I'm not your good buddy, and I've got reason not to be. You're high on more than whiskey. There's nothing you can do for me or to me.'

'Yeah, yeah, I'll cool it, Monk. You nervous? Mebbe carryin' a rod with no permit?' Eddie shook his head. 'Well, all right, Monk, there's too many damn jerks in here. There's a place out that door, open-air, where we kin yak: come on, Monk boy.' He showed Eddie into a kind of courtyard, the night sky above, and urged him into a rustic chair.

They were alone in dim light. Into the walls of this court were set pieces of carved stone from demolished buildings of the blighted neighborhood: the lintel of a bank's doorway, even part of the balustrade of some vanished house. It was all rather deathly, in a handsome way.

'Pretty fancy joint, eh, Monk?'

'Sure,' said Eddie. 'What do you have to say before I go?'

'You ain't goin', Monk; I gotta have your help.'

'You can't stop me; there isn't anything you can do to me now.'

Butte stared at him malignly. 'You was a lifer, Monk. I got parole while you was still in the infirmary, but you didn't have no connections. How'd you get parole, Monk?'

'I didn't.'

'You mean they pardoned you?'

'No.'

'That's what I thought, good buddy. It's easier gettin' away if you're in the infirmary than if you're in the yard, ain't it?'

Eddie was silent.

'They want you back there at the prison, Monk, so set down. I could turn you in.'

'You'd do that?'

'Hell, I could grab you right now an' tell the barkeep to call the pigs. You better believe it, Monk.'

The man was quite perfect, in his way: no spark of charity in him, not one. Butte had been serving a term for rape, back in the prison, but there had been a long string of felony-convictions before that, Eddie knew. And always Butte had been released after a few months: he did have connections, and it was advisable for certain people to make sure that Butte wouldn't talk too much behind bars.

'Anyhow,' Butte was saying, 'there's mebbe twenty grand for you in this, Monk. You sure could use money like that, pal; it'd be like I was payin' you back for what I done to you in prison. *Twenty grand*, buddy: all the dope an' whiskey an' women that money'll buy, Monk boy. Like the sound o' that? You ain't joined up with no Salvation Army, huh?'

'I don't like the sound of it,' said Eddie.

'Not like dope an' whiskey an' wild, wild women?' Butte suddenly reached across the table, as if to poke Eddie jocularly in the ribs — but actually to tell whether the Monk was wearing a gun, Eddie guessed. He drew back before Butte's huge hand could touch him.

'I'm not carrying an armory,' Eddie told him sharply, 'but watch yourself.'

'Okay, okay, no harm meant.' Butte grinned like a crocodile. 'But you can't put me on, friend, not old Butte. Why, what in hell's worth gettin' but them three things?'

*   *

Butte actually believed what he was saying, Eddie knew. Sickened by Butte's talk, Eddie let himself be swept back into the memory of the day he had stood up to Butte in prison. Here at the table, Butte growled on, sometimes wheedling, sometimes menacing; but Eddie ignored him, being lost in a frightful recollection of things past.

Eddie had kept to himself in prison, taken orders obediently, done his work; he had been regarded by most of the other convicts as a 'religious nut.' After a few months, the deputy warden — appreciative of model prisoners — had assigned Eddie to the prison library, having noticed a good deal of formal schooling on Eddie's records.

The way to survive in the terrestrial hell of the prison had been to keep uninvolved. He had been so counselled by his cellmate, a grim-faced gentle giant named Frank Sarsfield, practically the only other inmate who didn't lard every sentence with monotonous obscenities.

The actual lords of the prison had been Butte and his gang, deft at extortion and at cruel and unusual punishments. They had left Eddie the Monk pretty much unmolested: partly, he had known, because it was wise not to drive lifers to desperation — they did not have much to lose if it came to a showdown — and partly because 'religious nuts' had been looked upon as potentially dangerous to rational criminals.

But that one day Eddie had exploded. There had been a foolish smooth-faced boy, not bad by nature, sentenced for negligent homicide — held responsible for a car crash — and Butte and his gang liked having fun with that kind. Passing by the machine shop, Eddie had heard a rumpus, and had looked inside, and had seen what Butte was doing to the poor kid.

The blood-red tide, the raging anger of old kerns and gallow-glasses, had flooded into Eddie. He had been a lightweight boxer in the navy; and he had gone for Butte in the machine shop. For a few minutes, Eddie's old skill had driven Butte back. Then the big man's bulk and muscles had told, and Eddie had lost a tooth, and his face had become a pulp, but still he had fought on, mockingly ringed by Butte's chums, knocked down, rising again with a bubbling scream of fury, on and on, until at last Butte had ended it by drawing a knife. Eddie had fallen with the shiv between his ribs, and the gang kicking him about the head. Later, in the infirmary, he had been told that Frank Sarsfield had called the deputy warden and extricated his cellmate.

After that was some memory of operations, transfusions, complications, more operations, the news that Butte had been paroled, Sarsfield sitting by his bed quoting Omar Khayyám, coma, astounding visions, dim wakings, visions of grace, a wavering at the gates. . . . And here he was, face to face with Butte again; but Eddie Mahaffy, Eddie Cain, so changed, was now an instrument — no free agent. Saint Augustine said we ought to hate the sin but love the sinner. Such was the counsel of perfection. Who ever had loved Butte? Such magnanimity could be expected only of great saints; and, as Butte had observed, Eddie was no saint at all.

*   *

'You're the only guy that really stood up to me in prison, Eddie,' Butte was saying patronizingly, 'an' I give you credit. So when you walk in here tonight, I say to myself, "Brother, you're in luck. There's jest the boy I need for a helper."' Butte had two more shots of whiskey before him.

'What sort of help?' Eddie demanded, poker-faced. 'Your kind always has a pal or two around.'

'Well, I had me a pardner, but he got hisself picked up yesterday for somethin' that got nothin' to do with this here sure thing; an' so I set here, not wantin' to go it alone, an' the time I counted on jest a few hours off —

an' you showed up! Listen, Monk, I'll split even with you, an' there ain't no damn risk to it. You couldn't ask better'n that, hey?'

'What would I need to do?'

'Now you're talkin'! Here it is: there's one old house, great big place, with more'n forty grand stashed there, an' nobody livin' in it. It's jest five minutes' easy work, Monk, an' I got the tools for it in a swiped car outside. We hit the house at three tonight — there's nobody in the block 'cept mebbe some junkies sleepin' in wrecked houses — an' then me an' you is in the bucks, buster.'

'If it's that easy, why split with anybody?'

Butte, shifting in his chair, glanced aside. 'Feel a little easier that way, that's all. The house is from Deadsville, pal. Here, take a look at this, an' you'll git the picture.'

Butte produced from his billfold a newspaper clipping, the date on it three months old. It was a long story, and the heading ran: OLD COUPLE, PRETTY NIECE MURDERED IN PALATIAL SETTING.

Glancing through the article, Eddie gathered that a retired physician, an old-school doctor, had lived with his elderly wife and a sixteen-year-old niece in a big inherited house; the neighborhood, once splendid, had gone to pieces swiftly in little more than ten years, but the old doctor had stuck to his father's and grandfather's mansion. That house had been one of the few remaining pillars of order in the vicinity of Lafayette Square. The doctor's love for his house had been a fatal attachment.

For after five days during which no one had seen the old couple or the niece, the police had investigated, and had found in the deep cellar the bodies of all three. There had been a fourth corpse besides: that of a kind of handyman who had been given regular access to the house. There had been a kitchen knife in the handyman's back. The two women had been bound and tortured, the girl ravished, and their throats cut; apparently the old doctor had died of heart failure, under stress.

More than a thousand dollars in bills had lain scattered round the handyman's body. The police discovered that the handyman, who had used various aliases, had been a heroin addict, with a long string of arrests for other mischief.

So far as the police had been able to piece the affair together, it appeared that the handyman, Harry, had been caught in the act of robbing a wall safe. Presumably Harry had turned on his employers with a knife, murdering the two women; but the old doctor, vigorous for his years, somehow must have managed to stab Harry in the back — and then fallen dead from a heart attack.

The story went on to describe the antique furnishings, the former glories of the house (the doctor had been straitened by investment losses), and the speedy decline of the neighborhood. A score of similar homicides and rapes by armed robbers during the preceding four months were listed.

In this year of our Lord . . . Eddie crossed himself before handing back the clipping to Butte, who had lit a cigarette complacently. 'How do you come into this?'

'That thousand on the cellar floor was chicken feed, Monk, left there to fool the pigs.' Butte licked his lips. 'The real bundle's still in the house.' He spoke *sotto voce*. 'Me an' Harry had a real long interestin' session with that there high-school tease, while she lasted.'

Eddie closed his eyes. He had not been transformed utterly: the blood-red tide flooded upon him for a moment. His lids still shut, he asked, 'Why did you stick your helper?'

There came a silence; Eddie opened his eyes and stared inquisitively at Butte, who was looking at the tiles of the pavement.

'Hell, Monk boy, it was the other way round: I was Harry's helper; he knowed about the old doc keepin' so much cash in the wall safe 'cause he got hurt on the stock market. If I hadn't helped Harry, some other smart guy would. But Harry had to go, as things turned out in that Deadsville cellar. Buster, you should've seen the spiders down there! Well, this Harry was a junkie, real spaced-out that there night, you better believe me, an' so help me, Hannah, it was him that polished off the women while I was lookin' for more money. Honest to God, Harry went crazy wild, an' he might of give it to me, too; anyway, he'd of yakked about the fun he had. I couldn't of let him do that, could I?'

Eddie put his hands across his face. Now he knew that his presentiment earlier that night had been genuine. For his sins, he had been sent to this place and this brute, this torturing creature worse than an ape, this triumphant psychopath Butte. Eddie sighed audibly, guessing the end, and asked, 'How could you have left forty thousand dollars in the house?'

'It was in big bills — century notes, pal — an' at the time I hadn't no way to launder them. Would I want to be picked up with that stuff on me, or had them found in my pad? So what's the safest place for the loot? Why, that there house itself.

'I could allus go back; I'd taken keys offen Harry; jest let the heat die down, an' then git in again some night. I stashed the stuff in a place nobody'd guess, you better believe me. Like I figured, nobody'd rent or buy the place, after what happened there — not for a hell of a while, anyhow, an' not by a long shot in that there neighborhood. The house is all boarded up, Monk, an' the local kids ain't broke in — 'cause they think about haunts. But a coupla days ago I hear tell that the place is goin' to be knocked down, there bein' no sale for it. The wreckers might start in next week, an' the furniture's goin' out tomorrow, so I'm gittin' my bundle out tonight.

'See, I figured the whole damn thing right, good buddy: the pigs did pick me up for questionin', knowin' as I'd palled with Harry, but o' course I didn't know nothin' an' they didn't find nothin'. So after tonight, Monk, me an' you are ridin' high.'

Eddie, his chin in his right hand, studied Butte impassively. 'What's to stop you from going there alone? Do you figure there's something waiting for you in that cellar? Something creepy-crawly?'

'You could scream your head off in that street,' Butte grunted, 'an' the pigs wouldn't come, not there, not in the middle o' the night, mebbe not in the daylight.'

Eddie persisted. 'Thinking about — ghosts?'

The big man balled his fists. 'Shut up!'

Eddie smiled his thin-lipped smile and closed his eyes again. It's odd, he thought, how in many people the dread of spooks has outlasted the fear of God which is the beginning of wisdom. This debauched gorilla-man, believing in nothing else, still could quiver at a footfall on a stair, a glimpse of something white round a corner. Had Butte seen or heard something unsettling, something inexplicable, while hiding the money in that desecrated house?

'The old doctor and his wife and the girl seem to have been decent people,' Eddie resumed, aloud, taking no notice of Butte's curses; 'harmless alive, harmless dead. Those three innocents are gone to where they can't be touched; they won't lurk to catch an animal like you. As for dead Harry, he wouldn't be any tougher wrapped in a bedsheet, would he? Ghosts! The silly notions people have about ghosts. . . . Of course there are fundamentalist types who'd say you might find demons in that cellar, ready to pitchfork you in your own very private hell; but you couldn't meet a worse devil than yourself. At the core, you're a coward, Butte.'

He thought that Butte would leap at him — in which event, Butte would get more than he bargained for. But the man's heavy face, swollen suddenly by a rush of blood, subsided as swiftly. 'Come on, you religious nut,' Butte snarled. 'The car's in the lot jest outside.'

Eddie went with him unprotesting. No longer was this a mere matter of a grudge over what had been done to him in the prison; for whatever purpose, he had been sent to Butte.

*   *

They were driving, Eddie guessed, toward Lafayette Square. Butte, silent and brooding, now and then glanced from the corner of his eye at his partner-victim. Low cunning frequently underestimates the awareness of its intended prey. Eddie knew beyond any doubt that Butte meant to leave the corpse of this 'good buddy' in the abandoned house this night, or else in the river. Also he knew that Butte was not bright enough to surmise that his conscript partner saw through the scheme.

In justice, why shouldn't the cadaver of Eddie Mahaffy, Eddie Cain, be flung away like so much garbage? He was a killer himself, and for what he had done in O'Leary's Bar, he had not yet atoned in full.

From birth, perhaps, this essence called Eddie Mahaffy, Eddie Cain, had been a bundle of contradictions. He had aspired to be a saint, when quite small, and later, too; he had succeeded in becoming a practical sinner. The relish for risk, denial, experience far out of the ordinary, moves sinners and saints both. But though both saint and sinner thirst after adventures, the path for the sinner is broader and more trodden. Eddie had fallen into it, though sometimes turning back out of remorse.

A gunner on a destroyer; then a novice whose words flew up, whose thoughts remained below; next a merchant seaman; then, emulating Uncle Chris and high on dope, an armed robber; finally a jailbird. He had been passionate in his evil, equally passionate in what little good he ever had done. Now passion was spent, or almost all of it, and he was comrade to the beast called Butte.

'What you whistlin'?' Butte asked, annoyed.

'I didn't know I was. But it comes to me, good buddy; it's called "The Pig Got Up and Slowly Walked Away." Do you know the lyrics? "Yes, the pig got up and hung his head in shame. . . ."'

'Shut up!' Butte commanded. Butte drove on slowly, through dismal back streets of the half-gutted city, careful not to attract attention from any passing patrol-car, not meaning to reach the house before three o'clock, when even the neighborhood junkies should lie in the arms of Morpheus.

Eddie indulged himself in reverie. If he was not careful, sometimes reverie — as distinguished from meditation — whirled him back to the night at O'Leary's Bar. That happened now.

Chris Mahaffy had planned it. Uncle Chris, a humorous, ruinous man, grown gray in exciting crime, running fantastic risks for the risks' sake while burglarizing banks, had dared Eddie to prove his nerve. It was an idle unemployed time for Eddie, an hour of depression of spirit, of the noonday devil. Let him be tested by just a little stickup, Chris proposed. This was to be for the fun of it: they'd hurt nobody, and after buying themselves a good dinner with the proceeds, they might even put the surplus cash into an envelope and mail it back to O'Leary, he being a good enough sort. Was Eddie up to this? Sure he was; a wild mood was upon him that day and night, and he would take any man's dare. Also Uncle Chris had given him something from Turkey to reinforce his resolution.

Chris and the Indian waited outside, the motor of Chris's car running. Eddie Mahaffy manfully strode into the bar, thinking himself twenty feet tall, shot out the lights, bowled over the bartender, and snatched the money from the register. Everybody was yelling; Eddie didn't care. He swaggered back toward the car, but a burly man rushed out of the bar and hit him on the side of the head with a blackjack. Uncle Chris, with his iron nerves, slid agilely out of the driver's seat and grappled with the man; Joseph bundled dazed Eddie into the back seat.

Then Chris's gun went off. He hadn't meant it to — he had been trying to pistol-whip the burly man — but it happened, and the burly man fell, and Uncle Chris was back in the driver's seat, and they roared off.

They had been trapped at a roadblock some hours later, and several witnesses had been produced the next day. The three of them might have got clear, had it not been for the deliberate risks that Chris had chosen all along. Yet Chris hadn't counted upon the dead man having been an off-duty police office, which fact had intensified the pursuit.

Chris and Joseph solemnly had sworn that they had entertained no faintest notion that their companion Eddie had intended to rob, or did rob, O'Leary's Bar; Chris had been rather vexingly pious on the witness stand.

Those two had been acquitted — for Chris, like this Butte, had possessed connections and a talented mouthpiece — but Eddie had been sentenced to life imprisonment. He had pleaded guilty, and had not testified in his own defense; he had not hinted that Uncle Chris's gun had done the business. For, accidents aside, hadn't he been guiltier than Chris? He never had seen Chris after the trial. But the Indian had visited Eddie in the jail, before sentence had been passed, and had said simply — his black eyes regarding Eddie almost with affection — 'You are good of heart, Eddie.'

Chris Mahaffy had been born crooked; Eddie had not; therefore Eddie was the greater sinner. Within limits, in life the will is free, if only to choose among evils. Eddie had chosen the path to Avernus. This had been his first felony, though, and his last.

Now he was Eddie Cain, perfectly solitary; and so far as freedom of the will went, his play was played out. There was reserved for Eddie only the possibility of inexplicable infinite mercy; and the plea that he had sinned more from folly than from malice. Yet how far removed was he from this Butte? To linger forever in company with Butte — that would be Hell indeed, 'to sit by Satanas the fiend.' Pray now, Eddie, pray sitting here in this car beside as vile a man as may be found. Eddie Cain, praise Him from whom all blessings flow that here, but for the grace of God, drive you.

*　　　*

'This here is it, Monk,' Butte told him, his voice subdued. Butte drove the car stealthily into a short alley and then into a brick-paved yard beside a dilapidated carriage-house. As they got out, Eddie noticed that Butte's hands were shaking.

The tall dark house, more than a century old, required gutter-repairs and paint, but looked far sounder than its sad battered neighbors that Eddie had observed before they turned into the alley. There were extensive grounds, the gardens recently grown up to weeds, a damaged pergola standing in the midst of them.

Together Butte and Eddie went quietly up the back steps, Eddie carrying Butte's incongruous big briefcase full of burglars' tools. The back door had been padlocked by the estate's executor, but Eddie used a short crowbar to pry away the hasp. There were two good modern locks set in the strong door, but Butte had keys to both of them. What with Butte's fingers trembling so, Eddie had to take the keys; after probing and twisting, both locks yielded. Butte insisted that Eddie do all the prying and forcing; it didn't need saying that Butte meant to leave no fingerprints of his own.

It was well that the keys sufficed; for the ground-floor windows were permanently protected with iron bars, besides being boarded up, and at nearly any point except this kitchen entrance their activities could have been perceived from the street. It was a well-built old house, almost fortresslike, its walls faced with rusticated ashlar.

Then they were inside; Butte had Eddie lock the back door behind them, and snatched back the keys. 'In jest five or ten minutes, Monk boy,' Butte told him, 'you're gonna git what I brung you here for. Glad you come, pal?' Butte's face was whiter than any winding-sheet, his eyes a wild thing's, and he stared all round the archaic kitchen. With a trembling hand he extracted a bottle from a hip pocket and took a long swig; he did not offer the bottle to Eddie. The man was pulled fiercely in opposite directions by superstition and greed.

As for Eddie, he understood Butte's dread. This old house was permeated by violence and worse than mere violence, horror upon horror; and the presence of Butte was a catalyst to set everything bubbling. Eddie felt himself turning into an animated lump of ice.

Something toward the front of the house slammed sharply. 'My God, what's that?' Butte pulled a gun from inside his coat.

'A loose shutter in the night breeze, good buddy,' said Eddie. The rational explanation comforted neither Butte nor himself. 'Now put that artillery away, take hold of yourself, and sit down at the kitchen table,' he instructed Butte. 'We've got most of the night.'

'Oh, no we ain't!' Butte protested. 'We got to git the stuff an' git the hell out o' here!' Yet he submitted, taking from his pocket a rough sketch and spreading it upon the table. 'I'll show you where you got to go, Monk.'

The hidey-hole, it turned out, was in a kind of subcellar where there was an ash pit into which ashes from the fireplace fell. Butte simply had contrived to extract a brick from one of the side walls of the ash pit, stuff the big bills into a hollow space behind, and wedge the brick back into place, smearing soot over the places where mortar had been chipped away. Butte's drawing showed the precise brick and the position of the ash pit. If no one but the dead people had known that the wall safe had contained more than forty thousand dollars, presumably the money still lay behind the ash-pit wall.

Eddie studied Butte's sketch by the beam of one of the two big stand-up flashlights Butte had brought in the car, the utilities in this house having been turned off after the murders. 'No problem that I can see,' he said a trifle hesitantly. Something was about to happen now, but he was not sure what. What was he meant to do? Give me a sign! He was only an instrument. 'Shall we go right on down there and pull the stuff out?'

'*You* go on down,' Butte told him. 'I'll — I'll keep lookout up here. You can't tell: some o' them junkies down the street might hear us an' come bargin' in where they ain't got no right.'

Just then something clattered beyond the far door of the kitchen, perhaps in the dining-room.

'Oh, hell, hell, hell!' Butte gasped, his teeth chattering. He had that pistol out again.

'Probably a rat knocking over a tray,' Eddie offered, though the noise had startled him, too. 'The vermin must come over from the derelict houses. Butte, you're more frightened of spirits than a six-year-old girl in the Haunted House at the carnival. Come on, you poor scared rat named Butte: let's have a look at the rest of this place before we try the cellar.'

Butte rose from his kitchen chair as if he had been glued to it. 'Stay here, Monk.' He was almost whispering now.

'No, I'm going to see if there's anything out there,' Eddie declared. 'Stay here by yourself, if that's what you like.'

'No, I'm comin'.' Despite the gun in his hand, Butte followed Eddie like a child.

What a fine well-designed house — parlors and dining-room and library and all! The furniture, if a little shabby or scraped here and there, was old as the house, much of it, and as good; all would be taken away tomorrow. Eddie led the way up the beautiful staircase to search the big bedrooms, Butte right at his heels, muttering to himself softly and incoherently. Eddie reflected that nobody but himself would have moved about so confidently when Butte was at one's back with a gun in his hand.

Nothing stirred in those rooms, though once Butte suppressed a screech when he saw a face: it was his own satyr-face, reflected in a round mirror. Everything seemed in order. And yet even for Eddie, horror lurked invisible in every corner, pain and fright saturating all the neat rooms; Butte started whenever the flashlights revealed some harmless inanimate thing.

They descended the curving stairway. 'If anything means to jump out at you and yell "Boo!" it must be down below,' said Eddie. Butte no longer told him to shut up; in his eagerness to keep close, he nearly stumbled against Eddie.

'Don't touch me,' Eddie told him, 'don't touch me at all; you could get surprised and hurt. And watch out you don't blow your own foot off with that cannon. We haven't seen the entrance hall yet; come along.'

Doors set with stained glass divided the central staircase from the hall. Eddie pushed through. What a ceremonious entrance — 'the ceremony of innocence,' now drowned! There were walnut pillars, and a marble floor, and the walls were hung with family portraits. 'See anybody up there you knew?' Eddie inquired.

Most of the heavy-framed portraits were of past generations, but among them were hung three large recent photographs in color. 'Keep the light off them there!' Butte cried in dismay. But Eddie did not oblige; he merely shifted the big flashlight to his left hand and crossed himself with his right. These were pictures of the old doctor, his white-haired wife, and a wide-eyed girl, very pretty, perhaps sixteen. Tomorrow the movers would take these photographs away forever — possibly to the dump.

'May the Lord have mercy upon these three slain ones,' said Eddie. He knelt on the Persian carpet, put his hands together, and began to pray.

'Goddamn you, Monk, come on out o' here!' Butte was roaring, his back to the glass doors. But Eddie went on praying, and Butte did not venture to touch him. 'Holy Mary, Mother of God . . .' Eddie prayed aloud, ignoring Butte's flow of obscenities and pleas for action.

Swiftly, between formal prayers, Eddie thought of how throughout the land the ceremony of innocence was drowned. The quiet dignity of this house, profaned by creatures like Butte and Harry, soon was to be effaced altogether. The life of this house had nurtured generation upon generation. How he would have liked to enter, invited, at the front door, Eddie fancied, and be welcomed into such a household as this had been! These had been good people, he knew, kindly and faithful. But how they had ended! Yes, 'hereafter' was everything: without that prospect, all life would have been a nasty joke, and men like Butte the natural lords of life. Yet the Lord is not mocked, and vengeance is His alone.

At length Eddie rose, his eyes burning. 'March!' he said to Butte. In the midst of Eddie's prayers, a sign had been given to him internally, and now Eddie must drink from his cup. 'Get back to that kitchen!' Butte obeyed.

Aquiver in the kitchen, entreating rather than commanding, Butte whispered to him, 'For Christsake, git me that bundle quick!' The stairs to the cellar led down from the kitchen; by three strong bolts the cellar door was secured against any intruders who might force the bars over the cellar windows and come upward — not that such precautions had availed those murdered three. Eddie drew back those bolts, and motioned to Butte.

'Go on down there, down to the pit; the money's all yours, with all the blood on it,' Eddie ordered him.

Butte was trembling like a man in *delirium tremens*. The ghastliness of this polluted house, weighing heavily upon Eddie, crushed Butte down; and now Eddie could perceive in this killer's hard eyes a consuming dread of his 'good buddy.' '*You* gotta go down for it,' Butte contrived to say, staring at Eddie as if he suspected at last what Eddie had become. Butte raised his automatic in shivering menace. 'They won't take you, Monk.'

'No, Butte, anything that's down there, spooks or devils, can't take me, any more than you can.' Butte's shoes seemed nailed to the floor; Eddie shifted his position in the oppressive room so that he stood between Butte and the kitchen table, and Butte's back was to the open cellar doorway. 'But you're the one who has to go down — down to your private hell. The wreckers may smash this good old house you polluted, and fill in the cellar; yet you'll be there till the end of all things, Butte, trapped among your own horrors, in a cellar beyond time, in the ash pit, your Gehenna, screeching. Get down with you!'

For an instant, only half comprehending what had been said, Butte rallied. 'You go to hell, Monk!' He pointed the pistol at Eddie's heart.

Eddie did not flinch at all. 'You chose the wrong word: you should have said, "Purgatory." But I'm there already, Butte. Hadn't you begun to guess that? Didn't I look a little funny to you there in the bar, and here in the hall? I told you I wasn't paroled or pardoned, and you left me in no shape to go over the prison wall. No, good buddy, I left that prison feet first, for the boneyard.'

The gun fell from Butte's hand; Butte reached out desperately, reeling, and grasped a jamb of the cellar door-frame.

'The spook has been beside you all the time.' Eddie moved closer to the big man. 'You're scared of ghosts, buster; well, look at me.'

Some appalling change had come over his appearance, Eddie sensed; but what it was, only Butte's eyes could see. Butte began to scream at the top of his lungs. Eddie took one more step toward him, and then Butte pitched backward down the long cellar stairs, his heavy body thumping hideously. In the dark at the foot of the stairs, he could not be discerned at all. The screeching had ceased. Eddie closed and bolted the cellar door.

Before leaving the house, Eddie want back into the entrance hall and said another long prayer — praying even for the soul of Butte, for only the Lord knows His own mercies. Last of all, he prayed, 'Forgive me my transgressions, O Lord of Justice, even as the instrument of Thy wrath; and at Thy Last Judgment, out of Thine infinite compassion, remember if Thou wilt that if I did not serve Thee in my first state, yet I served Thee in my latter. O Author of all, Thou who made the shrew made me, and only Thou knowest why. Thus it was in the beginning, is now, and ever shall be, world without end, amen.'

That said, Eddie Mahaffy, Eddie Cain, went out of the house and sauntered across Lafayette Square in the perilous dark, invulnerable, wondering when another sign might be given up to him. Presently he began to whistle 'The Pig Got Up and Slowly Walked Away.' There are no dead, Saint Augustine of Hippo had written; all souls, all essences, endure forever; but where and in what condition? Aye, there's the rub. The first flush of dawn was glowing east of the river. '*Pax*,' said the Monk, aloud, and strolled obedient in that direction.

What Shadows We Pursue

What wild desires, what restless torments seize
The hapless man, who feels the book-disease!

John Ferriar
The Bibliomania

'Eleven thousand books,' said Mrs. Corr, mildly and factually. In her
clear old voice lingered no tone of affection for the vast dusty library, no hint of apprehension of its dignity. 'Or nearly eleven thousand.
Dr. Corr had Sarah make a card for every one. Why, that's less than thirty
cents a volume you're offering, isn't it, Mr. Stoneburner?' With a species of
gentle calculation, she let her dim glance slide along the interminable
Georgian spines of *A Universal History*. 'My . . . but I suppose that's the best
we can hope for.'

From thick, faded carpet to molded-plaster ceiling fifteen feet above,
Dr. Corr's books staunchly filled the walls of the long room. Beyond the
archway was another room nearly as large, and there books not only
jammed the shelves but lay in heaps upon tables, and were monumentally
stacked upon the floor. The grand, chill corridor upon which this second
room opened also was choked with books, while the shorter hall at right
angles, leading from the corridor to what had been Dr. Corr's bedroom,
held bound volumes of *The Edinburgh Review* and *Harper's Monthly*. Nor did
these comprehend the whole of the collection, for the great skylighted attic, up beyond the graceful curve of the mahogany stair rail, was a store-

house for countless periodicals never bound but neatly tied together in volumes; for obscure governmental reports; for a welter of cheap and damaged editions that Dr. Corr should have sold as waste. But, of course, Dr. Corr never had parted with a book, however wretchedly printed or wretchedly written. He would as soon have sold his daughter — sooner, old Mr. Hanchett said. Hanchett, who had been Stoneburner's cataloguer for five years and cataloguer to other booksellers decades before that, was given to uncharitable judgments. And for all these books, William Stoneburner, book dealer, was now writing a check.

'Not much more than a quarter each,' Stoneburner replied, with his apologetic nod, blowing upon the check. 'If you could find a man who wanted the collection for himself, Mrs. Corr, he could give you more than any of us dealers. But who'd have the space for them, in these days? Or the money? Or the leisure to read?' Stoneburner was a little vain of the mien with which he could deliver his genteel and recurrent sigh of *in hoc tempori*. It sat well upon a man who inhabited the valley of the shadow of books, even though he dwelt there as a bourgeois.

'A friend told me,' murmured Mrs. Corr, rocking her little chair softly and inspecting the buttons of her shiny shoes of a fashion forty years obsolete, 'that the old Bibles might be worth a great deal, just by themselves. There's a man somewhere who collects old Bibles, this friend said.' Despite her having tucked the check into her workbasket only this minute, already she was displaying the recriminations so frequently encountered among sellers of books. Stoneburner, knowing the mood, was tolerant.

'I'm sure some people must collect Bibles,' he assured the venerable Mrs. Corr in a voice nearly as artless as her own. 'Here's what you and I'll do: you can have all the old Bibles. Put them aside and keep them, and sell them to somebody else, if you like. I own too many old Bibles. The price for the library will stand. But I do want to take just one Bible — the Cranmer. I think I know where I can sell that. The rest are yours.'

A harsh tone, neither masculine nor feminine, broke in upon this colloquy: the voice of Miss Sarah Corr, who had entered by the door at Stoneburner's back. 'What Bible is that, Mr. Stoneburner?' She moved ponderously toward the window-seat where a half-dozen folio and quarto Bibles clustered, a black dust thick upon their exposed top edges. 'You'll get a lot of money for it, I imagine?' She poked unfeelingly the thick book in vellum that Stoneburner indicated.

And Miss Sarah Corr turned her set smile upon Mr. Stoneburner.

Larger far than Stoneburner, larger than most men, she was a massive spinster. Fifty? Sixty? Had she ever been young? Not to judge by her dress, which was as timeless as her frail mother's. To be beamed upon by Miss Sarah Corr was not altogether pleasant. When Stoneburner first had seen that broad smile, he had been standing upon the steps of the austere stone house of Dr. Corr, a house sombre even on an Indian-summer evening; and Miss Corr had opened to his ring with some caution, and then had said, with that peculiar smile, 'You're the gentleman who buys books? The one with the advertisement in the telephone directory?'

A month gone, that evening. The month had been a time of delicate negotiation with Mrs. Corr and Miss Corr, two recluses mightily ignorant of the contents of these eleven thousand volumes, mightily afraid of losing a fortune. It was a good library, but there was no fortune in it: the library of a man who read, not of a man who collected.

'It's going to bring me sixty or seventy dollars, Miss Corr,' Stoneburner told her, unruffled. 'Only that for a Cranmer Bible. On all these shelves, perhaps there are six or eight books people will pay that much for. The rest — why, they're good books, the kind of books Dr. Corr read. I think I'd have liked to know Dr. Corr.'

'Yes, yes?' replied Mrs. Corr, civilly, still rocking. She accepted Stoneburner's remark as a conventional compliment, apparently, and volunteered no comment upon her husband. Her *late* husband, Stoneburner had thought when initially he browsed through this house; but while the Corr women spoke of the doctor as one forever gone, they never seemed quite to use the past tense. So Stoneburner had inquired of old Hanchett, who knew something of every man within this century who had bought very many books in the city.

'Dr. Corr is one of those chaps that wither up and the wind blows away,' old Hanchett had said, being himself invincibly portly and rubicund. 'Haven't seen him in several years. He let his friends go because he liked the books better, and he came out into the light less and less. . . . Well, you've seen his wife and daughter. Books cost; the Corr women had to manage with one new dress a year, or every other year. And then they gave up their card-parties. As time went on, Corr decided that his women's mission in life was to make catalogue cards for his books and to do a bit of dusting. He used to take his wife for an hour's walk after supper; then back to his library, and she to her parlor to sew, until it was time for sleep — Corr to his bedroom (books helter-skelter on the floor), she to hers.

'The daughter? Oh, the girl was queer to begin with. You'll see it, Mr. Stoneburner: she has her little ways. Maybe she was one of the things that drove Corr away from people, into books. Corr was allergic — allergic to people. Ah, but books, though . . . I'll hand it to him there. No, it's been years since I had a word with him. As he dried up, even the evening walk got to be too long a vacation from his books. I wonder if he has books where he is now? I don't know exactly when they took him away, but Mrs. Corr told my cousin that they sent him out West for his health. They don't seem to expect him back. His *health*, eh?' Here Hanchett had tapped a plump finger against his forehead, uncharitably. 'One-way ticket, Mr. Stoneburner. And is the money nearly gone now, too? I suppose it costs to keep the doctor in the West for his *health*. Why, the doctor would be a screaming devil if he knew the library was being sold. He was a tall, white husk of a man, decent-spoken, a gold-mine for the dealers.'

Still Mrs. Corr rocked, soothing away this reference of Stoneburner's to her husband as she and her daughter were wont to pass over such comments — nothing of pride in their manner, nothing of resentment. 'Yes, yes? Well, now — the house will seem almost empty with the books gone, won't it? All sorts of people are looking for places to live these days, I hear. I suppose we could rent part of this great big house of ours. But who would want to live here? It's too dirty.' And Mrs. Corr laughed her delicate little laugh, and Miss Corr added her deep chuckle.

Candid, this. The Corrs were not deficient in a certain withered wit. Undoubtedly the Corr house was too dirty for anyone but the Corrs. From the parlor ceiling, the paper hung down in festoons that obscured the gilt-framed paintings on the walls. Plaster was falling in the attic, for the roof had begun to leak in Dr. Corr's time. One suspected that Dr. Corr's allergy toward humanity extended even to roofers and plumbers and paperers. Certain utilitarian improvements had been installed in his house only with extreme tardiness: the lighting, for instance. Apparently possessed of a reactionary confidence that the days of high old Roman virtue would return, Dr. Corr had cherished three systems of illumination, each ready to function in a pinch. Candelabra and kerosene lamps were to be seen, tarnished and topsy-turvy, in this corner or that; gas jets still protruded from plaster or panelling, and could be lit; but the actual artificial light came from naked bulbs dangling like hanged felons from the ceilings — many of them the early bamboo filament sort that terminate in a glassy spike, since the Corrs lived in three or four rooms and turned on these other switches scarcely more than twice in a month.

Not a practical man, Dr. Corr; nor was Mrs. Corr a practical woman; yet she seemed to have a canny eye for a dollar, possibly out of necessity. Her rocking uninterrupted, she continued, 'Now, Mr. Stoneburner, I don't suppose you mean the books in the attic are included, do you? Those still belong to us?'

Stoneburner certainly had thought they were his. All the same, they were trash, except for the periodicals, which needed binding. And it was unpleasant to deny a crumb of victory to an impractical lady in her eighties. He was about to say, 'You're quite welcome to them,' when Mr. Markashian entered. Mr. Markashian had overhead something of the conversation. Mr. Markashian had a habit of overhearing, Stoneburner reflected.

'Of course they belong to us, Mother,' pronounced Markashian, with emphasis.

Mrs. Corr obviously was not Markashian's mother, for he was a Levantine; despite the Armenian name, he had more the look of an Anatolian Greek. He was her son-in-law, nevertheless, a public accountant from Newark, firm in a decided opinion that he knew the world, and deserved well of it. 'Markashian never dared turn up while the doctor was in the house,' Hanchett had told Stoneburner. 'He married Lilly Corr on the sly. Both of them got cheated.'

But the vanishing of the doctor from the scene and the scent of a sale of family assets had drawn the worldly Mr. Markashian from his accustomed pursuits in New Jersey. He left his wife behind to tend the children, informing her that family honor and prosperity now were his responsibility. As a man of business, Mrs. Corr and Miss Sarah Corr appeared to reverence him unwillingly; but it was clear to Stoneburner that Markashian did not want the books to be sold at all, preferring the chance of inheriting the library to the chance of inheriting a remnant of the cash. As a man of business and as a simple man, Stoneburner loathed Markashian, who rejoiced in the best suits and the worst manners Stoneburner had observed for some years.

'You understand that, don't you?' went on Markashian, turning to Stoneburner. 'The books in the attic don't go with the others. There's highly valuable property upstairs.'

'What money you can extract from the books in the attic,' Stoneburner told him sourly, 'I make you a present of.'

'That's settled, then,' grinned Markashian, on a note of triumph. 'What's the book you're holding, Sarah?'

Miss Sarah Corr gave Markashian one of her long stares, and then a long smile, and suddenly came out with, 'An old Bible worth seventy dollars. Mr. Stoneburner wants this one.' A single bond of sympathy joined Stoneburner and Miss Corr: distrust of Markashian.

'What, this lovely old ancestral Bible?' groaned Markashian. 'An heirloom! Gutenberg Bible, isn't it? It mustn't leave the family.'

'It's not a Gutenberg, I'm sorry to inform you, Mr. Markashian; and it's my property. I can't have more books extracted from my purchase. Would you prefer to return the check to me, Mrs. Corr?' He extended his hand toward her. Though a cheery little man, Stoneburner was capable of firmness.

Patting her workbasket in alarm, Mrs. Corr declared she had no intention of breaking the bargain. 'Everything but the other Bibles, and the books in the attic, and the few things Mr. Markashian took for himself yesterday after you left — everything else is yours, Mr. Stoneburner. My, what a strange house this will be with the books gone! You'll take them all out yourself, Mr. Stoneburner? You won't bring anyone to help? We'd rather carry them for you ourselves than have strangers running upstairs.'

This was a matter of consequence with her and with Sarah Corr, who turned her stagnant look on him. The intensity of the appeal somewhat embarrassed Stoneburner and seemed to surprise even Markashian. But Stoneburner already had agreed to the stipulation. It was natural enough: dirty though they confessed their house to be, still they hardly would want it inspected by chance comers.

'All eleven thousand, Mrs. Corr — I'll lug them to the truck myself. I'll need a whole week, off and on. We'll have to take care with some of the folios: they're shaky. Heavy things, books — I'll be stiff when it's done. Will it suit you if I start at nine tomorrow morning?'

Sarah Corr went with him to the double-bolted front door, through the vaulted corridor where two walnut clocks ticked alternately amid the ashes of magnificence, and she let him out into the night. He swung away from that ponderous, ever-beaming face, with the close-cropped gray hair that turned it almost masculine. 'You've seen the attic,' she said. 'You won't need to go there again, after tonight?'

'Since those books aren't mine, no.'

'That's nice of you,' Miss Corr concluded, closing the door in his face.

He listened to her bolt it, hesitating for a moment on the steps. As he loitered, it occurred to him that he had not heard Sarah Corr's slow stride back through the corridor. She must be standing just inside the door, to make sure he was gone. Shrugging, Stoneburner went.

*   *

A light covered truck especially equipped with wooden racks was the property of Stoneburner's Bookshop. And this Stoneburner parked close by the porch of the Corr house next morning, ready to commence moving one tier of the books in the library proper. Greeting him with her invariable hesitant commendation of the weather, Mrs. Corr admitted him. She wore that black dress that hid her ankles — a dowdy figure, but not vulgar. Back into her parlor she tottered, and Stoneburner went his quiet way up the circling stairs to the library. As he trod the stair carpet, he heard feet hastily descending from a higher level — the attic, of course; and he took them for Mr. Markashian's feet. But when he reached the library floor, nothing was to be seen of Markashian. Perhaps he had ducked into one of the chilly bedrooms off the corridor. Markashian was given to judicious ducking.

Methodically dusting the top of each volume with a piece of flannel, Stoneburner took the books from a tier of shelves close to the window and stacked them in tidy heaps convenient for carrying downstairs. A gap appeared upon one of the shelves. The morning before, a set of Bacon had reposed there, and Stoneburner assumed it was part of his purchase. But finding it gone in the afternoon, he had inquired of Mrs. Corr, to be told that 'Mr. Markashian thought it ought to be his — useful in his work.' Stoneburner had waived the matter.

A decrepit little ladder enabled Stoneburner to reach the higher shelves: he balanced upon it, dusting. In this volume, or that, Dr. Corr had inserted neat slips of paper to mark favorite passages; small checks in the margins pointed to some mighty line or kernel of wit. Himself a leisurely man, Stoneburner now and then opened a book to glance at these passages, and generally was much taken with the doctor's choice. He began to form an image of Dr. Corr other than the 'sneer of cold command' that Hanchett's description had left in his mind. A solitary man, this Dr. Corr; but then how could he be other than alien to his mousy wife and queer daughter and infuriating son-in-law? Indeed, Stoneburner experienced the beginnings of awe for a noble mind in provincial obscurity. Corr's family may have paid back his disdain in that ferocious envy the vulgar feel toward the proud. Bound to them he may have been; but until now they had been his slaves.

Stoneburner took down Fuller's *Holy State and the Profane State* — a fine glossy seventeenth century binding. 'Cesare Borgia, His Life,' Corr had underlined in the index, and had marked the page by inserting a note-card. The bookseller ran his eye along the passages checked: 'The throne and the bed cannot severally abide partners. . . .' 'For he could neither lengthen the land nor lessen the sea in Italie. . . .' 'He preferred the state of his body to the body of his state.' Why, even a touch of fun in this Dr. Corr. Stoneburner put the quarto upon his dusted stack; and, having done with this shelf, glanced at the books on the window-seat. There was a gap among them.

What sort of fool did they think him? For the Cranmer Bible was gone. He was inured to pilferage and aware that the average person with whom he dealt thought a single volume hardly could be missed among so many. But in the present instance, Stoneburner had specifically claimed the Cranmer for his own the previous day, and it was too bulky and too valuable for them to suppose he would forget it wholly. This was more than Stoneburner was disposed to endure. Though angry, he was self-possessed, and he turned to face the room, wondering if they could have tucked the book into some drawer. They would not dare hide it absolutely, since that was theft; more probably they would endeavor to lose it in some pile of trash, trusting he might pass it by. And so he recalled the steps he had heard briskly descending from the attic when, an hour before, he had entered the house.

Mrs. Corr was downstairs, and Sarah Corr with her, no doubt; Markashian — for surely it was he who had scuttled from the attic — would not be inclined to face him at this moment, even supposing him only across the corridor. A quiet survey of the attic could do no harm.

Stoneburner walked into the corridor and turned up the spiralling stair. At the top the door stood ajar. Standing on the last step and resting his arm upon the balustrade, Stoneburner sent an exploratory glance within. One enormous room, this attic, into which the sun penetrated dully through a cupola skylight. Sundry boxes and articles of old furniture were scattered about the center of the floor, but Dr. Corr had kept the place fairly clear of rubbish so that he could get to his shelves of magazines along the walls. Right opposite the door, in line with Stoneburner's eyes, was a broad tier of worthless novels, no doubt bought by Dr. Corr with other books at some auction.

These novels had been disturbed. Six or seven had fallen to the floor, and another gap indicated that more had tumbled from the shelves. Had Markashian been sliding the Cranmer among this trash and been interrupted at his game? Stoneburner raised one foot to the final step of the staircase.

But he was prevented. Sharp and resistless, a grip pinned his arm against the balustrade. Half a second he paused to quiet his leaping nerves, and then looked round to see Miss Sarah Corr at his back, her great hand clamped upon his wrist, her face set in that inimitable smile. The smile grew broader. As it spread, her fingers dug into his wrist as if to find a passage through. She must have tiptoed painstakingly after him, weasel behind goose. And in her face there was no more of mercy than of sanity.

'Sarah!' whispered Mrs. Corr from the foot of the staircase, and commenced laboriously to climb toward them. At that soft cry, Miss Sarah Corr relaxed her clutch, and the smile sank into something nearer humanity, but still she did not speak.

Mrs. Corr ascended the infinite way to their side, and said to him, most politely and casually, 'Did you need something in the attic, Mr. Stoneburner?' Her old eyes cried out some awful disturbance. But what?

'Someone seems to have been looking over the Cranmer Bible,' Stoneburner answered, something of a quaver in his voice. 'Do you suppose it might have been left up here by mistake?'

Embarrassment he had expected, perhaps shamed denial; but not this assuagement that came into the faces of the Corr women. 'Oh, I'm sorry you have the trouble of looking for it,' said Mrs. Corr with a tiny sigh. 'Sarah and I will see if we can help.' And together they entered the attic.

To the left of the cupola skylight stood an imposing oak desk, a pile of old ledgers sprawled upon it. Stoneburner had noticed it before. But now the capacious drawers were pulled open, and bundles of letters and papers and photographs tossed out of them and spread in confusion beside the ledgers. Sarah Corr drew a heavy breath, and Mrs. Corr glanced round the big room, and then they went at the desk with a sort of horror-struck frenzy. Markashian's curiosity and covetousness extended beyond the library purchase to the property of his mother-in-law and sister-in-law, Stoneburner surmised; and doubtless his coming had interrupted Mr.

Markashian's prowling. As mother and daughter packed papers into drawers and cubby-holes with a gingerly haste, Stoneburner examined a photograph of a white-haired, hollow-cheeked man in a high collar that lay face upward. 'Oh, Dr. Corr?' he inquired. 'And these are his papers? A fine face.'

They stopped sorting the papers, and, wordless, looked at him. Sarah Corr raised a massive hand, and for a foolish moment he thought she meant to strike him; but instead she laid a finger upon her lips. Then she took the picture from his hand, turning it downward in the act, and laid it at the bottom of a drawer. This silence was contagious. Quite dumb, he stood by while they cleared away the confusion and shut the violated drawers and padded back toward the stairs. Then — 'Ah, there's the Bible,' said Stoneburner, seeing the quarto among a heap of the fallen novels and bending to retrieve it.

'My . . . Mr. Markashian must have been reading it,' murmured Mrs. Corr, touching his coat sleeve — almost tugging at him. As he rose with the Bible, he noticed a deep, an incalculably deep, space behind the gap from which the novels had tumbled.

'Why, what's happened here, Mrs. Corr? Have you lost some books down a hole?' He glanced into it. A hole, yes; a very great hole. A stairwell, with steps descending into a black abyss. This tier of shelves veiled, and sealed away, was some disused back way into the attic. When he leaned forward for a closer look, his shoulder brushed against a tottering novel, and that book, too, fell backward from its place, bounding four or five steps into the filthy gloom and then flopping to its rest upon the last visible tread.

'You! Don't you dare!' The stifled scream had come from Sarah Corr — the most nearly feminine expression he had heard from her. Her teeth were gritted, but she seemed beyond smiling. Mrs. Corr ran a hand along her daughter's arm.

'Those are the old stairs for the maids, Mr. Stoneburner,' Mrs. Corr explained, looking not at him but at the gap in the shelves. 'They've been boarded since I don't know when. That's one reason we hoped you wouldn't need the books up here: the stairs would seem so odd without books to hide them.

'I'm glad the Bible wasn't lost. Do you need us to help you dust downstairs?' She took his arm; he helped her down the staircase, Sarah closing the door tightly behind them. There was no key in it, and Stoneburner suspected that nearly every key in the house had been mislaid years before.

In the library, with the Corr women gone down to the parlor, Stoneburner placed his resurrected Bible among the dusted books and went on with his stacking. A pox upon the book-ignorant folk who think every dog-eared Victorian New Testament a collector's treasure beyond the dreams of avarice! How often had he heard over his telephone some hesitant voice inquiring, 'Do you buy old books? Really old books? What do you pay? I've got a *really* old Bible here. Authorized Version. London, 1884 . . .'

All too strong was this spirit in that nervous pair, the Corr women. Possibly, though, they were endowed with redeeming virtues. They had seemed genuinely shocked at Markashian's profanation of the doctor's papers, presumably left undisturbed, out of sentiment, ever since that gaunt shell of learning was sent somewhere into the West to linger out the little time still vouchsafed his wreck.

Now Stoneburner began taking down the volumes of a good set of Burke, their pages much marked and checked in the doctor's hand. Such pencilings impair the value of secondhand books; but since Stoneburner read books as well as sold them, he did not complain overmuch. What sort of thing had Corr favored in Burke? Opening at random, he found a sentence doubly underlined: 'What shadows we are, and what shadows we pursue.'

Just so, old doctor. And true for bookworms like you and me, most especially — thus Stoneburner to himself. You even more than I, thank God. He put the volume with the others and stretched his tired arms. As he rested, a noise of voices full of anger drifted faintly to him from the parlor below. Well, had the Corr women had enough of that reluctantly revered Setebos of a son-in-law, that dandy with the vulturine profile and the flaccid hand? The temptation to eavesdrop was overwhelming. Stoneburner bent over the stairwell, where the words could be made out sufficiently.

'. . . Only to look for the receipts, Mother.' Yes, it was Markashian, half the cocksureness gone out of his tones, a Markashian taken aback at such vehemence over a bout of snooping.

Sarah Corr was answering him, or rather drowning him out. 'Meddling, meddling, stirring things up! What do you want to poke into? What do you want to bring on us? Take your pictures, take your books, but don't poke. Take your money, but don't pry! No more sense . . .'

Markashian's reply was not wholly audible, but Stoneburner made out something about 'no harm' and 'a thousand miles away.' Miss Corr roared down the oily voice again, her mother's low entreaty interrupting her. Then a door was shut and Stoneburner was prevented from hearing the rest; but this he caught before the colloquy was suppressed: 'He always slept light, and he knew what you were after, and he could get into your dreams, and now he'll stir, the devil! That old white sneering creepy devil! That's what!'

Was it the absent Dr. Corr thus described by his daughter? A nice family, a cordial household. Well, time for lunch, Stoneburner realized. He skipped down the stairs and tapped at the parlor door and glanced within. The three were standing in the middle of the faded room, all taut at his knock. 'Back at two, if that's all right,' Stoneburner told them, and went his way. Yes, a jolly family.

*   *

The grimmest of all aspects of the book trade is the carrying of big volumes upstairs or down; and just this was to be Stoneburner's afternoon task. Commencing at two, he kept at it faithfully for more than an hour. The Corrs and Markashian stayed out of his way, withdrawn in their parlor with its dingy plush chairs. As Stoneburner lugged perhaps the fortieth stack of volumes towards the front door, there came a crash above. Had the books piled in the library fallen? Hardly. He had arranged them neatly, and the noise seemed more distant. From the parlor peered Markashian and Mrs. Corr.

'Perhaps some magazines in the attic toppled,' Stoneburner offered.

'My, no,' said Mrs. Corr, almost inaudibly, holding tight to the doorjamb. Markashian went up the stairs; Mrs. Corr opened her mouth as if to call after him, but no words followed. So remarkable was the look she sent up the stairwell that Stoneburner waited for Markashian's report.

He came down with his accustomed strut. 'Three shelves in the attic tipped over somehow,' Markashian informed them. 'Sarah ought to pick them up before long — some of the shelves in front of the closed-off stairs.'

Without a word, Mrs. Corr vanished back into the parlor, and Stoneburner went on with his load. But as he closed the house door, he heard from the parlor what sounded like an hysterical gurgle; and also it sounded like Sarah Corr.

When five o'clock was chimed by the two clocks in the hall, Stoneburner still was lugging books to his truck. For a moment's rest, he seated himself in a rickety chair amid his dusted stacks and leafed through the first collected edition of Harrington, *Oceana* Harrington. 'Dr. Randolph Corr,' with a flourish, was written upon the flyleaf. 'Purchased in Bristol, April 23, 1912.' Ah, how everything passes! The doctor had spent his life amassing these dead men's fancies, and here strove the undoer of the great library, dispersing in some days what Corr had built in as many decades. Perhaps it was as well that he had not known the doctor, Stoneburner reflected: had he ever seen Corr, this work of destruction might have weighed up on his conscience. One man's pleasure, another's agony . . . He lifted another stack, cradled it in his arms, and proceeded carefully downstairs.

Halfway down, an odor drifted round him. Undeniable — yes, gas. Stoneburner took the books to the stair foot and then tapped at the parlor.

'Who?' It was Mrs. Corr's voice, with a quaver. He entered. Mrs. Corr and Sarah Corr sat near to each other in two armchairs that faced the door. Markashian was not there. They looked at him with disturbing intensity.

'Could you have forgotten to turn off the kitchen range, Miss Corr? I smell gas somewhere.'

'Gas, gas, gas,' repeated Sarah Corr with a heave of her heavy body; but she did not rise, nor did her mother. Truly, Miss Corr had her ways.

A pregnant pause; then, from Mrs. Corr, 'Mr. Markashian is out. Might I ask you, Mr. Stoneburner, to see if the gas is turned on?'

Still they did not rise nor offer to assist, nor even to come so far as the door with him. And they watched him as he went into the corridor.

No, it was not the kitchen range. Now that he was on the ground floor, it seemed to Stoneburner that the faint gas-odor drifted to him from above. And when he was on the library floor, it came stronger still; and he thought it must emanate from the attic. Up the stair. As evening approached, the attic grew unpleasantly dark. Those books still lay tumbled from the shelves before the sealed staircase. Yes, the odor was most strong in this dim room. Three gas brackets in the attic: the first two securely turned off — indeed, screwed tight so firmly that he could not budge them with his bare hands. But the third was open, the gas pouring from it. Closing the jet, Stoneburner reflected upon his good fortune not to have been smoking. Had Markashian turned on a light while up here, blown it out, and forgotten to twist the little knob below the mantle? A man unfamiliar with gas mantles might well blunder. But why hadn't Markashian switched on the single electric bulb dangling near the skylight? A most eccentric ménage.

'Ah!' cried Stoneburner. And then, 'Who is it?' For two or three books had fallen suddenly, an earthquake in this attic silence. He jerked about; but there was no one, and surely there could have been no whisper. Yes, more books had dropped inward from those shelves before the dead-end staircase. He reached into that hole back of the novels to retrieve whatever volumes had escaped downward. But they had tumbled beyond his reach — he could make them out, vaguely, a half-dozen steps down, one flopped open on its spine, its pages slowly slipping from left to right as if turned by fingers indiscernible.

'By God, no!' muttered Stoneburner, low.

For no one could have whispered to him, whispered ever so slyly and incoherently, out of the abyss. Stoneburner shrugged uneasily, dusted off his trouser-knees, and fixed his mind resolutely upon book-prices current.

He trotted down to the library then, picked up his Cranmer Bible to ensure it against another misadventure, and proceeded to the ground-floor corridor. The Corr women still sat immobile in those lumpy chairs.

'Someone didn't close the jet in the attic, but it's all right now. I think I'll go to dinner. Will it inconvenience you people if I finish moving the section I'm on about seven o'clock or so?'

Sarah Corr had worn that smile so literally mordant, but without warning she said fiercely, 'Old devil! Old white creepy devil!'

Was it extreme old age or a genuine power of dissimulation that enabled Mrs. Corr so placidly to gloss over her daughter's outbursts? At any rate, she nodded politely to Stoneburner. 'We'll be glad to have you back this evening.' But ah, her eyes. And she did not accompany him to the porch. So Stoneburner left them in the moldy tattered parlor.

*   *

Nearer eight o'clock than seven, Stoneburner pulled the tarnished bellknob at Dr. Corr's house. No clang responded within, so far as he could tell; but he always had suspected that the bell did not work, and that Miss Corr had known of his presence only because she had been peering from some window. He knocked, and knocked again. No one came. And now he observed that the whole house was a darker mass of blackness against the night — not one window lit. Had the Corrs gone out? Too early for bed, surely. He tried the door: not locked, fortunately. Closing it behind him, Stoneburner felt for a light-switch, and could find none; everything in the Corr house was tucked out of sight.

Ah, well, he knew the stairs and could find the light in the library. Inside the library doorway his fingers encountered the switch, and the old-fashioned bulb sent its radiance into the corridor. And then, as he was about to cross the threshold into the sea of books, out of the corner of his eye he perceived something unfamiliar, something inappropriate, protruding between two posts of the stair rail to the attic. A chill went through him. For the unfamiliar thing was a flabby hand. Behind it? Whoever was behind it must be lying prone on the dark stairs. A quick-witted little man, Stoneburner thought of the miniature flashlight attached to his key-ring. Pulling it from his coat, he stepped to the stairs and sent the beam upward.

Markashian: nothing worse. Mr. Markashian lay with his unconscious face slanting downward, as if he had tripped and fallen — and the blood on one olive cheek seemed to confirm this. A closer look suggested that he was breathing, though thoroughly stunned. Kneeling in the dark by the accountant, Stoneburner listened for any step or rustle. But surely nothing moved within the house, and its stone walls barred the noise of the street. Mrs. Corr and Sarah Corr? Somehow Stoneburner dared not call out. He left Markashian, and slipped with infinite care down the carpeted treads to the ground floor, every hint of a creak from the old boards an agony to his nerves, his own faint shadow on the papered wall a hunched menace.

Hesitating at the parlor door, he still could detect no sound. None? Why, perhaps the gentlest of sounds, not a hiss, not a swish, but the suggestion of a breath of air. Stoneburner did not desire to turn that knob.

All the same, he turned it, and pushed open the door, and was met by a wave of gas, long pent within. Holding his breath, he fumbled for the light-switch. This time, luck being with him, the light came on. Mrs. Corr still sat in her chair, but Sarah Corr had slumped out of hers upon the rug. Their faces were toward him, unmistakably dead, faces with such a look as drifts through dreams.

*   *

Several curious and unpleasant matters concerning Mr. Markashian's past were known to the police captain who arrived at Dr. Corr's house ten minutes after Stoneburner's call. No one could doubt that Markashian had been quite as odd, on occasion, as had been his connections by marriage, nor that his mind was seriously impaired at present, nor that his case required not a trial, but committal to an asylum. At least, none could doubt these conclusions but Stoneburner, and he only confusedly. Why Mrs. Corr and Miss Corr had not risen from their chairs to shut off the jets remained unexplained, unless it was from terror of Markashian.

After two hours in the echoing house, the police discovered at the foot of the disused maids' stairs what remained of the doctor — Dr. Corr, who had gone West only figuratively, his body having been crammed into a closet, or large cupboard, in that sealed passage. Within the cupboard was a gas mantle, and the police captain speculated that the old man, still living, had been bound, pushed into the closet, and left for some hours with the gas turned on. He must have been a vigorous old man, Dr. Corr: great strength would have been required to subdue him. Passed from this life for many months, and that by what must have been an act of explosive violence, Corr bore the marks of a domestic hatred that had smoldered many a year. Markashian, rallying, disclaimed any knowledge of the doctor's death. And so far, but no farther, the police believed him.

The police put the livid Markashian on a sofa in what had been the doctor's office. After a time — he watching the closed door intently all the while — Markashian defiantly informed them (his slippery vanity somewhat reviving) that he had gone to the attic to rummage the doctor's desk for a will. 'My wife has her rights, after all' — and Dr. Corr, presumably never to return from the West, might have left behind a testament of sorts. Stoneburner watched that vulturine bravado pale and sag then; but Markashian went on, stumblingly, to say that he had run downstairs and had fallen, and knew nothing of what followed in the Corr house.

'Why did you hurry on the stairs?' the police captain demanded.

'Because it was coming up, up from behind the books,' Markashian cried out, gripping the sofa arm.

'What do you mean?' The captain was infected with this man's dread.

'Oh, it woke. The books falling, the mouth, the long hair, the dusty hands!' That said, Markashian sank sobbing to the floor. From the rim of one high shelf, past the leather spines of fine bindings that gleamed from their cases, a streamer of soot floated downward to settle upon his cheek.

The Cellar of Little Egypt

Where will we all be a hundred years from now?
Where will we all be a hundred years from now?
Pushing up the daisies, pushing up the daisies:
That's where we'll all be a hundred years from now.

The other morning I heard the little scamps across the street singing this, and it set me to thinking of Uncle Jake and Amos Trimble. You don't believe there's anything in a town like New Devon but asphalt pavements and supermarkets. Well, grow to be an old codger here, the way I have, and you'll come to know that life's as much a puzzle in New Devon as it is anywhere. And folks remember things they don't tell children. . . . But I'll tell you about Amos Trimble, as my Uncle Jake told me. That'll do for a sample.

When I was little we had eight shoemakers in town. Fifty years gone; but it could be a thousand, for the difference in New Devon. Eight shoemakers in town then, and nowadays never a one left. That old way of living was strangled by the factories and the cars. North along the river road, beginning where the town dump is now and stretching on for miles, were good farms — farms of the kind you can't find in the whole county these days. Look at the Millard place, what's left of it, and you'll have a notion. Most of the others are gone, every scrap of them, the square brick houses with cupolas, and carriage barns behind them, and scale houses. Next to the dump, you can see the foundation of one of the biggest: the house where Amos Trimble lived, and afterward — but that's another matter.

It's hard to think of New Devon without mills. On the south side you see as many smokestacks as I saw barns on the river road, when I used to steal my Uncle Jake's plug tobacco. Where the tube mill stands, Amos Trimble used to drive that surrey of his through the short cut to Little Egypt. A little red scar was over Mr. Trimble's right eye, that touched his eyelid and wrinkled if he looked sidewise at you; but he didn't often look at me — he wasn't the sort that boys ask pennies from.

Eight shoemakers, then; and Uncle Jake was one. The three of us, his nephews, used to sit in his shop, watching him nailing down soles. He'd put a nail where he wanted it, and raise the hammer, and pound three times. 'Hum, hum, hum!' he'd say; and when it went home, 'Hum, b'God!' When he wasn't looking, we'd stick his tobacco in our pockets. Jake was in his thirties, but he seemed like an old man to us; and he was old, too. Turning away from the liquor made a change in him, and keeping off the bottle took nerve for a man who belonged to my family. But from the day Dan Slattery died downstairs in Little Egypt, Jake wouldn't look at booze.

We had a different kind of men in New Devon those days. Could they work! But, then, that's all there was for them — work, or else drink. Never a day without a real fight — half of them at Little Egypt. No movies, no lodges, no women in bar-rooms — nothing but work and whiskey. The men were devils for both. After he had to leave the liquor, Uncle Jake could only work. You never see a man, these days, drive himself the way Jake did. He didn't leave himself time to think. There'd been a day when people called him a great reader — before he got in with the boys at Little Egypt. I suppose he'd have been happier if he had been a fool. Maybe that was why he loved the whiskey: it made a fool of him. When he was sober the thought of what he'd like to be and never could — too slow for the turf, too light for the plow. And so he was drunk all his life, first on rot-gut, then on work.

You and I have got our feet on the ground. Sometimes that's an advantage; sometimes not. There are things we miss. A dog hears sounds a man can't; a fellow like Jake who hasn't got his feet on the ground, who's drunk and weak and maybe a little off — why, how can you or I judge what they see or feel, these fellows, or how much truth they make out through a whiskey-fog? I don't know. Jake was no fool, and I think he never lied. He was drunk on the day Slattery died, and he wasn't afraid, much; but as he thought about it afterward, he froze. Nobody could get him to touch a body, after that time in the cellar of Little Egypt.

Most of what I know about this I learned from Jake one afternoon in his shop — Jake sitting cross-legged on the bench, a shoe half finished in his lap, his little blue eyes (hard as marbles) looking past me toward the window, as if he wanted to see who might peer in. Jake was cold sober when he told me, and had been that way for years.

My Uncle Jake was the first man in New Devon to see Amos Trimble. I think he was the last to see him, too. On a fall morning, Jake said, a square-built, bearded man, who might have been almost forty or might have been younger, came off the train from Detroit and put his bag on the cinders beside the depot. Along the railway siding New Devon was no beauty spot, even then; and I don't suppose Jake made it prettier — leaning against the depot, rough looking as they come, and needing a shave, as always. The man from off the train looked round as if he were saying, 'I'd straighten this up, fast,' and then eyed Jake. Jake wasn't the kind to kowtow to God Almighty, so he kept on leaning; but he said to me, there in the shop, 'Roy, that fellow made me squirm. He had green eyes that looked right into your damned rotten heart.'

'Well, sir,' said the stranger to Jake, 'I'm Amos Trimble, and I'm looking for the Devon House.' Jake stood up, though he wasn't naturally obliging, and nodded:

'All right, Mr. Trimble; I can take a walk that way.' When they got to the Devon House, Trimble stood Jake a drink. Amos Trimble was a drinking man, Jake said; but he was stone sober, all the same, day or night. 'Frightening collected, all the time,' were the words Jake used, 'except when he wanted to make you laugh. He could split your sides if he had a mind to. Fact is, he could make anybody do anything.' Jake took to him, right away, though Jake didn't care for many people.

Trimble came to New Devon from the West. Whether he had been born out there, he didn't say; and nobody asked Amos Trimble questions like that. I don't mean that Trimble had a Past, in the usual way of speaking. He lived his own life, that was all, and it may not have been happy. He could tell you stories for hours, but they weren't stories about himself. He was honest straight through, and when he told you to lick dirt, you licked. It leaked out that he had been a lumberman and a land speculator and a judge of probate; and now he was going to stay in New Devon, where he had bought a farm for himself and was going to buy and sell the farms of other people. He had some money and was likely to have more. Only the cellar hole is there by the dump, now, but what was the Adams place — the oldest big house in the township — was grand when Trimble came to New Devon, and he bought it. He made it his house right away, and it stayed Amos Trimble's house, even after he was gone, until it burned. Trimble cut his mark deep on everything. He lived alone; his tenants across the road took care of the farm. That house came to look like Trimble, square and shaggy and proud.

At Little Egypt, the boys didn't know what to make of Mr. Trimble — Dan Slattery and Jack Cane and Red Fellows and the rest. Cane thought he was a man to steer clear of; Fellows said Cane was yellow; and the two of them tangled about it one afternoon till Mrs. Johnston, who owned Little Egypt, had to come downstairs with a broom and get them both outside, her black wig falling off as she shoved them through the doorway, show- ing her old bald head to everybody at the depot. Where the Hotel Puritan is today, that's where Little Egypt stood. Sixty years before, it had been a first-rate tavern, one of the prettiest in the state; I've got a snapshot of it, taken the year they tore it down. Downstairs was a good solid taproom, and above that six or seven sleeping rooms; it had columns along the sec- ond storey, facing the street, like the Millard place. But when Mrs. Johnston, old Baldy Johnston, ran it, it was a filthy hole. It had been named the Madison, but after some of the boys went to the Exposition at Chicago, they called the saloon Little Egypt, because it was as free as that dancing girl in '92. In Baldy Johnston's time there was still a long oak bar, and Slattery was behind it.

Bloody Dan, my brothers and I used to call him after looking round to make sure he wasn't down the alley. Six feet four, almost, and built for it. He'd been a butcher, and liked the work, but he got free drinks behind the bar at Little Egypt. It was something curious to watch him knock a cow between the eyes or slit a pig's throat — one knock, one slice, and all over. Blood was slopped on him most days, since he butchered for Smith now and then even after he was hired by Baldy Johnston. At Little Egypt no- body minded a barkeeper with a little blood on him. It wasn't safe to mind Dan, anyway. He had more cunning in him than you'd think, to look at his big empty face with all the front teeth missing. Dan was an animal, with a beast's quickness and a beast's suspicions.

As for Red Fellows, he was a rough customer who'd crippled his mother with a couple of kicks one night after he lost his shirt at poker.

Jack Cane, who stuck with them, had served time for stealing; he was mostly muscle. Jake used to play cards with them a good deal — he was one man that dared to.

And Amos Trimble — it's odd enough — was in and out of Little Egypt some days. He seemed to have a liking for a bit of rough company. Good at poker, Trimble, as at everything; and even Bloody Dan forked over when he lost to him. I don't suppose Dan loved him, though.

But it was only some evenings that you could find Mr. Trimble at Little Egypt. Other times, he'd stick among the books at his old square house, his kerosene lamp burning all night. He read a lot, that was clear; but other nights, Jake thought, Trimble must have sat from sundown to sunup in his high leather chair, not moving, not reading, staring into some corner. He wasn't a man you could kid. Brice, the undertaker, came on business one evening, and found Trimble that way, sitting straight and solemn, his eyes open but not blinking. Brice had to shake Mr. Trimble two or three times before he stirred; and when he did wake, or speak, the whites of his eyes showed with anger, though he was polite enough, and Brice wished he never had touched him. A queer duck, in a fine house; but the house was dark and musty with only Trimble there. Jake said it would have given him the creeps to live in it alone; he got a look at the place the day he went with Brice and George Russell (who was deputy sheriff) to tell Amos Trimble what had happened to Jingo Criminy. When you needed any sort of help, Trimble was the man to look to. Russell needed it, and he remembered that Trimble had been a judge. They came up through the deep snow that covered the steps, that January, and Trimble led them to the upstairs parlor, and they told him about Jingo Criminy. It had been a dull winter in New Devon, until then.

What Jingo Criminy's real name was doesn't matter. 'Well, by Jingo Criminy!' the dirty old man would say, whether he'd taken in another dollar or dropped his glass eye. Jingo had lived alone in his cabin across the river for twenty years and more, and he didn't spend much on himself. The dollars came in, slowly, and Jingo Criminy hid them away. In twenty years, a heap of silver dollars can go into a box. There must have been a good many men in New Devon who thought about those dollars, because it was three miles from Jingo's cabin to town. Three men thought too long.

How did Jake know there were three? No, he wasn't one, for Jake had a heart; but talk comes out. There were three of them, and they took a cutter: three big men, faces hard as the ice on the road, and it was cold — too cold for anybody else to be out that evening. The snow crunched under the runners, and they came to Jingo's cabin, and they broke down the door. Crazy old coots like Jingo don't talk, even with matches at their feet, but sometimes they talk when they're strapped to the stove. Maybe Jingo Criminy talked, and maybe they found the hole in the floor without his help. They tore up the boards and emptied the box and went away in the cutter; but when they went, they left Jingo Criminy still strapped to the stove. A couple of days later, someone noticed the cabin door open, and looked in.

That meant a job for Uncle Jake. Brice was a good undertaker, but there were times when he needed help, and Jake was his man. Nothing turned Jake's stomach, which was cast iron. He and Brice took old Jingo off the stove, while Russell stood by; and as soon as they could, they went to Trimble's. Nothing was known, then, about the cutter and the three men, you understand: the snow had melted part way down, so there were no tracks.

If anybody knew men, Trimble did. Deputy Russell came to him for that and for something more. You could see that Trimble had power; some people said that he had powers. Russell believed in powers. Those were the big years for the Spiritualists. Russell believed in the whole kit and kaboodle, and nobody thought he was queer. Trimble didn't take too much stock in it, Jake said. Could he see things, though — things afar off, or done in the past? Yes, sometimes, Trimble told them. He would try. They sat in the dark of the upstairs parlor with their fingers pressed hard on the table top. Jake was across from Trimble. The sight of Jingo hadn't turned a hair of Jake's head, but Trimble's green eyes two feet away behind the candle flame was a sight he didn't like. For five minutes they sat, till Trimble's voice said, 'They tied him with his face to the stove.'

'That's true, Mr. Trimble,' Russell whispered. 'What about *their* faces?'

Amos Trimble stood up and lit the gas; Jake saw sweat running down his forehead. 'That's no evidence for you — not yet,' Trimble said. 'I'll see what I can find. I'm going to Little Egypt, once I write this note.' He scribbled something while Jake and the rest were getting on their coats, and tucked it away. 'I'll see you tonight, Mr. Russell,' he said. But he didn't.

Trimble had faith in himself, as he had a right to. Something slipped that evening — Jake never knew what; but for once, Trimble failed himself. He didn't make the mistake twice.

Down to Little Egypt Trimble went; and Jake, being thirsty and curious, went with him. Fellows and Cane and a couple of boomer switchmen were near the bar, Slattery and a helper behind it. Baldy Johnston was sick abed upstairs that day. One of the switchmen called Jake over for a drink, while Trimble walked halfway round the bar and looked at Slattery. There wasn't the man who could help being stared down by Amos Trimble.

'Well?' asked Dan. Nothing happened. 'Well, Mr. Trimble?' For him, Trimble was the only Mister in town, and he must have hated Trimble for it.

'What's roasting today, Slattery?' Trimble said. A vein swelled across Dan's forehead; he opened his mouth wide, but no words came.

Red Fellows, for once, thought faster than Dan. 'What do you say to a game, Mr. Trimble?' Fellows edged closer, till Trimble looked sidewise at him, the little scar on his eyelid puckering, then Fellows shifted back.

'I'll play your game,' said Amos Trimble.

'Let's go in the backroom, then,' growled Dan, who hadn't quite got his breath back. Trimble nodded and motioned to the three to go in ahead of him; he shook his head at Jake, who had started to rise; and then Trimble closed the door behind himself. Jake heard chairs scraping up to the table and made out Dan's voice every few minutes — whining first, then hoarse. But Jake had other fish to fry, because the boomer switchman was in the cash and the drinks were on him. Even Jake had his limit for whiskey, and he went past it.

Something roused Jake of a sudden. How long had he been lying with his head on the table, alone? He didn't know. It was a breaking noise that woke him, he thought, and he shook his head. The boomer switchmen were gone; there was no light in the taproom. He could see light coming from under the door of the back room, though. He headed for it and turned the knob, but the door was bolted. Jake gave it a kick. Nobody spoke. 'Come on!' said Jake, and nearly knocked a panel out. The door opened a crack, Dan showing his ugly face behind it. Jake gave him a shove and stepped in, nearly falling flat over the trap door to the cellar, which had been thrown open in the middle of the kitchen floor. Dan swore, and steadied Jake, who was blinking in the light. The room was empty except for Dan, who must have been washing, because water and suds were slopped over him. That surprised Jake a bit, soap not being in Dan's line.

'Where's Mr. Trimble and the rest?' Jake asked him.

'Gone home, long ago,' was all Dan said, slamming down the cellar trap and standing upon it.

Jake still didn't know what had waked him, but he was willing to forget. He told Dan to give him another bottle. 'Serve yourself,' said Dan, pushing him out into the bar. Jake obliged, and finally put his head down on the table for a minute.

Jake woke again, and found he was lying on the porch of Little Egypt in the snow — nothing for Jake — and it was sometime in the early morning and not a star out. Jake could walk, but he didn't feel like it. If Slattery had put him out, he'd try his luck with Slattery tomorrow. His bed was half a mile away. Just then, though, he heard a buggy coming out of the stable behind Little Egypt: a ride for him, maybe. Jake slipped down the steps and made for the corner of the tavern; just before he reached it, Amos Trimble's surrey, pulled by his smart bay, came into sight.

'How about a lift, Mr. Trimble?' called out Jake. The surrey moved on, the driver snuggled in a rug. 'Hey, Mr. Trimble, it's Jake,' Uncle Jake yelled. The bay started out at a brisk walk along the road beside the railway tracks. Jake stumbled and went into a drift; when he was up again, the surrey had gone round a turn. 'What did I do tonight that Trimble doesn't speak?' thought Jake. It was a cold half-mile home.

And it still was cold next morning when Brice pulled Jake out of bed to give him another job. 'A fellow got mixed up with a train at Tecumseh crossing, early today,' said Brice. 'That's what it looks like, though I can't figure out what train. He must have walked there — no sign of a horse. I don't know who. It's a mess, Jake; he's scattered for a hundred yards.'

Tecumseh crossing was halfway between the New Devon depot and Trimble's farm. The man, or what had been one, was only patches in the snow, Jake told me. Jake went along carefully with a basket, picking up everything; when he worked, he earned his pay. He and Brice came to a boot; Brice looked at it and gave a moan: 'Trimble's.' Jake never talked much. 'Can't be,' he said. 'Trimble's not the kind.' Jake found the other boot. 'Not his,' he said, but he didn't look at it closely.

It was Jake, too, who came to the head, with the black beard all stiff, and, in spite of dirt and blood, the scar still clear over the right eye. 'Oh, God, Mr. Trimble; oh, God, Mr. Trimble, not you,' was all Jake could say that day. The surrey was in the stable at Little Egypt; Trimble hadn't been sober enough to drive, the people there said. And what was Jake's word? He'd been lying in the snow on the porch like a sick hog. Brice had to go on with the work alone. He found everything, at last, except one thumb.

*   *

What was done? What you'd expect, with no more to go on. Russell could talk to Slattery, but Dan had his story. Lacking proof, there was no point in rousing Slattery's gang, in the lonely winter, with Russell the only officer in town. Jake might have done something, if he hadn't been married to the bottle. As it was, he kept clear of Little Egypt most of the time.

And here is where I fit into the picture — though I didn't know it was a picture, at the time. Spring came early that year. Sam Johnston — Baldy Johnston's little boy — and I were like a couple of cubs out of a cave, and got to wrestling in the mud of the back yard of Little Egypt. Sam was fatter, and got me down, and bounced on me. Jake came along and looked at us. 'What'll I do, Uncle Jake?' I asked him.

'If I was in your place, Roy,' he said, 'I'd eat my way out. Sam's nose is mighty close to you.' Sam gave a yell, and jumped off, and Jake walked on. Both Sam and I had had enough, so we started to plague Baldy Johnston's old cat, which was in the yard with us.

The cat was playing with something when Sam pulled it by the tail. I grabbed the thing it had been pushing around. At first I didn't know what it was. But when I turned it over, I saw the nail. It was shrunken and dry, but it was a man's thumb. I let it drop.

Sam bawled for his mother. She came out and took a look at the thing; you wouldn't have thought much could upset Baldy Johnston, but she opened her mouth to scream and then stopped herself, white as a table-cloth. 'Dan!' she screeched, instead. Dan stepped out of the taproom. His face didn't change. 'That damned cat's been in the cellar,' was all he said — all that I could make out. He muttered something else, lower, to Baldy.

'Why didn't you make sure?' said Baldy, furious.

'Don't worry,' Dan told her. 'The stove's hot.' He picked up the thing in the dirt. Old Baldy shivered.

'No, you don't, Dan,' she said. 'Get a spade.' She and Dan looked at us, and Sam and I made tracks out of there. Sam's mother must have taught him not to talk, and I didn't say anything. When I was a kid, I had nobody really to talk with, anyhow; and I was scared this time, though I didn't un-derstand why.

It could have been evidence, but no one else knew. There was one other piece of proof somewhere, maybe: Russell thought of the note Trimble had scribbled at his house, before he went to Little Egypt the last time. Russell and Jake and Brice had seen him write something. But where had he put it? It wasn't in the clothes they found along the tracks, and it didn't turn up at the house. Nobody had any idea of what Trimble had written. Russell was ready to quit.

As the months went by, Jake drifted back to Little Egypt and drowned himself in Baldy Johnston's raw whiskey. One afternoon early in July, Jake was playing poker with Fellows and two other boozers — a rough game, with plenty of money on the table. Cane was at the bar, talking with Slattery. A lucky day for Jake. After three hands, everything went his way. Ordinarily he was a bad player; this day it seemed to him as if someone were looking over his shoulder and giving him tips, the queer feeling that gamblers sometimes have. All said, something peculiar hung about Little Egypt that afternoon. Jake always could feel what was in the air; and Slattery seemed to know something was odd, too, shifting back and forth behind the bar, spoiling for a fight.

Red Fellows never could take a licking at cards. When Jake threw down the deuce, he set up a howl: 'What's going on, you midget? I already played the deuce.' It was all wind, but both he and Jake were ready to make something of it; Little Egypt was on their nerves.

'The hell,' said Jake, pushing back his chair and reaching for the money. 'My deuce.' Fellows picked up a big schooner of beer from the table and let fly at Jake's head.

Jake wasn't tall, but he was thick where it counted. The schooner scratched the red cap Jake wore. Jake reached across the table, hoisted Fellows up, spun him round, and let him fly into the front window. Fellows broke half a dozen bottles when he landed.

'If you're going to kill him, don't kill him in here,' yelled Slattery, coming over the bar. Jake was sick of Slattery. He heaved a chair at Bloody Dan.

The chair missed Dan; it brushed a lighted lamp and knocked it on the floor. Dan went after Jake, but Jake was quick for a man of his build, and side-stepped. They sparred round the floor while Fellows crawled out of the window, pulling glass from his pants. Then they started to cough, and found they couldn't see to fight — the smoke was too thick. The lamp had set Little Egypt afire.

Flame in one corner, smoke everywhere. The two other boys who'd been in the game got out the door and ran for help. Cane went for a bucket of water at the pump, and Jake and Fellows and Slattery tried smothering the flames with a couple of rag rugs. But it was old wood, Little Egypt. The fire spread, and all of a sudden an awful yowl came up from somewhere. 'My God, who's that?' asked Jake, coughing harder. Slattery swung round, but Jake couldn't see his face for the smoke. The yowl came again, and someone opened the door of the backroom, though Jake couldn't make out who was coming in — Cane, probably.

'Hell, it's only the cat, scared silly down below,' Fellows grunted, beating at the fire with a broom. He was at the far side of the room. 'Get a move on with that water, Cane!'

But Jack Cane didn't come in. The backroom door swung to again; and someone said, through the smoke, 'Why don't you get us out of the cellar, Slattery?' The closing of the door muffled whatever else was said, and Jake was too busy with his rug to pay much attention; but the voice was nothing like Cane's.

'Dan!' said Fellows. He had dropped his broom, and was leaning against the wall, too startled by something even to swear. 'Dan, who was that? It sounded like . . .'

'Shut up, damn you,' Dan told him; but he whispered it. Slattery was crouched in the middle of the floor, ignoring the fire, watching the backroom door. 'I couldn't see a thing. It must have been Jack.' The door did not open again.

'Come on, Dan!' howled Jake, who was getting hot, what with the fire gaining. 'Grab that rug!' But Dan stood there, staring at the door. Jake beat at the fire; and then a crowd of section-hands ran in with buckets of water. Little Egypt had one inside wall burnt nearly through, but nothing worse. By the time Jake got the smoke out of his eyes, Dan and Fellows were standing outside by the porch, saying nothing but letting other people finish the fire. 'Say, where's Cane?' asked Fellows, after a while.

They looked in the backroom, but found not hide nor hair of Jack Cane. Nobody in New Devon saw Cane from that time on. About two o'clock was the time the fire started in Little Egypt. At ten past two, the Detroit train came into New Devon. Just before it whistled — so Rowson, the ticket agent, told people — Cane ran into the depot and bought a ticket. He looked over his shoulder, and swore at Rowson for being slow, and grabbed his ticket and made the train. He didn't take anything with him. Why he went, nobody knew, and nobody ever had a chance to ask him. Two weeks later, Cane was dead in a rooming house in Chicago: some said bad liquor, some said carbolic acid. Nobody knew why.

Maybe Dan Slattery had some idea why Cane ran for the train. Dan kept mum during the next week. He took to shaking his head, as if he were saying 'no' to himself. He stood at a spot behind the old bar where he could see down Depot Street, in front of Little Egypt. He watched, but he didn't say what for. He watched all week. Nothing he was watching for came.

'Who you expecting, Slattery?' Jake said to him, when he was feeling high. 'You watching for Russell? Or Cane? Or who?'

'Shut up,' said Slattery. He kept on watching. When he thought Jake was looking the other way, he shook his head to himself.

*   *

Brice had been made executor of Mr. Trimble's estate; and it took him a long time to clear up some of Trimble's affairs. He spent a day, almost every week, going through receipts and vouchers and notes in the library at Trimble's dark old house, though he didn't like being there. Brice was used to dead bodies, but not to houses that seemed as if they were going to start talking any minute. Nearly a month after the fire at Little Egypt, Brice came puffing up the street toward Russell's office and saw Jake going the other way and told him to come along; there might be a job for him.

They hurried into Russell's place, Jake not knowing what it was all about; and Deputy Russell, seeing Brice's face, said, 'Something special?'

'I found something in a Bible at the Trimble house,' Brice told him, pulling a scrap of paper out of his vest pocket.

Russell took the paper, but didn't unfold it for a minute. 'Didn't know you were a Bible reader, Brice,' said Russell, who was one.

'It wasn't me that took the Bible off the shelf.' Brice said it as if someone were going to call him a liar. 'Somebody put it in the middle of Trimble's desk, open. I never touched a book in that house.'

'Anybody been there since you left last week?' Russell asked him. Not that he knew of, said Brice. Russell and Brice looked at each other a second. 'Just where was this paper stuck?' said Russell.

'What made you ask that?' Brice said. 'It's a funny thing. I wrote down the book, chapter, and verse: Ezekiel, eighth chapter, eighth verse, at the top of the page. Look it up.'

Russell took his own Bible from the whatnot in the corner, and read aloud to Brice and Jake:

'Now will I shortly pour out my fury upon thee and accomplish mine anger upon thee; and I will judge thee according to thy ways, and will recompense thee for all thy abominations.'

133

'Let's see that paper,' was all Jake had to say. Russell unfolded it. It didn't look as if it had been in a Bible for a while; it looked fresh, hardly creased. Russell said as much to Brice.

'I hope to die if that isn't where I found it,' Brice told them. 'I know what it says, but read it.'

Russell did: 'Jingo on the stove. Two men, backs turned; another at door. McCunn's cutter.'

'Whose writing?' asked Brice.

'Trimble's, looks like,' said Russell. 'Let's move. I'm going over to talk with Larry McCunn. You two get hold of some men and drift around Little Egypt. Watch the doors.'

Russell drove off, whipping up his horse, toward McCunn's; Jake was game for trouble, and he rounded up two other fellows, and with Brice they went toward Little Egypt.

Larry McCunn was a washed-out sort, scared of his shadow, and Russell didn't have to talk to him long. On the day Jingo Criminy died, McCunn's cousin Red Fellows had borrowed McCunn's horse and cutter. Fellows and Cane and Slattery weren't the boys McCunn could say no to, or the boys he could blab about afterward. McCunn told Russell all he knew, and then Russell let him go and rode for Little Egypt.

The saloon still was smoked up from the fire, and the door was sagging, and Russell never saw a fouler, tougher place. There wasn't a soul inside but Fellows, half asleep. Russell was glad of that. He sat down opposite Fellows and asked where Bloody Dan was. 'At the butcher shop, I guess,' Fellows told him.

'Then maybe you won't hang, Red,' said Russell. 'McCunn had a talk with me. There's you and Slattery. Slattery's enough to hang.'

Fellows gave in; something had been eating him since Cane ran away. He whined like an old hound. 'It was Dan planned it. Dan finished Jingo that way. It was Dan that got behind Trimble.' He talked on, while Russell nodded. Then, of a sudden, Russell knew somebody else was in the saloon, and he looked over Fellows' shoulder. The backroom door stood open; Bloody Dan had come in; he had his meat ax in his hand.

Russell knocked over his chair and ran for the door. Fellows twisted round, and squealed, and got up, but not soon enough. Slattery split him.

Russell went down the front steps like water over a dam. Jake and Brice picked him up, and the other men bunched together, watching the doorway. 'For God's sake,' Russell called to the men in the back of the tavern, 'don't let Dan slip out that way.' A crowd was outside now — women and boys, and half the men in town. 'Well,' said Russell, 'we better go after him, if we don't want him coming out on us.'

People looked at Jake, who was swinging a blacksmith's hammer. 'Come on,' said Jake, and went up the steps.

Fellows was in front of the bar, and his head was in two pieces. 'I thought Dan used that ax on Mr. Trimble,' was what Jake said. Dan? Nowhere. Not in the backroom or the kitchen. Four men with guns went through the rooms upstairs, peeking round corners; but they turned out only Baldy and little Sam. Everybody had his mind on that meat ax: Little Egypt was dark and Dan was fast.

'It'll be the cellar,' said Jake. They gathered around the trap in the backroom floor. 'Sure as hell he's down there.' Nobody spoke above a whisper.

'I think there's a little window to the cellar on the north side,' Russell said. 'I'll see if I can get through that way. Anybody willing to try the trap at the same time?' He and Brice looked at Jake, who spat and shifted to his other foot.

'Dan's got the ax and maybe a gun,' Jake told them. 'Burn the skunk out.' He reached for the oven door.

'No, it ain't lawful,' Russell said. 'We got to go after him.'

'All right,' said Jake. 'But break the glass in that window the minute you see my legs on the ladder. And close the trap behind me, boys; I don't want Dan sighting on me.'

Russell ran out. They opened the cellar door; Jake waited a bit, and then heard a pane break, and scooted down the ladder into the dark. And as he went down, and as the trap closed above him, everyone heard a screech: a screech that shook the floor and froze every man and made Jake slip when halfway down the ladder and fall to the dirt at the bottom.

'Not Slattery, if I know Slattery,' Brice said, up in the backroom. They had left the trap just a bit ajar, so that Jake could have a glint of light.

Jake huddled at the bottom, looking out for Dan's ax, and for whatever had screeched. It was an old stone cellar, full of cobwebs and broken bottles. Jake could see no one; but as his eyes became used to the darkness, he made out an open hole in the corner, probably a dry cistern, and not very deep. Had they put what was left of Trimble there, before they drove the surrey to the crossing? Jake crawled to the edge, expecting to feel that ax any second.

There they were: one man flat on the cistern bottom, looking as if he'd been broken in the middle, and the other tugging at him, so as to lift the body the five or six feet to the lip of the cistern. Dan was the smashed man; his ax was away at the far side of the hole. Jake took a real breath for the first time since he'd gone through the trap. 'That's a good job, Russell,' Jake said. 'Shove Dan up, and I'll pull.'

Now the man down in the dark below had Slattery's big body over his shoulders. He straightened slowly, and brought the dead man almost level with Jake's face. Dan's head flopped on one side: the neck was broken. Jake caught hold of the shoulders and began to pull. Just then, Russell said, 'Jake, are you there? Is that you? I can't get through the damned window.'

For a quarter of a second, Jake looked round to where Russell's voice came from. Yes, Russell was looking through the little window; he still was outside the cellar, too fat to crawl through. Jake snapped his head back toward the cistern as quick as an owl. The man in the hole was shoving Slattery's body toward him, and as he rose under the weight, he and Jake came face to face, a foot or two apart. The man in the cistern had a black beard; and he had green eyes; and he had a little puckering scar running up from one eyelid. Jake saw this, and he sucked in his breath, and let go Dan's body; and it fell back into the cistern. Then Jake was at the foot of the ladder, and up in two jumps, and into the backroom.

Jake broke the neck off a bottle of whiskey, and poured it down himself, but no one could get a word out of him except 'Trimble, Trimble, Trimble.' Brice and two other men went down the ladder; they found Dan dead with a broken neck and a broken back in the little cistern, and nothing else. Russell still was at the window, pointing a shotgun through: all he had seen was Jake, or somebody he took to be Jake, kneeling by the cistern and then diving for the ladder.

That's all. What do you expect me to tell you? Jake never drank again. No one lived in Trimble's house afterward, for his mark was on it. It's been twenty years since it burned. All the rest of his life Jake watched, the way Slattery watched for a week or two; but nothing ever came to him. They're all in the graveyard now, Uncle Jake and the lot, and before you know it, I'll be with them. And because I never had powers like Amos Trimble's, I'll lie easy there.

Fate's Purse

Thy money perish with thee, because thou hast thought that the gift of God may be purchased with money.

Acts 8:20

Four miles west of Bear City, Cubby Hasper splashed up the gravelly bed of Brownlee's Creek, casting for trout. Although swift, the creek was very shallow this dry summer. It was a remote spot, the woods of the Brownlee farmstead extending densely on either side of the stream. Cubby, thirteen years old, trusted that he wouldn't encounter old Fate Brownlee, who had a short way with trespassers. Fate! It was a funny name to have given a Brownlee baby — if one could imagine old Fate as a baby — but, as the man had turned out, the name was suitable enough.

Rounding a bend, Cubby saw something curious. A small tractor somehow had nosed down the low bank into the creek and stood there silent and unmoving, the clear water eddying round the forepart of it, as if the machine had given up the ghost. Cubby reeled in his line and made his way to the tractor. Then he perceived what turned him white and shaking all over.

Just under the surface of the fast-flowing water, shadowed by the branches of an ancient willow, a few feet beyond the tractor's nose, lay a man's face. Cubby almost had stepped upon the dead thing. It was old Fate Brownlee's face. Cubby screamed and turned and ran for home, falling into two or three creek-bed potholes on the way.

*   *

In the considered judgment of the coroner, Fate Brownlee's death, as an act of God, was a case for the judge of probate, not for the county prosecutor. Apparently the old miser had intended to cut yet more cords of firewood in preparation for winter — even though already there must have been a hundred cords stacked close beside his damp farmhouse, the earlier cords among them already fungi-covered and rotting to punk. As best the circumstances might be reconstructed, it seemed that Fate must have driven his rusty tractor along the woods trail to the creek, intending to cross the stream at his ford and fell dead elms on the far side; his chain saw had been hanging upon the tractor when his body was taken from the water.

At the creek, something must have happened to the tractor, the coroner speculated — one of its treads snagged on a dead water-logged branch, perhaps. Old Fate, presumably, had waded into the creek to clear the way. Then his tractor, its engine left running, must have begun to move again when Fate had freed the tread; or else the tractor may have slid down the bank, unexpectedly, so pinning Fate Brownlee to the creek bed, cruelly imprisoned under great weight nearly to his waist, but his head and arms and chest free to flounder in the stream.

It had been a hard way to go. For it appeared that Fate may have lain alive and conscious in the creek for some time — possibly for hours. There had been lacerations on his hands, as if he had tried to hold his head above water by grasping willow twigs that strayed down from the vast willow overhanging the ford; some willow branches had been broken off. But when Fate's strength had failed, and he had been able to grip the branches no longer, then his head had sunk beneath the shallow water.

The corpse may have lain there for as much as three days before little Cubby came upon it: Fate Brownlee, a loner, a bachelor all his life, sometimes had not gone into Bear City for weeks on end, and there had been no important reason why anyone should have bothered to seek him out. Fate's chickens, unfed, had scattered into the woods. His dog somehow had vanished altogether. The dead man's cattle had browsed unperturbed in the pastures, and the bees from his dozens of hives had buzzed about the honeysuckle hedges, at their business as usual. Few people in Bear City seemed more concerned at Fate's passing than had been the cows and the bees: in seventy years, Fate had made no friends, although he had accumulated (according to rumor) plenty of cash. 'An act of God,' the postmaster said in private, was just the right phrase for Fate's end.

Only one circumstance had puzzled the coroner a trifle: Fate's purse had been found nowhere. It had been a very big oldfangled leather change-purse or pouch with steel fasteners at the mouth, from the time when everybody used silver dollars, and it had been in evidence when Fate had deposited money in the bank or had sold honey at people's doors. Although Fate had carried the purse with him always — it had been fastened to his overalls by a contraption of chain — that big purse had not been found on his body, nor near the tractor, nor in the decayed farmhouse. Could it have come loose from his overalls and have been washed down the creek? Cubby was an honest boy who wouldn't steal pennies off a dead man. Two neighbours had gone down the creek bed with rakes, at the coroner's request, but had not found the purse. Presumably there would have been only small change in it, anyway, for Fate had been popularly supposed to bury at least as much of his money as he put into the bank and not to lug cash about with him recklessly. An odd circumstance, this, but a small one: one of God's little jokes, conceivably, poetic justice. So much for Fate's fate. With that witticism, the coroner resigned the business to the county judge of probate.

*   *

Mr. Titus Moreton, sometime lieutenant-colonel of cavalry in the Army of the United States, had been judge of probate in Pottawattomie County for more than a decade. He was a burly outdoor man, strong in defiance of his years, popular enough, who kept three horses, collected weapons, and understood how to manage young wards of the court competently and humorously. The judge had known Fate Brownlee slightly, as he knew most of the odd characters in Pottawattomie County. Niggardly old Fate, he suspected, must have stashed away a tolerable fortune somewhere: if a hard-fisted bachelor buys next to nothing for most of his life, and doesn't drink or smoke or treat, and owns a good farm and mortgages on other people's farms, and works his land as if somebody had him under the lash — why, in the nature of things, the money accumulates. The judge's wife couldn't believe that a ragged scarecrow in overalls like Fate Brownlee might have been by far the richest man in his rural township, but the judge could and did.

Judge Moreton had appointed as administrator of the estate of the late Fate Brownlee the township supervisor, Abe Redding, whose probity was undoubted: a sensible lean man with a weathered face, jolly and resourceful. There might be a will in Fate's safety-deposit box at the bank. Undoubtedly there was an heir presumptive — the dead man's brother, Virgil Brownlee, who lived in the big city and sold real estate. The judge had not seen this Virgil, but Abe Redding said that the brother, who dressed well enough and had made plenty of money on his own, was nearly as miserly as Fate had been, except that Virgil had indulged himself in a spouse and a daughter. Fate and Virgil, Redding went on, had not been at all fond of each other, but the city miser had visited the country miser two or three times a year, according to the neighbors; perhaps he had felt some attachment to the old family farmstead, though the house was sufficiently bleak. If Fate had died intestate, the inheritance would go to Virgil, his wife, and child; even had Fate made a will, Redding suggested, probably Virgil was the sole legatee.

'Why?' the judge wished to know. 'If, as you say, the brothers fought every time they met. . . .'

'Because, Judge, Fate knew that Virgil would save his money.'

'Save it for what?'

'Just to put a cool million into the hands of Virgil's daughter and Fate's niece, Judge — an ugly little thing called Dorcas.'

'And what would the niece do with it, Abe?'

'Save it, if she's a chip off the old block, and she is.'

The judge had snorted — he was openhanded to a fault, himself — and had bought Abe a drink. 'Here's to you, Administrator. If there's a will, it's up to you to unearth it. So far as I know, Fate had no lawyer. Do you think there's really a will?'

'Maybe, Judge. They say that after one or two fights the brothers had, old Fate threatened to draw up a new last will and testament and leave money, farm, and the whole kaboodle to the Salvation Army. He told Matt Heddle, at the post office, how he might do just that. Yet it wasn't in his nature: the Salvation Army would have spent the money on bums. Still, the talk of it was a good way to put the fear of God into Brother Virgil.'

Fate and Virgil, the judge reflected — what incongruous names! The Brownlee parents, with such classical affectations in the backwoods, must have been as odd as their precious offspring. Fate — *fatum* — destiny; and Virgil, the poet of destiny, mission! The brothers had looked much alike, Abe said, but Virgil had been the younger by ten years.

As matters had turned out, there *had* been an old will in the safety-deposit box; and everything had been bequeathed to 'my brother, Virgil H. Brownlee.' Also it had turned out that Fate's savings-account had been surprisingly small. Redding had contrived to track down certain very substantial investments of Fate's in stocks and bonds, made late in his life, and there were also the mortgages on half the farms in the township. All this had made the deceased's estate plump and happy, as the judge had expected, Fate's lifelong woeful façade of desperate poverty notwithstanding. Yet Redding suspected, and the judge agreed, that very possibly there lay concealed in the farmhouse, or round about, currency and coin exceeding all the tangible and intangible assets that Redding had uncovered so far. Persistent and long-standing report among the neighbors had it so. And before ruling upon that old will from the safety-deposit box, the judge meant to find what — or at least part of what — lay behind those rumors.

The Brownlee farm, isolated and unguarded, was more than four miles distant from little Bear City. But happily an under-sheriff, Buck Tuller, lived on a hardscrabble holding only half a mile distant from the dead man's house. Redding had prevailed upon Buck to keep an eye on the Brownlee place, feeding the cattle, taking the chickens into custody at his own chicken house, and making sure no rough boys might tip over the many beehives. (Redding had hinted to Tuller that perhaps the bee swarms might be given to him, on settlement day, as reward for these services.) Also, of course, Buck Tuller was to watch for any two-footed predators: two or three unoccupied lake cottages in the county had been plundered this season, a nocturnal burglary unsuccessfully attempted at the Bear City bank, and it was sufficiently notorious that old Fate had kept the green stuff and the silver dollars ready to hand. Money does not breed, but its proximity warms the cockles of miserly hearts that are too stingy to keep a fire burning on cold nights in a sooty old wood stove.

Still, Buck Tuller could not be always keeping a weather eye on the Brownlee place, round the clock; so some search of the premises ought to be made soon, Redding had declared. The judge had concurred. Mr. Virgil Brownlee, heir presumptive, had been invited to attend and witness on this occasion. On the appointed day, a Saturday, they had gathered at the Bear City post office to start out upon the formal search: Redding, the judge, and Virgil Brownlee. Buck Tuller would be waiting for them at the gaunt farmhouse, and Buck would be armed. The judge thoughtfully brought along a long spade and wore in a holster at his belt his old army revolver. In these days, precautions were prudent even in farm townships. The gang that had looted the cottages and attempted the bank in recent months just conceivably might turn up at the Brownlee farm, and the judge was a practiced quick-draw man.

They drove out to the farm in Redding's car, Virgil Brownlee talking volubly. He was a long-nosed man, in physiognomy and figure nearly the spit and image of Fate, but clean-shaven and attired in black suit and black tie, as if in mourning. Mourning did not quite become Virgil. Now and again, this Virgil Brownlee bit his nails, but he smiled a great deal, even when speaking of his brother's untimely end and the melancholy character of it. And how Virgil did run on — a compulsive talker if ever there was one! He babbled of the dear boyhood intimacy between him and his brother.

'I suppose, Mr. Brownlee, that you two got along famously all your long lives, eh?' inquired the judge, a trifle dryly.

Virgil Brownlee looked sharply at him. 'He left me everything, didn't he? Oh, brothers have their spats, you know, but deep down underneath, Judge Moreton, the bond lasted — right up to the end.' Here Virgil sniffed and put his right hand over his eyes, as if in sharp sorrow, peering between his fingers at the judge.

Redding turned the car into a rutted driveway. 'Here we are, gentlemen. You haven't seen the Brownlee place before, Judge?'

*   *

It was no delightful sight. The barns and sheds were well enough maintained; a perfectly astounding array of hives stood in long rows behind the chicken house, and fairly neat orchards stretched along either side of the honeysuckle-lined drive to the farmhouse. But that house itself was neither picturesque nor old, though it stood apparently upon the squared-boulder foundations of an earlier dwelling. The windows were uncurtained, and the afternoon sun glared back from their dull dirty panes. The chimney looked about ready to fall. It was a smallish house of a single storey, the paint long ago peeled from the warped siding.

'Your brother didn't bother much about appearances, Mr. Brownlee,' Abe Redding offered.

'If you fix up the outside of a house, they raise your property taxes. My brother saved his money.' Virgil spoke as if this retort were crushing. He kept up a flow of talk as they walked toward the house — having left their car near the road, the ruts of the farm lane being bone-bruising.

Meanwhile the judge was surveying the orchards on either side of the track. Here and there, under one old apple tree or another, he noticed a little heap of stones, and touched Virgil's arm. 'What do you suppose those stone piles are?'

'Just Fate's way of making it easier to plough,' Virgil told him, smoothly. But it had passed through the judge's mind that these might be cairns marking — or some of them, only Fate knew which — burials of something of value.

Taking a ring of keys from his pocket, Redding unlocked the front door. 'You first, friend, as next of kin,' he told Virgil Brownlee, motioning toward the doorway. Brownlee hesitated, shook his head, again covered his eyes with the fingers of one hand:

'Let somebody else step in first; it's too sad for me.'

What a rat's nest the place was! The judge had seen many filthy hovels in Pottawattomie County, but none so abominable as this. The four of them stared at the barren living-room, with old newspapers pasted on the walls instead of regular wallpaper, no carpet or linoleum on the bare floorboards, the scanty cheap furniture damaged or broken. What had been meant for the dining-room was perfectly empty. In the smeared cheerless kitchen was the house's only source of heat, the battered wood range, looking as if it might explode were a fire lit. There was one fairly new, fairly serviceable thing: a big white freezer was full to its brim with loaves of store bread.

'Fate used to buy week-old bread cheap at the supermarkets in the county seat,' Virgil commented, 'and keep it here for a year or more. He said he didn't grudge eating it if it was a year old, even if he'd had to pay cash for it. Fate didn't waste.' Virgil said this with fraternal pride.

To conceal anything in these squalid rooms, with their naked walls of unpainted plaster, would have been almost impossible, unless under the floorboards, which had many cracks; and besides, the judge ruminated, the place was a perilous firetrap, as even its owner must have perceived. Whatever Fate had hidden could not be above ground in this house.

The main bedroom was next for inspection, a dark hole. As they crowded in, some shape loomed at the foot of the bed. 'O God!' Virgil Brownlee cried; but he recovered swiftly.

Fate had possessed but two outer garments aside from his ragged black overcoat, and those two identical: pairs of worn blue overalls. He had been buried in one pair, decently laundered for the ceremony by Mrs. Tuller. The remaining pair of overalls, caked with dried sweat and grime so that they were permanently filled out to their owner's proportions, hung suspended on a coat hanger from a ceiling hook and swayed slightly in the draught caused by the opening of the bedroom door. In the dimness, it had seemed as if Fate himself had been swaying there.

'Gives a man a turn, don't it?' Virgil sighed. Indeed it did.

On the cot bed's thin mattress lay a single frayed blanket and a pillow without a slip. A cheap straight chair stood beside the bed. Some grimy underclothing, socks, and shirts lay on the floor of the closet. Otherwise the bedroom was empty. The man who had lived thus could have bought and sold nearly everybody in the county. The house, though some light bulbs dangled from their cords, had no running water, let alone a bathroom. 'Fate didn't complain about going out to the pump and using the backhouse,' Virgil explained.

All the money they found in these rooms was contained in a glass jar atop the kitchen range; one dime, one nickel, two pennies. Perhaps even that sum had been left exposed there in the hope of persuading conceivable burglars that it was the whole of Fate's savings.

'There's nothing here,' said Abe Redding. 'Where'd we ought to look, Mr. Brownlee?'

'Why, I couldn't just say.' Virgil's long nose twitched, and again he stared at the three of them through his fingers. 'I don't have the least idea where my brother kept his money — supposing he had any, and I don't know that he did. But if I was you, I'd go down into the cellar.'

It was an old Michigan cellar, surviving from the earlier farmhouse on this site — very deep and high-ceilinged, its walls in part rubble from the fields, in part packed earth rudely plastered over. As they went down the rickety stairs, the judge noticed here and there in the stone staircase-walls certain patches that looked as if holes had been opened and then sealed up again; the mortar round the stones at these spots was newer and of a different hue. But they had no picks ready to hand, and it was uncertain how much authority even a judge of probate and a duly appointed administrator held, when causing actual damage to a house's fabric was in question.

This cellar had several rooms, and all but one of them crammed with rough shelving, and on the shelves lay food enough to feed a cavalry regiment for a whole month. There were hundreds, perhaps thousands, of glass jars of preserves — meat, fruit, berries, vegetables, fish, jellies, jams. Some of this unmistakably had spoiled, and growths of exotic tints oozed from beneath their jar lids. This must be an accumulation of decades. 'Fate was the great one for home canning,' Virgil offered. Into the judge's mind came the image of old Fate: a bag of bones in overalls, an effigy of Famine. What power of self-denial — or, rather, denial of the flesh; what lunacy!

Another cellar room contained tier upon tier of combs of honey, thick with dust, enough concentrated sweet to sicken every child in Pottawatto-mie County for a year at least. 'Fate was handy with the bees,' Virgil con-tinued, 'though he didn't eat much honey himself, except for reasons of health. He liked to see the stuff available here in case of need.'

'About them bees,' Buck Tuller broke in, awkwardly. 'Now I could use the hives, and Mr. Redding here was suggestin' . . .'

Virgil spoke with abrupt force and venom. 'Yes, I sure heard what Abe Redding had in mind, and I can tell you, Buck Tuller . . . Well, look at the thing this way. For my part, you'd be welcome to Fate's bees. But I don't know for sure yet that they belong to me; and even if I did know, there's others to consider — my wife, and our kid Dorcas, and I don't know who else. Now it wouldn't be fair of me to just give away other folks' property, would it? Anyway, Buck Tuller, them hives is going to stay just where they set, and I'm not going to have you lay hand on them, officer of the law though you be.'

This at first surprised the judge. Giving Tuller the hives might have saved the estate the modest cash bill for services as watchman that Tuller could submit. But now it occurred to the judge — who kept his peace — that hives alive with stinging bees would be the last place that thieves might search for hidden money.

The four of them came to the last room in the cellar, a long narrow space running parallel with the front of the house. They had to use the flashlights that Redding and Tuller had brought. The floor here was of sand, and the room was empty of shelves or junk.

'I see you fetched a good spade, Judge Moreton,' Virgil Brownlee com-mented. 'Now, like I say, I don't have no notion as to where Fate buried his money, if he had any.' His speech had grown hurried and blurred, and his grammar rougher. 'But if I was you, Judge, I'd dig *right over there*.' He indi-cated the northern end of the room.

The judge thrust his spade into the sand. At the second spadeful of earth, the sharp spade-edge struck against something that rang. Bending down, the judge extracted from the sand a sealed glass jar. It was packed tight with little cylinders of something, sewn up neatly in newspaper. Redding held the jar, and the judge thrust in his spade afresh, again successfully. Altogether, he dug up some twenty-nine jars, buried fairly close together. Spade where he would in the rest of the cellar, he could discover no more.

They carried the jars to the living-room and set them on a pine table. Strong in his fingers, the judge screwed open the first jar, extracted the several cylinders, and cut them carefully with his pocketknife. Underneath the integument of stitched newspaper was a tight roll of hundred-dollar bills.

The judge let Abe Redding open the other jars. Not all contained hundred-dollar bills, but there was nothing so small as a one-dollar bill. All were currency issued during the twenties and thirties.

But when Redding removed the newspaper wrapping from the cylinders in the ninth jar, there were no notes inside. Instead the jar was packed with dry corncobs, sewn up as neatly as the rolls containing money.

'I'll be a monkey's uncle,' Buck Tuller declared. 'Now why did Fate save them old corncobs?'

Virgil Brownlee, previously so loquacious, had fallen silent, and his face was expressionless. But he did not seem really astonished or chagrined. The judge wondered cynically whether this fellow, years ago, might not have got into this cellar when his brother had been absent for a few hours, say, and have made substitutions not easy to detect, so many as he dared.

Only eight of the jars contained corncobs; the rest were stuffed with bills. Putting all the jars on the floor, Redding proceeded to count their take, jotting down the contents of each jar in his notebook. He had opened his mouth to announce the grand total when the boards of the porch floor creaked, and something rattled the knob of the front door.

'For Christ's sake, don't let him in!' Virgil Brownlee shrieked.

What Virgil meant, the judge did not know; for his own part, he thought immediately of the gang who had attempted the bank. Visions of an autumnal glory suffused his judicial imagination; he could see the headline in the county daily — 'Probate Judge Wipes Out Robber Band.'

Faster than Bat Masterson, as the front door swung inward and Virgil fled to the inner rooms, Judge Moreton had his pistol out and was thumbing back the hammer. A gray bulk occupied the doorway.

'Hold it, please, Judge!' Buck Tuller implored him. 'That's a federal man!'

So it was. With a slight sigh, the judge slid his gun back into its holster, not fancying a headline like 'Probate Judge Slaughters IRS Agent.'

'I was just seeing what might be up,' the federal man muttered apologetically. 'Afternoon, everybody. Judge, did you know that Fate Brownlee, for years back, had written "no income" on his federal returns?'

Virgil, his composure recovered, had returned from the back of the house. 'What you see here ain't income,' he put in, tartly. 'It's capital, and it's old money. And I don't need to tell you that there's a three-year limit on investigating income-tax returns.'

'I know that,' the federal man admitted, not happily. 'Judge Moreton, you're going to give this house a real thorough search?'

The judge, like other judges of probate whose authority is indefinite but ample, was easily put on his mettle; and he was zealous for state and local powers. 'You're intervening in the proceedings of a duly constituted court of probate,' he retorted in his colonel's tones of yesteryear, 'and I'll not allow it. You go out that door and sit on the porch until we've finished our business, or I might find you in contempt.'

The federal man having obeyed, Virgil Brownlee clapped the judge approvingly on the shoulder. 'That's the way to handle them meddlers, Judge.'

'Take your hand off me,' the judge said. 'Abe Redding, what's your total?'

In those glass jars there had been found the sum of $17,490. 'Deposit it in the bank under a special account for the estate, Abe,' the judge told Redding. 'Brownlee, don't stand so close to that table.'

Whatever might lie still behind those patches in the stone walls or under orchard cairns or in hives — why, this was a clammy house, a presence brooding over it, and already the sun was going down. And why should the Treasury get its fingers, through arrears of income tax or extortionate inheritance tax, upon the hoard for which dead old Fate had sacrificed comfort, pleasure, friends, even true humanity? Fate had paid for his ignoble treasure. Why, should he linger longer in this deathly house, the judge thought, he might turn miser himself.

As they left, Redding locking the door behind them, the judge told the waiting federal man, 'Unless you have a warrant, keep off this property, or I'll warrant *you*. Scat, now! Mr. Redding's in charge of all this.'

They lingered in the car until the federal man had driven off. Behind them, against its background of neglected woods, the farmhouse looked lonely enough to give anyone the shivers.

'You being in real estate, Mr. Brownlee,' Abe Redding said as they parted at the Bear City post office, 'I guess you'll be selling the old place once it's settled that it's all yours.'

'Wouldn't think of selling,' Virgil informed him. 'Not a farm that's been in the family a hundred years! Why, the wife and daughter may not care for the place, but I might spend a good deal of time up here by myself, just loafing around, thinking of Dad and Mom and — and Fate.'

'It has a hold on you, Brownlee?' The judge did not shake his hand. 'I can imagine why. Well, if Abe's work goes along smoothly, we should be able to settle this estate about a month from now. My clerk will send you a notice in sufficient time. Meanwhile, stay off that property. Keep everybody else off it, Tuller. It's not a healthy place to be alone.'

* *

On the day of the settlement, in September, everyone concerned with the Fate Brownlee estate met at the judge's chambers in the courthouse. The chambers were panelled in old oak, and portraits — well, photographs, mostly — of earlier judges of probate hung on the walls, in heavy frames, high up; and there was set into one wall the splendid painted cast-iron door of the old strongroom. The judge felt majestic here.

Virgil's wife and daughter were along with Virgil, the judge noticed; also a scruffy-looking lawyer whom Virgil Brownlee had fetched from the big city. The judge secretly regretted having to turn over so much money and land to such dubious-looking characters.

Fate's will was valid, no later will having been discovered, and everything was to pass to Virgil Brownlee after any charges against the estate had been paid in full. Abe Redding's labors as administrator had turned up a respectable fortune for the heir, quite as the judge had anticipated — a fortune subject to federal and state inheritance taxes necessarily. Virgil very privily might turn up a second fortune for himself, clear of taxes, mining that ancestral farmstead so dear to Virgil's sentimental heart. But the judge spoke no word of that. A curious thought came casually into his head, just before he opened the proceedings: why hadn't they found Fate's purse anywhere at all? It had been a big, rather conspicuous thing.

Virgil's city lawyer sat close beside his client as bills against the estate were presented for settlement. Fate had paid for everything by cash or check, lifelong; so the only charges against the patrimony were those incurred since Fate's drowning. Abe Redding, as administrator, presented his bill for a sum very tidy indeed — yet only the minimum fee authorized by statute for so substantial an estate. The judge rather had expected Virgil and his household to protest so whopping a deduction from their inheritance; but Virgil sat wooden-faced, allowing the bill to be approved; presumably his lawyer had advised him that Redding could have made bigger charges, had he been greedy, with an excellent chance for approval of the court; let well enough alone, Mr. Brownlee.

Buck Tuller's modest wage for watching over the farm, too, slipped by undiminished: Virgil did open his mouth, as if meaning to say something indignant, but thought better of it. Perhaps he recollected that he could have let Buck take the hives, by way of compensation, and did not care to have that alternative raised afresh.

And then Frank McCullough, who kept the garage and auto-parts emporium at Bear City, submitted his account for payment. Fate had been a customer of his ever since Frank had opened his garage — though not a very profitable patron. Once Fate had driven coughingly up to Frank's station and asked if Frank could repair his dragging ragged muffler. Frank had inspected it solemnly.

'I don't think so, Fate,' he had pronounced. 'Now I could sell you a new one. . . .'

'O Lord Jesus, man, don't say that!' Fate had ejaculated in anguish. 'Just give it a hit with a board or something, and maybe it'll be all right.'

Now Frank McCullough's bill went to the judge's desk. It had been Frank who had pulled the tractor off Fate Brownlee's corpse in the creek, had taken the murderous thing to his garage, had put it back in working order, and had returned it to the Brownlee farm. For these services he requested the compensation of twenty-nine dollars and seventy cents.

At that demand, Mr. Virgil Brownlee rose up in wrath, ignoring his city lawyer. 'Outrageous!' he shouted. 'Scandalous! We can't pay that much! Why, a bill like that just shows you what people won't do for money.'

*   *

Nearly a month after Virgil Brownlee had entered upon possession of his brother's goods and chattels, the judge, in an idle hour, decided to pay a visit to the Brownlee farm. It was his custom, nearly every Sunday, to saddle one of his horses and take a long ride along the back roads and sand trails of Pottawattomie County, often exchanging some pleasant words with farmers and pensioners he passed along the way — a tactic useful for one who meant to be reelected judge of probate, term upon term. It had been more than a year since he had ridden the country west of Bear City, and he felt a hankering to see what Virgil might have done with his tangible inheritance. If the judge himself had owned both the Brownlee farm and Hell, he would have rented out the Brownlee place and lived in Hell. He put into his pocket a detailed map of the county.

As he saddled his mare Diane, his wife came out to hand him a thermos of coffee for the ride on this brisk fall day. 'Titus, you silly,' said Charlotte, 'you've put on that nasty pistol of yours. You'd look a fool, and what if you fell off Diane and the gun shot you?'

It was the judge's long sorrow that Charlotte disliked horses and guns. 'There's a safety on it, my darling, and a hard trigger pull.' But not being quite sure why he had happened to belt on the revolver, anyway, the judge put the gun back on the shelf in his bedroom. Sometimes he called Charlotte by the pet appellation of Ozymandia, Queen of Queens — 'Look on my works, ye Mighty, and despair.'

She supplied him with a sandwich well wrapped, an orange, and a chocolate bar, and compelled him to don a heavy riding jacket, and would have thrust more impedimenta upon him until he protested that she meant to make him look like the White Knight. She demanded to know what way he was bound, and he told her that he would ride to Brownlee's.

'Why do you want to see that smirking Virgil Brownlee?'

'I don't want to see him, my darling; it's just that I want a long ride, and I might have a glance at what he's done to that sad house. They say he comes up alone from the city on weekends. I hear he's sold the herd and rents out the pastures and most of the fields, but threatens trespassers, like Fate before him.'

'Don't quarrel with him, if he's there; a judge is supposed to be above that. You're so aggressive and domineering, Titus.'

'Yes, my darling.'

Then the uxorious judge, astride Diane, went on his cheerful way to the west of Bear City, occasionally putting the mare to a canter or a trot, keeping to the gravel roads and sand trails, greeting an elector or an electress now and again — but not many, this township being scantily peopled. Halfway to his destination, he tied Diane to a tree, sat upon a stump, ate his sandwich and drank his coffee, and read an old pocket edition of Cicero's *Offices* — he had retained classical tastes from college — for more than half an hour.

He rode on. Finding himself about a mile, presumably, from the Brownlee homestead, he consulted his map and ascertained that he could approach the place by a forgotten lumbermen's road that must cross Brownlee's Creek a few hundred yards to the rear of the farmstead.

Kept open at all only by venturesome hunters and fishermen, this track was overgrown. Now he could hear the rippling of the creek, and he emerged upon a ford of sorts overhung by a giant willow. Why, this must be the very spot where old Fate had drowned; he never had happened upon it before.

Without warning, Diane neighed, and shied so violently that she almost threw him, inveterate rider though he was. Close at hand, on his left, something fairly big retreated through the thickets, more heard than glimpsed. A deer it must be, or just possibly a large raccoon. 'Easy, Diane!'

But the mare was behaving badly, almost hysterical. She reared and plunged; she did not mean to cross that ford. Ordinarily as gentle with good horses as with good women, the judge refrained from using his full strength on Diane's mouth. 'Why, girl! Easy, easy!' She tried to swing back toward the trail by which they had come.

He might as well humor her this once, as he humored Charlotte. Dismounting with some difficulty, he led Diane a hundred yards back from the creek and fastened her to a silver birch; he patted her, and she seemed more at ease away from the ford. It would be only a short walk to the farmstead.

In his riding boots, he crossed the creek without trouble and strolled up the track toward the Brownlee place. He ascended a low hogback; the woods ended on the far side of the ridge; and standing in scrub at the edge of the tangle, head and shoulders above a thick clump of wild blackberry bushes, he had a good view of the farm. On his rides he carried field glasses, and now he took these from their case at his belt and surveyed the field between him and the farm buildings.

He could see a part of one of the orchards; he thought he could make out piles of fresh earth under some trees. He could see very clearly that a number of the beehives back of the chicken house had been overturned and lay on the ground. Then across his line of vision a man moved: a man in old overalls, gaunt, with a rifle in his hand. He saw him in profile and was not perceived himself. For a silly instant, the judge took the man for Fate Brownlee *redivivus;* then he knew it must be Virgil. He was startled when the man abruptly brought the stock up to his shoulder and fired toward a sugarbush grove to the north. The rifle crack echoed mightily over the desolation.

What might Virgil be hunting with a rifle in October — deer out of season? The judge could not trust a city man's discretion or aim, and he didn't mean to be taken for a buck; he must make his presence known. 'Virgil!' the judge shouted, hoarsely.

The man started conspicuously, swung around, hastily took aim, and pulled the trigger before the judge grasped his intention. The judge felt a swift stinging blow, reeled, and fell forward to earth, among the bushes.

If he had fainted, it could have been only for a moment. He had been hit in the head: Virgil Brownlee was a crack shot, or a lucky one. How badly? Half-dazed, the judge sensed that blood was running thickly down his right cheek and his chin. He thought that he could have stood up, but he didn't mean to try it; for the moment he was invisible behind the blackberry bushes. He remembered, relevantly, how last December one deer hunter had fired at another, taking him for game; and when the wounded man had screeched, stood up, and tried to run, the whiskey-swigging first hunter had pumped bullet after bullet into him, blind with hunter's lust.

The judge heard a shrill voice, happily still some distance off. 'Come on out! Come on out of there, Fate!'

The judge had been wounded twice in New Guinea, and on one of those occasions had played possum while the Japanese poked about the jungle to finish him off. Four of his own men had come to his rescue then, but no one could help him here. He felt his bloody head with his right hand: there was a flesh wound on his cheek, and the cheekbone must be broken, and the lobe of his right ear was missing. As yet, the pain was surprisingly endurable, but the bleeding was profuse. Confound darling Charlotte for depriving him of his pistol! There was not even a stick or a big stone ready to hand — nothing to defend him against Virgil Brownlee's damned rifle. Would Virgil come into the brush after his trophy?

He would. Close now, too close, there came a second wild shout: 'Fate, you in there? You come on out of there, or I'll give it to you in your belly like I gave it to your dog after you got caught in the creek. I ain't scared of you, live or dead!' It was a maniac shriek.

There was a trampling in the brush; and peering eagerly through the lower part of the bushes without raising his head or stirring a finger, the judge could see a pair of muddy farm boots only a few yards distant from him. But he reckoned from the boots' angle that the man was staring somewhat to his left, his rifle at the ready. The judge held his breath.

'Fate,' the frantic voice cried, 'it's all mine now, by law. You think you can scare me out of it by peeking in windows and rattling knobs? You can't take it with you, Fate!'

At that moment there occurred some slight noise in the woods off to the left, and perhaps some slight movement, too; Virgil heard and perhaps saw, or thought he saw, and swung in that direction, crouching, so that his back was fully turned upon the judge. Staring at the man's boot heels, the judge tensed himself for action.

'Fate,' the shriek came, 'you let me off, I'll let you off. Hell, I didn't start up the tractor; all I done was walk away after you got caught. Fate, I wouldn't of done that if you hadn't said you'd give the whole shebang to them Salvationers. I ain't scared to look at you in daylight — come on out and show your dirty old face. Come on out, now, or I'll give it to you in the belly!'

Nobody answered. The judge rose on hands and knees, most stealthily. Blood was streaming down his arm and his side.

After what seemed like an hour but must have been seconds, the shouting was resumed. 'What you after, Fate? You want what I took off you in the creek? All right — take it, then!'

Something must have been flung toward the grove of maples, for there was a faint clinking thud. Then came a second rustling of bushes — from that deer or coon or possum that had frightened Diane at the ford? 'And take this, Fate!' Pow! The rifle cracked again and again and again.

Rising desperately to his feet, the judge hurled himself through the bushes and rushed at Virgil's back. He made it. Flinging all his weight upon the man, he hit Virgil's spine with his knee and clamped his blood-dripping hands over Virgil's averted face. In a voice that seemed like someone else's, the judge roared, 'Got you, Virgil!'

The man collapsed, the judge tumbling upon him, and the rifle fell just beyond Virgil's head. The judge pounded Virgil's face against the earth, and then he poked the lunatic. 'Get up, Brownlee: I'm taking you to jail.'

Virgil did not stir. Another possum? The judge tore off his own necktie and bound Virgil's wrists behind his back; still no resistance. Virgil's hands felt cold. 'Get up, you brother-killer!'

No movement at all. The judge rolled the man over and ripped open his clothes: he could detect no heartbeat, no breathing. Virgil's unattractive face was close to his, and the fixed, open eyes were sightless. No possum! In his time the judge had seen many dead men, but all the others had borne wounds.

Buck Tuller's house stood less than half a mile distant, the judge contrived to recollect in his confusion, and he thought he might get there before fainting from loss of blood. He had clamped his handkerchief to ear and cheek. Ride Diane? No, he was in no shape to force her across the creek. He must foot it to Tuller's, even if already his legs quivered ominously under him.

Keeping his handkerchief pressed hard against his cheek and ear, he took three or four steps; and then his foot struck something. Part of it glittered. It was Fate's old steel-mouthed purse, lying among ferns: this was what Virgil had flung out as bait to the invisible. Virgil must have taken it from his brother trapped in the creek, perhaps while Fate still had clung to the willow branches and begged for life. The judge nudged the thing with his foot; coins clinked inside.

Let it lie, for the moment: if he bent over, giddiness might undo him. Let it lie, for more reasons than one. Two months before, at the Brownlee house, there had come upon him the sense of a hungry presence; that sense descended again upon him now, more powerful and more malign, and he enfeebled. Was he alone with one corpse and two dead things?

Did those woods creatures stir again at the edge of the field? Deer or raccoon, of course; keep telling yourself that, Titus Moreton: coon or deer. Let the purse lay where it had fallen.

Come on, Titus: you walked out of the jungle at Buna, with grenade-fragments in both arms, and even now you can walk as far as Tuller's. Walk as fast as you can, not showing fear. Pay no heed to that deer, or that coon, or whatever it may be, scrunching somewhere behind you. A bullet to the head can inflict hallucinations even upon a steady-nerved man. Don't look back: walk!

*   *

154

Buck's eldest son and Buck's wife drove the judge to the hospital, and Buck Tuller and his second boy took the panel truck and went after Virgil Brownlee's body. It was there, all right, cold stone dead, clad in the pair of overalls that Virgil had inherited from his brother. Then Buck and his boy searched the ferns and elsewhere for Fate's purse, the judge having said it was a piece of evidence. They did pick up the judge's binoculars, fallen when he was shot, but no purse. They looked until sundown, glancing over their shoulders often, but they could not find it. Buck gave up when his son's teeth began to chatter.

When, a fortnight later, the judge had mended sufficiently, Charlotte drove him out to the Brownlee place, and he poked through the scrub for two hours or more, kicking aside masses of fallen maple leaves. He was perfectly sure of the spot. Defying Ozymandia's commands and entreaties, he went down on his hands and knees, feeling all over for the purse. No luck. With the coins in it, the purse would have been too heavy and awkward for any squirrel to carry off. Yet the thing had been taken, and no pack rats live in Pottawattomie County.

Charlotte now had grown as skittish as Diane had been at the ford, glancing back and forth from the judge among the leaves to the house so silent and derelict. 'Give it up, silly,' she demanded, almost *sotto voce*. 'Is anybody in that house?'

The judge straightened up and joined her at the car. 'Ask me what songs the sirens sang, darling.'

'Who wants that old purse, anyway?'

'I won't speak his name here, Charlotte, if you'll excuse me. I suppose he had his heart's desire, and the iron in his soul withal.'

'You make me angry when you're so obscure, Titus.' She started up their car. 'Oh! What's that toward the creek?' She stepped hard on the gas, and the car bounced so over the ruts that the alert judge, his head craned backward, could make out nothing.

'Did you see anything, darling?'

'Not exactly.' Her hands trembled on the wheel.

'I suppose it was some obscure hungry thing, Ozymandia, needing an obol or two for Charon. It was a poor thing; let it fade.'

The Princess of All Lands

Your soul deserves the place to which it came
If having entered hell, you feel no flame.

Every roadside stand, as Yolande drove swiftly northward, still displayed its pumpkins, its bunches of Indian corn, its jugs of cider. This was the last day of October, the weather clear and warm for the season, here and there bonfires of leaves sending up their pungent offering to the powers of dissolution. Once the schools let out at half-past three, the children of the villages along this old highway would straggle home, witches and Indians and marauders, bags of Hallowe'en-party candy clutched in their fists.

Yolande had become twenty-eight years old on this day, suffused with love of life amidst the commemoration of death, the virtue stirring within her, on her way home to her little baby and her big husband and tonight's jack-o'-lantern party. There almost never being any police-car along this bypassed route, Yolande stepped on the gas: it was a long drive up from the quarterly commission meeting at the state capital.

At a rural intersection, a traffic-light halted her. A young girl, perhaps sixteen, was standing on the shoulder — no baggage, but clearly hitchhiking. Across the road was a hamburger-stand, a pickup truck parked in front of it; two burly men loitered there, looking speculatively at the girl. Not liking their faces, Yolande rolled down her window and called out to the girl, 'Going north?'

The hitchhiker bounded into Yolande's station-wagon. She was swar-

156

thy, rather plump, and apparently wore only a loose sweater, jeans, and tennis-shoes: not ugly, but hard-faced and well over sixteen, Yolande saw at close range — perhaps twenty. Yolande whizzed through the green light toward home, still more than a hundred miles distant.

'If you hadn't of picked me up,' the girl said, 'I'd of got in with them truckers. You know what they'd prob'ly done to me after a few miles?' She proceeded to a frank and graphic description, omitting no obscenities. 'Men!' she concluded. 'Rats are better'n men.'

'Some are different,' Yolande commented mildly. Really she shouldn't have invited this girl; yet perhaps she had been sent to her for some purpose, as often people had been sent to her before. Already she could perceive that this one required discreet management. 'Where are you bound?'

'Pompey Eye,' the girl muttered.

This peculiar place-name stirred some dim memory in Yolande. Armies rose — or rather, they hadn't risen — where Pompeius Magnus stamped his foot. Wasn't it Pompey, slain on an Egyptian beach, who had no tomb? Where had she heard of Pompey Eye? 'I've never been there; it's not on this road,' she told the girl. 'If you'll open the glove-compartment, you'll find a map.'

Unfolding the road-map, the girl pointed to a dot on a side road, at least seventeen miles to the west of this highway. Yolande slowed down to observe. 'Pompeii' read the map's small print. 'Does everybody there pronounce it Pompey Eye?' Yolande cautiously inquired.

'What else?' The girl snorted. 'Think they'd call it Las Vegas? It's a hick place with a gas station and a grocery store.'

'Do you live there?'

'Not now. I been comin' up from Florida to see my daddy; he's got a place by Pompey Eye. It's my daddy's birthday.'

This was encouraging. 'Oh, it's my birthday too,' Yolande exclaimed. 'That's why I'm in such a hurry. We'll have a Hallowe'en party and a birthday party all in one, and it's our baby's first birthday party.'

The girl stared at her fixedly — but Yolande was used to that. 'You're pretty. You married?'

'Yes, for seven years, but just one baby.'

'I never had no baby,' the girl remarked, less harshly than she had spoken before. 'Babies are cute. I got married when I was fourteen, but they put seven slugs into my husband's head next day, an' I never had no babies. I bet men go crazy 'bout you.'

'One is, and I'll have a party with him tonight. I'm so sorry about your husband. What happened, or would it hurt to tell?'

'I had plenty of trouble with men before an' after that.' The girl's mouth twisted. 'My brother, too. Don't like no man but my daddy.'

'You poor kid!' Yolande stretched out her arm, meaning to put it round the girl's shoulders; but she shrank away, saying, 'I don't need no help.'

This was a hard case, Yolande reflected, conceivably beyond redemption. She and her husband took in unwed mothers, people out of prison, and more difficult types than those, but there existed limits beyond which one wasted the virtue. Still, this girl might have been sent to her; she would try — which would not be facile, for she already felt some aversion to this companion.

'This is a richy car,' the girl was saying. 'You and your husband in the bucks?'

'We cast our bread upon the waters.' Yolande laughed. 'He's a kind of doctor.' The girl had not given her name, and probably didn't mean to; nor would Yolande, not yet; this was a little creature who preferred anonymity, doubtless with reasons.

'Docs are rich,' the girl declared. 'Your husband do abortions?'

'Never. You might call him a doctor of souls. He makes his money by being a psychoanalyst, but it's parapsychology that interests him. That's why, in the beginning, he paid attention to me.'

'Souls!' The girl snorted again. 'Then he's doctor o' nothin'. There ain't no souls. You ask my daddy.' Here she stopped herself, as if thinking better of what she had meant to add, and then volunteered merely, 'He's an Indian.'

This was a bond of sorts — perhaps an opportunity for breaking down the girl's wariness. 'Why,' Yolande cried cordially, 'I'm part Indian myself!'

The girl inspected her afresh. 'Yeah, I kin see that.' She was surveying Yolande's high cheekbones, her long black hair worn in braids, the flair of her nostrils. 'But you're more a half-breed than me.'

'My great-great grandfather was an Indian prophet and conjuror, they say, great in the Ghost Dance.'

'Hell, there ain't no ghosts. When you're dead, you're dead an' you rot, that's all.' The girl seemed much irritated. 'What'd we do if ghosts went dancin' round?'

Yolande went on little discouraged. 'And my grandmother was a famous medium. My husband says that virtue may skip every other generation, but nobody really knows about that. Maybe our baby won't have the virtue.'

'Virtue! You show me a man with virtue!'

'I could,' Yolande murmured, 'but it's not that sort of virtue I mean. I'm talking about virtue as an essence, a power, something that flows into you and out of you, letting you do acts that are good or evil. Remember — "Jesus, at once knowing that *virtue* had gone out of him, turned him about in the press, and said, 'Who touched my clothes?'" That's according to Saint Mark.'

This girl didn't remember. 'You a Jesus freak?'

'Not as you mean. But sometimes my husband and I can heal. He has the wisdom, I the virtue. Without him to control me, I might be dangerous.'

'You dangerous?' The girl chuckled joylessly. 'I bet you never stuck a knife in nobody.'

'Have you?'

'My ma, she don't live with my daddy no more. I stopped by to see her, though, couple o' years ago. She's livin' in Chicago with six niggers and a wetback, soused most days. I come friendly-like, but she calls me bad names, an' I tell her to stop, but she keeps on. So I run the bread-knife into her backside.'

Was this true? Anything might be true of this one: handle with care. 'What did your mother say to that?' Yolande asked, composedly. She wondered if the mother had survived. With this girl, it was well to show no emotion on your face.

'She falls down on the floor and says, "Daughter, I'm sorry." Oh, she was sorry, all right. I ain't been back to see her since. What's your ma like?'

'She died when I was twenty-one, before I married.'

'What'd she die of?'

'Mother had a weak heart, and an Indian scared her, and she died in my arms that night, my birthday night. But she was brave.'

'You live on a reservation?'

'No, but it was half-wild country.'

'You act like you owned it.'

'I suppose I thought I did — all of it, and more besides. I've had to watch my pride. When I was little, they had a nickname for me: "the Princess of All Lands." They halfway meant it, for they saw the virtue begin to come to me early; indeed, I suppose it was in me from the first.'

'You mean you was a kook when you was a baby?'

'If that's what you like to call it,' Yolande answered, unperturbed. 'For one thing, very early I could see things that other people couldn't. I had a friend that nobody else ever beheld. He had a name: Doctor Cady. Perhaps he told me that name, but I rather think I gave it to him. He used to visit me when I was playing with dolls behind the woodshed. He seemed very big and strong, and he had a red beard. Sometimes I could make him come if I wished strongly enough; other times he came without being asked. After I started going to church, I began to think he was my guardian angel — though who ever heard of an angel named Cady? How does the little prayer go?

'Angel of God, my guardian dear,
To whom God's love commits me here,
Ever this day be at my side
To rule and guard, to light and guide.

'After I was seven, I didn't see him, but I felt that he was near some-times; and I still think that he, or some presence, is near when the virtue stirs in me. Certain people might call Doctor Cady a "familiar," but I know he's something nicer than that.'

'Oh, yeah? You were some nutty kid.'

'Perhaps. Still, a curious episode happened when I was five, and after that my grandmother and father and mother half believed in Doctor Cady. It was behind the woodshed, as usual, and Doctor Cady had come to amuse a lonely little girl. Then a rattlesnake crawled out of the woodpile. There weren't many rattlesnakes where we lived, and we kept pigs to per-secute those few, but this one snake came squirming out. I squealed, and Doctor Cady picked up the snake by the tail and flung him into the weeds. The snake simply lay there. A little later I told Father about it, and he went to see, even though he chuckled about Doctor Cady. The snake still was there — dead, all *seared,* as if a million volts of electricity had gone through him.'

'I git a charge out o' you, lady.'

'So did the snake. But why not? Aren't we all really collections of par-ticles of electricity, positive and negative charges held together by Lord knows what law or power? We seem substantial flesh and blood, but aren't we all just energy, body and soul? And some few, very few, can direct the energy, sometimes. I'm a ghost in a machine: now don't be frightened.'

'You don't skeer me.'

'My husband says that if he hadn't taken me in hand after I was fourteen, someone might have put me into a travelling show and sent me round the country as the Beautiful Witch. Or in an earlier time, they would have burnt me. "I don't know whether you're a sport or a mutant," he tells me. I fascinate him in more ways than one. He doesn't laugh at Doctor Cady. My husband says that it's right enough to call me the Princess of All Lands, because I might take the kingdoms of the earth if I abused my virtue. It can be a power for good or a power for evil, a power for healing or a power for blasting. Is that what Joan of Arc had?'

'If you talk like that they'll lock you up, lady.'

'Why, I suppose they might have done so already, if my husband hadn't taught me to repress myself — never, or almost never, to fall into a bad temper. It's such a worry, the virtue in me.' Yolande swerved the car to avoid a dead dog, and then talked on.

'I know it sounds silly — the Princess of All Lands, with power over the quick and the dead. Yet Doctor Cady wasn't purely imaginary. I think it was he who first called me Princess, and I passed on the name, haughtily, to my family. Shall I tell you something even stranger? My husband looks just like Doctor Cady, as I remember my big friend behind the woodshed — and of course he's a doctor, too. But I met Doctor Cady long years before the doctor who's my husband found me. Is my husband really my guardian angel? Sometimes I suspect that; yet angels don't father children, they say. It's a world of mysteries, isn't it? Oh, I'd be a risk to everybody if my husband didn't keep me under his thumb, even though I don't really want the kingdoms of this earth.'

The girl only grunted; she mustn't bore her. Why was she telling all this to a girl who couldn't understand one syllable of the mysteries? Why, to keep her from launching again into all that obscene and horrid talk. How many miles to the Pompeii junction? Too many. Yolande's memory ran giddily back to those strange years of her childhood. She had been able to make plates fly off the mantelpiece, without visible cause; she had compelled the poker and the tongs to dance. Her grandmother the medium had been impressed but not amazed; her parents had been frightened for her.

The notoriety of the 'racketing spirit' which little Yolande could raise had filtered, vaguely, all the way to universities and special institutes. And the famous doctor had come from the south to the log house on Lake Superior to see the juvenile witch. He had found her intelligent, cheerful, dutiful, enthusiastic — qualities rare in such people as are supposed to possess occult powers, or to be possessed by them. Also he had found her lovely, even at fourteen, when first he visited her family. More wondrous things occurred in that big log house, and round about it, than ever had happened to the Wesleys at Epworth Rectory.

The great doctor from the Institute, with his red beard, had instructed her mother in how to deal with Yolande — how to discipline her without crushing her. The doctor himself advanced no dogmatic theories about her 'virtue' then; he still didn't.

Yolande had been so remarkable a case that the famous doctor himself had put up half the money for sending her to a boarding-school kept by an especial order of nuns. She had done well in that school, and had not permitted her virtue to get out of hand.

When she had finished at the convent school, the doctor had found the money for her to spend four years in Switzerland, at a very good college for foreign girls; also it had been near a Swiss clinic where she had been tested politely, and had been studied intensively — though to nobody's satisfaction. When she returned home, in her twentieth year, the doctor with the red beard had been mightily pleased to find that she continued 'normal' in outward behavior, and that she was lovelier than before. She had been taught a good deal at the Swiss school — deportment, and piano, and even academic disciplines — these last in rather an old-fashioned nineteenth century style, she perceived now. That had been all to the good in learning literature; fairly harmless in learning history; not so wise in learning the natural sciences, for they had tried to stuff into her a mechanism and a materialism which her own precocious experiences belied. The red-bearded doctor, anyway, had come to love her; and she had loved him long before that.

'Hey, you goin' to sleep at the wheel?' Yolande came out of her reverie.

This sulky child beside her must be diverted. It was weary work, trying to scour vessels for dishonor. This girl was empty; for a little while it had seemed as if she weren't even there in the car beside her.

'We're both part Indian,' said Yolande, 'so you won't mind if I tell you about a certain bad Indian.' The girl probably would relish this particular true narration, and there would be time enough for it before the Pompeii junction. Yolande skilfully passed two cars and then began to spin her grim tale.

*   *

'I was born in a log house, very old, on Lake Superior,' Yolande said. 'The building had been a trading-post in the early days, and my grandfather and great-grandfather on my father's side had run it, and others of our family before that, all the way back to the beginning of the eighteenth century. We had a farm, too. I don't know how much Indian I am — those French-Canadian ancestors of mine intermarried generation after generation. There's Irish in me, too. My father could speak the patois, but I can't.

'Indians still came, when I was a little girl, sometimes, a few of them, mostly looking for handouts.'

'That sounds like my daddy. He wanders round a lot.' The girl drew from the pocket of her jeans a glue-bottle, unscrewed the cap, and began sniffing it. 'My daddy, he says, "Daughter, don' you sniff that there glue more'n once a week." But he ain't around right now.'

It had been a blunder to have picked up this girl, Yolande knew now, and Pompeii junction still was miles ahead. The thing to do was to keep her entertained. Well, I can talk all day, scarcely drawing breath, Yolande reflected. The girl's eyes were dilating.

'There was one Indian we dreaded,' Yolande went on, still smoothly, 'and he seemed to come just every seventh year. Do you know, he came the day I was born! Ours was a lonely farmhouse, and this Indian wanted money for whisky. He claimed to be some sort of distant cousin. All that my father gave him was a meal. The doctor didn't arrive in time to deliver me, so my father and grandmother and Aunt Susan were busy bringing me into the world. They kept an old bull bitch as a watchdog, and they heard her howling, but they didn't have time right then to find out why. Afterward they came upon her in the woods, dead, beaten with a club and then stamped to death. Father thought that Indian "cousin" did it.'

'Sounds like my daddy,' said the girl. 'He don' like dogs.'

'On my seventh birthday,' Yolande went on, rather hurriedly, 'that very same Indian came back. I think I can remember him in the kitchen. He walked in a kind of crouch, like a wildcat about to spring, and he was singing or chanting half the time.

'"Turn that man out of here," said my grandmother, the Indian woman, in her blunt way. "Turn him out now." She was the medium I told you about. Father wasn't perfectly sure that this Indian "relative" had killed our dog, so he let him sleep in the barn, though not in the house, that Hallowe'en. Just before dawn, we smelled smoke: the barn was afire. It nearly caught the house. The Indian was gone.'

'Sounds like my daddy,' the girl repeated. 'He likes to burn things.'

'And do you know,' Yolande continued, 'the Indian returned on my *fourteenth* birthday, really? That's what people call coincidence, but I suspect there aren't any coincidences. Everything may be some power's design, for good or ill.

'Father met him in the yard, and I was with Father. The Indian looked me over slowly. "Honeybun," he said, and reached out to stroke my hair, but Father pulled me back. The Indian had a string of trout that he'd caught, and Father gave him a dollar and told him to clear out. We couldn't prove anything about the barn-burning seven years before.'

'Sounds like my daddy,' the girl interjected, grinning — two teeth were missing — "cause he's gone fishin' more of'en than not.'

'Uuummm.' Yolande compressed her lips. 'My father died that night, in terrible pain; we lived a long way from any doctor. Afterward they said it may have been food poisoning. He had eaten the four trout because the rest of us didn't think those fish looked especially fresh. My virtue couldn't help him, though I tried. Maybe it was an accident. He was a good father. The Indian cousin wasn't to be found anywhere.'

'My daddy traps,' said the girl, 'an' he knows how to make poisons o' deadly nightshade an' sech-like plants, to set for varmints.'

'What's your father's name?'

'Some places he takes one name, some places he uses other names. Me too.'

There is more than one type of Daddy in this world, Yolande reflected. 'But the very worst thing,' she ran on, 'was on my twenty-first birthday, cross my heart and hope to die. Many things had happened during those seven intervening years. The "virtue" — that's what we ordinarily call it, for lack of a better word — grew stronger in me not long after Father died, and I began to play silly games with it. I could even make little flames appear in the middle of carpets — and they burned real holes. Already I had more virtue than ever my grandmother the medium had possessed.'

'You're kooky, real kooky,' said the girl, ferociously.

At her tone, Yolande started — though not noticeably, she hoped. For some reason she dreaded this girl, and not because of the glue-bottle and the dilated pupils only. Dogs could smell the human fear-scent; conceivably this girl, so close to the beast-realm, might have detected Yolande's disquiet if it hadn't been for the glue. She *must* keep on talking.

'Well, on my twenty-first birthday I was alone in the old house with Mother, and we went to bed, and about three in the morning Mother heard a noise downstairs, and then more noises — though I slept on for a time, because I'd run up and down the lake shore half that week, from joy of being home from Switzerland.

'What Mother had heard had been somebody throwing things around and stirring the fire in the fireplace. We were quite alone in the house, remember. Without waking me, Mother took the shotgun from the rack and tiptoed down the stairs.

'She found that same sinister Indian! He was drunk, and had forced open a window to get in, and was tossing more logs on the fire, making himself at home. Mother pointed the gun at him and asked what he wanted; I heard voices and came downstairs too.

'"Honeybun!" he grunted when he saw me in my nightgown, and just stood there, leering at me. But Mother told him to get out, the shotgun trembling in her hands; and he must have known that a gun is more dangerous than ever if it's held by a woman who doesn't really know how to use it — and has a finger on the trigger. So he went back out the window, and Mother contrived to lock and barricade it behind him, and we didn't see him after.

'"Oh, Mother!" I told her, holding her in my arms when she slipped to the floor, "why didn't you wake me? I could have managed him without the gun."

'"Yes, dear," she said faintly, trying to smile, "but that virtue of yours might have set the whole house ablaze. And I'd rather not meet your Doctor Cady."'

Yolande paused and then resumed. 'Sometimes I think that Indian is our family Azrael, separating body and soul. Doesn't anyone else ever see him? I can't get him out of my head: he swaying in the firelight, gabbling something or other, humming a tune while Mother threatened him, then dropping out the window without a sound. Even if the sheriff had caught him, I don't suppose he could have been charged with anything worse than unlawful entry.' Yolande stepped on the gas.

'It was too much for Mother: she'd suffered two heart-attacks earlier that year. We had a telephone, but the line had been cut, and I didn't dare leave Mother to go for the doctor. She collapsed on the parlor sofa. Toward morning I couldn't feel any pulse. She was buried beside Father and Grandmother and Aunt Susan in St. Anne's graveyard. What that Indian had wanted, I don't know: perhaps he was simply after food and liquor, but Mother thought he was after me.'

'Sounds like my daddy,' said the girl. 'He likes women. Two or three times they put him in jail for it, but they couldn't keep him.'

'A few days after the funeral,' Yolande concluded, trying to ignore two tears rolling down her cheeks, 'the red-bearded doctor from the Institute asked me to marry him. He was old enough to be my father, but I loved him the more for that. We've kept the old log house, and our dear baby will love it as she grows up. Our marriage has everything. We work together, and he knows how to direct the virtue so far as anybody knows. He's not afraid of me at all.'

'Yeah?' the girl said. She was growing restive.

But deliverance was at hand. Just ahead, a narrow gravel road joined the highway on the left, and the metal sign said, 'Pompeii 17 mi.'

Yolande slowed down. 'Here you are,' she announced. 'I'm sure you can get another ride soon. I've got to get home just as quickly as I can, because the woman who minds the baby has to leave by suppertime.' This was not precisely true, but Yolande had come to loathe the girl beside her — without knowing quite why.

'But I'm goin' to Pompey Eye,' the girl told her, ominously.

'I'd take you there if I possibly could,' Yolande said, still contriving to smile, 'but I simply haven't time. There'll be other cars. . . .'

'I'm goin' to Pompey Eye,' the girl repeated. She pulled up her sweater and pulled down the waistband of her jeans. From the region of her groin protruded an efficient-looking pistol.

Yolande hesitated. Then, without changing expression, she swung the station-wagon westward toward Pompeii.

*   *

This Pompeii road being rough and tortuous, Yolande had some excuse for driving slowly. The girl did not appear to notice the slackening of speed, for now she was dominating the conversation.

Yolande had surmised that directness would be best. 'Why are you carrying that gun?' she had asked.

'It's a present for my daddy: he likes to shoot things up. Anyways, I carry a gun most o' the time. Never know when you might want it. One time I git a ride in a truck with this here wise guy, an' he starts pawin' me. I warn him off, but he don' stop, so's I pull this baby an' shoot him in the leg.'

'Didn't they arrest you for that?' Yolande kept her eyes fixed on the winding road.

'Naw, it was after sundown at the edge o' a little burg, an' prob'ly, if anybody hears, they think it's a backfire. Anyways, he warn't hurt all that bad.

'"Git out, you!" I says to him, an' I shove over an' take the wheel while he's limpin' out o' the cab.

'"You gonna ditch me here bleedin' like a pig?" this wise guy says. I don' say nothin', but drive roun' the block an' come back to him again; nobody ain't turned up.

'"Git back in an' drive!" I tell him.

'"But I'm shot!" he says to me.

'"You kin still drive," I says. So I make him drive me ten more miles, all bleedin', till we get to a big town, an' then I git out an' run for it. He's pretty weak by then. Maybe he didn't report nothin'. Prob'ly he was in some racket an' didn't want nobody fussin' with his load. Men!'

She took another whiff of the glue-bottle, and then launched into renewed discourse concerning the iniquities of the opposite sex. Down to this girl, dull-witted and unschooled, somehow there had drifted the slogans and liberation-chic of bored bourgeois Women's Lib zealots, Yolande guessed; and in this girl those grudges were stoked by deeper resentments. What was the quip about modern society that Yolande had read somewhere? 'Like German beer — dregs at the bottom, scum at the top.'

The girl had not exhibited her pistol again: a thin pretense of amiability was maintained. But the girl's eyes were altogether wild now. This was a neglected road, only two or three farmhouses set back some rods, and those looking derelict. Yolande was terrified for the two of them, the girl and herself; most of all she feared for her baby and her husband, who might not see her again. Powers of darkness roam the world, she had read, seeking whom they may devour. Why should she be given to such?

Was there a purpose in all this? Could she be meant somehow to rescue this girl and her father and her brother, as she had helped others? Had she virtue sufficient for that task? To outward appearance unmoved, Yolande tried hard to dredge up from her retentive memory the echoes of that place-name Pompeii — Pompey Eye. What had she heard about it? Last days? Bulwer-Lytton? Golden House of Nero? Grottoes? No, something fairly recent and quite nasty in this particular word-association. Three swamp folk and Pompey Eye . . .

There came to Yolande, as the girl maundered on, one of her waking visions. She perceived in her mind's eye, in all detail, a place in the woods: dead elm trees, birches, a sprawling bog, in the foreground a shallow excavation. Yes, it was a grave. A spade was thrust into a heap of fresh wet soil. Was this a vision of what had been or of what was to be? The virtue did not tell her that. And now, from a distance, something limp and heavy was being carried toward the hole. Two men bore it. She could see them laboring between the naked trees and among the leafless shrubs, and she shivered.

Then everything fell into place, within her mind, and there came to her the memory for which she had been questing. Pompeii! She had evoked the name's associations, more horrid than any volcano. What had occurred at Pompeii, this little Pompeii, only last year — why, it had been in all the newspapers, though she did not read of such crimes more than she had to.

Her waking vision passed away, mercifully, and now Yolande knew; she knew what her peculiar perceptions had been trying to tell her ever since the girl entered the car; she knew what the girl was. Such an experience would be put upon the Princess of All Lands and none other. Yolande's loathing of this gabbling girl swelled even more monstrous than before. Without the virtue, she would have fainted then and there.

Nothing could be done for this girl: too late, irrevocably late. Then why had this trial been inflicted upon her, Yolande? Was she a pawn to be sacrificed in a game between Light and Darkness?

One conceivable sanctuary remained, before worst should come to worst: the village of Pompeii itself. There would be no dishonor in flight from this encounter. If she should brake the car abruptly in the main street and leap out, would the girl fire? And would she be vulnerable to the girl's bullets? There was no telling, in this debatable realm between quick and dead. If there should be many people in the street, or a policeman, she might chance it.

Slowly they drove into Pompeii, Pompey Eye. A filling station. 'I'll pull in here to gas up,' Yolande said, hoping her voice did not quaver overmuch.

The girl glanced at the fuel gauge. 'You don't need none yet,' she declared, 'an' anyways this here station's shut.' So it was. Pompeii was a shrinking hamlet, with no suggestion of Roman pleasures except the name itself. An old man and an older woman were the only folk on the short street: no help. But there was a grocery store — still open, for the old woman hobbled into it.

'Let's see if there's a cake for your father's birthday,' Yolande suggested timorously. 'Let me buy it.'

'My daddy don' eat no cake; what he wants is booze, an' they don' sell none o' that in Pompey Eye. Keep goin'.'

How far this lost girl's power might extend over her, here in this shadowy village of Pompeii, between two realms of being, Yolande could not tell. If sacrificing herself had offered salvation to someone, she might have tested that gun's power, or even gone on to the end of this journey for the final contest; but already the battle had been fought, so that her own destruction could not alter the judgment upon this girl. Even had it been otherwise, her duty lay with her husband and baby, not with the vessel for dishonor in the station-wagon beside her.

She would flee if the odds for survival seemed tolerable. 'Does your father live on a side street?' At the last moment, Yolande might abandon the car, run for it, seek shelter in some neighbor's house.

'Nope, his place is a piece out in the woods. Keep goin'; I'll show you where.'

That forlorn hope abandoned, Yolande obeyed in silence. She felt the weight of some invisible domination or power, not to be resisted. They turned from the narrow county road into a mere track, doubtless a lumberman's trail once. The second-growth forest closed round them. This was swamp-country, altogether desolate. And the farther they drove, groaning along ruts and through potholes, the more aggressive the girl grew — sure of her prey now.

'My brother'll be there too. He ain't bright, but he kin drink as much as my daddy. They beat each other up once a week or so. Daddy an' Brother'll like you a lot, 'cause you're gorgeous. You gotta come in an' meet 'em.'

It was like being invited to meet Grendel's mother, Yolande told herself. Could this girl's lost heart be touched at all? 'My baby will be crying for me, and my husband won't know what's happened to me,' she entreated. 'Can't I let you out here? I could turn around in that old clearing. You like babies — you told me you did.'

It might have been better for herself, Yolande thought in this moment, had she grown up less beautiful. There exist depraved natures, perhaps more numerous in this age than in other times, which pull the wings off butterflies and burn cats alive: they lie in wait for the innocent endowed with the fatal gift. Yet even such, if sometimes ones strikes the right chord in them at the right hour, may be dissuaded, God willing.

For a fraction of a second the girl's heavy face softened — and then soured. She pulled the gun out of her jeans. 'Keep goin', I told you. You're jest like the other woman we fetched here. I'm bringin' my daddy two birthday presents, this gun an' you. Daddy's goin' to have lots o' fun with you, an' my brother, too.' She sniffed her glue vigorously.

Yolande fought down an anger that would have been devastating. 'Wouldn't you rather have money than me? There's only a few dollars in my purse, but my husband . . .'

'Yeah, that's what the other woman said. We got both of 'em, the money, the woman.'

'Where is she now?'

The girl snarled like a brute, her broken teeth showing, and thrust the gun against Yolande's middle. 'Don' you ask no more questions! Ain't I told you there ain't no ghosts?'

Still the station-wagon lumbered along that trail, crunching over fallen limbs now and again; once, holding the gun on her, the girl compelled Yolande to get out of the car and drag the rotten trunk of a birch-tree from the faint track. Red-winged blackbirds, gathering in these marshes for southward flight, flapped up alarmed at the car's passage.

'You don't know what you're getting into,' Yolande ventured, gun or no gun. 'You're not clever enough to carry this off. The sheriff would trace us and . . .'

The girl poked her with the gun again, and shook her head complacently. 'Don' nobody know where you turned off the highway; don' nobody know where my daddy lives; don' nobody know we got you; don' nobody never come here till deer season. You ain't gonna be here then. Sheriff!' She spat on the floor of the car.

'There's something else,' Yolande insisted. 'I wish this cup would pass from me. But we're both in danger — you, too. And your danger is worse than my danger.'

'If you'd seed what happened to the other one, "Princess," you'd know there ain't no danger worsen your danger. She didn't do like she was tolt.'

Whatever the peril, Yolande must make a final attempt upon the girl's feelings. 'I think a devil has got inside you,' Yolande began, 'and he's eaten up nearly all of you. But if there's anything left to save, let me try to help. Let me touch you. . . .'

The girl jerked back and jammed the pistol into Yolande's belly. Yet for an instant, something intelligent had gleamed in the girl's eyes, perhaps some fragment of dreadful memory — as if the terror of her condition had been apprehended ever so briefly, and then blotted out. She cursed Yolande foully and at length. 'Keep on drivin'!'

The station-wagon came to the wreck of a wooden bridge, the planks of its floor carried off by some flood. 'Take the car down alongside,' the girl directed, 'an' head downstream.'

Yolande stared at her: 'You'd drown both of us?'

'You'll see. Gravel bed, an' shallow, an' only a hun'erd yards to go. Then swing left.'

Sure enough, the creek-bed, though broad, carried merely a trickle of water: just enough to efface the station-wagon's tracks. A front wheel went into a hole, but Yolande gunned the motor, and in second gear the car came out. Now on the left was a gently sloping gravel bank, a space between two oaks; after considerable twisting of the wheel and gunning, Yolande thrust the station-wagon up that bank, through bushes, to a sort of prairie.

'Not bad drivin',' the girl commented. 'Knew you could do it, 'cause we take the truck through. Who'd track a car here?'

So here Yolande was at the end of the world. When a little girl, she would have loved this secret place; now she was meant to be buried here.

Beware, beware the Bight of Benin:
Few come out though many go in.

That other woman had passed this way, not to emerge in this life.

On they drove, bumping across the vestige of a forty-acre field, young poplars overgrowing most of it. Beyond the far boundary, marked by a ragged stump fence, commenced a northern swamp-jungle, seemingly impenetrable. This must be some hardscrabble homestead abandoned decades ago, never truly fit for cultivation, now the lair of squatter predators.

Yolande made out the cabin and some tottering sheds, sepulchral as twilight settled upon them. 'Daddy'll git the surprise o' his life!' the girl was whooping. At her order, Yolande switched off the ignition at the dooryard.

The cabin's door hung crazily by one hinge. The windows were smashed. Bottles and tin cans littered the dooryard. A battered farm truck, looking inoperable, stood in front of what appeared to have been the entrance to a root-cellar. There was no sound: dead, dead, dead, death everywhere.

'Blow the horn!' Yolande obeyed energetically, for the blast of noise would be relief from this ghastly stillness. And as she pushed the horn-disc, extremity roused the virtue in her. What were those lines about the dastard who feared to draw the sword before he blew the horn? She felt the blood pour flaming into her pallid cheeks.

Two men slouched out of the cabin doorway. The first was gross and filthy, perhaps a little older than herself, his eyes dull slits. The second man, with a long knife in his belt — why, he was the Indian who had killed the dog, burned the barn, poisoned her father, put an end to her mother: that seven-year Indian, her animated jack-o'-lantern, waiting here for their birthday party on Hallowe'en. Hadn't she foreseen this culmination all along, though burying the hideous concatenation below the level of her consciousness?

*   *

'Daddy, Daddy, I'm home, and look what I brung you for your birthday! A real lady, better'n the other 'un!' The girl prodded Yolande out of the car.

Daddy, Daddy the Seven-Year Indian, gaped incredulous at Yolande. 'I know this one!' he shouted. 'Honeybun, I seed you in your nightie las' time, an' I been thinkin' o' you ever since.'

Be calm and cold, Yolande told herself sternly. Stepping from the station-wagon, she almost turned her ankle upon a little heap at the edge of the dooryard, beside a stray conglomerate boulder. Glancing down instinctively, she saw what the little heap consisted of: empty shotgun shells. It was as if — she had an instant vision of this, too — someone had lain half-protected behind this tall boulder, firing round after round at the cabin, furiously.

Averting her eyes from the men's stares, she paused at the front of the station-wagon and surveyed in a sweeping glance the panorama of ruin. The cabin door appeared to have been blasted from its heavy hinges; the whole face of the log cabin was splintered and pocked from gunfire; the window-frames had been shot away; there were bullet-holes, many of them, in the hood of the truck. There had occurred such a barrage as soldiers called a 'mad moment.' So her memory of the shocking Pompeii item in the newspapers had not played her false. Vengeance had been wreaked in this place.

Now she met the Indian's look, eye to eye. Daddy's glare was wilder even than his daughter's, but this catlike man was no dull thing. He was animated by a kind of skipping devilish gaiety, clapping his hands and crooning as he studied his prize. He was mad only west-northwest, Yolande perceived, malignly clever after his fashion, totally corrupt. There may have been in him, once, virtue of a sort: 'If thy light be darkness . . .' It was nearly extinguished now, but for years this one had worked complex mischief for mischief's sake.

Once he must have been handsome, too. And then it came to Yolande that his features were a caricature of her own. Had his claim to cousinship been true? She shuddered. Was this one also descended from the savage conjuror of the Ghost Dance? Was he her own reflection in a distorting glass?

When their eyes met, there passed between these two some impalpable understanding — between damned and blessed, brute and victim — striking both as if it were a physical blow, deep crying unto deep. 'Hell,' the Indian screeched, 'you're jest like me!'

What remote ancestral blood, what vestige of forgotten powers, what concatenation of the immortals, what chain of fatality, linked him and her? Yolande stood unmoving, struck silent by this final confrontation. This one, somehow akin to her, had marked her family for destruction, and at this last she had been brought to him.

The Indian, too, stood there openmouthed, some sense of the marvel in this breaking upon him. But round him capered the girl: 'Ain't you pleased! Daddy, ain't you pleased?'

He spoke. 'Yes,' said Daddy, slowly, gloatingly, 'I'm pleased you fetched this one. How'd you happen on her? You fetched a real lady: she's all growed up an' ready for harvest. She's the last one of 'em left. We'll take our time with her. Cousin, set down over there.'

He gestured toward a crumbling rustic wooden slat-chair with a high back, to one side of the cabin, and Yolande sank into it. Two or three feet from this chair was a picnic-table bench, with 'Property of County Park System' stencilled upon it; Yolande clutched at every insignificant detail of ordinary reality, that she might not slide into the realm of her captors. Daddy, Brother, and the girl seated themselves in a jack-o'-lantern row on the nearer split-log bench of the picnic-table, facing her directly.

Brother spoke slurringly: 'A real looker! You brung a real looker, Sis.' He pulled a bottle from his overalls and drank deeply.

'An' she's married to a rich doc,' the girl exulted. 'This time the fun really pays off.'

'Let's us have a purty good talk before the party starts,' Daddy said. 'Didn't never think I'd get you right here, Cousin Honeybun.'

'First we send the doc his wife's clothes,' Brother suggested.

'While we keep her, we'll keep her in the root-cellar,' Daddy decided. He snatched the bottle from Brother and finished it. Then he began to chant something tipsily, in mingled corrupt English and corrupt patois. All that Yolande could make out was the refrain, 'But I don' care!'

'She says she's a princess, Daddy,' the girl was crying. 'Is she richy! They call her the Princess o' All Lands!'

'Like the other time,' Brother grunted, 'if he don' pay up right after gittin' her clothes, then we send him a piece o' *her*.'

In the setting sun, Yolande's three captors rocked with mirth on their bench. Yolande, in that parting light, could see her own shadow but not theirs. Woods and swamp cribbed them, as if the whole derelict clearing were a grave. There was no place to flee, unless toward the swamp at her back; and they would catch her easily, should she try.

'She don' seem as much skeered as she might, but still she's awful skeered,' Daddy observed to son and daughter, as if Yolande already were only an unheeding lump of flesh. 'I scairt her ma to death.' His keen eyes may have detected the high flush on Yolande's cheeks; or some surviving sense within the man, akin to hers, might have perceived the virtue churning within her. For all his bravado, the Indian shifted on the bench, not wholly at ease, hesitating to strike.

Now Yolande spoke to these three damned ones. 'I don't know why it was permitted to fetch me here,' she said very distinctly, her chin held high, 'but possibly it's not too late for you to let me go.' A welling of last-minute pity for even these three swept through her. 'Perhaps you still have the choice: that may be why I was given to you — to offer you a last chance for mercy.'

'Lissen to the lady talk!' Brother crowed. 'Jest lissen to her! Real lady, all right, all right, but she won't be for long. Mercy! We'll titch her tricks that ain't so ladylike.'

'We kin sell her car for plenty, Daddy,' the girl put in. 'It's 'most new.'

As yet they had not tried to touch her, perhaps savoring this piquant interval before the violence, waiting for her to scream and beg, and then mastering her altogether. Yolande was resolved not to beg or scream. Or possibly her great black eyes held them off for the moment, and her strange erect dignity, sitting there before them as if invulnerable.

The Indian had ceased to laugh and croon. He was regarding Yolande intently, even soberly, as if pondering something. Clearly the son and the daughter were little more than emanations from the wizard-father, Yolande now understood. The virtue which once had flowed within this being, through labyrinthine dark channels, malignant and destructive, must not be wholly extinguished even in this terminal and phantasmal state of the Indian. What other power still could force these simulacra of mortality to cohere, after catastrophe had visited them?

Might it be that this obscene creature's vestigial consciousness misgave him, in awareness of the virtue pent within Yolande? The Indian shook himself in a feline way; then he leaped upon the picnic-table, flung himself into the air, bounded, pranced, emitted a falsetto wail, contorted his face, shivered and swayed rhythmically. It was the frenetic Ghost Dance of long ago, meant to raise the valiant from the dust. Looking upon this evocation of vanished slaughter, Yolande knew absolutely that the fierce old prophet-conjuror's blood and virtue must run in this human horror and in herself, both.

Abruptly as he had begun his dance, the Indian ceased. Poised upon the table, his unease brushed away, he directed a long finger toward Yolande: 'You was brung here for fun and money, Honeybun. I been after your people since you was born, an' now'll be the best time o' all. You an' me, we're akin, an' I'm goin' to make you know it in all the ways!' He slid supplely back from table to bench, snakelike. 'Go on, Honeybun, talk if you want to: you got a few minutes left.'

Were she to faint now, Yolande dreaded, she would fall into their antagonist world of madness, despair, and unavailing sorrow, everything lost. They awaited her first show of weakness. If they should spring, what would or could they do to her, on this their blood-soaked territory, on this particular immemorial evening, in this moment out of time? Would they wreak upon her everything they had done to the other woman? She did not know. She could not guess what powers were permitted them. For what they were, they retained amazing substantiality.

Yolande spoke a second time: 'There are demons in all three of you, but is there anything else? Must I do what I can?'

Captors and captive sat silent for a full minute, as if in stalemate. First the girl, with a kind of puzzlement, looked away from Yolande; then Brother's eyes shifted; finally Daddy ceased to stare balefully and fingered the hilt of his sheath-knife. They had not expected this resolute confrontation; it must have been quite otherwise with the other woman. Yolande had done to them, for the moment, what one may do with dogs, through the overweening authority of the confident eye.

The tension grew; that minute seemed forever. And the vehement virtue, so long held in check, began to engulf Yolande.

They were waiting for her to leap up and run for the swamp, Yolande sensed: then they would saunter chuckling after her, catch her knee-deep in slime, her back turned to them; tear at her clothes, begin the long torment. . . .

The hysterical girl snapped the tension. 'Daddy,' she was squealing, 'take her! Go on, Daddy, take her! I brung her for your birthday — grab her now!'

Still avoiding Yolande's eyes, the two men began to get up from the bench, heavily, as if some cautionary instinct impeded them. A second more and their hands would be upon her, which Yolande could not bear.

'I must do this!' Yolande cried to them. 'Don't you know you're dead? Don't you know you've all been dead for a year? The sheriff tracked you after you took that other woman, and you shot at them out of the cabin, so the sheriff's men blew you all apart. Why are you clinging here, you poor ghosts?'

In those three faces Yolande saw a fury and a ravaging doubt such as she never had glimpsed before. Risen from the bench, the three lost ones wavered before her, hands clutching at nothingness.

'Old friend, help me now!' the Princess of All Lands prayed aloud. She raised her arms in desperate supplication.

At once some consuming burst of energy swept round the four of them, a billowing airless wind, crackling and popping, fire without light. At the core of this field of force, the Indian screamed inhumanly, 'Who's come? Who's come?' For the most infinite fragment of consciousness, Yolande fancied that she glimpsed a tall fifth figure, black against greater blackness.

Then the Princess of All Lands uttered the ancient formula, shouting into the abyss: '*Go ye cursed into the fire everlasting, which is prepared for the devil and his angels!*'

Before her the three of them writhed, speechless in agony, seared, incandescent, disintegrating. Then, the virtue ebbing out of her, Yolande fainted in her chair.

*　　*

She did not know how many hours had elapsed before the cold roused her. She was slumped in the rude chair, quite alone, the moon illuminating cabin and clearing. Weak though she felt, she was able to rise.

She must be away from this place, driving through the night. Husband and baby calling her, enough virtue remained to her for that.

She compelled herself to look at the picnic-table, even running her fingers over the planks. Nothing was to be seen upon it, nor upon the ground beneath. But an odor of burning hung about it, and here and there the wood was charred. By the virtue that was given her, she had effaced the shadow of perfect evil, lest it cling longer and descend upon others.

Only her husband could believe her; she would tell him only. Despite the frightfulness of the place, Yolande knelt in the withered grass of autumn to pray that this cup might not be thrust upon her again.

Rising, she started at something bulky which scurried into the root-cellar. But it was only a raccoon or an opossum, she knew certainly. For such was her virtue, when retributive, that whatever it dispersed in fractured atoms could not trouble time and place ever after.

Sorworth Place

But the age of chivalry is gone. . . . The unbought grace of life, the cheap defence of nations, the nurse of manly sentiment and heroic enterprise is gone. It is gone, that sensibility of principle, that chastity of honor, which felt a stain like a wound, which inspired courage whilst it mitigated ferocity, which ennobled whatever it touched, and under which vice itself lost half its evil, by losing all its grossness.

Edmund Burke
Reflections on the Revolution in France

In defiance of a faint ancient charm that perfumes its name, Sorworth today is a dirty and dreary little town, fouled by the colliery since the pit was sunk and a blot of hideous industrial workers' houses began to spread about it. The lanes are half derelict, now that the pit approaches exhaustion. At a turn of the High Street, or down close off the Back Vennel, some fragments of old Scots masonry stand yet amidst a welter of hoardings and 'fish restaurants' and corrugated iron roofing.

To damp Sorworth, of all places, Mr. Ralph Bain, M.C., had contrived to drift at the end of a month of purposeless nights in 'family and commercial' hotels or bare village taverns across three counties. Drinks with strangers in one village, listless games of cards in the next town, inconsequential talks on buses or trains, dull glimpses of a pleasant wood there, an old church here: thus February had run out, and the next little pension check would be forwarded to him at Sorworth, which spot he had chosen at random as his address for the first few days of March.

Bain lounged by the door of The King's Arms in his old tweeds (with the cigarette-burns neatly darned) and felt the crack in his skull more vexatious than usual, and shifted his long legs languidly. Sorworth had nothing to show him. But what place had? He lit a cigarette, though he already had smoked three more this morning than he once resolved to allow himself out of the indispensable pension check.

At that moment, a girl came out of a provision shop across the square, walking obliquely past the market-cross in the direction of The King's Arms; and Bain, one hand cupped to shelter his match, his face inclined slightly downward, noticed the remarkable grace of her little feet. He glanced lazily up; then he threw away his match, let his cigarette go unlit, and instinctively straightened. He had not seen this lady before, but in that second it passed through his mind, whimsically, 'Perhaps she's what drew me to Sorworth.'

Surely a man might travel a great way without meeting such a face as hers — pale, very pale, with lips a glowing natural red, and black hair gathered with taste at the back of her head into a heavy roll that rested upon her firm shoulders. Her chin, too, was delicately firm. She carried herself with a dignity that seems to be dying from modern life, looking straight ahead, as if in some reverie that walled her away from the grossness of Sorworth — yet not (Bain judged from her mouth) a reverie wholly pleasant. Among the mill girls and shop-assistants and bedraggled housewives in Sorworth, there was none anything like her; and few anywhere else. As she passed by The King's Arms, she seemed to notice Bain; their eyes met, briefly; then she lowered her lashes, unsmiling, and was gone up the Vennel.

'Och, she's a bonnie one. Mrs. Lurlin.' Happening to come to the door as the girl passed by, old MacLeod, who kept The King's Arms, had followed Bain's long look. 'There wullna be her like for aye, Mr. Bain — not at auld Sorworth Place.' MacLeod shook his head portentously. In his youth he had been a gardener at some house of Lord Bute's, and he continued to hold the county families in profound respect, muttering sourly about Communists among the miners who drank in his bar.

'She's young to have the care of a big house,' said Bain, relapsed into lethargy, and lighting his cigarette at last.

'Aye, and wee tae be widowed, sir. Noo the hoose — she canna hope tae keep it in the auld way, ye ken. Twa maids, and they carlines fu' o' girnings, sir: sma' comfort in a cauld hoose that na sae canny, when a's said. It will be rack and ruin, forbye, wi' half the grand hooses in the county.' And MacLeod proceeded to expatiate on his favorite topics, the decay of old families and the follies of socialism.

'A widow?' put in Bain, lifting his heavy eyelids a bit. 'She couldn't have been married a great while. What was this Lurlin like?'

'Be wha' he was, sir, the gentleman's dead, dead the year noo, Mr. Bain; and sma' gude claverin' o' men in the grave.' That said, MacLeod turned back into his pub; but Bain, surprised at this reticence in a publican who ordinarily manifested a full share of Scottish censoriousness, followed him.

'He didn't die in the war?' inquired Bain.

'Na, na,' said MacLeod, thus brought to bay; and, presently, 'The drink, sir, the drink; that, and mair. Dinna mistake me, Mr. Bain. The Lurlins were braw auld blude; aye, but this Mr. Alastair Lurlin, he wasna o' the proper line, ye ken — na mair than a cousin. Mr. Hamish Lurlin, the auld laird, died seven years syne, and his twa sons were shot in Libya, first Alexander, then Hew. A' three death duties maun be paid, and the cousin comes tae wha's left. Last year, this Mr. Alastair dies; mair duties. Weel, Mrs. Lurlin keeps the hoose, and the policies, and a bit moor besides. Ninety thousand acres Lurlin o' Sorworth had, before the first war. Noo, but a hoose wha's unco cauld and clammy. Come awa' upstairs, sir, if ye be sae fascinated' — this a trifle spitefully — 'and ye can see the auld Place frae the attic, if ye ha' gude een.'

From a garret window of The King's Arms, they looked over the pantiles and corrugated iron roofs of the shabby town toward a serrate ridge some miles westward. On a flank of that hill, Bain just could make out the gray shape of a big ancient house, wraithlike against the heather and gorse and bracken. 'There'll be nane aulder in the county,' said MacLeod.

Bain went down alone to the parlor, sat some minutes before the doddering fire, and then addressed a note to Mrs. Lurlin, Sorworth Place. He was, he wrote truthfully enough, rather a dilettante in architecture; recently he had heard her house spoken of as remarkable; he would be glad to see it, if no inconvenience would be caused; and he would be in Sorworth the rest of the week. After some hesitation, he signed himself 'M.C.': the Military Cross, after all, was one of his few remaining links with decent society, and he had the right to use it.

This letter posted, he went up to his room, brushed his old tweed suit, and glanced at himself in the mirror: the heavy eyes, the long and regular features weakened by lines of indecision, the defiant half-grin of bravado. He grimaced, and the suture in the back of his head — a memento of the shell fragment that had given him his pension — winced in sympathy. To escape from self-dislike, he went down to the bar, very like fleeing from the cell into the jailyard.

*   *

Late the next afternoon an answer to his note came, written in a small round hand, which said that Mr. Bain would be shown about Sorworth Place if he should call on Thursday afternoon, and was signed 'Ann Lurlin.' The firm signature put Bain in mind of Mrs. Lurlin's elegant pale look; and he spent most of the intervening evening and night and morning in a reverie of nearly forgotten faces, men he had alienated by his negligence or his improvidence, women he had found hollow or who had found him exasperating. None of these ever thought of him now, even when dreaming before the fire. And why should they?

Shortly past noon on Thursday, he walked along an empty road toward the ridge called Sorworth Law; the road became a lane between high and crumbling stone dykes; and then he was at the entrance to a neglected park on the side of a hill, its gates vanished, its gatelodge empty, all its larger trees felled by some timber merchant and the stumps left among heaps of dead leaves. Bain turned up the drive, and soon he could see, on the bare slope above, the massive stone shape of the Place of Sorworth.

Two square towers, at either end; and between them, extending also far to the rear, an immense block of building, in part ashlar, but mostly rubble. None of this, except a fine large window above the entrance, was later than the seventeenth century, and most was far older. An intricacy of crowstepped gables, turrets, dormers, and chimneys confused one's eyes when they roved upward. All in all, the Place was an admirable example of the Scots mansion house unprettified by Balmoralism. A flight of heavy stone steps led up to the door, and on either side of the entrance projected a conical-capped turret, each supported at its base by an enormous corbel, curiously bevelled.

Some rods to the north could be made out to be what was left of a detached building, the roof of it gone — a chapel, perhaps. So far as Bain could see, there were only two entrances: the grand portal, and a small heavy door with a wrought-iron grille before it, that probably gave upon the kitchen. At the angles of either tower, musket-holes or arrow-loops, some blocked with mortar, the rest now closed with small panes of glass, flanked the entrance. The roofs were of ancient stone slabs.

Away at the back, the stout dykes of a walled garden closed the view, although Bain could hear the rushing of a burn somewhere in that direction. The lawn before the Place was unkempt, no better than pasture; and there, in one of the towers and even in the main block, a broken pane glinted in the afternoon sun, and all about the strong gray house hung a suggestion of neglect and impoverishment that would have been more clearly manifest, doubtless, had not the mansion been so severe and rugged in its very character. The huge window of what must be the great hall broke the solidity of the façade just above the main door. Between this window and the doorway below, Bain perceived, as he climbed the steps, a terribly weathered coat of arms executed in a soft red sandstone, appended to it some pious inscription in venerably barbarous Scots-Latin characters, most of them indecipherable. He could read only the two words which composed the last line:

L-A-R-V-A   R-E-S-U-R-G-A-T.

Larva Resurgat? Why *larva*, rather than *spiritus?* The old lairds sometimes put things quaintly. He found no bell and so banged at the oaken door with a rusty knocker.

After an interval of leaden silence, the door was pulled ajar a bit, and a sour woman's face peeked round it. Bain asked to be announced. The fat maid let him into a little round room with naked stone walls at the stair-foot, and locked the door again and then conducted him up a twisting stone stair in one of the entrance turrets — its treads scooped hollow by centuries of feet — to a gigantic vaulted chamber, well lighted: the hall. It was fitted with sixteenth century paneling, painted with heraldic symbols and family crests. The air was cold, the yawning medieval fireplace quite empty; here and there a Jacobean carved cupboard, or the polished surface of a table, or a tapestried chair endeavored to apologize for the emptiness of the Place. None of the furniture seemed in good repair. Bain sat gingerly on a Chippendale piece, while the maid scurried off to some hidie-hole in this labyrinth of a house.

After three or four minutes, Mrs. Lurlin came down to him, emerging from behind a door concealed by a hanging. A faint smile hovered on her fine lips, her eyes met his composedly, and Bain thought her most beautiful, in an antique fashion. 'I'll show you the curiosities of this draughty place, Mr. Bain,' she said, in a low voice with an agreeable suggestion of west coast accent about it, 'if you'll pledge yourself to ignore dust and damp. I've nothing left but the house and the policies and a bit of moor, you know — not even a home farm.'

Bain hardly knew what he said in reply, for she unsettled him, as if he had been shaken awake. Then Mrs. Lurlin led him up disused stairs and down into vaulted cellars and through chambers with moldering tapestries and Lord knows where else. Almost all these interminable rooms were empty.

'Most was gone before the place became mine,' said Mrs. Lurlin, without visible embarrassment, 'but I had to sell what was left of the furniture, except for a few sticks in the really necessary rooms. I suppose the wreckers will buy the house when I'm dead. You can sell an eighteenth century house, just possibly, in spite of rates, but not a behemoth like this. I can't afford to live here; but I can't afford to go away, either. Do you have some great barn of this sort, Mr. Bain?'

'I haven't even a cottage,' Bain told her, 'or a stick of furniture.' He thought her black eyes remarkably candid.

She took him up to the summit of one of the towers, where they stood in the wind and looked over the braes that parallel the den of Sorworth Water as it twists down to the sharp-toothed long skerries where it meets the sea. From this height they could see quite clearly the surf on the rocks, and, some distance south, smoke from the fishing village of Sorworthness. Sorworth Water was in spate. Just at the tower's foot, the den veered right up to the castle, so that a stone which Bain tossed over the rampart bounced down a steep slope into the roaring burn. In the rough old days, the lairds of Sorworth had the security of a strongly situated house. 'You're not afraid of heights, Mr. Bain?' asked the young woman.

'No,' he said, 'I've climbed a good deal.'

'I fancy you're afraid of very little,' she observed, lifting her eyebrows slightly. 'Do you know that I happened to see you in the square two days ago? I thought you looked like a soldier. What were you?'

He had been a captain, he told her.

'Come down into the policies, Captain Bain,' she said. As they descended, he bumped his head against the window ledge, and cried out involuntarily. She stopped, with an exclamation of sympathy.

'A mortar put a crack in my skull,' Bain apologized, 'and I'm still tender, and probably always will be.'

'Does it pain you much, Captain Bain?'

'No; but perhaps I ought to tell you that it makes me a trifle odd, now and then. Or so people seem to think.' He did not mind confiding this to her: perhaps it was the oddity he had just acknowledged, but at the moment they two seemed to him the only realities in an infinity of shadows.

'So much the better,' she said, still lower — either that or something of the sort.

'I beg your pardon, Mrs. Lurlin?'

'I mean this, Captain Bain: we seem to be birds of a feather. People hereabouts think I am rather odd. Sorworth Place is soaked in oddity. The maids won't stay. I've only one, now; the other went last week, and even Margaret, who's left, won't sleep in — she goes down to her son's cottage. I don't suppose you know why Janet went, unless someone at The King's Arms told you the gossip. Well, Janet wouldn't stay because she thought something whispered to her in the cellars. Poor timid creature! It was all fancy; for if anything were to whisper, you know, it would whisper to *me*. Would you like to see the garden? Most of it has gone back, of course.'

They poked about the overgrown walks of the policies, talking of trifles, and presently strayed near the chapel ruin. 'May I glance inside?' asked Bain.

'There's very little . . .' she answered, somewhat sharply. But Bain already had passed through the broken doorway. Some defaced sixteenth and seventeenth century monuments were fixed to the walls, and a litter of leaves encumbered the pavement. Where his feet scattered these, Bain noticed two or three ancient bronze rings fixed in stone slabs; and, being rather vain of his strength of arm, he bent, gripped one of them, and pulled upward. The stone lifted very slightly, though it was heavy, and when Bain let go the ring, the slab settled back with a dull reverberation.

'O, for God's sake, stop!'

He swung round to her. That delicate pallor of her young face had gone gray; she clutched at the door moulding for support. Bain took her hands in his, to save her from falling, and led her toward the house. 'What is it, Mrs. Lurlin?' He felt mingled alarm and pleasure thus to have a bond between them — even the terror in her eyes.

'You shouldn't have done that! He's under, just under!'

Of course! In his wool-gathering, Bain had nearly forgotten this girl ever had a husband. He muttered something awkward, in his contrition: 'I thought . . . with the leaves about, and everything so neglected, you know . . . I thought no one would have been laid there this century.'

She was calmer now, and they re-entered the house through the kitchen door. 'I know. They shouldn't have put anyone there, after all this time. His uncle and grandfather are in the kirkyard in the village, and his two cousins. But he had himself buried in the old crypt; he wrote it into his will. Do you understand why? Because he knew I'd loathe it. I think tea will be ready, Captain Bain.'

At the tea table, in a pleasant corner room of one tower, she was cool and even witty. Bain saw in her a girl become woman in some short space, a year or two, perhaps; she was charming and possibly wise. But something stirred woefully, now and again, beneath this pretty surface. The afternoon went rapidly and smoothly. When it was time for Bain to leave, she went with him to the great door; and she said, deliberately, 'Come to tea tomorrow, too, if you like.'

Startled, Bain hesitated; and she caught him up, with just the hint of a flash in her eyes, before he had said anything. 'But don't trouble, Captain Bain, if you're to be busy.'

'I'm never busy, Mrs. Lurlin,' he told her, unable to repress his old arrogant grin. 'Shall I be frank? I was surprised that you should ask me. I'm thoroughly *déclassé*.'

She looked at him steadily. 'I believe you're decent. I have no friends, and I hate to be solitary here, day on day. I'm afraid to be alone.'

'I wouldn't take you to be timid, Mrs. Lurlin.'

'Don't you understand? I thought you'd guessed.' She came a trifle closer to Bain; and she said, in her low sweet voice, 'I'm afraid of my husband.'

Bain stared at her. 'Your husband? I understood — I thought that he's dead.'

'Quite,' said Ann Lurlin.

Somewhere in that Minoan maze of a house, a board or table creaked; the wind rattled a sash; and this little room at the stairfoot was musty. 'You know, don't you?' Mrs. Lurlin whispered. 'You know something's near.'

*   *

Bain stayed on at The King's Arms, and every afternoon he walked up the barren lawn to Sorworth Place for tea. Some days he came early, and with Mrs. Lurlin he tramped over the Muir of Sorworth, talking of books and queer corners and the small things of nature. Ann Lurlin, he perceived, was one of those women, now unhappily rare, who delight in knowing about squirrels' habits and in watching field mice and peeking into birds' nests, with a childlike curiosity quite insatiable.

On one afternoon, they reached the summit of the Law and looked back upon the Place. A vast twisted oak, still bare of new leaves, stood halfway between them and the house, its black branches outlined like fingers against the gray of the distant mansion. This was the finest of many brave views on the Muir of Sorworth, and they could see the colliery, a dismal smudge far down in the valley, and the red roofs of Sorworth village, at this remove still seeming the douce market town that it once had been. In the several days that had elapsed since Bain's first call, Mrs. Lurlin had not touched upon the theme of her parting shot at the stairfoot, and Bain had been content to let that field lie fallow. But now she clutched his arm, and he sensed that the mood was upon her again.

She was looking intently toward a rise of ground this side of the oak. 'Do you — ' She checked herself, and said, instead, 'Do I seem rational to you, Captain?'

She did, he told her; but he said nothing of all the rest he felt about her.

'I am going to put your confidence to the test.' He observed that her charming lips were pressed tightly together, when for a moment she was silent. 'Do you think you see anything between us and that tree?'

Bain studied the face of the moor. At first he detected nothing; then, for just an instant, it seemed as if some large stooping creature had hurried from one hillock to another, perhaps its back showing above the bracken. 'I don't know, Mrs. Lurlin,' he said, a bit too quickly. 'A dog?'

'It didn't seem like a dog to you, now, did it?' She looked into his eyes, and then turned her sleek head back toward the moor.

'No. I suppose it's a man out ferreting.' But he let his inflexion rise toward the end of the sentence.

'No one keeps ferrets here, Captain Bain. I'm glad you saw it, too, because I feel less mad. But I don't think anyone else would have made it out. You saw it because you know me so well, and — and because of that crack in your poor head, perhaps. I fancy it makes you sensitive to certain things.'

Bain thought it kindest to be blunt: he asked her what way she was rowing.

'Let's sit down here on the heather, then,' she went on, 'where we can see for a good way round. I'd rather not talk about this when we're in the house. First I ought to say something about my husband.'

Perceiving that all this hurt her, Bain murmured that he had been told her late husband had been no credit to the family.

'No,' said Ann Lurlin, '*no*. Have you read Trollope, Captain? Perhaps you remember how he describes Sir Florian, in *The Eustace Diamonds*. Sir Florian Eustace had only two flaws — "he was vicious, and he was dying." Now Lizzie Eustace married Florian knowing these things; but I didn't know them about my husband when I married. I hadn't any money, and no relative left worth naming. Alastair — though he looked sick, even then — had manners. I don't suppose I wanted to look very closely. Afterward, I found he was foul.'

Bain dug his fingers into the heather.

'If we were to walk down toward that tree,' said Mrs. Lurlin, after a silence, 'I don't think we'd meet anything, not yet. I don't believe there's any — any *body* to what we saw. I fancy it was only a kind of presentiment. I've been alone here, more than once, and caught a glimpse of something and made myself hunt; but nothing ever was there.'

'Supposing a thing like that could — could rise,' Bain interjected, stealthily surveying the bracken, 'why should he have power over you? You're not foul.'

She did not seem to hear him. 'He wanted everything to be vile, and me to be vilest of all. Sometimes I think it was the pain of dying in him that made him try to befoul everything. When he found he couldn't break me, he cursed like a devil, really as if he were in hell. But I stayed with him, to his last day! I was his wife, whatever he was. Most of the time he lay with his eyes shut, only gasping; but in the evening, when he was nearly gone, I could see he was trying to speak, and I bent down, and he smirked and whispered to me, "You think you've won free, Ann? No. Wait a year. I'll want you then."'

'A year?' asked Bain.

'It will be a year next Friday. Now I'm going to confess something.' She turned her lithe body so that her eyes looked directly into Bain's. 'When I saw you in the square, I wondered if I could use you. I had some notion that I might stick a life between myself and . . . You looked no better than a daredevil. Do you mind my saying that? Something in me whispered, "He was made to take chances; that's what he's good for." I meant you to come to see me. I don't suppose it flatters you, Ralph, to have been snared by a madwoman.'

'No,' Bain answered her. 'You're not mad. We both may be dolls in someone's dream, Ann, but you're not mad.'

'And you'd best go, for good,' she told him. 'I don't want to stain you with this, now that I know you. I want you to go away.'

'You can't dismiss me,' Bain contrived to grin his old grin. 'I'm in your net. But how am I to get into your mind, Ann? How am I to stand between you and what your memory calls up?'

'If it were only memory and fancy, I could bear it.' She shut her eyes. 'A glimpse of him in a dream, a trick of imagination when I turn a dark corner, the shape dodging on the moor — those might pass away. But I think he's coming . . . Now you'll know I'm fit for Bedlam. I think he's coming — well, in the flesh, or something like.'

'Nonsense!' said Bain.

'Very well, then, I'm mad. But you'll bear with me, Ralph? Perhaps something in me calls him; possibly I even control him, after a fashion. But I think he'll be here Friday night.'

Believing she might faint, Bain put his big hand behind her head. 'If you really think that, Ann, leave the house, and we'll go to Edinburgh or London or where you like. We'll leave now.'

'Where could I live?' She nodded toward the gray castle. 'It's all I have — not even enough to pay my rent anywhere else. And then, it would make no difference. I think he'd follow me. He wants life to drag down with him. Either he must break me, or he must be broken somehow himself, before he'll rest.'

Bain sat awhile, and presently asked, 'Do you want me to watch in Sorworth Place on Friday night, Ann?'

She turned away her head, as if ashamed of her selfishness. 'I do.'

It passed through his mind that she might think he was making a rake's bargain with her, over this wild business. A bargain he might have made with another woman, or even with this one at another time, he admitted to himself, but not with a woman beside herself with terror. 'You understand, Ann,' he blurted, 'that I'm asking nothing of you, not now.'

'I know,' she whispered, her face still averted. 'I'm offering nothing — nothing but your death of fright.' Then she tried to laugh. 'Who'd think, to look at you, Captain Bain, that you're so very proper? I'd rather be scandalous than damned.'

Thus it was settled; and though they two walked and talked and drank their tea on the Tuesday and the Wednesday and the Thursday, they did not mention again her past or their future. Whatever sighed in some passage or cupboard of that old house, whatever shifted and faded across the moor — why, such intimations they ignored, speaking instead of the whaups that cried from the sky above them or of the stories they had loved as children.

*   *

Old Sorworth Place still was fit to stand a siege, Bain told himself as he mounted the staircase between the turrets on Friday afternoon. The lower windows could not be forced, the doors were immensely stout; anything that had substance might scrape and pound in vain outside, all night, once the bolts were shot home. Ann Lurlin herself admitted him, and they went to sit in her little study, and the hours fled, and their tea, untasted, grew cold; and at length they heard fat Margaret shuffle down the kitchen passage, open the door, and make her way through the policies toward the distant sanctuary of her son's cottage.

Then Ann's eyes seconded Bain's glance, and he ran down the stair to the kitchen door, locked it, and made sure the great door was well bolted. He returned to the study and the pale girl with the great black eyes. The night was coming on. They could think of very little to say. Here was Bain locked in for the night with the woman that he most desired, though he had known many women, too well. 'Yet Tantalus' be his delight . . .' Unless she sought him, he would not touch her, in this her hour of dismay.

'Where will you stay?' asked Bain, when the sun had sunk quite below the level of the little west window of the study.

'In my bedroom,' she said, drearily enough. 'There's no place safer.'

Her room was in the southern tower. Bain's mind reviewed the plan of the Place. 'Is there a way into the tower except through the great hall?'

She shook her sweet head. 'There were doors on the other levels, once, but they were blocked long ago.'

This made his work easier. 'Well, then, Ann, your bogle will have to swallow me whole before he opens the door behind the hanging, and I'm a sour morsel.' He didn't admit the possibility of fleshly revenants, Bain told himself, and if he could keep her safe from frenzy this one night, she might be safe forever after.

Solemn as a hanging judge, she looked at him for what seemed a long time. 'You shouldn't stay here, Ralph; I shouldn't have let you.' She ran her little tongue along her dry lips. 'You know I never can be anything to you.' This was said with a kind of frozen tenderness.

These words hurt him beyond belief; and yet he had expected them. He saw himself as if in a mirror: his shallow, tired, defiant face, his frayed clothes, every long lazy inch of himself, futile and fickle. 'No,' said Bain, managing a hoarse laugh, 'no, Ann, of course you can't — or not tonight. I meant to sit outside your door.'

Biting her lip, she murmured, 'Not tonight, nor any other night, ever.'

'Well,' Bain said, 'you needn't drive the point home with a hammer. Besides, you might care for me in better days.'

She continued to look at him as if beseeching mercy. 'You don't understand me, Ralph. It's not you: why, so far as I still can care for any man, I care for you. Anyway, I'm grateful to you as I've never been to anyone else, and I'd give myself to you if I could. It's not what you think. It's this: after having a year with him, I couldn't bear to be anything to a man again. It would be dreadful. I can't forget.'

'Don't tell yourself that.' Bain spoke slowly and heavily. 'It won't be true. Given time, this night and your life with that — that fellow will wash away. But I suppose I'll be gone, and good riddance.'

She lit a candle: paraffin lamps and candles were the only lighting in the Place. Now, he knew, their night of listening and guarding must commence. 'You still can go, Ralph,' she told him, softly. 'A moment ago I hinted that I felt something for you, but that was because I tried to be kind. Kind! Well, whatever makes you do this for me? In honesty, I don't love you, though I should.'

'Bravado,' Bain said, 'and boredom, mixed.' He was glad she could not see his eyes or his mouth in that feeble candlelight. 'Now up with you, and let me play my game of hide-and-seek, Ann Lurlin.' He went with her to the door behind the hanging, and watched her ascend to the first turn of the stair. Looking back upon him, she contrived a smile of understanding, and was gone to her room. Alone, he felt a swelling of confidence.

'Come on, if you like, Alastair Lurlin, Esq.,' he thought. 'I'm your man for a bout of creep-mouse.'

Before settling himself in the hall for the night, he must make sure that no one was playing tricks, a remote possibility he had kept at the back of his mind, by way of a forlorn link with the world of solid things. So, taking his little electric torch from a pocket, he proceeded to inspect every chill corner of the Place, apart from Ann's south tower, with a military thoroughness. Certain corners in this pile were calculated to make one wary; but they were empty, every one. After half an hour or so, he found himself looking from a loophole in the north tower, and across the main block of the house he saw a light glowing from Ann's window. There she would be lying in a passion of dread. But nothing should force itself upon her this night.

Returning to the main block, he listened: nothing. 'For a parson's son,' he thought, 'Ralph Bain gets into peculiar nooks.' Then he opened a door into the great hall.

O God! Something white was by the stair door, even then slipping out of the hall into the turret. He flung himself across the hall, down the stair, and leaped the last twist of the spiral to overtake that white fugitive. It was Ann Lurlin, pressing herself against the great door.

She shuddered there in her nightgown, her slim naked feet upon the damp flagstones. For a tremulous instant he thought his own desperate longing might have stirred some impulse in her: that she might have come to him out of love or gratitude. But a glance at her face undid his hope. She was nearly out of her mind, a tormented thing fumbling at the oak, and when he took her by the arms, she panted spasmodically and managed to say, 'I don't know why I'm here. I wanted to run out, run and run.'

For only a moment he pressed her body to his. Then, picking her up, he carried her to the door behind the hanging, and thrust her in. 'Go back, Ann: I've promised you.' She put both her chill hands in his, looked at him as if she were to paint his picture, and kissed him lightly with cold lips. Then she crept up the steps. He bolted the little tapestried door from his side.

Well, back to sentry-duty. What hadn't he inspected in this house? The cellars. Down you go, Captain Bain. They were fine old Scots vaults of flinty stone, those cellars, but he detested them this night. Outside, a light rain was falling. He sat upon a broken stool in the cellar that had been a medieval kitchen, shadowed by the protruding oven. This was the ragtaggle end of chivalry all right — a worn-out fool crouching in a crumbling house to humor a crazy girl. Then something crunched on the gravel outside the barred window. From old-soldierly habit, Bain kept stock-still in the shadow.

He saw it plain, so that there could be no possibility of illusion; and he asked himself, in a frantic sensation of which he was at once ashamed, 'What have you got into, Ralph Bain, for the sake of a pretty little thing that won't be yours?'

It was a face at the slit of a window, damn it: a sickening face, the nose snubbed against the glass like a little boy's at the sweetshop. The eyelids of this face were drawn down; but while Bain watched, they slowly opened, as if drawn upward by a power beyond themselves, and the face turned awkwardly upon its neck, surveying the cellar. Somehow Bain knew, with an immense temporary relief, that he was not perceived in his sanctuary back of the oven, supposing the thing could 'perceive' in any ordinary sense. Then the face withdrew from the window, and again Bain heard the gravel crunch.

Some little time elapsed before Bain could make his muscles obey him. The crunching grew fainter, and then, hearing with a preternatural acuity, he made out a fumbling at the small kitchen door down the passage. But it was a vain fumbling. Something groped, lifted the latch, pressed its weight against the barrier. The stout door did not budge. At this, Bain experienced a reckless exultation: whatever was outside in the night obeyed in some sort the laws of matter. 'Go on, you dead hands,' thought Bain, wildly. 'Fumble, damn you, push, scratch like a cat. You'll not get at her.' Rising from his stool, Bain tiptoed down the passage, and heard the stumbling feet in the gravel, moving on. Would it try the big door? Of course. Let it try.

Bain told himself he had to look at what was outside; and he made his way to the lowest loophole of the left-hand turret, which commanded the steps. There was moon enough to show him the stairs, and they were empty. But the great door, a trifle ajar, was just closing behind whatever had entered.

He sucked in his breath, and believed he would go mad. 'O Lord! O Lord! It's in, and I'm done for!' These phrases thrust through his consciousness like hot needles. Yet a dogged rationality contended against them. However had the door been forced? Then he thought of Ann in her nightgown. Before he had caught her, she must have drawn the bolt; and he, in his love-sick anxiety, had forgotten to try it. Collusion between the living and the damned: this conjecture of treachery woke in him, and he felt momentarily that all his days with Ann Lurlin had been part of a witch's snare. But he rejected the doubt. Whatever had moved Ann, whether simple terror and a foolish hope of flight, or some blind impulse forced upon her out of the abyss, no deceit lay in her.

These sterile reflections occupied no mensurable time. Face it out, Bain: nothing else for it. With luck, he could be in the hall first. He was up the kitchen stair and through an anteroom as fast as ever he had moved in his life. An uncertain moonlight showed him the hall, and he was alone in it, barring the way to the tapestried door; but then the door from the turret stair opened. Something entered.

Just inside the hall, the thing paused heavily. Light enough came from the great window to outline it; Bain had not the heart to pull out his torch; indeed, he could not move at all. Again he looked upon the sagging face he had seen at the cellar-loop. The thing was clothed in a black suit, all mildewed. Its slow body seemed to gather itself for new movement.

Who should be master, who should move first — these points might decide the issue, Bain hoped: perhaps a horrid logic governed this contest. Ralph Bain then compelled himself to take two steps forward, toward the middle of the hall. He looked at the dark shape by the window, and twice tried to speak, and on the third attempt a few broken words croaked from his throat: 'Time you were properly buried, old man.'

No answering sound came. Bain flexed his arms, but could not force himself to advance further. He could discern no expression upon the face: only a blackened mask obedient to some obscene impulse from a remote beyond. How long they two stood there, Bain did not know. But presently the thing swung about awkwardly, lurched over the threshold, and was gone back to the darkness of the stair-turret.

Bain thanked God with all sincerity. Now who was the hunter and who the quarry? The will was in him to make an end of this thing. Would it have gone back to the door and out into the rain? Bain listened. Yes, there came a stumbling on the stair — from above. What was it trying for? And then Bain knew. Ah, what a fool he was! It was ascending to the roofs, and would cross the slabs to the woman whose passionate terror perhaps animated its shape.

Bain went after it, slipping and bruising himself in his urgency; but as he leaped up the spiral toward the higher stories of the north tower, he felt a cold draught sweeping down upon him. The thing had got open a window, and must be upon the roof. Bain found that window, and stared into the night.

Now the rain fell heavily, and down at the foot of the wall, Sorworth Water moaned and gleamed. From Ann Lurlin's room, the candlelight cast some faint radiance upon the stone slabs of the sharp-peaked roof, and the glimmer was enough to show Bain a sodden bulk inching its way along the gutter toward the south tower, a footing precarious enough in daylight. The ruined face was averted from Bain, whatever power moved the thing being intent upon that piteous lighted window.

What propelled Ralph Bain then was an impulse beyond duty, beyond courage, beyond even the love of woman. He dropped from the window upon the wet and shimmering slabs, clambered along the gutter, and flung himself upon the dark hulk. Bain heaved with all the strength that was in him. Together, living and dead, they rolled upon the mossy old stones; together they fell.

A glimpse of the great stone wall; a flash of the savage burn; then explosion of everything, opening to the blessed dark.

*   *

Early on Saturday morning, a lone fisherman out of Sorworthness, rowing near the reefs that lie off the mouth of Sorworth Water, thought he perceived some unpleasant mass lying nearly submerged in the tangle of kelp among the rocks. But the sea boils nastily there, and the fisherfolk of Sorworthness are of the old legend-cherishing sort, and this man recalled certain things muttered by the arthritic old hag in the chimney corner, his mother. Rather than rowing closer in, then, he worked his boat round and made back toward the decayed little harbor.

Some hours later, having got two friends into his boat for company, he returned to the skerries for a closer look; but the tide had ebbed, and if anything human or human-like had lodged earlier among the rocks, now it was gone forever. Whatever ends in the boiling sea upon the reefs, having tumbled down the den of Sorworth Water, never wakes again.

Saviourgate

This ae nighte, this ae nighte,
— Every nighte and alle,
Fire and sleet and candle-lighte,
And Christe receive thy saule.

A Lyke-Wake Dirge

This old street, scarcely wider than a lane, could not be long; at the far end of it there loomed the Norman tower of a parish church. Mark Findlay had a notion that if he were to hurry the length of the street and turn to the right beyond the church, he might reach a modern square with cinemas and a taxi-rank. Needing to catch the midnight train for London, he must find a cab soon.

And, his cough growing worse, he must get out of the wet. In Northminster, this Christmas Eve, a light snow had fallen and then melted, lingering as fog. Between trains he had strolled the streets for nearly three hours, his head so filled with worries that he scarcely had noticed anything he passed. Looking back the way he had come, and coughing hard, he saw by the great clock on the cathedral tower that it was nearly half-past eleven. In more ways than one, he had lost his sense of direction; he was uncertain what way the railway station lay.

This was a charming narrow street of Georgian houses, or perhaps some of them from Queen Anne's time, two or three little white-washed steps going up to each door — that he could make out through the low-lying chilly mist. There seemed to be no shopfronts, and only one hanging signboard, a few yards directly in front of him, visible by gaslight (this being, perhaps, the only lane in Northminster still lit by gas-lamps):

THE CROSSKEYS
PAUL MARRINER, RESIDENT MANAGER

Above this gilt lettering was the well-painted symbol of two crossed keys. Decades ago, had he glimpsed this street sometime? He had been in Northminster only once before, early in the War: much of the town had been uglified since then, but this street — supposing it to be the same street — looked unchanged. Had he seen that pub-sign before?

As he lingered on the corner, coughing ferociously, a clergyman brushed past him in the dim light. 'Could you tell me . . .' Findlay began; but the parson hurried on, umbrella over his head. Perhaps he had taken Findlay for a tramp, what with his cough, his pale face, and his mud-splashed coat. Someone else, looking rather like a civil servant, was striding in the opposite direction on the other side of the street.

'I'm sorry, but could you help me?' Findlay called to him. A smug face was turned toward him briefly, but there was no slackening of pace, and the second man went round the corner.

Somewhere he must get directions. Should he go a few paces down that street, ring the bell for the porter — if there might be a night porter at a small hotel of this sort, nowadays — and ask his way to a cab-rank or to the station? He hesitated; for the past several months, he had evaded most decisions, big or small.

Yes, he had best try The Crosskeys. The stained-glass windows were alight in that church at the far end, Findlay noticed as he made his way past the Georgian doors, and a bell was tolling from the tower. Just as he was about to mount the stone steps, another coughing fit racked him. Bent and hacking, he leaned against the bow-front of The Crosskeys.

Then the hotel door opened, and down the steps to him came a lean man. 'That's a graveyard cough,' the man said, sympathetically. 'I could hear you in the parlor. "It wasn't the cough that carried him off, but the coffin they carried him off in." Do come in for a whisky.'

Startled, Findlay contrived to gasp, 'I need to catch a train.' The man had taken his arm: a forceful tall man with a whimsical handsome face.

'Hacking like that, you'd never reach the station,' this stranger — or was he quite a stranger? — told him. 'I'll see that you make your train, if you must.' He held open the heavy door. Within, the corridor was warm and colorful, with dark oak wainscoting and good framed prints on the walls.

'But it's after hours,' Findlay protested.

'Oh, the public bar is closed, but at The Crosskeys they always can serve something to a bona fide traveler like you.' The man was briskly helping him off with his muddy coat. 'Come into the residents' parlor. I've put up for the night, and the manager knows me.'

'I don't think that there's time,' Findlay muttered as he was propelled into the parlor. This insistent host, who seemed tolerably sober, spoke like an educated man and behaved like an officer.

'Time!' The lean man chuckled. '"It's time, gentlemen, time!" That's no problem for you and me, is it? I say, you're a Canadian, aren't you? I know you. You're Findlay, Mark Findlay. I was thinking of you — coincidence, I'd have said once — before I heard that cough of yours in the street.'

Findlay stared into that confident face. Had he known this man? A certain recklessness made those bold features memorable. Perhaps this man had been a soldier. To Findlay came some faint memory of an hour's tipsy talk, a curious conversation, with a man who had looked rather like this, long ago. Some chance acquaintance, but encountered where?

'Did we meet — why, right here, in '39?' Findlay inquired. 'I'm sorry, but I don't recall your name.'

'I'm Ralph Bain. Of course it's here. Take that chair, the leather one, Findlay. Jimmie!'

A corpulent florid-faced porter or waiter, in scarlet jacket and brass buttons, ambled toward them. 'Whisky-and-sodas, Jimmie,' Bain ordered, 'and put more coals on that fire. You remember Mr. Findlay, Jimmie. He's passing through Northminster — unless, after all, we can persuade him to take a room. Anyhow, he's a bona fide.'

'It's your sort that makes this job a pleasure, Mr. Findlay, sir,' said Jimmie, who was an Irishman. The fire blazed up on the broad hearth below the Adam chimneypiece; the whisky glasses came promptly on a heavy silver tray. Findlay had ceased to cough. Surely this was the jolly hotel of his dim memory, with the faded upholstery or shiny leather of its easy chairs, the green draperies of its tall windows, the solid dark furniture of yesteryear, the big Oriental rug a bit frayed, and especially that massive-framed painting of the Highland cattle. Now he even recalled the looming silver tea-urn on the mahogany sideboard.

A few people still sat in this residents' parlor, perhaps waiting for the midnight peal from the cathedral's bells. Several of them had nodded to him, or smiled at him, when Bain almost had forced him into an armchair, and an old lady had said, 'Good evening.' Could he have seen her before, and perhaps the granddaughter or girl companion beside her? Ralph Bain he did recollect fairly well, by this time: rather a wag, this Bain, he recalled, with a talent for telling stories that seemed tall. They had taken to each other, he and Bain, when in that year so long vanished they had happened to fall into talk in this very pub. The Bain of Findlay's memory had seemed no younger than the man who sat opposite him now; his host must be remarkably preserved, not a gray hair to his head. Did he dye?

Bain had been chatting with him lightly for several minutes, but Findlay — needing to catch that train and fretting about tomorrow's hard decisive conference — scarcely had paid attention. What a heartening room this was, everyone in it good-natured and healthy-looking! The sound of the ancient church-bell penetrated through the thick drapes of the bow-front; yes, it was a single bell tolling, not a peal. At any moment, Findlay feared, the tolling might be mingled with the chimes of the cathedral clock sounding the third quarter of the hour — which would mean that he'd have a narrow squeak to make his train, even though the trains generally ran late or lingered at the platform.

Bain noticed that his guest was listening to the bell. 'That's a good sound, isn't it, Findlay? Lord knows when that church commenced the custom. There was a Saxon or Danish church on the site, you know. The day before Christmas, from time out of mind, they've tolled that bell from early morning to midnight, one stroke for every year since the Nativity. The church is our friend Canon Hoodman's, you remember, besides his being chapter treasurer. They must be coming close to stroke one thousand, nine hundred, and thirty-nine. Shall we drink to that?'

'Thanks, Mr. Bain,' Findlay heard himself saying — he was drowsy in this cordial room, after the long ride down from Aberdeen and after tramping those Northminster streets in miserable vacillation — 'but no. I'd order another round for us, except for my train. I'm going to have to say good night. We keep a flat in Aberdeen now, and if ever you get to . . .'

'Call me Bain, or Ralph, or Rafe. That whisky's your medicine, Findlay; I told you so before your cough stopped. As for the train — why, you'll be aboard it, if you really mean to be; I give you my word. I'll see you to the cab. "We have heard the chimes at midnight, Master Shallow." Forgive me, but you've not been long this side of the Border, I take it?'

'I came down from Aberdeen today, Bain. And if I don't meet three important men for breakfast at the Hyde Park Hotel' — here Findlay grimaced — 'it's all up with me. I've been in oil rigs in Aberdeen for the past two years, and I'm not so young as I was, and my wife is in a bad way. Now I'm in deep trouble — not enough ready money, and the banks pressing me hard about overdrafts.'

The careless smile faded from Bain's mouth. Bain stared at him incredulously. 'Why, Findlay, that sort of thing doesn't signify for you and me here, you know. Overdrafts! Or don't you know? Don't you actually? The moment I dragged you in, I thought you seemed a bit odd. If you don't mind my saying so, it was as if I'd taken hold on a ghost. I'm told that some people scarcely are aware of the change when they've just crossed the Border. If you don't mind, Mark Findlay, old man — just how was it you died?'

Jimmie was setting two more whiskies before them on the little Indian table; Bain must have given him a sign. The cozy parlor went round for Findlay.

Hadn't he thought too often of dying, and dying swiftly, whatever the consequences? Hadn't he thought of that escape all the hours he'd walked those Northminster streets? Did the death-urge show in his face?

For a moment, the two commercial travelers in the corner, and the old lady with her girl companion, and smiling Jimmie, seemed to fade into nothingness. Findlay saw only Bain's daredevil face, gone sober and pallid on the instant. Had one whisky been too many for Bain, or for himself?

'What do you mean?' Findlay tried not to stammer. 'I'm no deader than you are. I might as well be dead, though, if I'm not in London eight hours from now.'

'Dead!' Bain laughed, though it seemed to require some effort from him — almost as if Bain were frightened. 'Of course we're not dead, old man. Here, do I seem dead?' Leaning forward, he gripped Findlay's hand. 'There, a good fleshy shake, eh? We wouldn't be just here if we were dead, truly dead, would we, Findlay? I put the question to you too bluntly — that's one of my silly habits, got in the army. What I meant to say was this: how did you cross the Border?' Bain drank, and then resumed.

'There's no harm in calling it "dying." We all have to pass through the jaws of death to reach The Crosskeys or any other good sort of place — corruption putting on incorruption, and all that. We all have to die so that we can rise, don't we? Was it hard, your crossing? Is The Crosskeys the first place you've come to, this side of eternity? If so, there's the more honor for me, as the first friend to greet you.'

Bain drained his glass. 'Now drink your dram, old man, because there's nothing left for us to fret about, never, never. "It wasn't the cough that carried him off, but the coffin they carried him off in." I say — could it have been that you crossed the Border just outside the door of this hotel, when I heard you hacking there?'

Findlay stood up. Was this host of his drunk, or was he a lunatic? Bain seemed neither, but he might be both. Had he and Bain talked of something like this, so long ago? Not this precisely, but something about death and eternity? Findlay couldn't be bothered, though Bain was rather amusing, not with that train to catch.

'Thanks again,' he told Bain. 'My train won't wait. And it's not just my own future depending on that breakfast tomorrow: there's my wife, my sick wife, to think of. Good night. If you're ever at Aberdeen . . .'

'You really don't follow me, do you, old man?' Bain frowned in seeming perplexity. 'If you leave now, you'll miss Canon Hoodman. Train won't wait? Why, any train you want will be waiting for you whenever you want it. I'll be taking a train myself to Ayrshire, after a night or two here at The Crosskeys; there's a young woman I mean to walk the moors with. Time doesn't signify: there's no Time for you and me, thank God, Findlay. Why, we've not even begun to talk. How can I explain? You and I aren't dead, though I died once, and I suppose you have, too. We've just begun to live fully. Look here, Mark Findlay: do you believe what you read in the papers?'

'Half the time. Excuse me, but where did you hang my hat and coat?'

'Jimmie!' Bain called. But he did not tell Jimmie to fetch his guest's coat and hat. 'Jimmie, find us today's *Post* — and *The Times,* too. Mr. Findlay needs to see them.'

Newspapers, inserted in those oldfangled wooden rods, were hanging by the sideboard. It passed through Findlay's mind that The Crosskeys Hotel, like a beetle of a hostelry preserved in amber, retained amenities that had vanished nearly everywhere else. Jimmie brought two papers. They were full of news about the military stalemate. On the front page of both, the date was 24th December, 1939.

'What in hell is this?' Findlay was two-thirds angry. 'It was 1939 when I came to Northminster the first time.'

'That is now,' said Bain. 'There's only now, praise be: whatever "now" you like, whatever "now" I like. Sit down, old man. You need somebody with a head and a tongue better than mine to inform you. I say, Jimmie: Canon Hoodman still is in the house, talking with Mr. Marriner. Could you give him my compliments and ask him to join us, if it's no trouble to him? Tell him that I may have a ghost to show him.'

Well, in any event he must have missed his train by this time, Findlay reckoned. After all, how much did that matter? Those three insufferable men at the Hyde Park Hotel would do nothing for him, as the odds stood. The intended meeting had been a last forlorn hope. Fortune had conspired against him, and the stars in their courses. He might as well finish this whisky; he might as well finish many whiskies. Now it was all over for him, and all over for Marian, poor sick Marian. She had told him he would fail; his nerve had failed him, and he had failed her.

In his bag, at the station luggage-room, there lay secreted a sufficient quantity of prescribed capsules, long hoarded. He had feared that he might require them, the whole lot of them, after that Hyde Park breakfast. After he should leave this hotel, he could swallow them at the station, without having to face that grim breakfast after all. Now he had all the time in the world. If a coroner should call it an overdose, there would be some insurance-money left for Marian, anyway, despite their having borrowed heavily these past six months. 'It is a far, far better thing I do . . .' Findlay sat down again. There were worse places to spend one's last evening than this snug and well-appointed hotel parlor, with this friendly madman to entertain him.

'Jimmie,' said Findlay, 'another round of drinks. Nothing matters now.'

Bain had been peering at him, as if doubting whether this guest were flesh and blood. 'Actually,' Bain said, 'it *does* matter, don't you know, old man. It matters if you've not yet crossed the Border. It matters if really you're here at The Crosskeys by some uncanny chance — or by providence, I should say. If you're to understand Canon Hoodman, who explains mysteries as well as anybody could, you're not to be half-seas over. I beg your pardon. Jimmie, forget those whisky-sodas, and bring us a pot of tea — and some sandwiches, Jimmie.'

His last slim hope of survival abandoned, Findlay was willing to humor this quizzical lunatic called Ralph Bain. He did feel hungry, after those vain bewildered hours in the foggy streets.

'All right,' he told Bain, 'have your fun with me. That was a clever ploy, putting those old newspapers on the racks. Were you merely hoping that some fool, any fool, might come in tonight to be teased by you? Or do you play these macabre tricks at this hotel every night? Why am I a ghost, and not you?'

'It's a private joke, very nearly, that "ghost,"' Bain said. 'The Canon and I call anybody a ghost who turns up here, or turns up anywhere else in eternity, but doesn't belong: anybody who hasn't properly crossed the Border, but gets into eternity somehow — for a moment, so to speak — and then passes back into Time again. Let me tell you, Findlay, you're a rarity: here at the old Crosskeys, on Christmas Eve, in the year of our Lord one thousand nine hundred and thirty-nine, reading in the papers about the Twilight War, you're experiencing a timeless moment. You're in two states of being simultaneously, I fancy.'

Bain leaned toward him earnestly. 'Yet I don't think you've passed through the jaws of death. The Canon says he's met such people more than once, but I haven't. You believe you're alive, and so you are — though not only in the way you think of "life." I fancy you'll leave this pleasant room, whenever you need to, and you'll catch that confounded train of yours, and you'll find yourself back in whatever year of grace you fancy you belong in. That's why I call you a ghost.' Bain grinned at him reassuringly.

'You don't belong here, and yet you do belong. To me, you're unreal: you frighten me a trifle, as ghosts are supposed to do. The next thing I know, I may be looking straight through you to the back of your chair. You needn't dread *me*. But here's the tea, and here's the Canon.'

The Canon's grip was as hearty as Bain's. Canon Hoodman was a cheerful north-countryman with a broad mouth and thick spectacles. 'You may not remember me, Mark Findlay,' he began, 'not just yet. Or you may recall only a few words we spoke to each other. If you like, I can offer you a good many more words now.'

'Canon,' Bain was saying, 'I lug in an old acquaintance from the street, and then find that he's not crossed the Border, or so he says: it's a conundrum. When first you and Findlay and I sat down together, I wished we could go on talking forever. And here that possibility's come to pass, but Findlay doesn't understand, and he wants to be off immediately to his private misery.'

Was this purported Canon some actor recruited by the whimsical

Bain? Certainly Hoodman looked his part, collar and black suit and all. Findlay forced himself to enter into the spirit of this rag.

'Here's the question,' Findlay told Hoodman: 'Is Ralph Bain crazy, or am I? And I'd like to know what sort of innkeeper puts 1939 newspapers into this residents' parlor.'

'You seem out of sorts, Findlay,' Hoodman said, 'but melancholy men are the wittiest. The manager of this hotel is a very sensible person, and he puts those papers there because he, like everybody else in this house, knows that tonight is Christmas Eve — the verger is nearly done tolling the bell in my old church — of the year of our Lord 1939.'

Another wag! Findlay chuckled mordantly, pouring himself another cup of tea with a shaking hand. 'Are you suggesting, Canon — if you really are a canon — that I'm in Hell, having coughed myself to death in the street outside, and that I'm condemned to spend eternity in this room, in a little pocket of Time called December the twenty-fourth, 1939?'

The Canon smiled a warm and humorous smile. '*Au contraire,* Findlay, if you and Bain and I were in Hell, I fancy we'd not be discussing these mysteries. The damned, as I understand it, have no past and no future; no memories, no expectations. You're in a very different state from that.'

This sly game was not unpleasant; and afterwards there would be those deadly capsules at the station, a door out of the prison-house of life, leading to the jail-yard. With that final ace in the hole, why not play up?

'Well, then, Canon Hoodman,' Findlay went on, 'if we three, and the other people in this parlor, are imprisoned forever in a cozy moment in Time, how is it that you and Bain talk of "remembering" me; and how can I remember Bain, though I've forgotten you — if I ever met you before? If we're all dead men, how can we talk about memories and expectations — especially expectations?'

'I told you, old man,' Bain thrust in, 'we're *not* dead, none of us. We've come fully alive. And we're not locked up here; it's just that we've chosen, or fallen into, this one timeless moment. It's a good particular timeless moment, isn't it? No especial significance to it, I suppose: simply three friends arguing comfortably before a fire on a winter's night. But we have our choices of moments to experience afresh. It's up to you and the Canon and me, separately. This moment is a random sample of timeless moments; there are stronger moments, far stronger, for any of us. Why, if he chose just now, the Canon might be praying in some "draughty church at smokefall," I suppose; or I could be trading stories with some good chaps in a tent in the Western Desert, say, instead of disputing with you. It's a question of what you wish to experience all over again.'

As they talked, the heavy tolling of that church-bell contributed to the illusion of timelessness that these two fantastics had contrived for him, Findlay thought. Outside in the street there sounded the footfalls and murmuring of a good many people, with now and again children's laughter: folk on their way to midnight service at that church. The hotel was real, the people outside were real, these two clever companions of his were real; Findlay wondered about his own reality.

The Canon was speaking now. 'Yes, all the good moments or hours or days that you ever experienced are forever present to you, whenever you want them, after you've crossed the Border. We were told that we shall have bodies; we have them. You say that you've not yet crossed the Border, Findlay. Well, once you have crossed — and if really you're still in Time, that may be a long while yet for you — then, God willing, you'll understand as we two can't make you understand.'

'What's wrong with the present everlasting moment?' Bain inquired. 'Ah, I know: no cigars. Jimmie, fetch that box of cigars.'

Findlay chose a cigar, presumably his last — a Burma cheroot. He seemed to recall that good Burma cheroots had been easier to find in 1939. Where nowadays did the resident manager of The Crosskeys obtain his supply?

'All right,' Findlay responded, keeping his temper despite this waggery, 'for the sake of argument I'll accept your metaphysics. We're not dead, but in eternity, you say. Well, what sort of great expectations are we supposed to indulge, aside from another sandwich and another cigar? You two talk well, but this occasion might turn boring if it were to run on forever.'

The Canon took him up. 'As Bain said, it's your choice of all you have experienced. Suppose that your wedding-day was among the best days of your life, Mark — of what you call your life. Think of this: you can experience that wedding whenever you like, for eternity.'

'You mean that I can *remember* my wedding-day? I don't need you to tell me that, Canon. You mean that "happiness is emotion recollected in tranquility"? That's not enough for me: I don't have any tranquility left.'

The Canon shook his head amicably. 'No, it's not memory that I mean. It's this, rather: if you are given grace, the good things of your life are *experienced*, in all the fullness of your senses, whenever you desire them. True, there's another side to the coin: if you have rejected the grace of God, then the evil things of your life are forever present, and you cannot escape them. This unexpected moment here in The Crosskeys may be a sign for you, Mark Findlay: a sign that you may know grace in death, if you choose it.'

Ah, how these two jesters, these masters of the dry mock, stuck to their hobgoblin consistency! Findlay laughed sardonically. 'So you two can convert yourselves into bridegrooms in the twinkling of an eye, whenever you're in that mood?'

'Not I,' Bain admitted. 'I never married. I joined my regiment a few weeks after we met here, Findlay, and I was good at killing but at nothing else. After El Alamein, where I took some bullets, they gave me the Military Cross. When the War was over, I got my little pension and drank hard every day. Any girl would have been an idiot to have married me. I asked one, and she said it never would do, and she was right. That's the young woman I mean to walk the moors with again, when I leave The Crosskeys.'

'Why trouble yourself with her?' Findlay objected, grinning. 'There's no marriage or giving in marriage, I'm told, where we three are supposed to be just now. Or can you have your fun all the same?'

'So far as marriage goes,' Bain said quietly, 'we don't *want* what we didn't know the other side of the Border. As for "fun," I found in the end that love was better.'

'Have you ever read Augustine?' the Canon asked Findlay. 'No? He learned that truth while he still was in Time.'

'I take it, Canon, that you can chat with Saint Augustine whenever the fit is on you,' Findlay scoffed, 'and that Bain can play games with Helen of Troy.'

'Oh, nothing of that sort.' The Canon paused. 'How may I make it clear? We live only once; and the experiences of that one active life are eternal. I don't meet Augustine in The Crosskeys Hotel, say, because he never was here, naturally, and because I wasn't at Hippo in the fifth century, naturally. Augustine and you and I are joined only through the Mystical Body. As for Bain — may I speak for you, Bain? — an hour's stroll on the moors with that lady, merely talking, means more to him than could the conquest of the face that launched a thousand ships. We don't long for the physical presence of Augustine or of Helen, because the reality which we know satisfies us — which it didn't when we were in Time. I don't mean that this fuller reality of ours is static. Instead, our awareness of every timeless moment grows deeper and takes on more meaning. For a small instance, though you and I talked in this room before, you don't remember a word I said. I suspect, however, that you'll not forget what I am saying to you now.'

'What about those "expectations" of yours, when there's nothing new under the sun for you — when you do nothing but enlarge the same experiences?' Findlay thought he had caught this subtle canon there.

'Expectations, Findlay? This living moment in The Crosskeys isn't the whole of the life eternal — hardly.' The Canon chuckled. 'Nor is the reenactment of the love of created beings the whole of what we expect. You know the phrase "the Beatific Vision." Well, that's not a phrase only. That vision is yet to come, for Bain and for me. Perhaps we experience the Provisional Judgment now, and so remain tied, in some sense, to experiences within Time. When the Last Judgment is done, perhaps all expectations will be fulfilled, so that there will be nothing left to long for. These are only words to you? Formerly they were not much more than words to me. Words are tools that break in the hand. After you cross the Border, you will know truths that I cannot put into words for you.'

There's the last desperate resort of parsons, Findlay thought: flight into bloodless abstractions, empty formulas. He would try another tack. 'I fancy you must have been a model of propriety, Bain, to deserve a comfortable berth in eternity like this, eh?'

'I don't deserve it at all.' Bain looked down at his strong hands. 'I told you that I was good for nothing but killing, and that was true to the very end. Until almost the last, I was all ego, loving nobody but myself. My last action was to destroy a man, or what had been a man. Men are always saying that they'd die for this woman or that one. I said it, too; but what mattered, I did it — for that young woman I mentioned. I did it to shield her from somebody. And I took him with me. It was a beastly business on a high roof, and we went down together — into a river.

'Do you know, Findlay, ordinarily we don't talk about crossing the Border; I took the liberty of asking you how you crossed, but only because I sensed that there was something peculiar about your coming. It's bad form, since nasty memories don't fit in here. Yet in its way, even that last fight of mine was a high experience. That one decent impulse of mine is why I'm in the same room with the Canon. Because of that violent act for love — she'd never have taken me — everything else that I'd done was forgiven.'

Except for the tolling of the bell, there was silence for a little space.

Findlay had to admire Bain for this consummate skill of straight-faced yarn-spinning. Then Bain added, 'Now, beyond desire, I'm her friend, and know her always.'

'Just like Dante and Beatrice,' Findlay commented, puffing dryly on his cheroot.

'Rather,' said the Canon, knocking the ash from his cigar. 'Like Dante and Beatrice.'

How often did these two saturnine comedians find the opportunity to pull some chance visitor's leg so systematically? 'You gave your life, too, for a female friend, Canon Hoodman?'

'No,' the Canon answered, 'I had no choice as to how I crossed. My wife and I crossed together; I believe a bomb struck our old house in the Close; so we've never been parted. She'll be in the congregation when I give the homily at the midnight service, and we'll walk back to the Close together. People who come after us in Time don't know that handsome old house of ours, more's the pity; but nothing that's in Time can endure forever. For my wife and me, nevertheless, every stick and brick of that house endures in Eternity.'

They couldn't really expect him to swallow all this farrago! Of course these two were aware that he knew they talked tongue in cheek; they hoped to provoke him into an outburst of indignation at such stuff and nonsense. Findlay wouldn't let them have that satisfaction. 'So you have the pleasure of your wife's company, Canon,' he said, smoothly, 'and you enjoy your lady-friend's conversation, Bain. That's pleasant. But what about souls you're not so fond of? That man who rolled off the roof into the river with you, for instance, Bain?'

'That foul chap!' Bain blew a smoke-ring. 'God only knows. You can be sure our paths don't cross. In our Father's house are many mansions, but they're not all on the same floor.'

Findlay yawned; the jest was wearing thin, and he was dog-tired, and in his luggage those capsules awaited him. These two jesters might be sobered by what they would read about him in tomorrow's papers. After all, his would be the cream of the jest.

'You're quite worn out, Findlay, I can see,' the Canon was murmuring, 'and we've been boring you. Jimmie, is Mr. Marriner still up? Good: ask him to come, if he has a moment.'

The manager of this old-fashioned hotel turned out to be a small quick man with deep-set eyes. 'Something for you, Captain Bain?'

'Marriner,' Bain said to him, 'our friend Findlay has come a long way. Show him one of your rooms, will you? He still thinks of taking a train, but he might be tempted. This is a very old house, Findlay, part of the building medieval — worth seeing, worth sleeping in.'

'Would you prefer a haunted chamber, Mr. Findlay?' Marriner offered. Apparently he was a confederate of Bain and Hoodman. 'I don't know that we can supply a spectral monk on demand, but there's a room available where Coleridge slept once.'

Marriner led the three of them up a short flight of carpeted stairs, down a longish corridor, up a longer and steeper flight, and round a corner. Behind the door which he opened was a snug single bedroom, massive beams in its low ceiling, papered in blue, with a glistening old bedstead of some rare wood. 'If you'd care to sleep deep, Mr. Findlay,' Marriner said, 'I'd wake you when you might require a call — supposing that you should want it at all.'

'I must have missed that train of mine long ago, thanks to these gentlemen,' Findlay answered. To sleep in that old bed for eternity! That prospect was far more attractive than were those capsules waiting at the station.

'It's your choice entirely,' Bain was saying in his ear. 'Free will, you know, old man.'

Yet why choose either bed or poison? These chance companions, with their long-faced wit, had cared enough about him to twit him for an hour; somehow they had put heart into him. His cough seemed to have faded away altogether, and these two friends, and the atmosphere of this old house, were invigorating. He wouldn't swallow those capsules tonight, after all, he decided; perhaps never.

For Marian must not be left to suffer alone, and there were the sensibilities of railway porters to think of. Hyde Park breakfast or no Hyde Park breakfast, something yet might be accomplished in London with somebody or other — given will, given spirit, given grace. Behind this evening's charade there had moved some quickening power, some hint or glimpse of hope. *How* a man dies, and with what justification: this absurd interval of talk had wakened Findlay to awareness of such matters. He would not plunge himself into nothingness without another effort or two.

Canon Hoodman had been watching him closely. 'If you feel ready for a bed,' the Canon remarked, laying a hand on Findlay's shoulder, 'you'll not find a better one than this, Mark. But if you've duties you can't ignore — why, there's always a London train for you.'

'No, thanks, gentlemen,' Findlay said, 'I've miles to go before I sleep.'

Bain nodded. 'You still have hostages to Fortune, eh? And after all, that bed can be yours whenever you need it. I'll walk you to the corner.'

At the front door, Findlay shook hands with the Canon and Marriner. The two of them — if Marriner was privy to the plot — kept up to the last their roguish elaborate pretense. 'We'll have more to discuss when you come to us,' the Canon told him.

'I don't expect to pass this way again.'

'Yet you shall.' Findlay and Bain went down the white steps and into the drifting mist; the Canon waved.

That short street, it turned out, was quite as lovely as Findlay had thought it to be, in his glimpses before Bain had drawn him into The Crosskeys. If only he could have lingered to inspect it more closely! Ahead of them, stragglers were hastening through the churchyard and into the lighted church. And that bell tolled on.

'Do you have any idea when the first morning train will leave, Bain?'

'It will be there for you, old man. And all of us at The Crosskeys will be there for you, when you look for us. Ask the cabbie.'

Then the bell ceased to toll. Findlay glanced at his watch; it must have stopped in The Crosskeys. He looked backward toward the cathedral tower. Yet surely the cathedral clock, too, had run down, and at the same time, for it stood at half-past eleven.

'Here you are, Mark,' Bain was telling him. 'Do you make out a cab-rank to the right? Just wave and shout. Wage the good fight, old man.'

Sure enough, there was a taxi a few yards distant, on the modern street which intersected this ancient lane. Findlay waved and shouted, and the taxi rolled toward him. 'To the station, sir?' the driver was asking now.

'Just a moment. Ralph, you rascal, you've given me a lively evening, though . . .' Findlay turned to face Ralph Bain.

Bain was not to be seen. Nor was The Crosskeys Hotel there — only a vacant site strewn with rubble.

The charming houses of the old street were gone, or at least most of them, and those which survived were ghastly derelicts. That street was wholly lifeless.

Findlay swung back toward the taxi. Beyond it was the church with the Norman tower, or rather the wreck of a church, all dark, no glass in what remained of the window-tracery. The nave was roofless. A mercury-vapor lamp in the modern street glowered over the churchyard, and by it

Findlay could make out a metal sign which read: 'Public Gardens, Custody of Ministry of Works.'

'Station, sir? Time enough to catch the midnight for London. You can hear it coming down from the North now.'

Findlay tumbled into the cab. 'Tell me — tell me, how long has that street been smashed?'

'Before my time — 1941, they say. Them German fire-bombs done for it. Some year, they say, the Corporation'll get round to buildin' council-houses there.'

'And what's the name of that street?'

'Saviourgate, sir.'

The Last God's Dream

Licinius lies in a marble tomb, Cato in a mean one,
And Pompey has none at all:
Who says that there are gods?

ere in the palace of Diocletian she and Arthur stood, tired and dusty
from sightseeing and shopping in the Old Town of Split — and no
place to sit down! Didi Ross again surveyed the little tables of the Café
Luxor, on the sunny pavement of the Peristyle, and despaired. Every chair
occupied, the waiters were busy with Germans, Greeks, Bulgarians, English people, Scandinavians, Swiss, Rumanians, Australians, Austrians,
Czechs, Egyptians, Poles, Spaniards, Hungarians, Japanese, Argentinians,
Arabs, French people, Turks, Brazilians, Indians, Mexicans, many Americans, and more Yugoslavs: half the world.

A tremendous handsome bare-bellied Swedish girl, dashing past in hot
pursuit of a native Yugoslav youth, nearly bowled over Didi as they waited
for somebody or other to get up from a table and stroll away. It was hot in
this Adriatic sunshine, and ever so noisy. Didi naturally had expected a palace to be roofed and cool, but Diocletian's Palace actually had turned out to
be an enormous complex of buildings, with streets and lanes and squares,
surrounded by a wall as much as seventy feet high. Long, long ago it had
been converted into a fortified town, she had found out. Really, she and Arthur must rest for a few minutes, and have some lemonade, before making
their way past that black Egyptian sphinx into the cathedral.

'Arthur,' she sighed, '*is* this the cathedral in front of us? It looks small for that. The map says "Mausoleum."'

Although judges are supposed to know everything, Arthur said he didn't know. He did remember, youngish judge that he was, about the Emperor Diocletian having something to do with administrative law, but it had been nearly ten years since he was at law school. At this juncture, a small party of Japanese tourists took photographs of Arthur and Didi, doubtless mistaking them for typical citizens of the People's Republic of Yugoslavia. Everything around them seemed infinitely old, except for the tourists: Didi began to wonder whether the Roman arcades of this piazza, or Peristyle, or whatever the square was called, might not tumble down upon her and Arthur without the slightest warning. So ancient, so noisy, so crowded! So many swarming people in this bewildering Palace that was a kind of open-air human beehive!

Didi turned. Some man had risen from a table in the alfresco café, and was bowing and speaking to her. With her husband right at her elbow, too! He was a stranger, swarthy, white-haired and white-bearded; Didi started and began to shake her head. But this stranger wore a beautiful light silk suit cut in a military fashion, and his English, his genuine English English, was exquisite.

She nudged Arthur, who probably could tell whether this stranger were just a black-marketeer. A second man, tall, with a patch over one eye, had risen now; there were two vacant chairs at their table. The whitebearded man drew back a chair for her, and his companion was offering one to Arthur. 'Will you be good enough to join us?' The swarthy man's voice blended authority and suavity.

She and Arthur sank gratefully into those chairs, even if these two men did look as if they could use the score of *The Third Man* movie as background music. The white-haired man smiled blandly upon them.

'Will you take Turkish coffee?' he was saying. 'I drink it passionately here in Dalmatia, for it's forever tea, tea, tea in my country.' He was curiously handsome, with a beak for a nose, looking considerably like an arctic owl. His skin, contrasting with hair and beard, seemed almost unwrinkled, rather as if he had undergone plastic surgery.

'I'll have lemonade, please.' Could this man be the café proprietor, or did he have some sinister motive in offering them free coffee and lemonade? 'Are you sure we're not intruding?' Didi asked him, brushing back her blonde hair. 'I'm Didi Ross, and this is my husband, Arthur.' She perceived that Arthur was ill at ease with their hosts, though it must have been a relief for him to hear lovely English after days and days of Serbo-Croat jabber. The tall grave man with the neat eye-patch had spoken sharply to a waiter, who abandoned one crowded table of Eastern Europeans and took their order instead.

The white-haired gentleman offered his graceful hand to Arthur, who shook it awkwardly. And then the gentleman took Didi's hand and kissed it, as if she had been in Vienna rather than in Split. These men couldn't be Communists, anyway, not with the hand-kissing.

'I am called Manfred Arcane,' their host told them. 'As for intruding — why, Colonel Fuentes and I like American ladies and American judges. Besides, had these chairs remained vacant longer, we might have been invaded by a covey of those naked Swedish hoydens, whose name is legion here, and they're infinitely boring, don't you know?'

Arthur opened his eyes wide, as if he were on the bench. 'Why do you say "American *judges*," Mr. Archance?'

'*Arcane*, if you please, Judge Ross,' the swarthy man corrected him, amicably; 'that's to say, "shadowy."' He laughed a pleasant discreet little laugh — pleasant but faintly ominous, Didi felt. 'Did I hit the mark in your case? It's a necessity for me, in my line of work, to guess men's occupations and characters. Besides, when we saw that you and your delightful young consort were lacking a table, I asked our neighbor about you.' Mr. Arcane nodded toward a glum-faced Yugoslav in dark clothes, seated at the next table; that man averted his hard eyes.

'That person is a secret policeman,' Arcane ran on, 'set to watch us, and I perversely put him to some use. He's commendably well informed about foreigners of influence who have stayed in Split for a few days. You've a suite at the Marjan, I believe — altogether too modern and hygienic for my taste, but I suppose some travel-agent lodged you there. The government wished to put me and my friend there, but we declined. Oh, do let me present Colonel Jesus Pelayo Fuentes y Iturbide, commanding the Interracial Peace Volunteers, a body of well-disciplined men-at-arms in the service of the Hereditary President of the Commonwealth of Hamnegri.'

The gentleman with the eye-patch inclined his narrow head ceremoniously, murmuring something in Spanish. Didi noticed that two fingers were missing from the Colonel's right hand.

She could tell that Arthur was surprised and annoyed, but he kept his judicial dignity. 'Yes, Mr. Armond, I'm a district judge. We're from Ohio. This is the first time my wife and I have been behind the Iron Curtain.'

'Alack!' Mr. Arcane raised a supple hand in mock deprecation. 'Not "Iron Curtain," I beg of you, Judge Ross! What would the venerable President of this People's Republic think of so cruel a phrase? Our friend with the hard eyes, over there, might record your remark, and the President's sensibilities would be wounded. After all, his regime is less ferrous than Bulgaria's, Hungary's, Czechoslovakia's, not to mention Russia's.'

Didi felt the color departing from her cheeks. 'Oh, do you mean that it's dangerous to speak . . . ?'

Mr. Arcane laughed easily. 'Why, tourists may say what they like, especially if they speak to one another in English. Besides, being with me, you and your husband may be as free and easy as you please.' He beckoned to the waiter, who swiftly brought another of those little brass coffee-pots to him.

'I waited upon the President, the Marshal, at his island villa, a week ago today,' Arcane resumed. 'He's a very elderly personage, you know, less formidable than once — as doubtless our imperial friend Diocletian, *dominus et deus*, mellowed in his closing years, before they entombed him here.' Arcane indicated with a slim forefinger the little cathedral that had been the Emperor's splendid mausoleum.

'Oh!' Didi decided that this man wasn't a confidence-man at all, but somebody important, and possibly quite powerful. 'What do you do, Mr. Arcane?' Colonel Fuentes smiled narrowly.

'I commenced,' said Arcane — was he really old, despite the white hair? — 'as a brutal and licentious soldier. But Fortune, conspiring on my behalf, has made me a minister of state, without portfolio, in the Commonwealth of Hamnegri. I suppose that Diocletian would have styled me a pretorian prefect. Have you heard of our African realm?'

'You've got plenty of oil, I've read,' Arthur put in. 'And didn't you have a civil war there a few years back?'

'*Si*, won by his Excellency at the Fords of the Krokul,' the Colonel murmured. His English wasn't nearly so good as Mr. Arcane's.

'You're too kind, Don Pelayo,' Arcane remarked. 'I shouldn't have managed it without you to lead the assault.' He sipped his coffee. 'Though I've enjoyed my twilight victories, I've not been so favored by Jupiter as was the Emperor Diocletian, rest his soul. You've come to see Diocletian's tomb, Judge Ross and Mrs. Ross?'

'Oh, yes,' said Didi, 'and I wonder why they buried him in a cathedral. Didn't he persecute the Christians? The cathedral has four stars in our guidebook, but I don't know how we're going to get in. Look!'

Beyond the black sphinx and the colonnade, the portal of the octagonal cathedral was jammed with tourists, filing in and out unceasingly, being lectured at beneath the dome: tourists in the strangest getups, wearing too much or too little, tourists old, tourists young, staring uncomprehendingly, tourists who looked as if they never had entered a church before and wore hats, biker tourists, Iron Curtain tourists, hippie tourists, showy tourists, beggarly tourists. With such a crowd, it must be sweaty inside, and impossible to see much of anything.

'That will be remedied, Mrs. Ross. I'll show you the last great imperial tomb.' Arcane beckoned to the hard-faced man at the next table, who rose promptly and bent over the Minister without Portfolio — and then strode toward the tomb-cathedral.

'Quite enough time to finish your lemonade,' Arcane assured her. 'We'll have the Mausoleum cleared; that will take five minutes, I suppose.'

Sure enough, surprised tourists were being turned away from the portal now, and some who had entered — the Jotun-like Swedish maiden of the conspicuous navel among them — were departing more speedily than they had been admitted to the church. Even the Japanese tourists, hung about with cameras, looked vexed.

Arthur was impressed. 'You can have this done, Mr. Arcane, just for us? Are you big in the Communist apparatus?'

'*Au contraire*.' Arcane beamed civilly upon them. 'But the President-Marshal smiles upon captains and kings of the Third World, even upon such pretorian prefects or grand viziers *de facto* as myself, fancying himself their chief and patron. Besides, he fancies still more the trade treaty that I am negotiating with his people on behalf of our President-Sultan Hamnegri: Hamnegri's petroleum for Yugoslavia's rifles. Ah, I do believe they're ready for us now!'

He inclined his head graciously toward the hard-faced man, who had returned and was behaving like a clumsy majordomo, gesturing toward the Mausoleum-Cathedral. Didi and Arthur arose along with Arcane and the Colonel. As they strolled through the antique colonnade, Didi noticed that they were followed by two wolflike little black men who must have been seated at some other table. Also they were trailed by three more men in dark clothes, presumably Yugoslav secret policemen.

'They're Cleon and Brasidas, my guards and foster-sons,' Arcane told her when she glanced at the strange little black men. 'I found them in a burnt desert village: everybody else there had been massacred — not by me. Don't you like their classical names — the mortar and the pestle of war? Aristophanes, you know. If I do say it myself, I was first in Classics in my form at boarding-school. Actually, Mrs. Ross, I'm no African; I was born in Vienna, before the crash of empires, and was schooled in England. I'm Othello reversed, a European *condottiere* in Africa, now blessed for my services to the Sultan with a certain percentage of the oil-royalties of Hanmegri.'

'I wish you'd tell me all about yourself,' Didi replied, altogether sincerely. What a charmer this white-haired man was! 'I'd rather hear about you, Mr. Arcane, than about this Emperor Diocletian. Or should I call you Mr. Arcane? Is it Your Excellency?'

'You are to call me Manfred, this being my holiday.' He pointed back at the sphinx. 'That's from Africa, too; Diocletian fetched it from Egypt, and it was two thousand years old when he put it here.'

Didi marvelled. 'I don't know much about ancient history. I still wonder why they buried a pagan emperor in a Christian cathedral.'

'Ah, but it wasn't a church then, dear lady.' Arcane had taken her arm and was ushering her through the ancient doorway. 'All this was built near the end of the third century, a few years before the triumph of the Emperor Constantine and the Christians. Diocletian, who erected this whole complex, meant this particular wondrous building for his tomb, and here he was buried in a porphyry sarcophagus. Somebody robbed the sarcophagus fifty years later, and was put to death for it. The local Christians made it their cathedral after the Avars and the Slavs had destroyed the great city of Salona, a few miles from here, centuries later. What they did with poor Diocletian's corpse, goodness knows: they detested his memory. Mark you, he was the last pagan god. How are the mighty fallen!

'"Licinius lies in a marble tomb, Cato in a mean one,
And Pompey has none at all:
Who says that there are gods?"'

As if Mr. Arcane weren't bewildering enough, Didi was confused by the classical and medieval magnificence of the domed church-tomb. Arcane was declaiming softly about progenitors of Christian baptisteries, peripteral porticos, free-standing shafts, Buvina the carver, Saint Domnius — muddling her altogether. Now he was pointing up to the frieze.

'Just here, Judge; there, Mrs. Ross — those two medallions. The man in the one is Diocletian, born to serfs a little way from here, and at his end the last emperor to be declared divine, posthumously, by the Senate of Rome. The woman in that other medallion is Prisca, his wife. Licinius took off her head, you may recall, and the head of their daughter Valeria, too, for all that a husband and a father who had ruled the world could say or do. After that, with no consolation but cultivating cabbages here in his palace garden, Diocletian could not have desired to survive.'

They could make out dimly the Emperor Diocletian: an austere lean face, strong and alert, not at all like the gross persecutor that Didi had fancied. He looked rather like a judge, this Diocletian — rather like Arthur, indeed, though older. Arthur was honest and hard-working, but he did not know how to play. Mr. Arcane, on the other hand, must have been playful from boyhood up. . . .

Their host had been looking for a long time at that medallion in the frieze, almost as if he were venerating it. What was Mr. Arcane murmuring as he turned away — *dominus et deus?* 'Too many wonders in a single day blur one's impressions horridly, don't you think, Judge Ross?' A scraping priest showed them out; the security-man ignored this ecclesiastical custodian, but Arcane shook his hand at parting.

Like sheep or geese, they all followed this surprising Mr. Arcane out of the Mausoleum and across the Peristyle. 'Just before you is the Vestibule, the entrance to Diocletian's throne-room — that fine circular hall,' he was saying. 'Back of it . . . But enough of antiquities for the moment! I mean to give you dinner, if you've no objection. I can't tell you how delightful I find it to entertain two chance companions, your estimable selves, who undoubtedly are not terrorists plotting to put an end to me. And American innocence invariably tickles my fancy — if you don't mind my saying so. Colonel Fuentes and I are carefree for a few days, a rare condition for us. He is taciturn; I'm loquacious. Do you find it unpleasant to be my audience for an evening? Last night and today I completed an experience which you might find mildly amusing: I'm full of it, and require auditors. Now we go down these stairs, but don't think that I'm carrying you off to a subterranean fate worse than death. This is our quickest way out of the Palace.'

He led them into great vaults. 'The Emperor's cellars, on the harborside. Do you know, much of these vaults under the Emperor's private apartments hasn't been excavated even yet? Fifteen centuries of rubbish — what may they find? We'd best saunter along the quay and re-enter the Grad, the Old Town, but outside the Palace walls.'

The whole party, black guards and security police bringing up the rear, emerged from the Palace complex through the Brass Gate, the ancient watergate. Here they were by the deep blue harbor of Split, walking along the Titova Obala, the waterside esplanade. 'We go beyond that medieval tower,' Arcane indicated. Colonel Fuentes was being interrogated by facts-and-figures Arthur as they strolled parallel with the Palace wall.

Manfred Arcane had taken her arm again — why, this was almost a flirtation, Didi thought, not displeased. 'How can you possibly spare the time for strangers like us?' Didi asked him — and promptly feared that she had been arch. 'You're being so good to Arthur and me.' Was she imprudent in a foreign land? Was this man actually a kind of Grand Vizier, almost out of the *Arabian Nights?* Anyway, this Mr. Arcane scarcely could mean to drag her into one of those medieval lanes and deprive her of her virtue and her money — he must have plenty of the latter himself. She was not exactly rejoiced by the presence of those grim security-men, but there was safety in numbers, she hoped. Though Mr. Arcane seemed very nice and amusing, still he was a little — a little — well, *eerie.*

'By nature, Didi,' said Arcane, 'I am a *cicerone,* a tourist-guide, my dear. You don't protest at my avuncular "Didi"? We shall get on famously. Where was I just now? Ah, yes: cruel necessity compelled me to turn first mercenary and then statesman, despite my natural propensity for moping about ruins. Diocletian resigned the mastery of the world, when less than sixty, that he might raise cabbages in peace. Were I to retire from my exalted offices, I would hang about the Piazza San Marco, in Venice, or back there in the Peristyle of Spalato, eager to be of service, a useful tool, perhaps a bit obtuse, muttering antiquarian lore to the unwary, fixing them — especially beautiful ladies like yourself — with my glittering eye, pocketing their coins or begging their kisses, *grazie, grazie!* In fine, being cheerfully idle and secure in this old town for some days, Didi Ross, I thank the gods for this providential opportunity to bore a delicious young woman and a sober jurist with my dry-as-dust monologues.'

His melodious voice ran on, caressing, teasing, telling her the history of the Palace, and of Spalato or Split: of how twenty thousand people had crowded permanently within the walls of the former Palace, in the

Darkest Age, fleeing from Avar and Slav; of how there were still thousands living within the Grad; of how perhaps the human anthill of the Palace of Diocletian was the oldest continuously inhabited domestic complex in Europe. Even Arthur seemed quite interested, now that he and the Colonel were walking alongside them. I could listen for hours on end to Manfred Arcane, Didi thought. And it appeared that she was going to do just that.

'*Aqui, Excellentissimo,*' Colonel Fuentes said to Arcane. Their party turned into a small eating-house in the maze of the Grad which lay to the west of the Palace. A neat table was found for the four of them; a longer table in a corner was provided for their retinue of secret police and savages.

'This small *trattoria* is privately owned,' Arcane instructed them, 'and the powers of a Communist regime dine here, for the sake of the *cuisine bourgeois* and the decent service. You'll find the food basically Austrian. I discovered this retreat yesterday. You'll take Slovenian wine? May I ply you with it, smiling Didi?'

'You must have visited Split many times, Mr. Arcane — Manfred, I mean,' Didi ventured. She supposed he had been everywhere a great many times. The very ebony walking-stick that Mr. Arcane carried so jauntily apparently came from remotest Barbary — an elephant's head carved upon its handle, but an Arab or a Berber touch to the craftsmanship.

'Only thrice, including this present occasion. First I was brought here by my mother, when I was a small boy. No Yugoslavia existed then, nor ever had, and Spalato was Spalato still — not Split: under Austrian rule, as it had been for a century. Thousands of Viennese took their holidays on this shore. We spent a fortnight here, my pretty mother and I.

'She had been a dancer, but had acquired some antiquarian interests under my father's influence. He was a British officer, among other things, and did not marry her, but kept her well supplied annually with money. After all, in the long intervals between my father's visits, how could she have been more innocently occupied than in poking about old towns and reading a little history?

'She had been born in the mountains south of Spalato, as Diocletian had been, so many centuries earlier. Gypsy mother though my mother had, she came to take almost a kinswoman's interest in the dead Emperor, and imparted some of it to me. She made a hero of romance of the ruler who endowed the world with Giant Bureaucracy. To a small boy's fancy, the long-buried Diocletian became a Bayard, a Sidney, of the dying Empire.'

'Why did she bring you here just once, then?'

'Because of a bad fright I got within the Palace walls, I fancy. It was no great matter, but she was tender with me. How fortunate that she doesn't know of how I have supped long on horrors, in three continents, since she died! The African terrors have been the worst; I have been a kind of mayor of the palace in one of the more turbulent African countries since a year or two after the Second World War ended. But why conjure up raw head and bloody bones in this tranquil *trattoria*? For me, as for Diocletian, the object of war is peace.'

He drained his glass of wine and filled it again, and filled Didi's too. 'Yes, I was frightened the first time I visited Spalato, and I nearly ended my days here on the second occasion.'

'I'm so glad you didn't,' said Didi. She was conscious of blushing a little. This man, old enough to be her grandfather, talking of wars that had ended before she had been born, had what they called — *charisma*, that was it. And he was timeless.

'Three or four times, later, I was still closer to extinction,' Manfred Arcane added, 'but the devil protects his own. You seem to like this wine, Didi. That second visit came long later, when the Italians held this port during the Second World War. In those days I was a double agent — but don't look so shocked, young lady, without knowing my motives. Something very startling indeed happened to me that second time. I don't suppose you'd care to hear about it. Shall we begin dinner with a soup? Oh, you *would* care to hear — really?'

Colonel Fuentes, glancing toward the longer table, said something in Spanish to his superior, *sotto voce*.

'Ah, that's of no consequence, Don Pelayo,' Arcane told him, in English. 'Let the police agents listen! They'll not apprehend me, not even my moral. As for what I was then — why, the President-Marshal doubtless would promulgate a general act of oblivion, for the sake of the precious treaty I am negotiating with him. Do you fancy, old friend, that I'm senile? Not yet, not yet, even though you find me in my anecdotage.'

He patted Didi's hand, not surreptitiously, and laid his other hand on Arthur's arm. 'This is a longish tale, and I don't expect you to believe it, you American materialists. With your permission, Judge? With your gracious permission, Didi? You both must be impatient already at my garrulity, my pert loquacity. But you do conceal your exasperation so mercifully! Are all your fellow-citizens of the sovereign state of Ohio so courteous? Well, then, if you insist, and promise that you'll not be frightened. . . .' Arcane drew an ugly-looking cigar, rather like a small torpedo, from an elegant leather case.

'You'll not mind my lighting this, Mrs. Ross — Didi? Honor bright? Why, you're as kind as you are lovely. Perhaps Diocletian's high-minded daughter Valeria was like you. The world fell to pieces after Diocletian abdicated — he had kept the lid upon chaos for more than twenty years — and even Valeria wasn't spared, and even that masterful father, Master and God, couldn't save her.

'I have taken you outside the Palace proper to offer you this True Narration of mine, because even now I am uneasy at talking of my curious experience within those ghostly precincts. The stones cry out, the walls have ears — and I don't refer to the electronic devices of our thin-lipped companions at the other table.'

He addressed Arthur. 'One of these Burma cheroots for you, Judge Ross? Your first? Permit me to light it. It won't be your last: I'll have a box or two posted to you, if you'll leave me your card, and if you don't suspect me of endeavoring to corrupt the bench.'

Didi sat at his right hand. As Arcane's flow of talk grew more intense, she edged closer and closer to this marvellous man, until she found herself nearly nose to nose with Mr. Arcane. She understood now what was meant by the phrase 'hanging on his words.'

'Taste your wine, friends,' Arcane had begun, 'settle well into your chairs, await your soup — they take an unholy time in this house to cook anything, I suspect — and I will lull you into somnolence. Don Pelayo, you never have heard this particular misadventure of mine.' Under his heavy and tufted white eyebrows, Arcane's pupils seemed to dilate as night descended upon the Grad of Split.

*   *

'What with my childhood being spent in Vienna,' Arcane observed, 'I came to Alice, her Wonderland, and her Looking-Glass later than I suppose you did, Arthur and Didi. One encounter of Alice impressed me when first I read Carroll at my English school, and it has an especial significance for me now. I mean the Red King's dream. The Red King snores, and Alice is told that should he wake, she and everything else would vanish, annihilated: for Alice, Tweedledum, and Tweedledee are figments of the King's dream. Does that notion terrify you? It jolly well terrifies me. It's worse than solipsism, to which I never was addicted. To be nothing better than a figure of somebody else's nocturnal fancy, at the mercy of the vagrant imagination of a dreaming god, perhaps . . . what horror! "If that there King was to wake," says Tweedledum, "you'd go out — bang! — just like a candle!" Alice replies that she wouldn't. Yet on a certain occasion I didn't share Alice's confidence.'

Arcane paused to knock ash from his cheroot. 'Here in Spalato, thirty-five years ago, I came upon such an omnipotent dreamer — just thirty-five years ago last night. And last night I endeavored to look him up again, but failed. I suspect that he still dreams, for all that.'

'*La vida es sueño, y los sueños son,*' Colonel Fuentes suggested sibilantly.

'My old comrade knows his Calderón,' Arcane told the Judge and Didi. 'Yes, "life is a dream, and dreams are dreams" — though you do well to ignore that insight when there's shooting to be done, Don Pelayo. Well, my particular dreamer was no Sleeping Beauty. But I must bore you with a prologue, for my curious experience with the grand dreamer commenced when I first stayed in this city.

'It was 1913 when my mother brought me here for a holiday — to a town more Austrian and Italian in tone, then, than it was Croatian. My mother was parsimonious, though well supplied with money every year. She took with us from Vienna a single servant-girl, and engaged rooms at a small hotel within the walls of the Palace. That hotel stands still. It must have been a merchant-noble's house in the beginning, a rambling old place, built and altered over the centuries, growing like a saprophyte out of the wreck of one of Diocletian's structures. At least one of its walls must be a fourth century Roman wall of limestone. I have slept there, after a fashion, for the past three nights, and will sleep there again tonight.

'Our rooms, in 1913, before those shots at Sarajevo ushered in our time of troubles, were along a corridor within a confused mass of building: a warren of a place, that hotel, the whole interior plastered over with eighteenth and nineteenth century decor. Because already I was an adventurous and willful boy, my mother put me into the biggish room at the very end of that hallway: I would have to pass her door, and our maid's, if I ventured upon a solitary expedition at some eccentric hour.

'My room, irregular in shape, was sparsely furnished with solid old pieces. It had only one window, and that looking through bars upon a tiny courtyard, scarcely more than a well, far below. The innkeeper seemed hesitant to assign that particular room to us; on being pressed, he said that some guests had not slept soundly there. Doubtless perceiving in Mother a superior sort of patron, he did not wish to allow her any cause for complaint. She disregarded his murmurs: precisely because that room was almost a prison, with no escape except past her own more cheerful chamber, she found it a very good place to lodge a very naughty boy.

'At our house in the Vienna Woods, I had been given to nocturnal rambles about the premises, because I am one of that small minority of the human species who are sleepiest at three in the afternoon but very wide awake indeed at three in the morning. Not meaning to have me stroll the Grad in the small hours, she locked me into my room after our supper — having had the hotel servants provide a tray of refreshments for me, on the chance that I might wake in the night and be hungry. I suffer from total recall: I am quite sure that upon the tray were some pieces of cold chicken on a bed of lettuce, two large Dalmatian figs, and three or four bonbons.

'But I digress. I did wake that first night in the little hotel, and at three o'clock. I woke up sharp, with a small boy's intuition of something being wrong. I was famished, ravenous, hungrier than ever before in my short life. Yet I did not reach at once for my tray. For it seemed to me as if someone or something else were in my room, or perhaps about to enter.

'The furniture did not include an *armoire*. Instead — unusual at that time and in this country — a kind of closet was set into one wall, draperies concealing it. The servants had hung or lain my clothes within that recess. It seemed to my puerile imagination that the uncanny element I sensed somehow emanated from that veiled closet.

'I had acquired early the habit, so useful later in life, of confronting danger directly, before the peril might undo one's resolution. So I threw off my feather-comforter, leaped from my bed, dashed at the recess, and thrust aside its draperies.

'Except for hooks, shelves, and my clothes, the recess was empty. But set into the rear wall of this closet was a battered classical doorway of stone, still very handsome in its decrepitude, fluted and ornamented. Had I been older, I would have recognized the carving as Roman. This doorway was closed by a massive ancient wooden door, studded with brass, probably medieval; presumably this led, or had led, into another suite of apartments — perhaps into another building which had a common wall with the hotel, for such forgotten connections are common enough in this beehive of a town, where for many centuries thousands of townsfolk were crowded together insufferably out of dread of Slav or Turk. This door was secured on my side of it by rusty iron bolts, shot home into the stonework.

'Being a mischievous boy, of course at once I attempted to draw the bolts — despite the oppressive or menacing atmosphere of the room, strongest here in this tall recess, which already had beset me. The bolts withstood my young fingers. Perhaps the door had settled immovably into place through many generations of disuse.

'I gave up the endeavor. Perfect hunger, like perfect love, casts out fear. Returning to my bedside, I gobbled down the chicken, the lettuce, the figs, the bonbons. Yet still I remained ferociously, intolerably hungry.

'And still the room was horrid, though clean and decently white-washed. I could not get out the window, fortunately for me — the distance to the ground being considerable. I was so frightened in my solitude that I did a shameful thing: I pounded upon the locked bedroom door and screamed for my mother. She heard me after two or three minutes, res-cued me, and let me into her own bed for the rest of the night. I was not troubled nocturnally for the rest of our fortnight in Spalato.'

Even though the anecdote seemed pointless, Didi was fascinated. 'Lit-tle kids get moods like that,' said Arthur.

The soup had been served, and Arcane consumed his speedily, as if the hunger of 1913 still were upon him. Then he took a different tack.

'Gaius Aurelius Valerius Diocletianus, "son of gods and creator of gods," born plain Diocles the son of a serf or a slave, built nobly,' he de-clared. 'The Palace is only the most enduring of his creations in stone. The first thing one sees in Rome, if one arrives by train, is the Baths of Diocletian — gigantic even in their disintegration, still housing churches, convents, museums, everything but bathers. Do you know that the Mau-soleum, to which I took you just now, is the best-preserved work of antiq-uity? After Diocletian, form began to decay: consider the Arch of Constantine, and that monstrous stone head of Constantine in a court-yard on the Capitoline — how rapid a descent of art!'

'Why did he persecute the Christians?' Didi asked.

'Nobody knows, my dear. He didn't mean to shed their blood: Galerius, Valeria's fierce husband, did that. I suppose his urgent need for unity in the empire which he had re-created was his underlying motive. Without him, *Romanitas* would have been destroyed in the third century, rather than the sixth. He was a just man, imaginative, more merciful than most, a grand general, a great administrator. In the reconstituted Empire, everything depended upon loyalty to the person of the Emperor, and the Christians preferred one other loyalty above that — even the Christian nobles of the complex bureaucracy that Diocletian had organized.

'Or he may have been misled by the intriguing courtiers about him: no one knew better than Diocletian the corruption of imperial courts. It's quite the same nowadays in the "emergent nations," I assure you. What was it that Diocletian told a friend? It's in Vopiscus somewhere. Yes, I have it now; I do pride myself upon my memory.

'"How often is it the interest of four or five ministers to combine together to deceive their sovereign," Diocletian said. "Secluded from mankind by his exalted dignity, the truth is concealed from his knowledge; he can see only with their eyes, he hears nothing but their misrepresentations. He confers the most important offices upon vice and weakness, and disgraces the most virtuous and deserving among his subjects. By such infamous arts, the best and wisest princes are sold to the venal corruption of their courtiers."'

Arcane took a coin from his pocket and let his fingers play with it. 'I have quoted those sentences more than once to His Sublimity Achmet ben Ali, Hereditary President of Hamnegri and Sultan in Kalidu; but they are words upon the wind. I also, after all, am one of those intriguing ministers to the isolated great. Of course you have no such problems in your democratic America, Judge Ross — or have you?'

Arthur opened his mouth to say something, but already Arcane had resumed.

'Though a Papist myself, I say that the Christian writers of Constantine's time grossly libelled old Diocletian, and his wife Prisca too. They even accused him of cowardice at the end — of "procuring his own death." In reality he was utterly fearless. He did what no emperor before him had dared to essay: having ridden the tiger for more than twenty years, he dismounted. Having given peace to all the provinces, from Britain to Syria, he relinquished authority to his subordinates, settled in this Palace, grew cabbages, and prayed to the gods.

'Diocletian was a pious man, in the old Roman sense of that word, a champion of worship, of loyalty, of family, of private property. Nor was he vain. The diadem with pearls that he wore, the buskins, the imperial purple robes, were not effeminate affectations. Not sycophancy for himself, but reverence for the office of emperor, were their purpose. They were symbols of order, justice, peace; they meant that the emperor was more than a rude demagogic master of soldiers — even though Diocletian himself had been little more than that when he took power and beat back the barbarians.'

'But didn't he say he was a god?' Didi was proud of her little learning. 'That wasn't very modest.'

'The last god of the classical world?' Arcane nodded. 'He was apotheosized by the Senate after his death: the last man-created god. And even during his life, on his coins — he reformed the currency prudently — he was called *dominus et deus*, Master and God. What Diocletian himself understood by this glorification, I take it, was that Jupiter, lord god of hosts, had imparted to his humble and obscure servant Diocles some little spark of divinity, that he might uphold Rome in an hour of dreadful need. How else to account for Diocletian's great gifts, and his astounding successes — the lowness of the man's origins considered? In my own small way, I am tempted to embrace Diocletian's theory of inspiration — being, as I am, the bastard son of a half-gypsy dancer.'

Arcane lit a second cheroot. 'Diocletian was true to such light as was given him. The high old Roman virtue was reborn in him. In religion, he may have been a Mithraist at bottom; we know that he dedicated the Temple of Mithra at Carnuntum, on the Danube, and Mithraism was the soldier's fate then. Mithra's votaries may have pushed him into his persecution of the Christians: because of their close similarities, Mithraists and Christians hated each other, and the Christians took their retribution in Constantine's reign. However that may be, the Christian zealots of the fourth century shouted that Diocletian must burn eternally for his wickedness. In those times no one talked of merciful salvation on the ground of "invincible ignorance."'

'You said that his wife and daughter were beheaded, and he couldn't stop it,' Didi interjected. 'So how much of a god was he?'

'That, Didi, came a decade after Diocletian's abdication, and it was done by one of the hard men upon whom his imperial powers had devolved. "Power tends to corrupt, and absolute power corrupts absolutely." That was true of Diocletian's successors, though not of himself. The heirs to his power made certain that the heirs of Diocletian's body were extirpated.   '

'And when Constantine the Great had eliminated most rivals, he determined to eradicate the weary old man in the Palace near Salona — though Constantine's family owed everything to Diocletian. Constantine commanded Diocletian to attend a wedding at Milan. The old emperor knew that he never would be permitted to return to this Palace alive, and so he declined the invitation. Then Constantine and Licinius — the one who had murdered Diocletian's wife and daughter — sent him menacing letters. He was sixty-eight years old, and there was nowhere he could turn — not in this world, of which he had been absolute master. The panegyrists of Constantine say that Diocletian, craven at the end, had himself killed in his own house. I know that he died most honorably, as an antique hero should — better even than did Cato of Utica.'

Didi was being taught more than she needed to know about the Emperor Diocletian, enthralling though this antiquary from Africa was. 'But you were going to tell us about what happened to you in Split during World War II.' Was she being rude?

Arcane patted her hand again. 'Forgive the ramblings of an ancient, child of America: I must seem as old to you as Diocletian himself, now don't protest — I know you think me totally decrepit, a dotard, a eunuch, a dolt. You weren't born when the second episode of my True Narration came to pass. Let me plead that what I've just told you isn't altogether irrelevant to my interminable yarn. If you'll forgive me — you Americans and your passion for "relevance"! Relevance is to truth as price is to real worth. Now eat your veal before it's quite cold, and I'll approach the climax.'

He put down beside his plate the coin with which he had been playing as he talked, and took up knife and fork. 'Do you know, every one of us has too much ego in his cosmos. Here I fill my belly before tearing a passion to tatters. Wasn't it your President John Adams who said that every man must have first his dinner and then his girl? Meanwhile, as we feast and couple, our neighbors expire in agony — girl lost, dinner wanting. How right Augustine was about our universal corruption! Do try those lentils — not half bad, if one adds a little salt.'

The restaurant was full of people now, nearly all of them Yugoslavs, Didi noticed. Mr. Arcane had sent more bottles of wine to those secret police in the corner. In the lane outside, the evening crowd laughed and bantered and quarreled, as crowds had done here since Diocletian's death.

'Don't you think we ought to get back to our hotel?' Arthur whispered to her.

'No!' said Didi.

Having finished his *pièce de résistance*, Manfred Arcane called for finger-bowls. 'I demand such amenities on principle in Marxist lands, along with *cuisine bourgeois,*' he told Didi. 'It's a pity you're traveling by car: motor-vessel along the Dalmatian shore is ever so much more pleasant. Do you know, Colonel Fuentes and I have been voyaging *first*-class, quite comfortably, on a Communist ship called the *Proletarska* — the female proletarian? All animals are equal, remember, but some are more equal than others. I suppose you've heard enough and to spare of my memories. What shall we choose for dessert? They compound a reasonably appetizing chocolate soufflé here, I'm told.'

'Oh, please, please, go on with the story!' Didi insisted. 'I just adore the way you talk, Manfred. It makes me feel like a little girl hearing the *Arabian Nights* for the first time.'

'And I adore you in turn, Didi Ross — that is, with your generous permission, Judge Ross. I'm sure you're tired, Arthur: hadn't we best consume some brandy and then escort you back to the glittering splendors of the Hotel Marjan?'

'Don't you dare!' Didi cried. 'Arthur will get his second wind after coffee.' Too late, it occurred to her that she shouldn't have spoke quite so forcefully. Manfred had refilled her wine-glass several times.

'Then once more into the breach, dear friends.' Arcane ordered the soufflé all round, not forgetting the black henchmen and the security-men. 'How bored those unfortunate tight-lipped chaps must be! But when duty whispers low, *Thou must,* the flic replies, *I can.* I shall keep them up to all hours, guarding me and spying upon me.

'So be it, good companions. My second expedition to Spalato — Split, if you must — was far more lively than my first, and just thirty years later. Where had I been meanwhile? Why, having finished school in England, and having idled about Vienna, I was commissioned in the cavalry of a native prince in India; tired of that after some years; took a house in Spain, having plenty of money, thanks to my mother's frugality and the munificence of my father on the wrong side of the blanket — who never visited us after 1914. Presently the Civil War engulfed me at Toledo, and I fought, willy-nilly, on the illiberal side. Then I lived in Rome for a time, fell in love with a countess . . .'

'Did you marry her?' Didi wanted that story, too. The wine had made her forget, for a moment, that the countess might have had a count-husband already.

Arcane's dark ageless face ceased to be bland and turned impassive. 'No, my dear lady. She died in torment, a prisoner, a saint. In hope of ransoming her life, I turned double agent in Italy and Germany and other lands, during the War. No occupation for a gentleman, you may be thinking? Too true. But then, like dear Daisy Ashford's Mr. Salteena, I am not quite a gentleman, though you would hardly notice — or would you?

'It was as double agent, with a Spanish passport and a quasi-consular commission from the Spanish government, that I arrived in Spalato in 1943. An Italian garrison, not driven out until two years later, held this city. It would take too long for me to describe the secret business I was about, or how that business had some connection with my private motive.

'It was a risky errand for me, my Machiavellian notoriety having preceded me in certain knowledgeable quarters. The Italian administration suspected me; so did Tito's people, underground in Spalato, fancying that I was a courier to the Chetniks; while the Chetnik agents entertained grave doubts of my reliability, the German representatives in Spalato were not at all sure whether I was on their side, and the Croatian Ustachi wondered if I sympathized with the Serbs. My Spanish papers and connection were some protection against prompt open arrest — but not against being spirited away secretly to one brutal interrogation-chamber or another. What game I really was playing I may tell you another time, Didi — and of course you, too, Arthur — if you are at leisure.

'The Spanish consul feared to put me up, and the city was jammed with refugees and with Italian troops, many of the officers quartered upon the hotels. No room at any inn, no pillow where a self-respecting spy might lay his weary head! A young woman strolling the quays kindly invited me to share her lodging, for a reasonable fee; but I had come to spy out the nakedness of the land, not the nakedness of its women. Then I recalled the name, and the street, of the quaint hotel where Mother and I had stayed three decades before — by coincidence, three decades to the very day.

'The clerk at the counter protested that he had no room at all. But I jingled in my hand some gold pieces — nobody desiring inflated banknotes then — and said to him, "There is always a bed somewhere, if in a room not wholly desirable. May I have that biggish room at the end of the corridor on the upper floor — at a premium?" I laid my gold on the counter.

'The clerk started. "It does happen to be empty tonight, sir," he confessed. I told him to have me shown up.

'Except for the whitewash having turned dingy, that room was unaltered. Entrenched within, I looked to the door-fastenings, which seemed insufficient. So I propped a chair against the knob, and reinforced it with a heavy chest. I was exhausted from my long and hazardous trip all the way from Barcelona. I slipped my short pistol under my pillow, thrust my long knife into the money-belt I always wore about my waist, and went to sleep.

'As if time had had a stop, I woke at three in the morning, filled with dread as I had been thirty years earlier. How furiously hungry I was — and no chicken, no figs, no bonbons this night! In my diverse shadowy occupations, steady nerves are necessary. But I was all on edge, without ascertainable cause except the general recklessness of my mission. It was chilly and damp; I rose, put on my dressing-gown. . . .

'Only just in time. For at that moment I heard masculine whispers outside my door, and a key inserted in the lock; the knob was turned cautiously.

'I suppose you know that both our hard-faced companions at that long table, and practiced terrorists, prefer to take captives in the small hours, when the victims are befuddled by sleep. Mid-afternoon, on the other hand, is a kind of time-sanctuary for the hunted. I had learned not to parley with gentlemen of that kidney, at that fatal hour of three o' the morning, when most dying people give up the ghost. In such circumstances, the best recourse is to flee incontinent, forsaking goods and chattels.

'There remained one forlorn hope — that stubborn old door at the back of the recess. I did not even snatch up my pistol, which would have been useless against such odds in a cul-de-sac. I bounded for those closet draperies as the men outside forced my door and stumbled in the dark over chair and chest. My fingers found the door-bolts that had defied me thirty years before. Concealed behind the draperies, I tugged at those bolts with bleeding fingers. I heard someone lurch against my bed. One bolt gave, and I was crouched down fighting with the lower bolt when the curtains were ripped away and men groped in the blackness for me.

'Something struck my head. But the second bolt had yielded. I forced the creaking disused door part of the way open. Another bludgeon-blow fell upon me. Writhing snakelike, I crept through. . . .'

'They didn't catch you, Manfred!' Didi squealed. Even Arthur, having gained that second wind of his, was listening open-mouthed. 'Santiago de Compostela!' Colonel Fuentes muttered.

Arcane waited for them to subside. 'What followed is difficult to express in words,' he sighed in his musical voice. 'Coffee now? Plum brandy? A pale liqueur for you, blonde Didi?'

Except for their party, the restaurant had nearly emptied by this time, and the two waiters had on their faces that expression of Stoic apathy not uncommonly encountered in Dalmatia, as in Spain — perhaps a legacy from centuries of feud and hatred, every man's hand against every other man's. They regarded the remaining diners unsmilingly.

'We must appease these proletarian comrades of the private sector,' Arcane remarked. Colonel Fuentes produced several hundred-franc Swiss bank-notes — as if his superior owned all the money in the world except fourteen francs — and handed them to the waiters. 'Let us not be disturbed,' Arcane told them — at least that was what Didi surmised he must be saying in Serbo-Croat — and the waiters brightened perceptibly. The coffee, the brandy, the liqueurs were produced, and their tables were left in peace.

'Though earth be mixed with fire,' Arcane confided to Didi, 'one constant is not corrupted by rust or moth: the generous gratuity. As it was in the beginning, is now, and ever shall be, world without end, the tickling of the palm works all manners of wonders.' What an amusing fantastic this cosmopolite was — Austrian-cum-Englishman-cum-Spaniard-cum-Italian-cum-African!

Didi tugged at his silken lapel; she would have liked to have tugged at his silky beard — this old-young tormentor's, playfully teasing. 'Go on, go on, please, pretty please! What was behind that old door?'

'Did Guinevere bully Launcelot thus — begging your indulgence, Arthur? I'll tell the tale out, if you'll promise not to choke me, dearest lady. What happened is infinitely troublesome to account for.'

Arcane sipped his brandy, then his coffee. The four police agents, and even the two scarred black men, were listening unabashedly. Everyone else, the very waiters, had departed. It had grown almost cold and quite silent in the room, except for the urbane voice of the subtle Minister without Portfolio.

*   *

'Beyond that door I stumbled upon a short flight of brick steps,' Arcane said. 'I reeled up them. Blood was trickling thickly down my head and neck.

'At the top of the steps was a second door — a huge one, of bronze. Flinging my weight upon it, I made it yield. I slipped through, and it swung shut soundlessly behind me. On the far side of that door hung a kind of bronze bar, attached somehow to the door itself. I fixed that bar in place, fumbling in my haste. To my astonishment, there came no noise of pursuit.

'I was horribly giddy and distraught. Even so, the marvelous beauty of the high, long room in which I found myself still is fixed in my mind's eye. The tessellated pavement under my bare feet was all one vast colored mosaic. From floor to ceiling, elaborate frescoes and more mosaics covered the walls. There was no interior illumination, but light came from several small windows high up, and from skylights of a sort, two or three of them, set into the roof.

'I was barefoot, wearing only robe and pyjamas, armed only with the sheath-knife thrust into my money belt. I was wounded, and friendless in a strange town. Even so, for a moment I was lost in wonder at the classical perfection of this secret place.

'And this salon was well furnished, with what I took for superb copies of the Roman couches, tables, and chairs that one sees in the classical mosaics and frescoes. How can I give you some concept of their curious richness? Do you know your New York Metropolitan Museum? And perhaps the Roman rooms to the left, as one enters, on the principal floor? Good! Then you have seen the sort of thing I found that night.

'So far as I could reflect at all in this moment of peril, I took it that some magnificent virtuoso of Spalato must have commissioned or collected these reproductions, and have had floor and walls decorated, at unthinkable expense, in antique fashion. The building itself, butting against the old hotel, must be one of several medieval or renaissance family palaces — most of them slums now — which survive in the Grad.

'But I never had imagined that such a gem of mock-antiquity had existed anywhere in Dalmatia. The nearest thing to it that I have seen anywhere is on the Thames, of all situations — Syon House, whose interiors Robert Adam fitted up in Roman style for the Percys in the eighteenth century, with columns fished from the bed of the Tiber, mosaics transported from Roman ruins, all those priceless fragments he gathered. It was Adam, don't you know, who rediscovered Diocletian's Palace for the eighteenth century world of scholarship, taste, and fashion, and made his splendid drawings of the Palace, and tried to excavate Diocletian's cellars — and was expelled from Spalato by the Venetians, who thought him a spy! But of course I wasn't thinking about that remarkable Scot Robert

Adam, architect, of Kirkcaldy, as I stood dazed and bloody in this enchanted great hall.

'There was no one in the immense shadowy room — not surprising, the hour considered. It was totally silent. At any moment my adversaries might seize me. I had no notion of whether the occupants of this palace could, or would, shelter me from the gang that had burst into my hotel room.

'My head ached hideously, yet my stomach ached worse. The gnawing ravenousness which had oppressed me in the hotel, thirty years earlier and again this violent night, was inexpressibly worse here in this salon. I had not known that living man ever could be so hungry as I was at that moment — and when in imminent danger of capture or death, too! Had there been a blessed bowl of fruit in this room, I would have devoured it all like a wolf, right then, regardless of the hounds on my heels. But there was nothing at all to eat, so far as I could tell.

'I must get out of this place, as much to satisfy my appetite as to evade killers! I couldn't go back the way I had come, of course; but two massive marble doorways, with double doors of bronze, stood along the wall to my right. I dashed at the first of them. The handles or massive knobs had been removed from the inner side of those doors. Heedless of risk, I shook the doors, pried at them: they would not stir, and perhaps they had been fastened immovably on their outer sides. I scurried to the second doorway — and was frustrated again. This place was like a sealed tomb.

'During the few moments I had spent in this precarious sanctuary, a storm had begun to rise over the Adriatic — bellows and crashes of thunder, gigantic flashes of lightning, though no rain seemed to be falling yet. By one bright thunderbolt, I made out an open doorway in the further wall of the sala; presumably it led to other apartments. I passed through that doorway.

'On the right-hand side of the corridor, several beautiful closed doors were visible; I was able to open none of them. To my left was a long doorless wall, covered with mosaics, probably parallel with the harbor; the windows were too high up for me to glance out. I trotted stealthily the length of that corridor, and entered another large room.

'Here stood two marble statues, painted in part, on pedestals: both were twice life-size. I had seen no picture of either of them before, and their condition was so perfect that they must be successful modern imitations of classical sculpture, carved in the finest stone. One figure unmistakably was a tremendous Jupiter. The other, with a Phrygian cap and a knife in his hand, must be a representation of the god Mithra.

'I had no leisure to admire them. Beyond the images of the gods was yet another open doorway. Once I passed through that, I smelt the faint odor of burning oil. To my right was a doorway, apparently of porphyry, with a curtain hanging across it; and from behind that curtain came a slight glimmer of lamplight.

'In such a house as this, a half-naked intruder might be turned over to the police, but it was improbable that he should be beaten, tortured, or slain instantly. I parted the curtains, and could make out a silver lamp of the antique form burning on a marble table, but nothing else except some pieces of furniture. Might there be something to eat in this room? I went in.

'There came a faint suppressed groan which made me forget aching head and aching belly. Then a low masculine voice spoke, a touch of sardonic humour in it:

'"*Pastor, arator, eques, pavi, colui, superavi*
Capras, rus, hostes, fronde, ligone, manu."'

Didi gripped Manfred Arcane's wrist, sharply, at this point. 'Oh! What did that mean!'

The old adventurer had spoken almost in a trance: at Didi's clutch, he shook his white head as if to clear it. 'Forgive me, I had forgotten the decay of Latin in Ohio,' he said, tartly, rubbing his wrist — which Didi's long nails had scratched. 'But why should I blame you? I did not recognize the lines myself, though they had something Virgilian in them. I did catch the meaning, which runs much like this:

'"As shepherd, ploughman, knight, I've pastured, tilled, subdued
Herds, farms, and enemies, with herbage, hoe, and arms."'

Arcane was pale. He seemed to take hold upon himself, and continued.

'Beyond the silver lamp was a couch; and on that couch a tall man was lying, a purple mantle thrown over him. He did not rise; soon I found that he could not. He spoke in Latin. As I mentioned to you, I was a tolerable scholar in that language once. Yet I found difficulty in following him — not only because he spoke feebly, but because the pronunciation and some of his words were strange to me.

'How shall I put it? Why, suppose you were a Bantu who had studied painstakingly the plays of Shakespeare, but no other English. And suppose you abruptly found yourself confronted by an elderly general of the twentieth century, from San Francisco, speaking colloquial American. How well would you, the Bantu, understand the general? I had been schooled in Cicero, and I was hearing the Latin of a time as remote from Cicero as our time is remote from Shakespeare.

'I stood there frozen. The man upon the couch murmured in his exhaustion and delirium. "I have raised legions and cabbages. Have you been sent by Constantine and Licinius to strangle me? It is late for that."

'Another fierce flash of lightning showed me his face, ghastly thin and pallid, the face of a man starved and dying. I saw the broad forehead, the long prominent nose, the weary eyes, the lined cheeks, the severe mouth, the strong chin. I knew him.

'I flung myself down upon the mosaic pavement beside the couch. "Dominus!" I gasped.'

Arcane stroked his beard meditatively, paused, resumed with an effort. 'I suppose I was in ecstasy. This word "ecstasy" signifies "sensual joy" to nearly everybody nowadays: ours is a corrupt time, with corrupt meanings. Actually, "ecstasy" means to be extended, transported out of one's self. I was transported out of time and space, out of the body, out of the sensual world. I was overwhelmed with feeling, yet not terrified. I was beyond fear.

'"Ah, you are a friend then, a foolish friend, though I do not know your face," said the feeble voice with its undertone of high authority. "I think that you are a soldier. Have you come to tempt me? It is late for that also. I shall eat nothing, and in a little time I shall be spirit only. I no longer even desire a morsel of bread, nor an olive, nor could I contain them. Constantine and Licinius shall not take me. I have failed in living; I shall not fail in dying."

'"Imperator!" I whispered.

'"Rise up, foolish friend," said Diocletian.

'I contrived somehow to stand. His eyes must have been keen enough still, for all his extreme debility.

'"I see that you are wounded, friend," the Emperor went on. "I think that you are dying, as I am." His slow voice was like a distant gong. "Do you come to me for justice? I could not do justice upon Licinius for murdering Prisca and Valeria. What could I do for you? Justice also is dying in this world. You and I must appeal to the God of All, for only with him justice abides."

'Rain had begun to patter in at a high window. The blue lightning outside blazed in sheets now, near at hand. The Emperor was saying something more, but thunder drowned his words. In my ecstasy I was not denied memory.

'Staring at the man upon the couch, I remembered how the Emperor Carinus, on campaign against the Persians, had been struck by lightning in his litter; and how to Carinus's power there had succeeded one of his bodyguards — Diocles, or Diocletian. I remembered in that icy moment, too, that when Diocletian had published his edict against the Christians, lightning twice had struck his palace at Nicomedia, nearly destroying it, burning his bedchamber. And Diocletian had taken to himself the divine name of Jove, Jupiter of the thunderbolts, proclaiming himself one predestined to participate in Jupiter's eternal nature. Amidst strokes of lightning Diocletian had lived, and now he was expiring among them.

'Despite the frightful electrical storm then striking about the Palace, the starved master of the world did not shudder or start. His lips moved, and I bent close to him.

'"Where are we, friend?" he sighed. "Are we between Heaven and Earth, between time and eternity? It seems to me that I have been dreaming here age upon age." He muttered then some sentences I could not follow, closed his eyes, slowly opened them again, spoke once more.

'"Fasting to death here, I have dreamed of all times and all lands. I have dreamed of all follies and vanities. I have dreamed of my Prisca and my Valeria, who knew how to live and to die with honor. I have dreamed of Maximian, Galerius, Constantius Chlorus, with whom I shared the burden of empire — all gone down to death before me."

'With a forefinger he could only just move, he beckoned to me to come closer still. "Are you a phantom, friend? Your face is strange to me. Was everything always dream? How can you answer me, if you are but a creature of my long dream. Did I summon you, ghost calling to ghost? You cannot have entered as fleshly man enters, for I have sealed the doors. When I cease to dream, will you cease to be? Am I to dream in this room until the sun and all the stars grow cold, until the gods themselves are dead? Father Jove, give me a sign!"

'Then the lightning came in at a high window, destroying all shadow, revealing mercilessly the Emperor's face of agony. A tremendous sparkling fireball, particles innumerable, all at war with one another, ran frenziedly about the chamber, spitting, consuming, and struck Diocletian there on the couch. Amid that indescribable electrical blaze, I fell, and the ecstasy was ended.'

*   *

Didi gazed stupefied at Manfred Arcane. 'That was quite a dream!' Arthur offered. Colonel Fuentes was crossing himself.

'A dream?' Arcane shook his head. 'An experience. True, my body did not pass through that old door. Nor did I awake in the hotel. After some days, I woke in a military hospital, and remained there a good deal longer. I wouldn't have survived, had it not been for the chance, or providential circumstance, that when I was carried to the hospital with a broken skull I was recognized by an Italian military surgeon who had known me in Rome. He patched me up skillfully. Even so, after being deported from Dalmatia, I had to lie resting for three months in my house at Toledo, while the world tore itself to pieces.'

'Then those men actually did break into your room?' Didi demanded. 'And you didn't get away?'

'Precisely. Whoever they were, they beat me about the head and left me for dead in the closet. They took my pistol and my papers — though the documents can't have been of much benefit to them, for the more important part of my mission I had committed to memory only.'

Fuentes raised his eyebrows. 'They were . . . ?'

'The Italian military said it hadn't been their work, and I believed them. Were the gang the Marshal's partisans? Probably. I did not raise that tender subject with the venerable President last week, and it's unlikely that he knows himself, for I was of no great consequence at the time, and he has slain his myriads. I babbled much during my stay in the hospital, out of my head, but the Italians concluded that though perhaps something of a spy, I was more of a harmless lunatic; so they were content to expel me from Spalato.'

'But what about the rooms behind the door in the closet?' Didi was flushed and wonder-struck. 'Didn't you ever find out?'

'Not until this morning, my dear. I was transferred from hospital to ship, on being deported, without stay or ceremony, and I hadn't set foot again in Spalato until this week. Must you have the epilogue? What a little glutton for punishment you are! Very well: if you and Arthur don't object to a stroll after this prolonged dinner of ours, I'll lead you up through Veli Varos, which is more or less on the way to your hotel: an eighteenth century suburb of peasants, labyrinthine as the Grad, on slopes. On the way you shall have my sequel.'

They all left the restaurant, the woman cook locking the door behind them. They said little to each other for some minutes, marveling or embarrassed. Arcane spoke a few words to the security-man, who took the lead as they walked uphill. 'I recall vaguely a spot where my mother and I sat once, looking down at the Grad, somewhere high in Veli Varos, and that chap thinks he can take us there,' Arcane told Didi. He fell silent again.

Arthur — who, as Didi knew too well, grew uncomfortable when other people narrated their dreams — was walking ahead, beside the security chief; she guessed that he was asking him about crime and punishment in Yugoslavia. Flanked by Manfred and Fuentes, Didi made her way upward through the dreamy night, picturesque stone cottages on either side of their tortuous route. Their retinue of grim men loitered in the rear.

'Manfred,' she ventured with hesitation, 'you've done everything, and you've been everywhere, even out of the world. Why have you bothered with us? Arthur is so dull, and I'm so silly!'

There came a low laugh. 'How you undervalue yourself, young woman! Yet I confess that I chose you two for reasons. For one, you are *substantial*, both of you. I don't mean plump — perish the thought! Arthur is a fine figure of a man, and you are a finer figure of a young woman, Didi Ross. I mean, rather, that indubitably you two are flesh and blood, healthily normal, not given to illusions, not in love with shadows, not phantoms yourselves: sound sensible folk.'

Privately, Didi was not quite sure she relished the latter part of that description. Sensible? What about feeling?

'Now my duties, African and European, bring me into the company of human grotesques — people warped, bent, eccentric. You and the Judge are centric: what a relief! My usual companions — I exempt stout Fuentes — are afflicted by Augustine's three lusts: by cupidity, passion for possessions; by the lust for power, usurping the throne of God; by the lust for women's bodies — or men's. Such folk cannot be trusted with confidences, candid memoirs, and I love to be frank. You can be trusted; and besides, being out of my world, there's no one to whom you could betray me. How strange and pleasant to talk with the innocent! Centricity, all hail!'

She didn't know that she relished this praise, either. Could she win a personality contest as Mrs. Centricity of 1978? Arcane held her arm tightly, lest she stumble on the cobbles; he was strong still.

'More than that, Didi, the experiences of yesterday that I have promised to describe to you, and my boring reminiscences of this evening, have cast my consciousness into the realm of phantoms. In Hamnegri, the vulgar call me "the Father of Shadows" — signifying that I have slain many in war, and that my ways are crepuscular. You and the Judge, so substantial, fetch me back from the antagonist world of madness and despair to the ordered world — or what remains of it — that is supported by custom and convention: the sort of world that Diocletian vainly fought to shore up. Have I answered your question, Fair One?'

This man, with his playfulness, also was the man who dared to sleep again, night after night, in the Hungry Room where the violence and horror had come upon him. She'd never have poked her nose within that chamber door — unless Manfred Arcane was with her. Brave as Diocletian! Had Diocletian flirted? Probably not. There was a Latin word, she thought, for what Diocletian had possessed and what Manfred didn't: *gravitas*, that was it. Arthur had considerable *gravitas*. She hadn't reflected on that when she had accepted his ring.

Manfred glanced at her slyly. 'And besides, you are so very pretty! I possess a collection of grotesques, and another collection of pretty things — among the latter, my antique medallions and coins, my Italian primitive paintings, my ivories — some kept in Spain, some in Hamnegri. Would that I were a Moslem! Then I might keep a harem in the old slavers' lair of Haggat, and carry you off, a Sabine prize, from the good Judge. But, Papist that I am and pillar of righteousness that in recent years I have tried to become, all I may do is to present a pretty thing to a pretty creature.'

He took from his pocket the coin with which he had been playing in the restaurant, and pressed it into Didi's surprised palm. 'There! When I am lapped in lead, which should occur not many years from now, take this from your jewel-case now and again, and recollect me — and the Emperor, too.'

It was a Roman medallion of gold, in splendid condition, almost as if it had been minted yesterday. On the face was Diocletian in clear profile, wearing a solar crown — a massive head, beautifully delineated, the Emperor's eyes weary, his expression composed and confident. On the obverse was a superb Jupiter, with thunderbolt and scepter, his foot upon a barbarian; winged Victory was offering him a globe.

They had paused under a streetlamp, Fuentes having walked on ahead, to examine the little treasure. 'For me!' Didi exclaimed. 'But this ought to be in a museum!'

'Clap it in your boudoir-museum, young madam.'

'Wherever did you get this, Manfred?' A wild surmise rose in Didi's mind; her lips parted in wonder.

'Would you believe me, Didi Ross, if I told you that Diocletian thrust it into my palm, as just now I pressed it into your little hand?'

'*Really?* I'd believe almost anything you might tell me.'

'Would you? Then you *would* be rather silly. I'm crammed with guile: thus I survive in Africa. But I shan't deceive you tonight. No, there's a great gulf fixed between the realm of matter and the realm of spirit, and such light trinkets as this can't be tossed across that gulf. The Emperor gave me no aureate mementoes — only an apologue of sorts.

'This medallion I happened upon day before yesterday, in a curio-shop of the Grad. The proprietor fetched it out from under the counter, surreptitiously, and would not say where he'd acquired it. I suspect it may have been found by some light-fingered laborer in the cellars of the Palace, under the imperial apartments, where the excavations still are going on. This fine thing lay buried in dung, century upon century.

'If I didn't like you heartily, Didi, I should have played upon your in-genuousness and have told you that the Emperor defied nature to endow me with this souvenir. Yet isn't it nearly as marvelous that I contrived to pick up such a rarity just when I was about to make my romantic attempt upon that clay-sealed bronze door, once penetrated in vision? Now look at the obverse again. The figure of Jupiter on this medallion is identical with the statue of Jupiter I saw in the Emperor's halls, that night I was knocked on the head.'

'Oh, Manfred! How . . .'

From a little higher up the lane, the security-man called something discreetly. 'He's found the bench!' Arcane rejoiced.

There was a small open space by a great old fig-tree, and in it was a marble seat, chipped and worn. 'Do rest here, and I'll conclude my True Narration,' Arcane told them. 'I'll be Ancient Pistol for you.'

The seat had room for four, but Arcane stood before them, his ebony stick held like a sword, self-mockingly playing Bobadill. Cleon and Brasidas squatted on the ground, their liquid round eyes fixed upon their foster-father. The security-men leaned against a garden wall, pretending to hear nothing. Below them, to the east, were the lights of the Grad. They could make out the dim bulk of the Palace, and the medieval campanile was illuminated.

'I told you, Judge,' Arcane began, 'that my misadventure of 1943 — the strangest part of it — was no dream, but an *experience*. I must have been very near to physical extinction, lying beaten about the head in that closet. But the soul — *animula*, the Romans would have said, that which animates the carcass — somehow flitted. My *animula* burst from time into timelessness. Remember another great emperor's lines — *"Animula vagula, blandula . . ."* You don't? Let me put it into English:

> 'Little, gentle, wandering soul,
> Guest and comrade of the body,
> Who departest into space,
> Naked, stiff, and colorless,
> All thy wonted jests are done.

So the magnificent Hadrian, dying.'

'You really did find the Emperor there, then?' Didi bent forward toward Arcane in her intensity. 'You *went* there, without a body?'

'I *know* it, Judge's wife. But what proof might I offer scoffing Diogenes — or your Judge here? Yet what is our word "there," and what our word "then"? He and I were in space of a sort — reconstituted or restored space, if you will, but seemingly tangible space. Energy cannot be created, nor can it be destroyed: it merely alters its forms and expressions. The thunderbolt, the fireball, are energy pure and chaotic, agglomerations of atoms which assume patterns more infinitely varied than the patterns of a child's kaleidoscope. And why should we disbelieve that some inscrutable Will may shape again, for some moments, a pattern discarded long ago?

'As for "then" — why, according to the greatest of your American poets, time present and time past are both perhaps contained in time future, and time future contained in time past. In some fashion, this nocturnal happy moment in Veli Varos which we share, just "now" is a timeless moment. Beyond the frontiers of time, we may live it afresh.'

'I believe that,' said Didi, and little tears ran down her cheeks.

'I don't,' said Arthur. 'I won't buy that.'

'I'm not offering it at auction, Judge Ross. "At the Devil's booth all things are sold. . . ." No one can traffick in love and eternity. Am I turning sententious?' Arcane abruptly flung his ebony stick with the elephant's head high into the air, caught it like a juggler, brandished it as if it were a baton. 'I'm no doctor of the schools, but a clown. Had I stayed longer, I would have essayed to make the Emperor himself laugh. One may as well laugh as cry.'

Could this agile man, with his skipping energy, really have been born before the crash of empires, as he declared? Didi was dabbing at her cheeks with her handkerchief; Arthur looked vexed at that.

'So what did you find in that hotel of yours last night and this morning, Arcane?' Arthur sounded like Doubting Thomas.

Arcane put his stick behind his back and leaned upon it, like a Victorian dandy. 'On the first two nights, this week, I was restless and disquieted, nothing more: I suppose that is what most hotel-guests experience in that particular room. Last night, however — my anniversary night, so to speak — I woke suddenly at three, and the frightful hunger came upon me. It was not quite so intense, I think, as on the first and second occasions, but it was trying enough.

'I looked into that closet. The ancient door was unaltered, and those bolts had not stirred from their sockets: I could not pretend even to myself that I had succeeded in forcing them in 1943 — not physically. But the *animula* drew them that year, I assure you. That was all which happened last night, and I didn't go so far in my enthusiasm for mysteries as to hire thugs to bash in my head for me all over again. My dread last night was less, because I *knew*. The truly horrid terrors are the unknown terrors.'

'But the door!' Didi entreated. 'Are those rooms actually behind that door?'

Arcane came over and sat beside her on the bench. 'I had decided not to tamper with the door in the recess until I had made my scouting expedition of last night. It might not have done to alter the physical conditions; we don't know what laws govern such phenomena. Incidentally, almost nothing seems to have changed in that room since 1943, except that the walls are painted pink now. But I arranged, yesterday afternoon, for two curators from the Municipal Museum in the Papalic palace to visit me in my room this morning; also two joiners.

'The curators were surprised and delighted to find the battered stone doorway — of a limestone that blackens with age, a stone used elsewhere in portions of the Palace — back of the recess. They'd had no notion it was there. How many other curiosities lie undiscovered in the Grad, even though archeologists and architects and artists had been poking about energetically ever since Adam — since Robert Adam that is? The curators pronounced that doorway very late third century work, probably part of Diocletian's original construction.

'Yet there could be nothing behind the old door, they declared. "Let me see, then," I told them. You will understand that I hadn't informed them about what had happened to me in this room during the War; I didn't wish them to think me madder than I am. This was unseemly haste for members of the museum-bureaucracy, but I had in my pocket a formal letter of commendation from the President-Marshal, so they could not well say me nay. I set the joiners to work.

'They could not budge the rusted bolts without damaging the door, so they labored upon the hinges, and after three-quarters of an hour took off the door intact. Behind it was a short flight of brick steps, leading upward, as in my Experience. What say you to that, Judge? Yet there was no great bronze door at the top of the stair: instead, an old timber ceiling closed the way.'

'And you broke through?' Arthur asked, obviously stirred despite himself.

Arcane shook his head. 'The hotel manager, who had come up to watch our vandalism, humbly implored me not to take the roof off his establishment if that possibly could be averted. And the curators — who were slightly miffed at there being *something*, the brick steps behind the door, after all — assured me that they knew the roof which lay beyond. It was on their charts and plans, which they displayed to me.

'"Show me, learned colleagues," I told them — and bestowed gratuities, under the guise of adding to the funds of the Municipal Museum. So they took me outside, and upstairs in an adjoining house — not older than the seventeenth century, I judged, if that — and then out a window to a low-sloping tiled roof. It became clear even to me that we three were standing just above the head of the brick steps, and that whatever once had extended beyond that vanished bronze door must have gone to wrack and ruin long ago.'

'*Nada?*' Fuentes asked.

'Nothing but a few little fragments are left today of the Emperor's private apartments — a doorway of the library and lesser scraps. Beyond the Vestibule that fronts on the Peristyle, all the upper level of that quarter of the Palace, which contained the imperial suite, was pulled down for building-material sometime in the Dark Ages by the citizenry of Spalato. Gone, all gone — throne room, reception hall, dining hall, bedrooms, library, everything. Nobody, two curators included, has any clear idea even of the plan of Diocletian's private apartments — though they hope they may learn a good deal more from excavation of the cellars immediately below.

'Without confessing my Experience to those pedantic curators, I suggested to them that I had conceived a notion of what the rooms may have looked like. Then I described, under a slight veil, what I had seen in my brief Experience — my vision, if you will, Judge Ross. The first hall through which I passed, I take to have been the reception-salon; the second, the room with the statues, I fancy to have been the dining hall. *Vision* at least, mark you, Judge: definitely not *dream*. It was through the gates of horn that I passed, not through the gates of ivory. Well, the curators were astounded: my "suggestions" very nearly coincided with their own speculations, arrived at after decades of prying into the remains of the Palace. They were overly eager to learn where I had picked up my theory that great statues of Jupiter and Mithra had stood in one hall; Mithra especially. I smiled mysteriously. I'm certain that they now fancy me to be some famous archeologist, a rival in their trade, disguised as a statist. When I would tell them no more, they must have yearned to expel me as the Venetian masters of Spalato had expelled innocent Robert Adam.'

In the shadows under the fig-tree, Didi put her hand on Arcane's hand, as if to make sure that he was quick, not dead. 'Then you truly did see . . .'

'What no man may have seen for a thousand years or more — yes. And why was I given that uncanny glimpse? Why should the Emperor speak to me? Only God knows. Perhaps it all was a caution to me that I should never dismount the African tiger that I ride — and have ridden as long as Diocletian rode his Roman tiger. Perhaps because he and I, in some respects, are sib in mind and character — he in his great way, I in my small one. Soldiers and statists, struggling to hold the state together when Dinos is lord of creation, having overthrown Zeus — men of good intentions and some talents, compelled by necessity to be harsh in a bent time, to govern more than one heart of darkness — why, such was his lot, such mine. He had a great civilization to uphold, I a barbarous principality. Pray for us sinners now and at the hour of our death.

'Then, too, I had thought about him since I was a small child; and when my consciousness passed through that door, I was almost as nigh unto death as he. Deep may have cried unto deep.'

'*Excellentissimo*, was the Emperor in Hell?'

'That's better discussed, Don Pelayo, in Spanish, when our friends have gone to bed. Spanish is the language of faith, Didi. In Hell? In Purgatory? Our theological formulas cannot suffice us when we encounter such glimpses as mine, because we created beings are time-bound, here below. Lactantius and Eusebius and the whole crew of Constantinian ecclesiastic writers were eager to chuck Diocletian into the fire eternal, for he had authorized the last Roman persecution of Christians. But it is not the Constantines of this world, nor even the learned clerics, who sit upon the bench at the Last Judgment.'

'They taught us in Sunday school,' Didi volunteered, 'that you can't be saved unless you've taken Christ for your savior, and Diocletian didn't do that.'

'Ah, you delightful dogmatist! Is Licinius in glory because he tolerated Christians? I recall an American lyric that I used to play on the gramophone — something like "ever'body talks about Hebben ain't gwine dere." Does Constantine sit on the left hand of God because of that alleged deathbed baptism? Is that kindly beauty Valeria tormented hereafter, as here, because she did not see the Light before they took off her head? And is Diocletian, a man just and pious according to his ancient lights, damned because he did not understand the New Dispensation? What would you make of a human Supreme Justice, Judge Ross, who handed down such verdicts? God knows what we cannot — the heart. By that knowledge He judges.

'The meaning of my Experience I do not comprehend. Some tinge or echo of an ancient agony broods over the Palace of Diocletian, detected on rare occasions by such a one as I. For a very few minutes — if one may speak of "minutes" beyond Time — I, like an intruding ghost, shared the Emperor's despair. I entered with my wandering consciousness into the past. It was a fragment of Diocletian's experience, and a fragment of my experience, coinciding. But as for the eternal state of Diocletian, *dominus et deus*, the last man of the classical age to be declared a god — why, ask the angels.

'I know only that he died with the high old Roman virtue, as became a great emperor. He would not beg for mercy from his own creatures, men merciless. He would not do violence upon his own body, because Jove's divine spark inhabited it. Thus, with every luxury about him, he accepted no food, letting Nature reclaim his atoms. So resolute a man may be forgiven much, on high.'

'But the Red King's dream, Manfred — where does that come in?' Didi hadn't forgotten one sentence that this charismatic man had spoken.

'Aye, there's the rub, young sibyl of Ohio. Suppose that my imperial host — to him I must have been a spectral guest — was sound in his dying intuitions, and that your servant is nothing more than a phantom character in the Emperor's dream. Then am I here with you at all? If Diocletian ceases to dream in his palace beyond Time, will I cease to be — as *corpus*, as *animula*? I do wish he'd not suggested that: the fancy haunts me. Yet only in the last delirium might he have spoken so. I'd almost assent to my own annihilation, would that redeem the Emperor from the utter desolation of his dream. Yet let us suppose the contrary: that he was mistaken, and his dream is ended already, and Diocletian freed of agony. That Jovian thunderbolt in his chamber — why, I think of Eliot's lines:

'The only hope, or else despair
    Lies in the choice of pyre or pyre —
    To be redeemed from fire by fire.

Diocletian appealed to the God of All, asking for a sign, and a sign was given. After all, may he not have been a dying god, as the old Romans understood godhood? His talents were more than human, and his energies. What modern man could rule all the lands he ruled, with such instruments as he possessed then, and bring to them justice and peace? Wasn't he driven down to dusty death, like wife and daughter before him, because he was righteous in a criminal age? And wasn't he crucified, so to speak: that long agony of starvation, with no sop of vinegar carried to him? No, I'll not believe, my friends, that Diocletian's dream — "why has thou forsaken me?" — will have been inflicted upon Diocletian forever.'

*   *

Meekly for so hard-faced a man, the principal security agent came up behind Arcane and whispered something in his ear. The Minister without Portfolio drew from his waistcoat a handsome gold watch. 'My father's,' he confided to Didi, flourishing the watch. 'What is this Time it ticks away?'

He turned toward Fuentes. 'Midnight, Don Pelayo! These bold devotees of Holy Marx, Lenin, and Tito work in shifts as if they were wage-slaves of decadent capitalism. We must let them go. And poor Judge Ross, too, entombed in my foolish mausoleum of talk! Come, it's but a little way to the hotel: we'll walk you there, and then take cabs back into the Grad.'

He extended his hand and raised Didi from the stone seat. 'It's a clear night, Pride of Ohio: look at the sea. Do you think this Dalmatian shore the loveliest coast in the world? I do. Yet its people are sour, and its history bloody. There's a puzzle for us. Now look over there, by the campanile — we can see the roof of the Mausoleum. He built for the ages, and that must count for something in the Book of Judgment.'

'I don't know how to thank . . .' Didi began. 'Oh, I'm saying shallow things again! I mean, I never knew anybody like you. Oh, dear, that's equally silly, isn't it — because there isn't anybody like you to know.' She noticed without sorrow that Arthur had rejoined the security-man, doubtless hoping to obtain more solid information, and so was proceeding already up the lane to the Marjan.

'It might be a wilder world if there were many like me,' Arcane answered. 'Smile, Proud Beauty! Do remain centric, Didi Ross, I beg of you. Centricity, lovely centricity! Diocletian had that, and so kept the peace for twenty years. One lapse into eccentricity, the Persecution, undid everything. Had I been centric, I might — but then, grown centric, I suppose I'd not divert you.'

Taking her right hand, he raised it to his lips and imprinted upon it several small Viennese kisses, up to the wrist. She didn't know what to say. Was she supposed to extend the left hand for similar treatment? She wouldn't have minded.

'Say good night to Diocles, my dear, wherever he may be.' His hand on her elbow, he faced Didi toward the Grad, the Palace, the Mausoleum. She saw that his face had grown solemn, its blandness cast aside as if it had been a mask. He moved his arm as if to salute; then changed his mind, it seemed, and instead crossed himself.

'Good night, Diocletian, Imperator, wherever you may be,' she breathed obediently, and without mockery.

'May I die so well as you did, Dominus,' Arcane murmured. 'And not, I hope, chopped up by pangas on some tour of inspection in the south.' Leading Didi in the direction of the big hotel, 'Remember me in your orisons, child.'

'And in my dreams?' Oh, she shouldn't have said that.

'What an honor to be one of your figments, dear Didi Ross — well worth annihilation at your waking! Alas, now here we are, approaching your monstrous inn: what a ghastly flood of electric light from the place! Half the guests come from Eastern Europe, I suppose, where they strain their eyes beneath fifteen-watt bulbs, despite Lenin's aphorism that communism is socialism plus electricity. So this garishness is paradisiacal for them, poor things. When they depart from here — why, "Dark, dark, dark; they all go into the dark."'

She was holding in her hand the medallion of Diocletian. 'Don't throw away that imperial trinket, Didi,' he told her. 'Give it to your daughter, when you bear one, and call her Valeria.'

'But if it's a boy baby?'

'In Ohio, if you christen him Manfred, he'll be turned democratically into plain Freddie.'

Blushing, she had not hit upon a witty retort when Arthur came down the steps to collect her. 'No ghosts here, Mr. Arcane,' Arthur said, indicating the brilliant hotel, still noisy at this hour.

'There will be, Judge Ross. Every age leaves its specters to posterity. Doubtless those from our era will be mean enough, thin wailing ghosts like the Greeks' χῆρες, impotent in death as in life. This hotel will be pulled down, or blown up, centuries before Diocletian's Mausoleum finally crumbles. No gods or demigods of our century will defy Cronos. Still, some puny specters from the Age of Anxiety will walk the night even in the ruins of this hotel, in the next Dark Age.' He shook Arthur's hand.

'That was a good dinner and a good yarn, Mr. Arcane. Maybe we'll get together again sometime.' Arthur did not sound wholly sincere. One of the security-men was holding open the door of a cab for the Minister without Portfolio; Fuentes already was inside it.

'Oh, Manfred! Wait! wait!' Didi cried, ignoring Arthur's frown. Then she didn't know what to say. 'I mean — you're vanishing as if you really were something in somebody's dream. It isn't right!'

'You're not dreaming, Didi Ross,' Manfred said to her, with a parting smile that would haunt her like a strong ghost of ancient times. 'Nor will we lose each other, child. Dreams? It's death that is the insubstantial dream. You're glowing with life; and it's people who never knew vitality that are extinguished like spent candles. Diocletian starved to a skeleton was more alive than most human creatures ever are. Be a goddess, Didi, meant for immortality!'

He touched her hand a last time, with fingertips only. 'There! I endow you with eternal awareness! We're wrapped in mysteries always; if that weren't so, it would be better not to be born. And the grandest mystery is this: that certain moments of temporal experience defy the tooth of time — not moments of dream, but moments of truth. Such moments of agony occur, and such moments of love: agony greater than flesh could bear, love more intense than flesh could express.'

Didi was clinging to the window-frame of the taxi; Arthur was shaking hands with the chief security-man, who was about to enter the second taxi.

'Did there come upon you tonight, Didi Ross, such moments?' Manfred Arcane asked her, his eyes luminous, not twinkling. 'I see the look upon your face. Those moments, mark me, will be re-experienced in their fullness, perhaps countless times, beyond the limits of this sensual decaying world of ours. Do you follow me, my Didi? Why, if not now, later you will. Throughout eternity, you and I will meet by the Mausoleum, laughing together.'

He slid into the cab, his eyes still fixed upon hers; waved, and was gone — gone back to the Hungry Room within the Palace, gone perhaps to jest with shadows as he jested with the living.

'Like an emperor himself,' Didi murmured, her eyes wet. 'Good night, Imperator! Almost like a god himself.'

Arthur yawned. 'What did you say? Do you think that man has all his marbles?' Arthur asked. Arthur's slang always was redolent of yesteryear.

'From Roman quarries,' said Didi.

The Peculiar Demesne
of Archvicar Gerontion

The imagination of man's heart is evil from his youth.

Genesis 8:21

Two black torch-bearers preceding us and two following, Mr. Thomas Whiston and I walked through twilight alleys of Haggat toward Manfred Arcane's huge house, on Christmas Eve. Big flashlights would have done as well as torches, and there were some few streetlamps even in the lanes of the ancient dyers' quarter, where Arcane, disdaining modernity, chose to live; but Arcane, with his baroque conceits and crotchets, had insisted upon sending his linkmen for us.

The gesture pleased burly Tom Whiston, executive vice-president for African imports of Cosmopolitan-Anarch Oil Corporation. Whiston had not been in Haggat before, or anywhere in Hamnegri. Considerably to his vexation, he had not been granted an audience with Achmet ben Ali, Hereditary President of Hamnegri and Sultan in Kalidu. With a sellers' market in petroleum, sultans may be so haughty as they please, and Achmet the Pious disliked men of commerce.

Yet His Excellency Manfred Arcane, Minister without Portfolio in the Sultan's cabinet, had sent to Whiston and to me holograph invitations to his Christmas Eve party — an event of a sort infrequent in the Moslem city of Haggat, ever since most of the French had departed during the civil wars. I had assured Whiston that Arcane was urbane and amusing, and that under the Sultan Achmet, no one was more powerful

250

than Manfred Arcane. So this invitation consoled Tom Whiston considerably.

'If this Arcane is more or less European,' Whiston asked me, 'how can he be a kind of grand vizier in a country like this? Is the contract really up to him, Mr. Yawby?'

'Why,' I said, 'Arcane can be what he likes: when he wants to be taken for a native of Haggat, he can look it. The Hereditary President and Sultan couldn't manage without him. Arcane commands the mercenaries, and for all practical purposes he directs foreign relations — including the oil contracts. In Hamnegri, he's what Glubb Pasha was in Jordan once, and more. I was consul here at Haggat for six years and was made consul-general three years ago, so I know Arcane as well as any foreigner knows him. Age does not stale, nor custom wither, this Manfred Arcane.'

Now we stood at the massive carved wooden doors of Arcane's house, which had been built in the seventeenth century by some purse-proud Kalidu slave trader. Two black porters with curved swords at their belts bowed to us and swung the doors wide. Whiston hesitated just a moment before entering, not to my surprise; there was a kind of magnificent grimness about the place, which might give one a grue.

From somewhere inside the vast hulking old house, a soprano voice, sweet and strong, drifted to us. 'There'll be women at this party?' Whiston wanted to know.

'That must be Melchiora singing — Madame Arcane. She's Sicilian, and looks like a *femme fatale*.' I lowered my voice. 'For that matter, she *is* a *femme fatale*. During the insurrection four years ago, she shot a half-dozen rebels with her own rifle. Yes, there will be a few ladies: not a harem. Arcane's a Christian of sorts. I expect our party will be pretty much *en famille* — which is to say, more or less British, Arcane having been educated in England long ago. This house is managed by a kind of chatelaine, a very old Englishwoman, Lady Grizel Fergusson. You'll meet some officers of the IPV — the Interracial Peace Volunteers, the mercenaries who keep your oil flowing — and three or four French couples, and perhaps Mohammed ben Ibrahim, who's the International-Security Minister nowadays, and quite civilized. I believe there's an Ethiopian noble, an exile, staying with Arcane. And of course there's Arcane's usual ménage, a lively household. There should be English-style games and stories. The Minister without Portfolio is a raconteur.'

'From what I hear about him,' Tom Whiston remarked *sotto voce,* 'he should have plenty of stories to tell. They say he knows where the bodies are buried, and gets a two percent royalty on every barrel of oil.'

I put my finger on my lips. 'Phrases more or less figurative in America,' I suggested, 'are taken literally in Hamnegri, Mr. Whiston — because things are done literally here. You'll find that Mr. Arcane's manners are perfect: somewhat English, somewhat Austrian, somewhat African grandee, but perfect. His Excellency has been a soldier and a diplomat, and he is subtle. The common people in this town call him "the Father of Shadows." So to speak of bodies . . .'

We had been led by a manservant in a scarlet robe up broad stairs and along a corridor hung with carpets — some of them splendid old Persians, others from the cruder looms of the Sultanate of Kalidu. Now a rotund black man with a golden chain about his neck, a kind of majordomo, bowed us into an immense room with a fountain playing in the middle of it. In tolerable English, the majordomo called out, after I had whispered to him, 'Mr. Thomas Whiston, from Texas, America; and Mr. Harry Yawby, Consul-General of the United States!'

There swept toward us Melchiora, Arcane's young wife, or rather consort: the splendid Melchiora, sibylline and haughty, her mass of black hair piled high upon her head, her black eyes gleaming in the lamplight. She extended her slim hand for Torn Whiston to kiss; he was uncertain how to do that.

'Do come over to the divan by the fountain,' she said in flawless English, 'and I'll bring my husband to you.' A fair number of people were talking and sipping punch in that high-ceilinged vaulted hall — once the harem of the palace — but they seemed few and lonely in its shadowy vastness. A string quartet, apparently French, were playing; black servingmen in ankle-length green gowns were carrying about brass trays of refreshments. Madame Arcane presented Whiston to some of the guests I knew already: 'Colonel Fuentes . . . Major MacIlwraith, the Volunteers' executive officer . . . Monsieur and Madame Courtemanche . . .' We progressed slowly toward the divan. 'His Excellency Mohammed ben Ibrahim, Minister for Internal Security . . . And a new friend, the Fitaurari Wolde Mariam, from Gondar.'

The Fitaurari was a grizzle-headed veteran with aquiline features who had been great in the Abyssinian struggle against Italy, but now was lucky to have fled out of his country, through Gallabat, before the military junta could snare him. He seemed uncomfortable in so eccentrically cosmopolitan a gathering; his wide oval eyes, like those in an Ethiopian fresco, looked anxiously about for someone to rescue him from the voluble attentions of a middle-aged French lady; so Melchiora swept him along with us toward the divan.

Ancient, ancient Lady Grizel Fergusson, who had spent most of her many decades in India and Africa, and whose husband had been tortured to death in Kenya, was serving punch from a barbaric, capacious silver bowl beside the divan. 'Ah, Mr. Whiston? You've come for our petrol, I understand. Isn't it shockingly dear? But I'm obstructing your way. Now where has His Excellency got to? Oh, the Spanish consul has his ear; we'll extricate him in a moment. Did you hear Madame Arcane singing as you came in? Don't you love her voice?'

'Yes, but I didn't understand the words,' Tom Whiston said. 'Does she know "Rudolph, the Red-Nosed Reindeer"?'

'Actually, I rather doubt — ah, there she has dragged His Excellency away from the Spaniard, clever girl. Your Excellency, may I present Mr. Whiston — from Texas, I believe?'

Manfred Arcane, who among other accomplishments had won the civil war for the Sultan through his astounding victory at the Fords of Krokul, came cordially toward us, his erect figure brisk and elegant. Two little wolfish black men, more barbaric foster-sons than servants, made way for him among the guests, bowing, smiling with their long teeth, begging pardon in their incomprehensible dialect. These two had saved Arcane's life at the Fords, where he had taken a traitor's bullet in the back; but Arcane seemed wholly recovered from that injury now.

Manfred Arcane nodded familiarly to me and took Whiston's hand. 'It's kind of you to join our pathetic little assembly here; and good of you to bring him, Yawby. I see you've been given some punch; it's my own formula. I'm told that you and I, Mr. Whiston, are to have, tête-à-tête and candidly, a base commercial conversation on Tuesday. Tonight we play, Mr. Whiston. Do you fancy snapdragon, that fiery old Christmas sport? Don't know it? It's virtually forgotten in England now, I understand, but once upon a time before the deluge, when I was at Wellington School, I became the nimblest boy for it. They insist that I preside over the revels tonight. Do you mind having your fingers well burnt?'

His was public-school English, and Arcane was fluent in a dozen other languages. Tom Whiston, accustomed enough to Arab sheikhs and African pomposities, looked startled at this bouncing handsome white-haired old man. Energy seemed to start from Arcane's fingertips; his swarthy face — inherited, report said, from a Montenegrin gypsy mother — was mobile, nearly unlined, at once jolly and faintly sinister. Arcane's underlying antique grandeur was veiled by ease and openness of manners. I knew how deceptive those manners could be. But for him, the 'emergent' Commonwealth of Hamnegri would have fallen to bits.

Motioning Whiston and me to French chairs, Arcane clapped his hands. Two of the serving-men hurried up with a vast brass tray, elaborately worked, and set it upon a low stand; one of them scattered handfuls of raisins upon the tray, and over these the other poured a flagon of warmed brandy.

The guests, with their spectrum of complexions, gathered in a circle round the tray. An olive-skinned European boy — 'the son,' I murmured to Whiston — solemnly came forward with a long lighted match, which he presented to Arcane. Servants turned out the lamps, so that the old harem was pitch-black except for Arcane's tiny flame.

'Now we join reverently in the ancient and honorable pastime of snapdragon,' Arcane's voice came, with mock portentousness. In the match-flame, one could make out only his short white beard. 'Whosoever snatches and devours the most flaming raisins shall be awarded the handsome tray on which they are scattered, the creation of the finest worker in brass in Haggat. Friends, I offer you a foretaste of Hell! Hey presto!'

He set up his long match to the brandy, at three points, and blue flames sprang up. In a moment they were ranging over the whole surface of the tray. 'At them, brave companions!' Few present knowing the game, most held back. Arcane himself thrust a hand into the flames, plucked out a handful of raisins, and flung them burning into his mouth, shrieking in simulated agony. 'Ah! Ahhh! I burn, I burn! What torment!'

Lady Fergusson tottered forward to emulate His Excellency; and I snatched my raisins, too, knowing that it is well to share in the play of those who sit in the seats of the mighty. Melchiora joined us, and the boy, and the Spanish consul, and the voluble French lady, and others. When the flames lagged, Arcane shifted the big tray slightly, to keep up the blaze.

'Mr. Whiston, are you craven?' he called. 'Some of you ladies, drag our American guest to the torment!' Poor Whiston was thrust forward, grabbed awkwardly at the raisins — and upset the tray. It rang upon the tiled floor, the flames went out, and the women's screams echoed in total darkness.

'So!' Arcane declared, laughing. The servants lit the lamps. 'Rodriguez,' he told the Spanish consul, 'you've proved the greatest glutton tonight, and the tray is yours, after it has been washed. Why, Mr. Texas Whiston, I took you for a Machiavelli of oil contracts, but the booby prize is yours. Here, I bestow it upon you.' There appeared magically in his hand a tiny gold candle-snuffer, and he presented it to Whiston.

Seeing Whiston red-faced and rather angry, Arcane smoothed his plumage, an art at which he was accomplished. With a few minutes' flattering talk, he had his Texan guest jovial. The quartet had struck up a waltz; many of the guests were dancing on the tiles; it was a successful party.

'Your Excellency,' Grizel Fergusson was saying in her shrill old voice, 'are we to have our Christmas ghost story?' Melchiora and the boy, Guido, joined in her entreaty.

'That depends on whether our American guests have a relish for such yarn-spinning,' Arcane told them. 'What's dreamt of in your philosophy, Mr. Whiston?'

In the shadows about the fountain, I nudged Whiston discreetly: Arcane liked an appreciative audience, and he was a tale-teller worth hearing.

'Well, I never saw any ghosts myself,' Whiston ventured, reluctantly, 'but maybe it's different in Africa. I've heard about conjure-men and voodoo and witch-doctors. . . .'

Arcane gave him a curious smile. 'Wolde Mariam here — he and I were much together in the years when I served the Negus Negusti, rest his soul — could tell you more than a little of that. Those Gondar people are eldritch folk, and I suspect that Wolde Mariam himself could sow dragons' teeth.'

The Abyssinian probably could not catch the classical allusion, but he smiled ominously in his lean way with his sharp teeth. 'Let us hear him, then,' Melchiora demanded. 'It needn't be precisely a ghost story.'

'And Manfred — Your Excellency — do tell us again about Archvicar Gerontion,' Lady Fergusson put in. 'Really, you tell that adventure best of all.'

Arcane's subtle smile vanished for a moment, and Melchiora raised a hand as if to dissuade him; but he sighed slightly, smiled again, and motioned toward a doorway in line with the fountain. 'I'd prefer being toasted as a snapdragon raisin to enduring that experience afresh,' he said, 'but so long as Wolde Mariam doesn't resurrect the Archvicar, I'll try to please you. Our dancing friends seem happy; why affright them? Here, come into Whitebeard's Closet, and Wolde Mariam and I will chill you.' He led the way toward the door in the thick wall, and down a little corridor into a small whitewashed room deep within the old house.

There were seven of us: Melchiora, Guido, Lady Fergusson, Whiston, Wolde Mariam, Arcane, and myself. The room's only ornament was one of those terrible agonized Spanish Christ-figures, hung high upon a wall. There were no European chairs, but a divan and several leather stools or cushions. An oil lamp suspended from the ceiling supplied the only light. We squatted or crouched or lounged about the Minister without Portfolio and Wolde Mariam. Tom Whiston looked embarrassed. Melchiora rang a little bell, and a servant brought tea and sweet cakes.

'Old friend,' Arcane told Wolde Mariam, 'it is an English custom, Lord knows why, to tell uncanny tales at Christmas, and Grizel Fergusson must be pleased, and Mr. Whiston impressed. Tell us something of your Gondar conjurers and shape-shifters.'

I suspect that Whiston did not like this soirée in the least, but he knew better than to offend Arcane, upon whose good humor so many barrels of oil depended. 'Sure, we'd like to hear about them,' he offered, if feebly.

By some unnoticed trick or other, Arcane caused the flame in the lamp overhead to sink down almost to vanishing point. We could see dimly the face of the tormented Christ upon the wall, but little else. As the light had diminished, Melchiora had taken Arcane's hand in hers. We seven were at once in the heart of Africa, and yet out of it — out of time, out of space. 'Instruct us, old friend,' said Arcane to Wolde Mariam. 'We'll not laugh at you, and when you've done, I'll reinforce you.'

*   *

Although the Ethiopian soldier's eyes and teeth were dramatic in the dim lamplight, he was no skilled narrator in English. Now and then he groped for an English word, could not find it, and used Amharic or Italian. He told of deacons who worked magic, and could set papers afire though they sat many feet away from them; of spells that made men's eyes bleed continuously until they submitted to what the conjurers demanded of them; of Falasha who could transform themselves into hyaenas, and Galla women who commanded spirits. Because I collect folktales of East Africa, all this was very interesting to me. But Tom Whiston did not understand half of what Wolde Mariam said, and grew bored, not believing the other half; I had to nudge him twice to keep him from snoring. Wolde Mariam himself was diffident, no doubt fearing that he, who had been a power in Gondar, would be taken for a superstitious fool. He finished lamely: 'So some people believe.'

But Melchiora, who came from sinister Agrigento in Sicily, had listened closely, and so had the boy. Now Manfred Arcane, sitting directly under the lamp, softly ended the awkward pause.

'Some of you have heard all this before,' Arcane commenced, 'but you protest that it does not bore you. It alarms me still: so many frightening questions are raised by what occurred two years ago. The Archvicar Gerontion — how harmoniously perfect in his evil, his "unblemished turpitude" — was as smoothly foul a being as one might hope to meet. Yet who am I to sit in judgment? Where Gerontion slew his few victims, I slew my myriads.'

'Oh, come, Your Excellency,' Grizel Fergusson broke in, 'your killing was done in fair fight, and honorable.'

The old adventurer bowed his handsome head to her. 'Honorable — with a few exceptions — in a rude *condottiere*, perhaps. However that may be, our damned Archvicar may have been sent to give this old evildoer a foretaste of the Inferno — through a devilish game of snapdragon, with raisins, brandy, and all. What a dragon Gerontion was, and what a peculiar dragon-land he fetched me into!' He sipped his tea before resuming.

'Mr. Whiston, I doubt whether you gave full credence to the Fitaurari's narration. Let me tell you that in my own Abyssinian years I saw with these eyes some of the phenomena he described; that these eyes of mine, indeed, have bled as he told, from a sorcerer's curse in Kaffa. O ye of little faith! But though hideous wonders are worked in Gondar and Kaffa and other Ethiopian lands, the Indian enchanters are greater than the African. This Archvicar Gerontion — he was a curiously well-read scoundrel, and took his alias from Eliot's poem, I do believe — combined the craft of India with the craft of Africa.'

This story was new to me, but I had heard that name 'Gerontion' somewhere, two or three years earlier. 'Your Excellency, wasn't somebody of that name a pharmacist here in Haggat?' I ventured.

Arcane nodded. 'And a marvellous chemist he was, too. He used his chemistry on me, and something more. Now look here, Yawby: if my memory serves me, Aquinas holds that a soul must have a body to inhabit, and that has been my doctrine. Yet it is an arcane doctrine' — here he smiled, knowing that we thought of his own name or alias — 'and requires much interpretation. Now was I out of my body, or in it, there within the Archvicar's peculiar demesne? I'll be damned if I know — and if I don't, probably. But how I run on, senile creature that I am! Let me try to put some order into this garrulity.'

Whiston had sat up straight and was paying sharp attention. There was electricity in Arcane's voice, as in his body.

'You may be unaware, Mr. Whiston,' Manfred Arcane told him, 'that throughout Hamnegri, in addition to my military and diplomatic responsibilities, I exercise certain judicial functions. To put it simply, I constitute in my person a court of appeal for Europeans who have been accused under Hamnegrian law. Such special tribunals once were common enough in Africa; one survives here, chiefly for diplomatic reasons. The laws of Hamnegri are somewhat harsh, perhaps, and so I am authorized by the Hereditary President and Sultan to administer a kind of *jus gentium* when European foreigners — and Americans, too — are brought to book. Otherwise European technicians and merchants might leave Hamnegri, and we might become involved in diplomatic controversies with certain humanitarian European and American governments.

'So! Two years ago there was appealed to me, in this capacity of mine, the case of a certain T. M. A. Gerontion, who styled himself Archvicar in the Church of the Divine Mystery — a quasi-Christian sect with a small following in Madras and South Africa, I believe. This Archvicar Gerontion, who previously had passed under the name of Omanwallah and other aliases, was a chemist with a shop in one of the more obscure lanes of Haggat. He had been found guilty of unlicensed trafficking in narcotics and of homicides resulting from such traffic. He had been tried by the Administrative Tribunal of Post and Customs. You may perceive, Mr. Whiston, that in Hamnegri we have a juridical structure unfamiliar to you; there are reasons for that — among them the political influence of the Postmaster-General, Gabriel M'Rundu. At any rate, jurisdiction over the narcotics-traffic is enjoyed by that tribunal, which may impose capital punishment — and did impose a death sentence upon Gerontion.

'The Archvicar, a very clever man, contrived to smuggle an appeal to me, on the ground that he was a British subject, or rather a citizen of the British Commonwealth. "To Caesar thou must go." He presented a *prima facie* case for this claim of citizenship; whether or not it was a true claim, I never succeeded in ascertaining to my satisfaction; the man's whole life had been a labyrinth of deceptions. I believe that Gerontion was the son of a Parsee father, and born in Bombay. But with his very personal identity in question — he was so old, and had lived in so many lands, under so many aliases and false papers, and with so many inconsistencies in police records — why, how might one accurately ascertain his mere nationality? Repeatedly he had changed his name, his residence, his occupation, seemingly his very shape.'

'He was fat and squat as a toad,' Melchiora said, squeezing the minister's hand.

'Yes, indeed,' Arcane assented, 'an ugly-looking customer — though about my own height, really, Best Beloved — and a worse-behaved customer. Nevertheless, I accepted his appeal and took him out of the custody of the Postmaster-General before sentence could be put into execution. M'Rundu, who fears me more than he loves me, was extremely vexed at this; he had expected to extract some curious information, and a large sum of money, from the Archvicar — though he would have put him to death in the end. But I grow indiscreet; all this is *entre nous*, friends.

'I accepted the Archvicar's appeal because the complexities of his case interested me. As some of you know, often I am bored, and this appeal came to me in one of my idle periods. Clearly the condemned man was a remarkable person, accomplished in all manner of mischief: a paragon of vice. For decades he had slipped almost scatheless through the hands of the police and a score of countries, though repeatedly indicted — and acquitted. He seemed to play a deadly criminal game for the game's sake, and to profit substantially by it, even if he threw away most of his gains at the gaming tables. I obtained from Interpol and other sources a mass of information about this appellant.

'Gerontion, or Omanwallah, or the person masquerading under yet other names, seemed to have come off free, though accused of capital crimes, chiefly because of the prosecutors' difficulty in establishing that the prisoner in the dock actually was the person whose name had appeared on the warrants of arrest. I myself have been artful in disguises and pseudonyms. Yet this Gerontion, or whoever he was, far excelled me. At different periods of his career, police descriptions of the offender deviated radically from earlier descriptions; it seemed as if he must be three men in one; most surprising, certain sets of fingerprints I obtained from five or six countries in Asia and Africa, purporting to be those of the condemned chemist of Haggat, did not match one another. What an eel! I suspected him of astute bribery of record-custodians, policemen, and even judges; he could afford it.

'He had been tried for necromancy in the Shan States, charged with having raised a little child from the grave and making the thing do his bidding; tried also for poisoning two widows in Madras; for a colossal criminal fraud in Johannesburg; for kidnapping a young woman — never found — in Ceylon; repeatedly, for manufacturing and selling dangerous narcotic preparations. The catalogue of accusations ran on and on. And yet, except for brief periods, this Archvicar Gerontion had remained at a licentious liberty all those decades.'

Guido, an informed ten years of age, apparently had not been permitted to hear this strange narration before; he had crept close to Arcane's knees. 'Father, what had he done here in Haggat?'

'Much, Guido. Will you find me a cigar?' This being produced from a sandalwood box, Arcane lit his Burma cheroot and puffed as he went on.

'I've already stated the indictment and conviction by the Tribunal of Post and Customs. It is possible for vendors to sell hashish and certain other narcotics, lawfully, here in Hamnegri — supposing that the dealer has paid a tidy license fee and obtained a license which subjects him to regulation and inspection. Although Gerontion had ample capital, he had not secured such documents. Why not? In part, I suppose, because of his intense pleasure in running risks; for one type of criminal, evasion of the law is a joyous pursuit in its own right. But chiefly his motive must have been that he dared not invite official scrutiny of his operations. The local sale of narcotics was a small item for him; he was an exporter on a large scale, and Hamnegri has subscribed to treaties against that. More, he was not simply marketing drugs but manufacturing them from secret formulas — and experimenting with his products upon the bodies of such as he might entice to take his privy doses.

'Three beggars, of the sort that would do anything for the sake of a few coppers, were Gerontion's undoing. One was found dead in an alley, the other two lying in their hovels outside the Gate of the Heads. The reported hallucinations of the dying pair were of a complex and fantastic character — something I was to understand better at a later time. One beggar recovered enough reason before expiring to drop the Archvicar's name; and so M'Rundu's people caught Gerontion. Apparently Gerontion had kept the three beggars confined in his house, but there must have been a blunder, and somehow in their delirium the three had contrived to get into the streets. Two other wretched mendicants were found by the Post Office Police, locked, comatose, into the Archvicar's cellar. They also died later.

'M'Rundu, while he had the chemist in charge, kept the whole business quiet; and so did I, when I had Gerontion in this house later. I take it that some rumor of the affair came to your keen ears, Yawby. Our reason for secrecy was that Gerontion appeared to have connections with some sort of international ring or clique or sect, and we hoped to snare confederates. Eventually I found that the scent led to Scotland; but that's another story.'

Wolde Mariam raised a hand, almost like a child at school. 'Ras Arcane, you say that this poisoner was a Christian? Or was he a Parsee?'

The Minister without Portfolio seemed gratified by his newly conferred Abyssinian title. 'Would that the Negus had thought so well of me as you do, old comrade! Why, I suppose I have become a kind of *ras* here in Hamnegri, but I like your mountains better than this barren shore. As for Gerontion's profession of faith, his Church of the Divine Mystery was an instrument for deception and extortion, working principally upon silly old women; yet unquestionably he did believe fervently in a supernatural realm. His creed seemed to have been a debauched Manichaeism — that perennial heresy. I don't suppose you follow me, Wolde Mariam; you may not even know that you're a heretic yourself, you Abyssinian Monophysite: no offense intended, old friend. Well, then, the many Manichees believe that the world is divided between the forces of light and of darkness; and Gerontion had chosen to side with the darkness. Don't stir so impatiently, little Guido, for I don't mean to give you a lecture on theology.'

I feared, nevertheless, that Arcane might launch into precisely that, he being given to long and rather learned, if interesting, digressions: and like the others, I was eager for the puzzling Gerontion to stride upon the stage in all his outer and inner hideousness. So I said, 'Did Your Excellency actually keep this desperate Archvicar here in this house?'

'There was small risk in that, or so I fancied,' Arcane answered. 'When he was fetched from M'Rundu's prison, I found him in shabby condition. I never allow to police or troops under my command such methods of interrogation as M'Rundu's people employ. One of the Archvicar's legs had been broken; he was startlingly sunken, like a pricked balloon; he had been denied medicines — but it would be dis-

tressing to go on. For all that, M'Rundu had got precious little information out of him; I obtained more, far more, through my beguiling kindli-
ness. He could not have crawled out of this house, and of course I have
guards at the doors and elsewhere.

'And, do you know, I found that he and I were like peas in a pod — '

'No!' Melchiora interrupted passionately. 'He didn't look in the least
like you, and he was a murdering devil!'

'To every coin there are two sides, Best Beloved,' Arcane instructed
her. '"The brave man does it with a sword, the coward with a kiss." Not
that Gerontion was a thorough coward; in some respects he was a hero of
villainy, taking ghastly risks for the satisfaction of triumphing over law
and morals. I mean this: he and I both had done much evil. Yet the evil that
I had committed, I had worked for some seeming good — the more fool I
— or in the fell clutch of circumstances; and I repented it all. "I do the evil
I'd eschew" — often the necessary evil committed by those who are made
magistrates and commanders in the field.

'For his part, however, Gerontion had said in his heart, from the beginning, "Evil, be thou my good." I've always thought that Socrates spoke
rubbish when he argued that all men seek the good, falling into vice only
through ignorance. Socrates had his own δαίμων, but he did not know the
Demon. Evil is pursued for its own sake by some men — though not,
praise be, by most. There exist fallen natures which rejoice in pain, death,
corruption, every manner of violence and fraud and treachery. Behind all
these sins and crimes lies the monstrous ego.'

The boy was listening to Arcane intently, and got his head patted, as
reward, by the Minister without Portfolio. 'These evil-adoring natures fascinate me morbidly,' Arcane ran on, 'for deep cries unto deep, and the evil
in me peers lewdly at the evil in them. Well, Archvicar Gerontion's was a
diabolic nature, in rebellion against all order here below. His nature
charmed me as a dragon is said to charm. In time, or perhaps out of it, that
dragon snapped, as you shall learn.

'Yes, pure evil, defecated evil, can be charming — supposing that it
doesn't take one by the throat. Gerontion had manners — though something of a chichi accent — wit, cunning, breadth of bookish knowledge, a
fund of ready allusion and quotation, penetration into human motives
and types of character, immense sardonic experience of the world, even
an impish malicious gaiety. Do you know anyone like that, Melchiora —
your husband, perhaps?' The beauty compressed her lips.

'So am I quite wrong to say that he and I were like peas in a pod?' Arcane spread out his hands gracefully toward Melchiora. 'There existed but one barrier between the Archvicar and myself, made up of my feeble good intentions on one side and of his strong malice on the other side; or, to put this in a different fashion, I was an unworthy servant of the light, and he was a worthy servant of the darkness.' Arcane elegantly knocked the ash off his cigar.

'How long did this crazy fellow stay here with you?' Tom Whiston asked. He was genuinely interested in the yarn.

'Very nearly a fortnight, my Texan friend. Melchiora was away visiting people in Rome at the time; this city and this whole land were relatively free of contention and violence that month — a consummation much to be desired, but rare in Hamnegri. Idle, I spent many hours in the Archvicar's reverend company. So far as he could navigate in his wheelchair, Gerontion had almost the run of the house. He was well fed, well lodged, well attended by a physician, civilly waited upon by the servants, almost cosseted. What did I have to fear from this infirm old scoundrel? His life depended upon mine; had he injured me, back he would have gone to the torments of M'Rundu's prison.

'So we grew almost intimates. The longer I kept him with me, the more I might learn of the Archvicar's international machinations and confederates. Of evenings, often we would sit together — no, not in this little cell, but in the great hall, where the Christmas party is in progress now. Perhaps from deep instinct, I did not like to be confined with him in a small space. We exchanged innumerable anecdotes of eventful lives.

'What he expected to gain from learning more about me, his dim future considered, I couldn't imagine. But he questioned me with a flattering assiduity about many episodes of my variegated career, my friends, my political responsibilities, my petty tastes and preferences. We found that we had all sorts of traits in common — an inordinate relish for figs and raisins, for instance. I told him much more about myself than I would have told any man with a chance of living long. Why not indulge the curiosity, idle though it might be, of a man under sentence of death?

'And for my part, I ferreted out of him, slyly, bits and pieces that eventually I fitted together after a fashion. I learnt enough, for one thing, to lead me later to his unpleasant confederates in Britain, and to break them. Couldn't he see that I was worming out of him information which might be used against others? Perhaps, or even probably, he did perceive that.

Was he actually betraying his collaborators to me, deliberately enough, while pretending to be unaware of how much he gave away? Was this tacit implication of others meant to please me, and so curry favor with the magistrate who held his life in his hands — yet without anyone's being able to say that he, Gerontion, had let the cat out of the bag? This subtle treachery would have accorded well with his whole life.

'What hadn't this charlatan done, at one time or another? He had been deep in tantric magic, for one thing, and other occult studies; he knew all the conjurers' craft of India and Africa, and had practiced it. He had high pharmaceutical learning, from which I was not prepared to profit much, though I listened to him attentively; he had invented or compounded recently a narcotic, previously unknown, to which he gave the name *kalanzi*; from his testing of that, the five beggars had perished — "a mere act of God, Your Excellency," he said. He had hoodwinked great and obscure. And how entertainingly he could talk of it all, with seeming candor!

'On one subject alone was he reticent: his several identities, or masks and assumed names. He did not deny having played many parts; indeed, he smilingly gave me a cryptic quotation from Eliot: "Let me also wear / Such deliberate disguises / Rat's coat, crowskin, crossed staves . . ." When I put it to him that police descriptions of him varied absurdly, even as to fingerprints, he merely nodded complacently. I marveled at how old he must be — even older than the broken creature looked — for his anecdotes went back a generation before my time, and I am no young man. He spoke as if his life had known no beginning and would know no end — this man, under sentence of death! He seemed to entertain some quasi-Platonic doctrine of transmigration of souls; but, intent on the track of his confederates, I did not probe deeply into his peculiar theology.

'Yes, a fascinating man, wickedly wise! Yet this rather ghoulish entertainer of my idle hours, like all remarkable things, had to end. One evening, in a genteel way, he endeavored to bribe me. I was not insulted, for I awaited precisely that from such a one — what else? In exchange for his freedom — "After all, what were those five dead beggars to you or to me?" — he would give me a very large sum of money; he would have it brought to me before I should let him depart. This was almost touching: it showed that he trusted to my honor, he who had no stitch of honor himself. Of course he would not have made such an offer to M'Rundu, being aware that the Postmaster-General would have kept both bribe and briber.

'I told him, civilly, that I was rich already, and always had preferred glory to wealth. He accepted that without argument, having come to understand me reasonably well. But I was surprised at how calmly he seemed to take the vanishing of his last forlorn hope of escape from execution.

'For he knew well enough by now that I must confirm the death sentence of the Administrative Tribunal of Post and Customs, denying his appeal. He was guilty, damnably guilty, as charged; he had no powerful friends anywhere in the world to win him a pardon through diplomatic channels: and even had there been any doubt of his wickedness in Haggat, I was aware of his unpunished crimes in other lands. Having caught such a creature, poisonous and malign, in conscience I could not set it free to ravage the world again.

'The next evening, then, I said — with a sentimental qualm, we two having had such lively talk together, over brandy and raisins, those past several days — that I could not overturn his condemnation. Yet I would not return him to M'Rundu's dungeon. As the best I might do for him, I would arrange a private execution, so painless as possible; in token of our mutual esteem and comparable characteristics, I would administer *le coup degrâce* with my own hand. This had best occur the next day; I would sit in formal judgment during the morning, and he would be dispatched in the afternoon. I expressed my regrets — which, in some degree, were sincere, for Gerontion had been one of the more amusing specimens in my collection of lost souls.

'I could not let him tarry with me longer. For even an experienced snake-handler ought not to toy overlong with his pet cobra, there still being venom in the fangs. This reflection I kept politely to myself. "Then linger not in Attalus his garden. . . ."

'"If you desire to draw up a will or to talk with a clergyman, I am prepared to arrange such matters for you in the morning, after endorsement of sentence, Archvicar," I told him.

'At this, to my astonishment, old Gerontion seemed to choke with emotion; why, a tear or two strayed from his eyes. He had difficulty getting his words out, but he managed a quotation and even a pitiful smile of sorts: "After such pleasures, that would be a dreadful thing to do." I was the Walrus or the Carpenter, and he a hapless innocent oyster!

'What could he have hoped to get from me, at that hour? He scarcely could have expected, knowing how many lives I had on my vestigial conscience already, that I would have spared him for the sake of a tear, as if he had been a young girl arrested for her first traffic violation. I raised my eyebrows and asked him what possible alternative existed.

'"Commutation to life imprisonment, Your Excellency," he answered, pathetically.

'True, I had that power. But Gerontion must have known what Hamnegri's desert camps for perpetual imprisonment were like: in those hard places, the word "perpetual" was a mockery. An old man in his condition could not have lasted out a month in such a camp, and a bullet would have been more merciful far.

'I told him as much. Still he implored me for commutation of his sentence. "We both are old men, Your Excellency: live and let live!" He actually sniveled like a fag at school, this old terror! True, if he had in mind that question so often put by evangelicals — "Where will you spend eternity?" — why, his anxiety was readily understood.

'I remarked merely, "You hope to escape, if sent to a prison camp. But that is foolish, your age and your body considered, unless you mean to do it by bribery. Against that, I would give orders that any guard who might let you flee would be shot summarily. No, Archvicar, we must end it tomorrow."

'He scowled intently at me; his whining and his tears ceased. "Then let me thank Your Excellency for your kindnesses to me in my closing days," he said, in a controlled voice. "I thank you for the good talk, the good food, the good cognac. You have entertained me well in this demesne of yours, and when opportunity offers I hope to be privileged to entertain Your Excellency in my demesne."

'*His* demesne! I suppose we all tend to think our own selves immortal. But this fatuous expectation of living, and even prospering, after the stern announcement I had made to him only moments before — why, could it be, after all, that this Archvicar was a lunatic merely? He had seemed so self-seekingly rational, at least within his own inverted deadly logic. No, this invitation must be irony, and so I replied in kind: "I thank you, most reverend Archvicar, for your thoughtful invitation, and will accept it whenever room may be found for me."

'He stared at me for a long moment, as a dragon in the legends paralyzes by its baleful eye. It was discomfiting, I assure you, the Archvicar's prolonged gaze, and I chafed under it; he seemed to be drawing the essence out of me. Then he asked, "May I trouble Your Excellency with one more importunity? These past few days, we have become friends almost;

and then, if I may say so, there are ties and correspondences between us, are there not? I never met a gentleman more like myself, or whom I liked better — take that as a compliment, sir. We have learnt so much about each other; something of our acquaintance will endure long. Well" — the intensity of his stare diminished slightly — "I mentioned cognac the other moment, your good brandy. Might we have a cheering last drink together this evening? Perhaps that really admirable Napoleon cognac we had on this table day before yesterday?"

'"Of course." I went over to the bellpull and summoned a servant, who brought the decanter of cognac and two glasses — and went away, after I had instructed him that we were not to be disturbed for two or three hours. I meant this to be the final opportunity to see whether a tipsy Archvicar might be induced to tell me still more about his confederates overseas.

'I poured the brandy. A bowl of raisins rested on the table between us, and the Archvicar took a handful, munching them between sips of cognac; so did I.

'The strong spirit enlivened him; his deep-set eyes glowed piercingly; he spoke confidently again, almost as if he were master in the house.

'"What is this phenomenon we call dying?" he inquired. "You and I, when all's said, are only collections of electrical particles, positive and negative. These particles, which cannot be destroyed but may be induced to rearrange themselves, are linked temporarily by some force or power we do not understand — though some of us may be more ignorant of that power than others are. Illusion, illusion! Our bodies are feeble things, inhabited by ghosts — ghosts in a machine that functions imperfectly. When the machine collapses, or falls under the influence of chemicals, our ghosts seek other lodging. *Maya!* I sought the secret of all this. What were those five dead beggars for whose sake you would have me shot? Why, things of no consequence, those rascals. I do not dread their ghosts: they are gone to my demesne. Having done with a thing, I dispose of it — even of Your Excellency."

'Were his wits wandering? Abruptly the Archvicar sagged in his wheelchair; his eyelids began to close; but for a moment he recovered, and said with strong emphasis, "Welcome to my demesne." He gasped for breath, but contrived to whisper, "I shall take your body."

'I thought he was about to slide out of the wheelchair altogether; his face had gone death-pale, and his teeth were clenched. "What is it, man?" I demanded. I started up to catch him.

'Or rather, I intended to rise. I found that I was too weak. My face also must be turning livid, and my brain was sunk in torpor suddenly; my eyelids were closing against my will. "The ancient limb of Satan!" I thought in that last instant. "He's poisoned the raisins with that infernal *kalanzi* powder of his, a final act of malice, and we're to die together!" After that maddening reflection I ceased to be conscious.'

* *

Mr. Tom Whiston drew a sighing breath: 'But you're still with us.' Melchiora had taken both of Arcane's hands now. Wolde Mariam was crossing himself.

'By the grace of God,' said Manfred Arcane. The words were uttered slowly, and Arcane glanced at the Spanish crucifix on the wall as he spoke them. 'But I've not finished, Mr. Whiston: the worst is to come. Melchiora, do let us have cognac.'

She took a bottle from a little carved cupboard. Except Guido, everybody else in the room accepted brandy too.

'When consciousness returned,' Arcane went on, 'I was in a different place. I still do not know where or what that place was. My first speculation was that I had been kidnapped. For the moment, I was alone, cold, unarmed, in the dark.

'I found myself crouching on a rough stone pavement in a town — not an African town, I think. It was an ancient place, and desolate, and silent. It was a town that had been sacked — I have seen such towns — but sacked long ago.

'Do any of you know Stari Bar, near the Dalmatian coast, a few miles north of the Albanian frontier? No? I have visited that ruined city several times; my mother was born not far from there. Well, this cold and dark town, so thoroughly sacked, in which I found myself was somewhat like Stari Bar. It seemed a Mediterranean place, with mingled Gothic and Turkish — not Arabic — buildings, most of them unroofed. But you may be sure that I did not take time to study the architecture.

'I rose to my feet. It was a black night, with no moon or stars, yet I could make out things tolerably well, somehow. There was no one about, no one at all. The doors were gone from most of the houses, and as for those which still had doors — why, I did not feel inclined to knock.

'Often I have been in tight corners. Without such previous trying experiences, I should have despaired in this strange clammy place. I did not know how I had come there, nor where to go. But I suppose the adrenalin began to rise in me — what are men and rats, those natural destroyers, without ready adrenalin? — and I took stock of my predicament.

'My immediate necessity was to explore the place. I felt giddy and somewhat uneasy at the pit of my stomach, but I compelled myself to walk up that steep street, meaning to reach the highest point in this broken city and take a general view. I found no living soul.

'The place was walled all about. I made my way through what must have been a gateway of the citadel, high up, and ascended with some difficulty, by a crumbling stair, a precarious tower on the battlements. I seemed to be far above a plain, but it was too dark to make out much. There was no tolerable descent out of the town from this precipice; presumably I must return all the way back through those desolate streets and find the town gates.

'But just as I was about to descend, I perceived with a start a distant glimmer of light, away down there where the town must meet the plain. It may not have been a strong light, yet it had no competitor. It seemed to be moving erratically — and moving toward me, perhaps, though we were far, far apart. I would hurry down to meet it; anything would be better than this accursed solitude.

'Having scrambled back out of the citadel, I became confused in the complex of streets and alleys, which here and there were nearly choked with fallen stones. Once this town must have pullulated people, for it was close-built with high old houses of masonry; but it seemed perfectly empty now. Would I miss that flickering faint light, somewhere in this fell maze of ashlar and rubble? I dashed on, downward, barking my shins more than once. Yes, I felt strong physical sensations in that ravaged town, where everyone must have been slaughtered by remorseless enemies. "The owl and bat their revel keep. . . ." It was only later that I became aware of the absence of either owl or bat. Just one animate thing showed itself: beside a building that seemed to have been a domed Turkish bathhouse, a thick nasty snake writhed away as I ran past; but that may have been an illusion.

'Down I scuttled like a frightened hare, often leaping or dodging those tumbled building-stones, often slipping and stumbling, unable to fathom how I had got to this grisly place, but wildly eager to seek out some other human being.

'I trotted presently into a large piazza, one side of it occupied by a derelict vast church, perhaps Venetian Gothic, or some jumble of antique styles. It seemed to be still roofed, but I did not venture in then. Instead I scurried down a lane, steep-pitched, which ran beside the church; for that lane would lead me, I fancied, in the direction of the glimmering light.

'Behind the church, just off the lane, was a large open space, enclosed by a low wall that was broken at various points. Had I gone astray? Then, far down at the bottom of the steep lane which stretched before me, I saw the light again. It seemed to be moving up toward me. It was not a lantern of any sort, but rather a mass of glowing stuff, more phosphorescent than incandescent, and it seemed to be about the height of a man.

'We all are cowards — yes Melchiora, your husband too. That strange light, if light it could be called, sent me quivering all over. I must not confront it directly until I should have some notion of what it was. So I dodged out of the lane, to my left, through one of the gaps in the low wall which paralleled the alley.

'Now I was among tombs. This open space was the graveyard behind that enormous church. Even the cemetery of this horrid town had been sacked. Monuments had been toppled, graves dug open and pillaged. I stumbled over a crumbling skull, and fell to earth in this open charnel house.

'That fall, it turned out, was all to the good. For while I lay prone, that light came opposite a gap in the enclosing wall, and hesitated there. I had a fair view of it from where I lay.

'Yes, it was a man's height, but an amorphous thing, an immense corpse-candle, or will-o'-the-wisp, so far as it may be described at all. It wavered and shrank and expanded again, lingering there, lambent.

'And out of this abominable corpse-candle, if I may call it that, came a voice. I suppose it may have been no more than a low murmur, but in that utter silence of the empty town it was tremendous. At first it gabbled and moaned, but then I made out words, and those words paralyzed me. They were these: "I must have your body."

'Had the thing set upon me at that moment, I should have been lost: I could stir no muscle. But after wobbling near the wall-gap, the corpse-candle shifted away and went uncertainly up the lane toward the church and the square. I could see the top of it glowing above the wall until it passed out of the lane at the top.

'I lay unmoving, though conscious. Where might I have run to? The thing was not just here now; it might be anywhere else, lurking. And it sent into me a dread more unnerving than ever I have felt from the menace of living men.

'Memory flooded upon me in that instant. In my mind's eye, I saw the great hall here in this house at Haggat, and the Archvicar and myself sitting at brandy and raisins, and his last words rang in my ears. Indeed I had been transported, or rather translated, to the Archvicar's peculiar demesne, to which he consigned those wretches with whom he had finished.

'Was this ruined town a "real" place? I cannot tell you. I am certain that I was not then experiencing a dream or vision, as we ordinarily employ those words. My circumstances were actual; my peril was genuine and acute. Whether such an object as that sacked city exists in stone somewhere in this world — I do not mean to seek it out — or whether it was an illusion conjured out of the Archvicar's imagination, or out of mine, I do not know. *Maya!* But I sensed powerfully that whatever the nature of this accursed place, this City of Dis, I might never get out of it — certainly not if the corpse-candle came upon me.

'For that corpse-candle must be in some way the Archvicar Geronion, seeking whom he might devour. He had, after all, a way out of the body of this death; and that was to take my body. Had he done the thing before, twice or thrice before, in his long course of evil? Had he meant to do it with one of those beggars upon whom he had experimented, and been interrupted before his venture could be completed?

'It must be a most perilous chance, a desperate last recourse, for Geronion was enfeebled and past the height of his powers. But his only alternative was the executioner's bullet. He meant to enter into me, to penetrate me utterly, to perpetuate his essence in my flesh; and I would be left here — or the essence, the ghost of me, rather — in this place of desolation beyond time and space. The Archvicar, master of some Tantra, had fastened upon me for his prey because only I had lain within his reach on the eve of his execution. And also there were those correspondences between us, which would diminish the obstacles to the transmigration of Geronion's malign essence from one mortal vessel to another: the obverse of the coin would make itself the reverse. Deep cried unto deep, evil unto evil.

'Lying there among dry bones in the plundered graveyard, I had no notion of how to save myself. This town, its secrets, its laws, were Geronion's. Still — that corpse-candle form, gabbling and moaning as if in extremity, must be limited in its perceptions, or else it would have come through the wall-gap to take me a few minutes earlier. Was it like a hound on the scent, and did it have forever to track me down?

'"Arcane! Arcane!" My name was mouthed hideously; the vocal *ignis fatuus* was crying from somewhere. I turned my head, quick as an owl. The loathsome glow now appeared behind the church, up the slope of the great graveyard; it was groping its way toward me.

'I leaped up. As if it sensed my movement, the sightless thing swayed and floated in my direction. I dodged among tall grotesque tombstones; the corpse-candle drifted more directly toward me. This was to be hide-and-seek, blindman's buff, with the end foreordained. "Here we go round the prickly pear at five o'clock in the morning!"

'On came the vague shape of phosphorescence, with a hideous fluttering urgency; but by the time it got to the tall tombstones, I was a hundred yards distant, behind the wreck of a small mausoleum.

'I have never been hunted by tiger or polar bear, but I am sure that what I experienced in that boneyard was worse than the helpless terror of Indian villager or wounded Eskimo. To even the worst ruffian storming an outpost at the back of beyond, the loser may appeal for mercy with some faint hope of being spared. I knew that I could not surrender at discretion to this *ignis fatuus*, any more than to tiger or bear. It meant to devour me.

'Along the thing came, already halfway to the mausoleum. There loomed up a sort of pyramid-monument some distance to my right; I ran hard for it. At the lower end of the cemetery, which I now approached, the enclosing wall looked too high to scale. I gained the little stone pyramid, but the corpse-candle already had skirted the mausoleum and was making for me.

'What way to turn? Hardly knowing why, I ran upward, back toward the dark hulk of the church. I dared not glance over my shoulder — no tenth of a second to spare.

'This was no time to behave like Lot's wife. Frantically scrambling, I reached a side doorway of the church, and only there paused for a fraction of a second to see what was on my heels. The corpse-candle was some distance to the rear of me, drifting slowly, and I fancied that its glow had diminished. Yet I think I heard something moan the word "body." I dashed into the immensity of that church.

'Where might I possibly conceal myself from the faceless hunter? I blundered into a side-chapel, its floor strewn with fallen plaster. Over its battered altar, an icon of Christ the King still was fixed, though lance-thrusts had mutilated the face. I clambered upon the altar and clasped the picture.

'From where I clung, I could see the doorway by which I had entered the church. The tall glow of corruption had got so far as that doorway, and now lingered upon the threshold. For a moment, as if by a final frantic effort, it shone brightly. Then the corpse-candle went out as if an extinguisher had been clapped over it. The damaged icon broke loose from the wall, and with it in my arms I fell from the altar.'

*   *

I felt acute pain in my right arm: Whiston had been clutching it fiercely for some minutes, I suppose, but I had not noticed until now. Guido was crying hard from fright, his head in Melchiora's lap. No one said anything until Arcane asked Grizel Fergusson, 'Will you turn up the lamp a trifle? The play is played out; be comforted, little Guido.'

'You returned, Ras Arcane,' Wolde Mariam's deep voice said, quavering just noticeably. 'What did you do with the bad priest?'

'It was unnecessary for me to do anything — not that I could have done it, being out of my head for the next week. They say I screamed a good deal during the nights. It was a month before I was well enough to walk. And even then, for another two or three months, I avoided dark corners.'

'What about the Archvicar's health?' I ventured.

'About ten o'clock, Yawby, the servants had entered the old harem to tidy it, assuming that the Archvicar and I had retired. They had found that the Archvicar had fallen out of his wheelchair and was stretched very dead on the floor. After a short search, they discovered me in this little room where we sit now. I was not conscious, and had suffered some cuts and bruises. Apparently I had crawled here in a daze, grasped the feet of Our Lord there' — nodding toward the Spanish Christ upon the wall — 'and the crucifix had fallen upon me, as the icon had fallen in that desecrated church. These correspondences!'

Tom Whiston asked hoarsely, 'How long had it been since you were left alone with the Archvicar?'

'Perhaps two hours and a half — nearly the length of time I seemed to spend in his damned ruined demesne.'

'Only you, Manfred, could have had will strong enough to come back from that place,' Melchiora told her husband. She murmured softly what I took for Sicilian endearments. Her fine eyes were wet, though she must have heard the fearful story many times before, and her hands trembled badly.

'Only a man sufficiently evil in his heart could have been snared there at all, My Delight,' Arcane responded. He glanced around our unnerved little circle. 'Do you suppose, friends, that the Archvicar wanders there still, among the open graves, forlorn old ghoul, burning, burning, burning, a corpse-candle forever and a day?'

Even the Fitaurari was affected by this image. I wanted to know what had undone Gerontion.

'Why,' Arcane suggested, 'I suppose that what for me was an underdose of his *kalanzi* must have been an overdose for the poisoner himself: he had been given only a few seconds, while my back was turned, to fiddle with those raisins. What with his physical feebleness, the strain upon his nerves, and the haste with which he had to act, the odds must have run against the Archvicar. But I did not think so while I was in his demesne.' Arcane was stroking the boy's averted head.

'I was in no condition to give his mortal envelope a funeral. But our trustworthy Mohammed ben Ibrahim, that unsmiling young statesman, knew something of the case; and in my absence, he took no chances. He had Gerontion's flaccid husk burnt that midnight, and stood by while the smoke and the stench went up. Tantric magic, or whatever occult skill Gerontion exercised upon me, lost a grand artist.

'Had the creature succeeded in such an undertaking before — twice perhaps, or even three times? I fancy so; but we have no witnesses surviving.'

'Now I don't want to sound like an idiot, and I don't get half of this,' Whiston stammered, 'but suppose that the Archvicar could have brought the thing off. . . . He couldn't, of course, but suppose he could have — what would he have done then?'

'Why, Mr. Whiston, if he had possessed himself of my rather battered body, and there had been signs of life remaining in that discarded body of his — though I doubt whether he had power or desire to shift the ghost called Manfred Arcane into his own old carcass — presumably he would have had the other thing shot the next day; after all, that body of his lay under sentence of death.' Arcane finished his glass of cognac and chuckled deeply.

'How our malicious Archvicar Gerontion would have exulted in the downfall of his host! How he would have enjoyed that magnificent irony! I almost regret having disobliged him. Then he would have assumed a new identity: that of Manfred Arcane, Minister without Portfolio. He had studied me most intensely, and his acting would have adorned any stage. So certainly he could have carried on the performance long enough to have flown abroad and hidden himself. Or conceivably he might have been so pleased with his new identity, and so letter-perfect at realizing it, that he merely could have stepped into my shoes and fulfilled my several duties. That role would have given him more power for mischief than ever he had known before. A piquant situation, friends?'

Out of the corner of my eye, I saw the splendid Melchiora shudder from top to toe.

'Then how do we know that he failed?' my charge Tom Whiston inquired facetiously, with an awkward laugh.

'Mr. Whiston!' Melchiora and Grizel Fergusson cried with simultaneous indignation.

Manfred Arcane, tough old charmer, smiled amicably. 'On Tuesday morning, when we negotiate our new oil contract over brandy and raisins, my Doubting Thomas of Texas, you shall discover that, after all, Archvicar Gerontion succeeded. For you shall behold me in a snapdragon, Evil Incarnate.' Yet before leading us out of that little room and back to the Christmas waltzers, Arcane genuflected beneath the crucified figure on the wall.

There's a Long, Long Trail A-Winding

Then said he unto the disciples, It is impossible but that offences will come: but woe unto him, through whom they come! It were better for him that a millstone were hanged about his neck, and he cast into the sea, than that he should offend one of these little ones.

Luke 17:1-2

Along the vast empty six-lane highway, the blizzard swept as if it meant to swallow all the sensual world. Frank Sarsfield, massive though he was, scudded like a heavy kite before that overwhelming wind. On his thick white hair the snow clotted and tried to form a Phrygian cap; the big flakes so swirled about his Viking face that he scarcely could make out the barren country on either side of the road.

Somehow he must get indoors. Racing for sanctuary, the last automobile had swept unheeding past his thumb two hours ago, doubtless bound for the county town some twenty miles eastward. Westward among the hills, the highway must be blocked by snow-drifts now. This was an unkind twelfth of January. 'Blow, blow, thou winter wind!' Twilight being almost upon him, soon he must find lodging or else freeze stiff by the roadside.

He had walked more than thirty miles that day. Having in his pocket the sum of twenty-nine dollars and thirty cents, he could have put up at either of the two motels he had passed, had they not been closed for the winter. Well, as always, he was decently dressed — a good wash-and-wear suit and a neat black overcoat. As always, he was shaven and clean and civil-spoken. Surely some farmer or villager would take him in, if he knocked with a ten-dollar bill in his fist. People sometimes mistook him for a stranded well-to-do motorist, and sometimes he took the trouble to unde-ceive them.

But where to apply? This was depopulated country, its forests gone to the sawmills long before, its mines worked out. The freeway ran through the abomination of desolation. He did not prefer to walk the freeways, but on such a day as this there were no cars on the lesser roads.

He had run away from a hardscrabble New Hampshire farm when he was fourteen, and ever since then, except for brief working intervals, he had been either on the roads or in the jails. Now his sixtieth birthday was imminent. There were few men bigger than Frank Sarsfield, and none more solitary. Where was a friendly house?

For a few moments, the rage of the snow slackened; he stared about. Away to the left, almost a mile distant, he made out a grim high clump of buildings on rising ground, a wall enclosing them; the roof of the central building was gone. Sarsfield grinned, knowing what that complex must be: a derelict prison. He had lodged in prisons altogether too many nights.

His hand sheltering his eyes from the north wind, he looked to his right. Down in a snug valley, beside a narrow river and broad marshes, he could perceive a village or hamlet: a white church-tower, three or four commercial buildings, some little houses, beyond them a park of bare ma-ple trees. The old highway must have run through or near this forgotten place, but the new freeway had sealed it off. There was no sign of a freeway exit to the settlement; probably it could be reached by car only along some detouring country lane. In such a little decayed town there would be folk willing to accept him for the sake of his proffered ten dollars — or, better, simply for charity's sake and talk with an amusing stranger who could re-cite every kind of poetry.

He scrambled heavily down the embankment. At this point, praise be, no tremendous wire fence kept the haughty new highway inviolable. His powerful thighs took him through the swelling drifts, though his heart pounded as the storm burst upon him afresh.

The village was more distant than he had thought. He passed panting through old fields half-grown up to poplar and birch. A little to the west he noticed what seemed to be old mine-workings, with fragments of brick buildings. He clambered upon an old railroad bed, its rails and ties taken up; perhaps the new freeway had dealt the final blow to the rails. Here the going was somewhat easier.

Mingled with the wind's shriek, did he hear a church-bell now? Could they be holding services at the village in this weather? Presently he came to a burnt-out little railway depot, on its platform signboard still the name 'Anthonyville.' Now he walked on a street of sorts, but no car-tracks or footprints sullied the snow.

Anthonyville Free Methodist Church hulked before him. Indeed the bell was swinging, and now and again faintly ringing in the steeple; but it was the wind's mockery, a knell for the derelict town of Anthonyville. The church door was slamming in the high wind, flying open again, and slamming once more, like a perpetual-motion machine, the glass being gone from the church windows. Sarsfield trudged past the skeletal church.

The front of Emmons's General Store was boarded up, and so was the front of what may have been a drugstore. The village hall was a wreck. The school may have stood upon those scanty foundations which protruded from the snow. And from no chimney of the decrepit cottages and cabins along Main Street — the only street — did any smoke rise.

Sarsfield never had seen a deader village. In an upper window of what looked like a livery-stable converted into a garage, a faded cardboard sign could be read:

REMEMBER YOUR FUTURE
BACK THE TOWNSEND PLAN

Was no one at all left here — not even some gaunt old couple managing on Social Security? He might force his way into one of the stores or cottages — though on principle and prudence he generally steered clear of possible charges of breaking and entering — but that would be cold comfort. In poor Anthonyville there must remain some living soul.

His mittened hands clutching his red ears, Sarsfield had plodded nearly to the end of Main Street. Anthonyville was Endsville, he saw now: river and swamp and new highway cut it off altogether from the rest of the frozen world, except for the drift-obliterated country road that twisted southward, Lord knew whither. He might count himself lucky to find a stove, left behind in some shack, that he could feed with boards ripped from walls.

Main Street ended at that grove or park of old maples. Just a sugarbush, like those he had tapped in his boyhood under his father's rough command? No: had the trees not been leafless, he might not have discerned the big stone house among the trees, the only substantial building remaining to Anthonyville. But see it he did for one moment, before the blizzard veiled it from him. There were stone gateposts, too, and a bronze tablet set into one of them. Sarsfield brushed the snowflakes from the inscription: 'Tamarack House.'

Stumbling among the maples toward this promise, he almost collided with a tall glacial boulder. A similar boulder rose a few feet to his right, the pair of them halfway between gateposts and house. There was a bronze tablet on this boulder, too, and he paused to read it:

SACRED TO THE MEMORY OF
JEROME ANTHONY
JULY 4, 1836–JANUARY 14, 1915
BRIGADIER-GENERAL IN THE CORPS OF ENGINEERS,
ARMY OF THE REPUBLIC, FOUNDER OF THIS TOWN
ARCHITECT OF ANTHONYVILLE STATE PRISON
WHO DIED AS HE HAD LIVED, WITH HONOR

'And there will I keep you forever,
Yes, forever and a day,
Till the walls shall crumble in ruin,
And moulder in dust away.'

There's an epitaph for a prison architect, Sarsfield thought. It was too bitter an evening for inspecting the other boulder, and he hurried toward the portico of Tamarack House. This was a very big house indeed, a bracketed house, built all of squared fieldstone with beautiful glints to the masonry. A cupola topped it.

Once, come out of the cold into a public library, Sarsfield had pored through a picture-book about American architectural styles. There was a word for this sort of house. Was it 'Italianate'? Yes, it rose in his memory — he took pride in no quality except his power of recollection. Yes, that was the word. Had he visited this house before? He could not account for a vague familiarity. Perhaps there had been a photograph of this particular house in that library book.

Every window was heavily shuttered, and no smoke rose from any of the several chimneys. Sarsfield went up to the stone steps to confront the oaken front door.

It was a formidable door, but it seemed as if at some time it had been broken open, for long ago a square of oak with a different grain had been mortised into the area round lock and keyhole. There was a gigantic knocker with a strange face worked upon it. Sarsfield knocked repeatedly.

No one answered. Conceivably the storm might have made his pounding inaudible to any occupants, but who could spend the winter in a shuttered house without fires? Another bronze plaque was screwed to the door:

TAMARACK HOUSE
PROPERTY OF THE ANTHONY FAMILY TRUST
GUARDED BY PROTECTIVE SERVICE

Sarsfield doubted the veracity of the last line. He made his way round to the back. No one answered those back doors, either, and they too were locked.

But presently he found what he had hoped for: an oldfangled slanting cellar door, set into the foundations. It was not wise to enter without permission, but at least he might accomplish it without breaking. His fingers, though clumsy, were strong as the rest of him. After much trouble and with help from the Boy Scout knife that he carried, he pulled the pins out of the cellar door's three hinges and scrambled down into the darkness. With the passing of the years, he had become something of a jailhouse lawyer — though those young inmates bored him with their endless chatter about Miranda and Escobedo. And now he thought of the doctrine called 'defense of necessity.' If caught, he could say that self-preservation from freezing is the first necessity; besides, they might not take him for a bum.

Faint light down the cellar steps — he would replace the hinge-pins later — showed him an inner door at the foot. That door was hooked, though hooked only. With a sigh, Sarsfield put his shoulder to the door; the hook clattered to the stone floor inside; and he was master of all he surveyed.

In that black cellar he found no light-switch. Though he never smoked, he carried matches for such emergencies. Having lit one, he discovered a providential kerosene lamp on a table, with enough kerosene still in it. Sarsfield went lamp-lit through the cellars and up more stone stairs into a pantry. 'Anybody home?' he called. It was an eerie echo.

He would make sure before exploring, for he dreaded shotguns. How about a cheerful song? In that chill pantry, Sarsfield bellowed a tune formerly beloved at Rotary Clubs. Once a waggish Rotarian, after half an hour's talk with the hobo extraordinary, had taken him to Rotary for lunch and commanded him to tell tales of the road and to sing the members a song. Frank Sarsfield's untutored voice was loud enough when he wanted it to be, and he sang the song he had sung to Rotary:

'There's a long, long trail a-winding into the land of my dreams,
Where the nightingale is singing and the white moon beams;
There's a long, long night of waiting until my dreams all come true,
Till the day when I'll be walking down that long, long trail to you!'

No response; no cry, no footstep, not a rustle. Even in so big a house, they couldn't have failed to hear his song, sung in a voice fit to wake the dead. Father O'Malley had called Frank's voice 'stentorian' — a good word, though he was not just sure what it meant. He liked that last line, though he'd no one to walk to; he'd repeat it:

'Till the day when I'll be walking down that long, long trail to you!'

It was all right. Sarsfield went into the dining-room, where he found a splendid long walnut table, chairs with embroidered seats, a fine sideboard and china cabinet, and a high Venetian chandelier. The china was in that cabinet, and the silverware was in that sideboard. But in no room of Tamarack House was any living soul.

*   *

Sprawled in a big chair before the fireplace in the Sunday parlor, Sarsfield took the chill out of his bones. The woodshed, connected with the main house by a passage from the kitchen, was half filled with logs — not first-rate fuel, true, for they had been stacked there three or four years ago, to judge by the fungi upon them, but burnable after he had collected old newspapers and chopped kindling. He had crisscrossed elm and birch to make a noble fire.

It was not very risky to let white woodsmoke eddy from the chimneys, for it would blend with the driving snow and the blast would dissipate it at once. Besides, Anthonyville's population was zero. From the cupola atop the house, in another lull of the blizzard, he had looked over the icy countryside and had seen no inhabited farmhouse up the forgotten dirt road — which, anyway, was hopelessly blocked by drifts today. There was no approach for vehicles from the freeway, while river and marsh protected the rear. He speculated that Tamarack House might be inhabited summers, though not in any very recent summer. The 'Protective Service' probably consisted of a farmer who made a fortnightly inspection in fair weather.

It was good to hole up in a remote county where burglars seemed unknown as yet. Frank Sarsfield restricted his own depredations to church poor-boxes (Catholic, preferably, he being no Protestant) and then under defense of necessity, after a run of unsuccessful mendicancy. He feared and detested strong thieves, so numerous nowadays; to avoid them and worse than thieves, he steered clear of the cities, roving to little places which still kept crime in the family, where it belonged.

He had dined, and then washed the dishes dutifully. The kitchen wood-range still functioned, and so did the hard-water and soft-water hand pumps in the scullery. As for food, there was enough to feed a good-sized prison: the shelves of the deep cellar cold-room threatened to collapse under the weight of glass jars full of jam, jellies, preserved peaches, apricots, applesauce, pickled pork, pickled trout, amid many more good things, all redolent of his New England youth. Most of the jars had neat paper labels, all giving the year of canning, some the name of the canner; on the front shelves, the most recent date he found was 1968, on a little pot of strawberry jam, and below it was the name 'Allegra' in a feminine hand.

Everything in this house lay in apple-pie order — though Sarsfield wondered how long the plaster would keep from cracking, with Tamarack House unheated in winter. He felt positively virtuous for lighting fires, one here in the Sunday parlor, another in the little antique iron stove in the bedroom he had chosen for himself at the top of the house.

He had poked into every handsome room of Tamarack House, with the intense pleasure of a small boy who had found his way into an enchanted castle. Every room was satisfying, well-furnished (he was warming by the fire two sheets from the linen closet, for his bed), and wondrously old-fashioned. There was no electric light, no central heating, no bathroom; there was an indoor privy, at the back of the woodshed, but no running water unless one counted the hand pumps. There was an oldfangled wall telephone: Frank tried, greatly daring, for the operator, but it was dead. He had found a crystal-set radio that didn't work. This was an old lady's house, surely, and the old lady hadn't visited it for some years, but perhaps her relatives kept it in order as a 'holiday home' or in hope of selling it — at ruined Anthonyville, a forlorn hope. He had discovered two canisters of tea, a jar full of coffee beans, and ten gallons of kerosene. How thoughtful!

Perhaps the old lady was dead, buried under the other boulder among the maples in front of the house. Perhaps she had been the General's daughter — but no, not if the General had been born in 1836. Why those graves in the lawn? Sarsfield had heard of farm families, near medical schools in the old days, who had buried their dead by the house for fear of body-snatchers; but that couldn't apply at Anthonyville. Well, there were family graveyards, but this must be one of the smallest.

The old General who built this house had died on January fourteenth. Day after tomorrow, January fourteenth would come round again, and it would be Frank Sarsfield's sixtieth birthday. 'I drink your health in water, General,' Sarsfield said aloud, raising his cut-glass goblet taken from the china cabinet. There was no strong drink in the house, but that didn't distress Sarsfield, for he never touched it. His mother had warned him against it — and sure enough, the one time he had drunk a good deal of wine, when he was new to the road, he had got sick. 'Thanks, General, for your hospitality.' Nobody responded to his toast.

His mother had been a saint, the neighbors had said, and his father a drunken devil. He had seen neither of them after he ran away. He had missed his mother's funeral because he hadn't known of her death until months after; he had missed his father's, long later, because he chose to miss it, though that omission cost him sleepless nights now. Sarsfield slept poorly at best. Almost always there were nightmares.

Yet perhaps he would sleep well enough tonight in that little garret room near the cupola. He had found that several of the bedrooms in Tamarack House had little metal plates over their doorways. There were 'The General's Room' and 'Father's Room' and 'Mama's Room' and 'Alice's Room' and 'Allegra's Room' and 'Edith's Room.' By a happy coincidence, the little room at the top of the back stair, on the garret floor of the house, was labeled 'Frank's Room.' But he'd not chosen it for that only. At the top of the house, one was safer from sheriffs or burglars. And through the skylight — there was only a frieze window — a man could get to the roof of the main block. From that roof, one could descend to the woodshed roof by a fire-escape of iron rungs fixed in the stone outer wall; and from the woodshed, it was an easy drop to the ground. After that, the chief difficulty would be to run down Main Street and then get across the freeway without being detected, while people searched the house for you. Talk of Goldilocks and the Three Bears! Much experience had taught Sarsfield such forethought.

Had that other Frank, so commemorated over the bedroom door, been a son or a servant? Presumably a son — though Sarsfield had found no pictures of boys in the old velvet-covered album in the Sunday parlor, nor any of manservants. There were many pictures of the General, a little roosterlike man with a beard; and of Father, portly and pleasant-faced; and of Mama, elegant; and of three small girls, who must be Alice and Allegra and Edith. He had liked especially the photographs of Allegra, since he had tasted her strawberry jam. All the girls were pretty but Allegra — who must be about seven in most of the pictures — was really charming, with long ringlets and kind eyes and a delicate mouth that curved upward at its corners.

Sarsfield adored little girls and distrusted big girls. His mother had cautioned him against bad women, so he had kept away from such. Because he liked peace, he never had married — not that he could have married anyway, because that would have tied him to one place, and he was too clumsy to earn money at practically anything except dishwashing for summer hotels. Not marrying had meant that he could have no little daughters like Allegra.

Sometimes he had puzzled the prison psychiatrists. In prison it was well to play stupid. He had refrained cunningly from reciting poetry to the psychiatrists. So after testing him they wrote him down as 'dull normal' and he was assigned to labor as 'gardener' — which meant going round the prison yards picking up trash by a stick with a nail in the end of it. That was easy work, and he detested hard work. Yet when there was truly heavy work to be done in prison, sometimes he would come forward to shovel tons of coal or carry hods of brick or lift big blocks into place. That, too, was his cunning: it impressed the other jailbirds with his enormous strength, so that the gangs left him alone.

'Yes, you're a loner, Frank Sarsfield,' he said to himself, aloud. He looked at himself in that splendid Sunday-parlor mirror, which stretched from floor to ceiling. He saw a man overweight but lean enough of face, standing six feet six, built like a bear, a strong nose, some teeth missing, a strong chin, and rather wild light-blue eyes. He was an uncommon sort of bum. Deliberately he looked at his image out of the corners of his eyes — as was his way, because he was non-violent, and eye-contact might mean trouble.

'You look like a Viking, Frank,' old Father O'Malley had told him once, 'but you ought to have been a monk.'

'Oh, Father,' he had answered, 'I'm too much of a fool for a monk.'

'Well,' said Father O'Malley, 'you're no more fool than many a brother, and you're celibate, and continent, I take it. Yet it's late for that now. Look out you don't turn berserker, Frank. Go to confession, sometime, to a priest that doesn't know you, if you'll not go to me. If you'd confess, you'd not be haunted.'

But he seldom went to mass, and never to confession. All those church boxes pilfered, his mother and father abandoned, his sister neglected, all the ghastly humbling of himself before policemen, all the horror and shame of the prisons! There could be no grace for him now. '*There's a long, long trail a-winding into the land of my dreams....*' What dreams! He had looked up 'berserker' in Webster. But he wouldn't ever do that sort of thing: a man had to keep a control upon himself, and besides he was a coward, and he loved peace.

Nearly all the other prisoners had been brutes, guilty as sin, guilty as Miranda or Escobedo. Once, sentenced for rifling a church safe, he had been put into the same cell with a man who had murdered his wife by taking off her head. The head never had been found. Sarsfield had dreamed of that head in such short intervals of sleep as he had enjoyed while the wife-killer was his cellmate. Nearly all night, every night, he had lain awake surreptitiously watching the murderer in the opposite bunk, and feeling his own neck now and again. He had been surprised and pleased when eventually the wife-killer had gone hysterical and obtained assignment to another cell. The murderer had told the guards that he just couldn't stand being watched all night by that terrible giant who never talked.

Only one of the prison psychiatrists had been pleasant or bright, and that had been the old doctor born in Vienna who went round from penitentiary to penitentiary checking on the psychiatric staffs. The old doctor had taken a liking to him, and had written a report to accompany Frank's petition for parole. Three months later, in a parole office, the parole officer had gone out hurriedly for a quarter of an hour, and Sarsfield had taken the chance to read his own file that the parole man had left in a folder on his desk.

'Francis Sarsfield has a memory that almost can be described as photographic' — so had run one line in the Vienna doctor's report. When he read that, Sarsfield had known that the doctor was a clever doctor. 'He suffers chiefly from an arrest of emotional development, and may be regarded as a rather bright small boy in some respects. His three temporarily successful escapes from prison suggest that his intelligence has been much underrated. On at least one of those three occasions, he could have eluded the arresting officer had he been willing to resort to violence. Sarsfield repeatedly describes himself as non-violent and has no record of aggression while confined, nor in connection with any of the offenses for which he was arrested. On the contrary, he seems timid and withdrawn, and might become a victim of assaults in prison, were it not for his size, strength, and power of voice.'

Sarsfield had been pleased enough by that paragraph, but a little puzzled by what followed:

'In general, Sarsfield is one of those recidivists who ought not to be confined, were any alternative method now available for restraining them from petty offenses against property. Not only does he lack belligerence against men, but apparently he is quite clean of any record against women and children. It seems that he does not indulge in autoeroticism, either — perhaps because of strict instruction by his R.C. mother during his formative years.

'I add, however, that conceivably Sarsfield is not fundamentally so gentle as his record indicates. He can be energetic in self-defense when pushed to the wall. In his youth occasionally he was induced, for the promise of five dollars or ten dollars, to stand up as an amateur against some traveling professional boxer. He admits that he did not fight hard, and cried when he was badly beaten. Nevertheless, I am inclined to suspect a potentiality for violence, long repressed but not totally extinguished by years of "humbling himself," in his phrase. This possibility is not so certain as to warrant additional detention, even though three years of Sarsfield's sentence remain unexpired.'

Yes, he had memorized nearly the whole of that old doctor's analysis, which had got his parole for him. There had been the concluding paragraphs:

'Francis Sarsfield is oppressed by a haunting sense of personal guilt. He is religious to the point of superstition, an R.C., and appears to believe himself damned. Although worldly-wise in a number of aspects, he retains an almost unique innocence in others. His frequent humor and candor account for his success, much of the time, at begging. He has read much during his wanderings and terms of confinement. He has a strong taste for good poetry of the popular sort, and has accumulated a mass of miscellaneous information, much of it irrelevant to the life he leads.

'Although occasionally moody and even surly, most of the time he subjects himself to authority, and will work fairly well if closely supervised. He possesses no skills of any sort, unless some knack for wood-chopping, acquired while he was enrolled in the Civilian Conservation Corps, can be considered a marketable skill. He appears to be incorrigibly footloose, and therefore confinement is more unpleasant to him than to most prisoners. It is truly remarkable that he continues to be rational enough, his isolation and heavy guilt-complex considered.

'Sometimes evasive when he does not desire to answer questions, nevertheless he rarely utters a direct lie. His personal modesty may be described as excessive. His habits of cleanliness are commendable, if perhaps of origins like Lady Macbeth's.

'Despite his strength, he is a diabetic and suffers from a heart murmur, sometimes painful.

'Only in circumstances so favorable as to be virtually unobtainable could Sarsfield succeed in abstaining from the behavior-pattern that has led to his repeated prosecution and imprisonment. The excessive crowding of this penitentiary considered, however, I strongly recommend that he be released upon parole. Previous psychiatric reports concerning this inmate have been shallow and erroneous, I regret to note. Perhaps Sarsfield's chief psychological difficulty is that, from obscure causes, he lacks emotional communication with other adults, although able to maintain cordial and healthy relations with small children. He is very nearly a solipsist, which in large part may account for his inability to make firm decisions or pursue any regular occupation. In contradiction of previous analyses of Sarsfield, he should not be described as "dull normal" intellectually. Francis Xavier Sarsfield distinctly is neither dull nor normal.'

Sarsfield had looked up 'solipsist,' but hadn't found himself much the wiser. He didn't think himself the only existent thing — not most of the time, anyway. He wasn't sure that the old doctor had been real, but he knew that his mother had been real before she went straight to Heaven. He knew that his nightmares probably weren't real; but sometimes, while awake, he could see things that other men couldn't. In a house like this, he could glimpse little unaccountable movements out of the corners of his eyes, but it wouldn't do to worry about those. He was afraid of those things which other people couldn't see, yet not so frightened of them as most people were. Some of the other inmates had called him Crazy Frank, and it had been hard to keep down his temper. If you could perceive *more* existent things, though not flesh-and-blood things, than psychiatrists or convicts could — why, were you a solipsist?

There was no point in puzzling over it. Dad had taken him out of school to work on the farm when he hadn't yet finished the fourth grade, so words like 'solipsist' didn't mean much to him. Poets' words, though, he mostly understood. He had picked up a rhyme that made children laugh when he told it to them:

> Though you don't know it,
> You're a poet.
> Your feet show it:
> They're Longfellows.

That wasn't very good poetry, but Henry Wadsworth Longfellow was a good poet. They must have loved Henry Wadsworth Longfellow in this house, and especially 'The Children's Hour,' because of those three little girls named Alice, Allegra, and Edith, and those lines on the General's boulder. Allegra: that's the prettiest of all names ever, and it means 'merry,' someone had told him.

He looked at the cheap wristwatch he had bought, besides the wash-and-wear suit, with his last dishwashing money from that Lake Superior summer hotel. Well, midnight! It's up the wooden hill for you, Frank Sarsfield, to your snug little room under the rafters. If anybody comes to Tamarack House tonight, it's out the skylight and through the snow for you, Frank, my boy — and no tiny reindeer. If you want to survive, in prison or out of it, you stick to your own business and let other folks stew in their own juice.

Before he closed his eyes, he would pray for Mother's soul — not that she really needed it — and then say the little Scottish prayer he had found in a children's book:

'From ghosties and ghoulies, long-leggitie beasties, and things that go bump in the night, good Lord deliver us!'

*   *

The next morning, the morning before his birthday, Frank Sarsfield went up the circular stair to the cupola, even before making his breakfast of pickled trout and peaches and strong coffee. The wind had gone down, and it was snowing only lightly now, but the drifts were immense. Nobody would make his way to Anthonyville and Tamarack House this day; the snowplows would be busy elsewhere.

From this height he could see the freeway, and nothing seemed to be moving along it. The dead village lay to the north of him. To the east were river and swamp, the shores lined with those handsome tamaracks, the green gone out of them, which had given this house its name. Everything in sight belonged to Frank.

He had dreamed during the night, the wind howling and whining round the top of the house, and he had known he was dreaming, but it had been even stranger than usual, if less horrible.

In his dream, he had found himself in the dining-room of Tamarack House. He had not been alone. The General and Father and Mama and the three little girls had been dining happily at the long table, and he had waited on them. In the kitchen an old woman who was the cook, and a girl who cleaned, had eaten by themselves. But when he had finished filling the family's plates, he had sat down at the end of the table, as if he had been expected to do that.

The family had talked among themselves and even to him as he ate, but somehow he had not been able to hear what they said to him. Suddenly he had pricked up his ears, though, because Allegra had spoken to him.

'Frank,' she had said, all mischief, 'why do they call you Punkinhead?'

The old General had frowned at the head of the table, and Mama had said, 'Allegra, don't speak that way to Frank!'

But he had grinned at Allegra, if slightly hurt, and had told the little girl, 'Because some men think I've got a head like a jack-o'-lantern's and not even seeds inside it.'

'Nonsense, Frank,' Mama had put in, 'you have a very handsome head.'

'You've got a pretty head, Frank,' the three little girls had told him

289

then, almost in chorus, placatingly. Allegra had come round the table to make her peace. 'There's going to be a big surprise for you tomorrow, Frank,' she had whispered to him. And then she had kissed him on the cheek.

That had waked him. Most of the rest of that howling night he had lain awake trying to make sense of his dream, but he couldn't. The people in it had been more real than the people he met on the long, long trail.

Now he strolled through the house again, admiring everything. It was almost as if he had seen the furniture and the pictures and the carpets long, long ago. The house must be over a century old, and many of the good things in it must go back to the beginning. He would have two or three more days here until the roads were cleared. There were no newspapers to tell him about the great storm, of course, and no radio that worked; but that didn't matter.

He found a great big handsome *Complete Works of Henry Wadsworth Longfellow,* in red morocco, and an illustrated copy of the *Rubaiyat.* He didn't need to read it, because he had memorized all the quatrains once. There was a black silk ribbon as marker between the pages, and he opened it there — at Quatrain 44, it turned out:

Why, if the Soul can fling the Dust aside,
And naked on the Air of Heaven ride,
    Were't not a Shame — were't not a Shame for him
In this clay carcass crippled to abide?

That old Vienna doctor, Frank suspected, hadn't believed in immortal souls. Frank Sarsfield knew better. But also Frank suspected that his soul never would ride, naked or clothed, on the Air of Heaven. Souls! That put him in mind of his sister, a living soul that he had forsaken. He ought to write her a letter on this the eve of his sixtieth birthday.

Frank traveled light, his luggage being mostly a safety razor, a hairbrush, and a comb; he washed his shirt and socks and underclothes every night, and often his wash-and-wear suit, too. But he did carry with him a few sheets of paper and a ballpoint pen. Sitting down at the library table — he had built a fire in the library stove also, there being no lack of logs — he began to write to Mary Sarsfield, alone in the rotting farmhouse in New Hampshire. His spelling wasn't good, he knew, but today he was careful at his birthday letter, using the big old dictionary with the General's book-plate in it.

To write that letter took most of the day. Two versions were discarded. At last Frank had done the best he could.

Dearest Mary my sister,

Its been nearly 9 years since I came to visit you and borrowed the $78 from you and went away again and never paid it back. I guess you dont want to see your brother Frank again after what I did that time and other times but the Ethiopian can not change his skin nor the leopard his spots and when some man like a Jehovahs Witness or that rancher with all the cash gives me quite a lot of money I mean to send you what I owe but the post office isnt handy at the time and so I spend it on presents for little kids I meet and buying new clothes and such so I never get around to sending you that $78 Mary. Right now I have $29 and more but the post office at this place is folded up and by the time I get to the next town the money will be mostly gone and so it goes. I guess probably you need the money and Im sorry Mary but maybe some day I will win the lottery and then Ill give you all the thousands of dollars I win.

Well Mary its been 41 years and 183 days since Mother passed away and here I am 60 years old tomorrow and you getting on toward 56. I pray that your cough is better and that your son and my nephew Jack is doing better than he was in Tallahassee Florida. Some time Mary if you would write to me c/o Father Justin O'Malley in Albatross Michigan where he is pastor now I would stop by his rectory and get your letter and read it with joy. But I know Ive been a very bad brother and I dont blame you Mary if you never get around to writing your brother Frank.

Mary Ive been staying out of jails and working a little here and there along the road. Now Mary do you know what I hate most about those prisons? Why not being on the road you will say. No Mary the worst thing is the foul language the convicts use from morning till night. Taking the name of their Lord in vain is the least they do. There is a foul curse word in every sentence. I wasnt brought up that way any more than you Mary and I will not revile woman or child. It is like being in H—— to hear it.

Im not in bad shape except the diabetes is no better but I take my pills for it when I can buy them and dont have to take needles for it and my heart hurts me dreadfully bad sometimes when I lift heavy things hours on end and sometimes it hurts me worse at night when Ive been just lying there thinking of the life Ive led and how I ought to pay you the $78 and pay back other folks that helped me too. I owe Father O'Malley $497.11 now altogether and I keep track of it in my head and when the lottery ticket wins he will not be forgot.

Some people have been quite good to me and I still can make them laugh and I recite to them and generally I start my reciting with what No Person of Quality wrote hundreds of years ago

Seven wealthy towns contend for Homer dead
Through which the living Homer begged his bread.

They like that and also usually they like Thomas Grays Elegy in a Country Churchyard leaving the world to darkness and to me and I recite all of that and sometimes some of the Quatrains of Omar. At farms when they ask me I chop wood for these folks and I help with the dishes but I still break a good many as you learned Mary 9 years ago but I didnt mean to do it Mary because I am just clumsy in all ways. Oh yes I am good at reciting Frosts Stopping by Woods and his poem about the Hired Man. I have been reading the poetical works of Thomas Stearns Eliot so I can recite his The Hollow Men or much of it and also his Book of Practical Cats which is comical when I come to college towns and some professor or his wife gives me a sandwich and maybe $2 and maybe a ride to the next town.

Where I am now Mary I ought to study the poems of John Greenleaf Whittier because theres been a real blizzard maybe the biggest in the state for many years and Im Snowbound. Years ago I tried to memorize all that poem but I got only part way for it is a whopper of a poem.

I dont hear much good Music Mary because of course at the motels there isnt any phonograph or tape recorder. Id like to hear some good string quartet or maybe old folk songs well sung for music hath charms to soothe the savage breast. Theres an old Edison at the house where Im staying now and what do you know they have a record of a song you and I used to sing together Theres a Long Long Trail A Winding. Its about the newest record in this house. Ill play it again soon thinking of you Mary my sister. O there is a long long night of waiting.

Mary right now Im at a big fine house where the people have gone away for awhile and I watch the house for them and keep some of the rooms warm. Let me assure you Mary I wont take anything from this good old house when I go. These are nice people I know and I just came in out of the storm and Im very fond of their 3 sweet little girls. I remember what you looked like when I ran away first and you looked like one of them called Alice. The one I like best though is Allegra because she makes mischief and laughs a lot but is innocent.

I came here just yesterday but it seems as if Id lived in this house before but of course I couldnt have and I feel at home here. Nothing in this house could scare me much. You might not like it Mary because of little noises and glimpses you get but its a lovely house and as you know I like old places that have been lived in lots.

By the way Mary once upon a time Father O'Malley told me that to the Lord all time is eternally present. I think this means everything that happens in the world in any day goes on all at once. So God sees what went on in this house long ago and whats going on in this house today all at the same time. Its just as well we dont see through Gods eyes because then wed know everything thats going to happen to us and because Im such a sinner I dont want to know. Father O'Malley says that God may forgive me everything and have something special in store for me but I dont think so because why should He?

And Father O'Malley says that maybe some people work out their Purgatory here on earth and I might be one of these. He says we are spirits in the prisonhouse of the body which is like we were serving Time in the world here below and maybe God forgave me long ago and Im just waiting my time and paying for what I did and it will be alright in the end. Or maybe Im being given some second chance to set things right but as Father O'Malley put it to do that Id have to fortify my Will and do some Signal Act of contrition. Father O'Malley even says I might not have to do the Act actually if only I just made up my mind to do it really and truly because what God counts is the intention. But I think people who are in Purgatory must know they are climbing up and have hope and Mary I think Im going down down down even though Ive stayed out of prisons some time now.

Father O'Malley tells me that for everybody the battle is won or lost already in Gods sight and that though Satan thinks he has a good chance to conquer actually Satan has lost forever but doesnt know it. Mary I never did anybody any good but only harm to ones that loved me. If just once before I die I could do one Signal Act that was truly good then God might love me and let me have the Beatific Vision. Yet Mary I know Im weak of will and a coward and lazy and Ive missed my chance forever.

Well Mary my only sister Ive bored you long enough and I just wanted to say hello and tell you to be of good cheer. Im sorry I whined and complained like a little boy about my health because Im still strong and deserve all the pain I get. Mary if you can forgive your big brother who never grew up please pray for me some time because nobody else does except possibly Father O'Malley when he isnt busy with other prayers. I pray for Mother every night and every other night for you and once a month for Dad. You were a good little girl and sweet. Now I will say good bye and ask your pardon for bothering you with my foolishness. Also Im sorry your friends found out I was just a hobo when I was with you 9 years ago and I dont blame you for being angry with me then for talking too much and I know I wasnt fit to lodge in your house. There arent many of us old real hobos left only beatniks and such that cant walk or chop wood and I guess that is just as well. It is a degrading life Mary but I cant stop walking down that long long trail not knowing where it ends.

Your Loving Brother
Francis (Frank)

P.S.: I dont wish to mislead so I will add Mary that the people who own this house didnt exactly ask me in but its alright because I wont do any harm here but a little good if I can. Good night again Mary.

Now he needed an envelope, but he had forgotten to take one from the last motel, where the Presbyterian minister had put him up. There must be some in Tamarack House, and one would not be missed, and that would not be very wrong because he would take nothing else. He found no envelopes in the drawer of the library table: so he went up the stairs and almost knocked at the closed door of Allegra's Room. Foolish! He opened the door gently.

He had admired Allegra's small rosewood desk. In its drawer was a leather letter-folder, the kind with a blotter, he found, and in the folder were several yellowed envelopes. Also lying face up in the folder was a letter of several small pages, in a woman's hand, a trifle shaky He started to sit down to read Allegra's letter that was never sent to anybody, but it passed through his mind that his great body might break the delicate rosewood chair that belonged to Allegra, so he read the letter standing. It was dated January 14, 1969. On that birthday of his, he had been in Joliet prison.

How beautifully Allegra wrote!

Darling Celia,

This is a lonely day at Tamarack House, just fifty-four years after your great-great-grandfather the General died, so I am writing to my grand-niece to tell you how much I hope you will be able to come up to Anthonyville and stay with me next summer — if I still am here. The doctor says that only God knows whether I will be. Your grandmother wants me to come down your way to stay with her for the rest of this winter, but I can't bear to leave Tamarack House at my age, for they might have to put me in a rest-home down there and then I wouldn't see this old house again.

I am all right, really, because kind Mr. Connor looks in every day, and Mrs. Williams comes every other day to clean. I am not sick, my little girl, but simply older than my years, and running down. When you come up next summer, God willing, I will make you that soft toast you like, and perhaps Mr. Connor will turn the crank for the ice-cream, and I may try to make some preserves with you to help me.

You weren't lonely, were you, when you stayed with me last summer for a whole month? Of course there are fewer than a hundred people left in Anthonyville now, and most of those are old. They say that there will be practically nobody living in the town a few years from now, when the new highway is completed and the old one is abandoned. There were more than two thousand people here in town and roundabout, a few years after the General built Tamarack House! But first the lumber industry gave out, and then the mines were exhausted, and the prison-break in 1915 scared many away forever. There are no passenger trains now, and they say the railway line will be pulled out altogether when the new freeway — they have just begun building it to the east — is ready for traffic. But we still have the maples and the tamaracks, and there are ever so many raccoons and opossums and squirrels for you to watch — and a lynx, I think, and an otter or two, and many deer.

Celia, last summer you asked me about the General's death and all the things that happened then, because you had heard something of them from your Grandmother Edith. But I didn't wish to frighten you, so I didn't tell you everything. You are older now, and you have a right to know, because when you grow up you will be one of the trustees of the Anthony Family Trust, and then this old house will be in your charge when I am gone. Tamarack House is not at all frightening, except a little in the morning on every January 14. I do hope that you and the other trustees will keep the house always, with the money that Father left to me — he was good at making money, even though the forests vanished and the mines failed, by his investments in Chicago — and which I am leaving to the Family Trust. I've kept the house just as it was, for the sake of the General's memory and because I love it that way.

You asked just what happened on January 14, 1915. There were seven people who slept in the house that month — not counting Cook and Cynthia (who was a kind of nannie to us girls and also cleaned), because they slept at their houses in the village. In the house, of course, was the General, my grandfather, your great-great-grandfather, who was nearly eighty years old. Then there were Father and Mama, and the three of us little sisters, and dear Frank.

Alice and sometimes even that baby Edith used to tease me in those days by screaming, 'Frank's Allegra's sweetheart! Frank's Allegra's sweetheart!' I used to chase them, but I suppose it was true: he liked me best. Of course he was about sixty years old, though not so old as I am now, and I was a little thing. He used to take me through the swamps and show me the muskrats' houses. The first time he took me on such a trip, Mama raised her eyebrows when he was out of the room, but the General said, 'I'll warrant Frank; I have his papers.' Alice and Edith might just as well have shouted, 'Frank's Allegra's slave!' He read to me — oh, Robert Louis Stevenson's poems and all sorts of books. I never had another sweetheart, partly because almost all the young men left Anthonyville as I grew up when there was no work for them here, and the ones that remained didn't please Mama.

We three sisters used to play Creepmouse with Frank, I remember well. We would be the Creepmice, and would sneak up and scare him when he wasn't watching, and he would pretend to be terrified. He made up a little song for us — or, rather, he put words to some tune he had borrowed:

> Down, down, down in Creepmouse Town
> All the lamps are low,
> And the little rodent feet
> Softly come and go
>
> There's a rat in Creepmouse Town
> And a bat or two:
> Everything in Creepmouse Town
> Would swiftly frighten you!

Do you remember, Celia, that the General was State Supervisor of Prisons and Reformatories for time out of mind? He was a good architect, too, and designed Anthonyville State Prison, without taking any fee for himself, as a model prison. Some people in the capital said that he did it to give employment to his county, but really it was because the site was so isolated that it would be difficult for convicts to escape.

The General knew Frank's last name, but he never told the rest of us. Frank had been in Anthonyville State Prison at one time, and later other prisons, and the General had taken him out of one of those other prisons on parole, having known Frank when he was locked up at Anthonyville. I never learned what Frank had done to be sentenced to prison, but he was gentle with me and everybody else, until that early morning of January 14.

The General was amused by Frank, and said that Frank would be better off with us than anywhere else. So Frank became our hired man, and chopped the firewood for us, and kept the fires going in the stoves and fireplaces, and sometimes served at dinner. In summer he was supposed to scythe the lawns, but of course summer didn't come. Frank arrived by train at Anthony-ville Station in October, and we gave him the little room at the top of the house.

Well, on January 12 Father went off to Chicago on business. We still had the General. Every night he barred the shutters on the ground floor, going round to all the rooms by himself. Mama knew he did it because there was a rumor that some life convicts at the Prison 'had it in' for the Supervisor of Prisons, although the General had retired five years earlier. Also they may have thought he kept a lot of money in the house — when actually, what with the timber gone and the mines going, in those times we were rather hard pressed and certainly kept our money in the bank at Duluth. But we girls didn't know why the General closed the shutters, except that it was one of the General's rituals. Besides, Anthonyville State Prison was supposed to be escape-proof. It was just that the General always took precautions, though ever so brave.

Just before dawn, Celia, on the cold morning of January 14, 1915, we all were waked by the siren of the Prison and we all rushed downstairs in our nightclothes, and we could see that part of the Prison was afire. Oh, the sky was red! The General tried to telephone the Prison, but he couldn't get through, and later it turned out that the lines had been cut.

Next — it all happened so swiftly — we heard shouting somewhere down Main Street, and then guns went off. The General knew what that meant. He had got his trousers and his boots on, and now he struggled with his old military overcoat, and he took his old army revolver. 'Lock the door behind me, girl,' he told Mama. She cried and tried to pull him back inside, but he went down into the snow, nearly eighty though he was.

Only three or four minutes later, we heard the shots. The General had met the convicts at the gate. It was still dark, and the General had cataracts on his eyes. They say he fired first, and missed. Those bad men had broken into Mr. Emmons's store and taken guns and axes and whisky. They shot the General — shot him again and again and again.

The next thing we knew, they were chopping at our front door with axes. Mama hugged us.

Celia dear, writing all this has made me so silly! I feel a little odd, so I must go lie down for an hour or two before telling you the rest. Celia, I do hope you will love this old house as much as I have. If I'm not here when you come up, remember that where I have gone I will know the General and Father and Mama and Alice and poor dear Frank, and will be ever so happy with them. Be a good little girl, my Celia.

The letter ended there, unsigned.

*   *

Frank clumped downstairs to the Sunday parlor. He was crying, for the first time since he had fought that professional heavyweight on October 19, 1943. Allegra's letter — if only she'd finished it! What had happened to those little girls, and Mama, and that other Frank? He thought of something from the Holy Bible: 'It were better for him that a millstone were hanged about his neck, and he cast into the sea, than that he should offend one of these little ones.'

Already it was almost evening. He lit the wick in the cranberry-glass lamp that hung from the middle of the parlor ceiling, standing on a chair to reach it. Why not enjoy more light? On a whim, he arranged upon the round table four silver candlesticks that had rested above the fireplace. He needed three more, and those he fetched from the dining-room. He lit every candle in the circle: one for the General, one for Father, one for Mama, one for Alice, one for Allegra, one for Edith — one for Frank.

The dear names of those little girls! He might as well recite aloud, it being good practice for the approaching days on the long, long trail:

I hear in the chamber above me
    The patter of little feet,
The sound of a door that is opened,
    And voices soft and sweet. . . .

Here he ceased. Had he heard something in the passage — or 'descending the broad hall stair'? Because of the wind outside, he could not be certain. It cost him a gritting of his teeth to rise and open the parlor door. Of course no one could be seen in the hall or on the stair. 'Crazy Frank,' men had called him at Joliet and other prisons: he had clenched his fists, but had kept a check upon himself. Didn't Saint Paul say that the violent take Heaven by storm? Perhaps he had barked up the wrong tree; perhaps he would be spewed out of His mouth for being too peaceful.

Shutting the door, he went back to the fireside. Those lines of Longfellow had been no evocation. He put 'The Long, Long Trail' on the old phonograph again, strolling about the room until the record ran out. There was an old print of a Great Lakes schooner on one wall that he liked. Beside it, he noticed, there seemed to be some pellets embedded in a closet door-jamb, but painted over, as if someone had fired a shotgun in the parlor in the old days. 'The violent take it by storm . . .' He admired the grand piano; perhaps Allegra had learned to play it. There were one or two big notches or gashes along one edge of the piano, varnished over, hard though that wood was. Then Frank sank into the big chair again and stared at the burning logs.

Just how long he had dozed, he did not know. He woke abruptly. Had he heard a whisper, the faintest whisper? He tensed to spring up. But before he could move, he saw reflections in the tall mirror.

Something had moved in the corner by the bookcase. No doubt about it; that small something had stirred again. Also something crept behind one of the satin sofas, and something else lurked near the piano. All these were at his back: he saw the reflections in the glass, as in a glass darkly, more alarming than physical forms. In this high shadowy room, the light of the kerosene lamp and of the seven candles did not suffice.

From near the bookcase, the first of them emerged into candlelight; then came the second, and the third. They were giggling, but he could not hear them — only see their faces, and those not clearly. He was unable to stir, and the gooseflesh prickled all over him, and his hair rose at the back of his big head.

They were three little girls, barefoot, in their long muslin nightgowns, ready for bed. One may have been as much as twelve years old, and the smallest was little more than a baby. The middle one was Allegra, tiny even for her tender years, and a little imp: he knew, he knew! They were playing Creepmouse.

The three of them stole forward, Allegra in the lead, her eyes alight. He could see them plain now, and the dread was ebbing out of him. He might have risen and turned to greet them across the great gulf of time, but any action — why, what might it do to these little ones? Frank sat frozen in his chair, looking at the nimble reflections in the mirror, and nearer they came, perfectly silent. Allegra vanished from the glass, which meant that she must be standing just behind him.

He must please them. Could he speak? He tried, and the lines came out hoarsely:

'Down, down, down in Creepmouse Town
All the lamps are low,
And the little rodent feet . . .'

He was not permitted to finish. Wow! There came a light tug at the curly white hair on the back of his head. Oh, to talk with Allegra, the imp! Reckless, he heaved his bulk out of the chair, and swung round — too late.

The parlor door was closing. But from the hall came another whisper, ever so faint, ever so unmistakable: 'Good night, Frank!' There followed subdued giggles, scampering, and then the silence once more.

He strode to the parlor door. The hall was empty again, and the broad stair. Should he follow them up? No, all three would be abed now. Should he knock at Mama's Room, muttering, 'Mrs. Anthony, are the children all right?' No, he hadn't the nerve for that, and it would be presumptuous. He had been given one moment of perception, and no more.

Somehow he knew that they would not go so far as the garret floor. Ah, he needed fresh air! He snuffed out lamp and candles, except for one candlestick — Allegra's — that he took with him. Out into the hall he went. He unfastened the front door with that oaken patch about the middle of it, and stepped upon the porch, leaving the burning candle just within the hall. The wind had risen again, bringing still more snow. It was black as sin outside, and the temperature must be thirty below.

To him the wind bore one erratic peal of the desolate church-bell of Anthonyville, and then another. How strong the blast must be through that belfry! Frank retreated inside from that unfathomable darkness and that sepulchral bell which seemed to toll for him. He locked the thick door behind him and screwed up his courage for the expedition to his room at the top of the old house.

But why shudder? He loved them now, Allegra most of all. Up the broad stairs to the second floor he went, hearing only his own clumsy footfalls, and past the clay-sealed doors of the General and Father and Mama and Alice and Allegra and Edith. No one whispered, no one scampered.

In Frank's Room, he rolled himself in his blankets and quilt (had Allegra helped stitch the patchwork?), and almost at once the consciousness went out of him, and he must have slept dreamless for the first night since he was a farm boy.

*　　　*

So profound had been his sleep, deep almost as death, that the siren may have been wailing for some minutes before at last it roused him. Frank knew that horrid sound: it had called for him thrice before, as he fled from prisons. Who wanted him now? He heaved his ponderous body out of the warm bed. The candle that he had brought up from the Sunday parlor and left burning all night was flickering in its socket, but by that flame he could see the hour on his watch: seven o'clock, too soon for dawn.

Through the narrow skylight, as he flung on his clothes, the sky glowed an unnatural red, though it was long before sunup. The prison siren ceased to wail, as if choked off. Frank lumbered to the little frieze-window, and saw to the north, perhaps two miles distant, a monstrous mass of flame shooting high into the air. The prison was afire.

Then came shots outside: first the bark of a heavy revolver, followed irregularly by blasts of shotguns or rifles. Frank was lacing his boots with a swiftness uncongenial to him. He got into his overcoat as there came a crashing and battering down below. That sound, too, he recognized, wood-chopper that he had been: axes shattering the front door.

Amid this pandemonium, Frank was too bewildered to grasp altogether where he was or even how this catastrophe might be fitted into the pattern of time. All that mattered was flight; the scheme of his escape remained clear in his mind. Pull up the chair below the skylight, heave yourself out to the upper roof, descend those iron rungs to the woodshed roof, make for the other side of the freeway, then — why, then you must trust to circumstance, Frank. It's that long, long trail a-winding for you.

Now he heard a woman screaming within the house, and slipped and fumbled in his alarm. He had got upon the chair, opened the skylight, and was trying to obtain a good grip on the icy outer edge of the skylight-frame, when someone knocked and kicked at the door of Frank's Room.

Yet those were puny knocks and kicks. He was about to heave himself upward when, in a relative quiet — the screaming had ceased for a moment — he heard a little shrill voice outside his door, urgently pleading: 'Frank, Frank, let me in!'

He was arrested in flight as though great weights had been clamped to his ankles. That little voice he knew, as if it were part of him: Allegra's voice.

For a brief moment he still meant to scramble out the skylight. But the sweet little voice was begging. He stumbled off the chair, upset it, and was at the door in one stride.

'Is that you, Allegra?'

'Open it, Frank, *please* open it!'

He turned the key and pulled the bolt. On the threshold the little girl stood, indistinct by the dying candlelight, terribly pale, all tears, frantic.

Frank snatched her up. Ah, this was the dear real Allegra Anthony, all warm and soft and sobbing, flesh and blood! He kissed her cheek gently.

She clung to him in terror, and then squirmed loose, tugging at his heavy hand: 'Oh, Frank, come on! Come downstairs! They're hurting Mama!'

'Who is, little girl?' He held her tiny hand, his body quivering with dread and indecision. 'Who's down there, Allegra?'

'The bad men! *Come on*, Frank!' Braver than he, the little thing plunged back down the garret stair into the blackness below.

'Allegra! Come back here — come back now!' He bellowed it, but she was gone.

Up two flights of stairs, there poured to him a tumult of shrieks, curses, laughter, breaking noises. Several men were below, their speech slurred and raucous. He did not need Allegra to tell him what kind of men they were, for he heard prison slang and prison foulness, and he shook all over. There still was the skylight.

He would have turned back to that hole in the roof, had not Allegra squealed in pain somewhere on the second floor. Dazed, trembling, unarmed, Frank went three steps down the garret staircase. 'Allegra! Little girl! What is it, Allegra?'

Someone was charging up the stair toward him. It was a burly man in the prison uniform, a lighted lantern in one hand and a glittering ax in the other. Frank had no time to turn. The man screeched obscenely at him, and swung that ax.

In those close quarters, wielded by a drunken man, it was a chancy weapon. The edge shattered the plaster wall; the flat of the blade thumped upon Frank's shoulder. Frank, lurching forward, took the man by the throat with a mighty grip. They all tumbled pell-mell down the steep stairs — the two men, the ax, the lantern.

Frank's ursine bulk landed atop the stranger's body, and Frank heard his adversary's bones crunch. The lantern had broken and gone out. The convict's head hung loose on his shoulders, Frank found as he groped for the ax. Then he trampled over the fallen man and flung himself along the corridor, gripping the ax-helve. 'Allegra! Allegra girl!'

From the head of the main stair, he could see that the lamps and candles were burning in the hall and in the rooms of the ground floor. All three children were down there, wailing, and above their noise rose Mama's shrieks again. A mob of men were stamping, breaking things, roaring with amusement and desire, shouting filth. A bottle shattered.

His heart pounding as if it would burst out of his chest, Frank hurried rashly down that stair and went, all crimson with fury, into the Sunday parlor, the double-bitted ax swinging in his hand. They all were there: the little girls, Mama, and five wild men. 'Stop that!' Frank roared with all the power of his lungs. 'You let them go!'

Everyone in the parlor stood transfixed at that summons like the Last Trump. Allegra had been tugging pathetically at the leg of a dark man who gripped her mother's waist, and the other girls sputtered and sobbed, cornered, as a tall man poured a bottle of whisky over them. Mrs. Anthony's gown was ripped nearly its whole length, and a third man was bending her backward by her long hair, as if he would snap her spine. Near the hall door stood a man like a long lean rat, the Rat of Creepmouse Town, a shotgun on his arm, gape-jawed at Frank's intervention. Guns and axes lay scattered about the Turkey carpet. By the fireplace, a fifth man had been heating the poker in the flames.

For that tableau-moment, they all stared astonished at the raving giant who had burst upon them; and the giant, puffing, stared back with his strange blue eyes. 'Oh, Frank!' Allegra sobbed: it was more command than entreaty — as if, Frank thought in a flash of insane mirth, he were like the boy in the fairy tale who could cry confidently, 'All heads off but mine!'

He knew what these men were, the rats and bats of Creepmouse Town: the worst men in any prison, lifers who had made their hell upon earth, killers all of them and worse than killers. The rotten damnation showed in all those flushed and drunken faces. Then the dark man let go of Mama and said in relief, with a coughing laugh, 'Hell, it's only old Punkinhead Frank, clowning again! Have some fun for yourself, Frank boy!'

'Hey, Frank,' Ratface asked, his shotgun crooked under his arm, 'where'd the old man keep his money?'

Frank towered there perplexed, the berserker-lust draining out of him, almost bashful — and frightened worse than ever before in all his years on the trail. What should he shout now? What should he do? Who was he to resist such perfect evil? They were five to one, and those five were fiends from down under, and that one a coward. Long ago he had been weighed in the balance and found wanting.

Mama was the first to break the tableau. Her second captor had relaxed his clutch upon her hair, and she prodded the little girls before her, and she leaped for the door.

The hair-puller was after her at once, but she bounded past Ratface's shotgun, which had wavered toward Frank, and Alice and Edith were ahead of her. Allegra, her eyes wide and desperate, tripped over the rung of a broken chair. Everything happened in half a second. The hair-puller caught Allegra by her little ankle.

Then Frank bellowed again, loudest in all his life, and he swung his ax high above his head and downward, a skilful dreadful stroke, catching the hair-puller's arm just below the shoulder. At once the man began to scream and spout, while Allegra fled after her mother.

Falling, the hair-puller collided with Ratface, spoiling his aim, but one barrel of the shotgun fired, and Frank felt pain in his side. His bloody ax on high, he hulked between the five men and the door.

All the men's faces were glaring at Frank, incredulously, as if demanding how he dared stir against them. Three convicts were scrabbling tipsily for weapons on the floor. As Frank strode among them, he saw the expression on those faces change from gloating to desperation. Just as his second blow descended, there passed through his mind a kind of fleshly collage of death he had seen once at a farmyard gate: the corpses of five weasels nailed to a gatepost by the farmer, their frozen open jaws agape like damned souls in Hell.

'All heads off but mine!' Frank heard himself braying. 'All heads off but mine!' He hacked and hewed, his own screams of lunatic fury drowning their screams of terror.

For less than three minutes, shots, thuds, shrieks, crashes, terrible wailing. They could not get past him to the doorway.

'Come on!' Frank was raging as he stood in the middle of the parlor. 'Come on, who's next? All heads off but mine! Who's next?'

There came no answer but a ghastly rattle from one of the five heaps that littered the carpet. Blood-soaked from hair to boots, the berserker towered alone, swaying where he stood.

His mind began to clear. He had been shot twice, Frank guessed, and the pain at his heart was frightful. Into his frantic consciousness burst all the glory of what he had done, and all the horror.

He became almost rational; he must count the dead. One upstairs, five here. One, two, three, four, five heaps. That was correct: all present and accounted for, Frank boy, Punkinhead Frank, Crazy Frank: all dead andd accounted for. Had he thought that thought before? Had he taken that mock roll before? Had he wrought this slaughter twice over, twice in this same old room?

But where were Mama and the little girls? They mustn't see this blood-splashed inferno of a parlor. He was looking at himself in the tall mirror, and he saw a bear-man loathsome with his own blood and others' blood. He looked like the Wild Man of Borneo. In abhorrence he flung his ax aside. Behind him sprawled the reflections of the hacked dead.

Fighting down his heart-pain, he reeled into the hall. 'Little girls! Mrs. Anthony! Allegra, oh, Allegra!' His voice was less strong. 'Where are you? It's safe now!'

They did not call back. He labored up the main stair, clutching his side. 'Allegra, speak to your Frank!' They were in none of the bedrooms.

He went up the garret stair, then, whatever the agony, and beyond Frank's Room to the cupola stair, and ascended that slowly, gasping hard. They were not in the cupola. Might they have run out among the trees? In that cold dawn, he stared on every side; he thought his sight was beginning to fail.

He could see no one outside the house. The drifts still choked the street beyond the gateposts, and those two boulders protruded impassive from untrodden snow. Back down the flights of stairs he made his way, clutching at the rail, at the wall. Surely the little girls hadn't strayed into that parlor butcher-shop? He bit his lip and peered into the Sunday parlor.

The bodies all were gone. The splashes and ropy strands of blood all were gone. Everything stood in perfect order, as if violence never had touched Tamarack House. The sun was rising, and sunlight filtered through the shutters. Within fifteen minutes, the trophies of his savage victory had disappeared.

It was like the recurrent dream which had tormented Frank when he was little: he separated from Mother in the dark, wandering solitary in empty lanes, no soul alive in the universe but little Frank. Yet those tremendous ax-blows had severed living flesh and bone, and for one moment, there on the stairs, he had held in his arms a tiny quick Allegra; of that reality he did not doubt at all.

Wonder subduing pain, he staggered to the front door. It stood unshattered. He drew the bar and turned the key, and went down the stone steps into the snow. He was weak now, and did not know where he was going. Had he done a Signal Act? Might the Lord give him one parting glimpse of little Allegra, somewhere among these trees? He slipped in a drift, half rose, sank again, crawled. He found himself at the foot of one of those boulders — the further one, the stone he had not inspected.

The snow had fallen away from the face of the bronze tablet. Clutching the boulder, Frank drew himself up. By bringing his eyes very close to the tablet, he could read the words, a dying man panting against deathless bronze:

IN LOVING MEMORY OF
FRANK

A SPIRIT IN PRISON, MADE FOR ETERNITY
WHO SAVED US AND DIED FOR US
JANUARY 14, 1915

'Why, if the Soul can fling the Dust aside,
And naked on the Air of Heaven ride,
Were't not a Shame — were't not a Shame for him
In this clay carcass crippled to abide?'

Watchers at the Strait Gate

I am for the house with the narrow gate, which I take to be too little for pomp to enter. Some that humble themselves may, but the many will be too chill and tender, and they'll be for the flow'ry way that leads to the broad gate and the great fire.

All's Well That Ends Well

The rectory at St. Enoch's, Albatross, was in poor repair. That did not much matter to Father Justin O'Malley, who felt in poor repair himself, and meant to leave the money-grubbing for a new rectory to the New Breed pastor who would succeed him here.

No doubt the New Breed types at the chancery would insist upon erecting a new church, as well as a new rectory, once Justin O'Malley was put out to pasture. They had succeeded in exiling him to the remotest parish in the diocese — to Albatross, away north among the pines and birches. The handsome simple old boulder church of St. Enoch, built with their own hands by the early farmers of this infertile parish, could have stood with little repair for another two or three centuries; but the New Breed meant to pull it down 'to facilitate the new liturgy' once Justin O'Malley was disposed of. Meanwhile St. Enoch's bell, at Father O'Malley's insistence, still was rung daily.

No, Justin O'Malley did not much heed the shutter that banged at his study window in this night's high wind, nor even the half choked chimney that sent an occasional streamer of smoke toward his desk from the oak-

308

limb fire flickering in the fireplace. He sat writing his sermon at three in the morning, or almost that, a decanter of whiskey on the corner of the desk, a handful of cigars beside it, and five battered volumes of Cardinal Newman stacked precariously before him. Now and again he hummed wryly when the shutter gave a particularly ferocious crack, mumbling the lyrics:

> This old house once rang with laughter,
> This old house knew many shouts;
> Now it trembles in the darkness
> When the lightning walks about . . .

He wasn't sure he had those lines quite right, but it was better to mangle lyrics than to mutilate dogmata. Sister Mary Ruth had called him a 'dogmatist' before she had shaken the dust of Albatross from her sandals — as if heterodoxy were ordained of God. Sister Mary Ruth had demanded that she be permitted to exhort from the pulpit of St. Enoch's, and Father O'Malley had said her nay, dogmatically; so she had gone away to the world — and, he suspected, to the flesh and the devil. St. Enoch's Elementary School had only two nuns left now, and he supposed that the next pastor would close it.

On Father O'Malley's study wall hung a Hogarth engraving, *The Bathos*, concerned with the end of all things. Father Time himself lay expiring in the foreground, amidst cracked bells and burst guns, and the word 'Finis' was written upon the tobacco smoke that issued from Time's dying lips. A broken tower rather like the tower of St. Enoch's hulked in the background. If only Hogarth had drawn also a torn-up missal and a roofless schoolhouse, the relevance to St. Enoch's parish would have been perfect. From the sublime to the ridiculous! So the Church, or at least this diocese, had descended in some fifteen years.

Father O'Malley sipped his whiskey and drew long on his thick cigar. He *must* stick to only one cigar an evening; otherwise the angina would come on worse than before. He had fought as best he could in this diocese, had been thrashed, and now lay eyeless in Gaza, otherwise Albatross. Defeat in the battle against innovation had left him a wreck — to mix metaphors — stranded on the barren shingle of the world. Perhaps, just conceivably, the Church might come to know better days; but he would not behold them. On he hummed:

Got no time to fix the shingles or to mend the windowpane;
Ain't gonna need this house no longer . . .

Oh, come now, Justin! You've got a sermon to finish; put the nonsense out of your head. Should he blast the New Breed one more time? *Come one, come all, this rock shall fly from its firm base as soon as I . . .* Yes: give them a dose of Newman, whom they never had read, actually.

He took up his copy of Newman's *Dream of Gerontius.* In Newman's spirit, very nearly, Vatican II had been conceived and convened; but that council had led, vulgarized, to much that Newman would have found anathema. Like Newman's Gerontius, the Reverend Justin O'Malley bent 'over the dizzy brink of some sheer infinite descent.' He asked now for little but to depart in peace.

Well, what should he call this comminatory sermon of his, here at the back of beyond, to his little congregation of aging faithful? Should it be 'Prospect of the Abyss'? Would they be shocked, or would they notice at all — especially those among them who were in the habit of slipping out of the church door right after the Sacrament? What would they think if he should quote certain chilling lines from *Gerontius?*

> And, crueller still,
> A fierce and restless fright begins to fill
> The mansion of my soul. And, worse and worse,
> Some bodily form of ill
> Floats on the wind, with many a loathsome curse
> Tainting the hallowed air, and laughs, and flaps
> Its hideous wings,
> And makes me wild with horror and dismay.

Rather a strong dose for the old ladies who frequently confessed the great sin that their thoughts wandered at mass? Father O'Malley put the slim volume *Gerontius* aside and took up the fat *Development of Doctrine.* But the words blurred before his eyes. How he could use a catnap! Nevertheless he persisted, covering half a page of paper with notes. He should have commenced this job earlier in the evening, and have abstained from even one whiskey. He ought to get outdoors more often, he knew, even in a winter so fierce as this, for the sake of his circulation. Why didn't he fetch those snowshoes out of the cellar? An hour or two of following a woods trail would put him in a better temper.

Once upon a time, he recollected, somebody had said that O'Malley was the one priest in the diocese who had a joke for every occasion. Had it been the bishop before this one? Well, why not laugh?

Life is a jest, and all things shew it;
I thought so once, but now I know it.

Should he put it in his will that they were to cut John Gay's epitaph on O'Malley's gravestone? But here, what was he scribbling on his sheet of sermon notes? 'O'Malley's a jest, and all things . . .' And he couldn't read half the sentences he had scrawled above that remark. Really, he must have a five-minute nap.

It required some force of will to remove the glass, the bottle, and the ashtray to a side table, sleepily, and to pile the books on the floor. Then Father O'Malley laid his face on his forearms, there on the old mahogany desk, and closed his eyes. High time it was for the nap, he reflected as consciousness drifted away: the pain in his chest had been swelling as he grew fatigued, but now it must ebb. The blessed dark . . .

*   *

Was it a really tremendous bang of the loose shutter that woke him? He could have slept only for a few minutes, but he felt rested. Then why was he uneasy? He glanced round his study; the desk lamp showed him that nothing had changed. Getting up, he went to the window. Indeed that shutter was being torn loose altogether by the storm outside. The blizzard had increased, so that the snowflakes positively billowed against the panes. Why was he so uneasy? He had lived alone in the rectory for decades. Newman's line crept back into his mind: *Some bodily form of ill* . . . He crossed himself.

Then something rattled and fell in the little parlor, adjacent to the study, where usually he had parishioners wait if he was busy when they came to talk with him. In that parlor was an umbrella stand, and presumably some stick or umbrella had fallen. But what had made it fall, at this hour? Some strong draught?

With a certain reluctance, he opened the parlor door. The light from the desk lamp did not show him much. Was that a bulk in the further arm-chair?

'Father,' said a deep voice, 'I didn't mean to disturb you. I can just sit here till you're ready, Father. Ah, it's a blessing to be off that long, long trail and snug indoors this night. This chair of yours is like a throne, Father O'Malley . . .

> 'Up from Earth's Centre through the Seventh Gate
> I rose, and on the Throne of Saturn sate,
> And many a Knot unravel'd by the Road
> But not the Master-knot of Human Fate.'

Justin O'Malley had sucked in his breath when the bulk in the tall chair stirred, but now he knew who it was: Frank Sarsfield, no other, with his quoting of the *Rubáiyát*. Frank had not come to him for more than a year. Now he would be wanting a bed, a meal, and a few dollars before he set out again. Oh, Frank was an old client, he was. Father O'Malley crossed himself again; this visitant could have been a different type. Only last month two priests had been hacked to death in their beds, at a house in Detroit.

'Frank,' he said, 'you gave me a turn. Come into my study and I'll see what I can do for you.'

'I think I was dozing off myself, Father, and my foot touched that um-brella stand, and something fell. I'm sorry. A little while ago, I peeked in and saw you resting at your big desk, and I said to myself, "Nobody de-serves his rest more than Father O'Malley," so I took the liberty of occupy-ing that throne-chair of yours till you should wake. I'm not asking any-thing, Father; it's just that I came out of the blizzard, thinking we both might profit from a few words together. I know what I owe you already, Father Justin O'Malley, having kept track of it in my stupid head, year in, year out: it's a long-standing debt, most of it, coming altogether to the sum of four hundred and ninety-seven dollars and eleven cents. Is that the right sum, Father? Well, as the bums say when they're hauled before the bar of justice: "Jedge, I've had a run o' hard luck." My ship didn't come in, Father, and none of my lottery tickets won big. But I know what I owe you, more than I owe anybody else in this world, and I've come here to square ac-counts, if that's all right with you, Father O'Malley.'

Perhaps Frank was careful with his diction when addressing the clergy;

but his speech must be very good for a tramp, in any company. What damaged his polished address was the accent — and the intonation. There was a strong salt flavor of 'down east' — Sarsfield had been born on the Maine coast, O'Malley knew — blended with flop-house accents. ('Bird' became 'boid.') The man had been a tramp since he was fifteen years or younger, Father O'Malley had found out, and he must be past sixty now. When not on the road during those weary decades, he had been in prisons chiefly. He must have slept here in the rectory nearly a dozen times, on his endless aimless peregrinations. Sarsfield professed to be a Catholic of sorts: if he should pilfer church poor-boxes, he preferred Catholic poor-boxes.

'Settle up?' Father O'Malley offered Sarsfield whiskey, as he always did; and as always Sarsfield declined the glass. 'Settle up, Frank? I'll believe that when you settle down, which you won't do until Judgment Day, I suppose. Have a cigar, then.'

'Get thee behind me,' Sarsfield answered, chuckling at his own wit. 'You know I never did smoke, Father, and only once I drank a bottle of wine — Mission Bell it was — and it made me sick, as my mother said it would; so I'm not tempted, thank you.' At O'Malley's gesture, Sarsfield resumed his seat in the tall chair he had called a throne; apparently he did not intend to enter the pastor's study. It took a strong great chair to sustain Frank. For Sarsfield was a giant, almost, with a great Viking head, carrying more weight than was good for him. Yet he had a good color now, Father O'Malley noticed, and seemed less elephantine in his movements than he had the last time he called at St. Enoch's.

'Then you'll be wanting to raid the refrigerator, Frank? Mrs. Syzmanski left some cold chicken there, I know. And you must be worn out, afoot on a night like this. There's a bed for you — the little room with the yellow wallpaper, if you're ready to turn in. How far did you come today — or yesterday, rather?'

'Far, Father, farther than ever — and found your door unlocked, as if you'd been expecting some tramp or other. Begging your pardon, Father Justin, I wouldn't leave the rectory open to all comers at night. Nowadays there's desperate characters on the move everywhere. You heard what was done to those two priests in Detroit, Father? And I could tell you about other cases . . . But I guess you're like that French bishop — *nisi Dominus custodierit domum, in vanum vigilant qui custodiunt eam.* What good are watchers, unless the Lord guards the house?'

Frank Sarsfield had succeeded several times in startling Father O'Malley with his scraps of learning and his faculty for quotation, which ran to whole long poems; yet this Latin, wretchedly pronounced though it was, staggered his host. He knew that this strange man, whose hair was perfectly white now, had been subjected to only four or five years of schooling; his knowledge of books came from public libraries in little towns, Christian Science reading rooms, prison libraries. 'Frank, I've told you before that you'd have made a good monk, but it's too late for that.'

'Ah, Father, too late for that or for anything else, or nearly anything. Yet there's one thing, Father Justin O'Malley, that you've urged me to do time and time again, and I've not done it, but I'll do it now, if you say it's not too late. If it pleases you, Father, it's one way of paying you back. It's this: will you hear my confession?'

What had come over this man? What had he done lately? During the several years of their intermittent acquaintance, Sarsfield had sat through masses at St. Enoch's, but never had taken communion or gone to confession. 'At this hour, Frank? Right here?'

'As for the hour, Father, I know you're a night person; and I never sleep well, whatever the hour. As for the place — well, no, Father, I'd rather confess to you in that handsome old walnut confessional in the church. You'll know who I am — that can't be helped — but I won't see your face, nor you mine, and that'll make things easier, won't it? I hear that nowadays they call it "reconciliation," Father, and sometimes they just sit face to face with the priest, talking easy like this, but that's not what I want. I want you to hear everything I did and then absolve me, if you can. What's the old word for it, out of King Arthur and such? You know — *shriven*, that's it. I want to be shriven.'

Father O'Malley never had expected this. He supposed that a psychiatrist might call Frank Sarsfield an 'autistic personality'; certainly Frank was a loner, an innocent of sorts, sometimes shrewd, sometimes very like a small boy, indolent, unmachined, guilt-ridden, as weak of will as he was strong of body. Like Lady Macbeth, Sarsfield was forever washing himself, using up the rectory's rather scanty hot water, as if there were immaterial stains not to be washed away; he was every day clean-shaven, his thick hair well brushed, his clothes neat and clean. Sarsfield had been concentered all in self, his seeming joviality a mere protective coloration that helped him to beg his way through the world. He had been no solipsist, the priest judged, but had withdrawn ever since childhood within a shell — a mollusc of a man. *This* one was ready to confess to him at half-past three in the morning?

'It'll be cold in the church, Frank . . .'

'Why, this coat of mine is warm, Father — I bought it with my dishwashing pay, never fear — and you can put on your overcoat, if it's not too much trouble, and your gloves, and we needn't go outside, for there's that passage between the rectory here and the church that I scrubbed for you three years and seven months ago. You don't mind going into your own church, do you, Father, with a man who looks rougher than Jean Valjean, in the dead of the night?'

Suddenly Father O'Malley did mind. There had come into his memory of this man a recollection of a certain evening — yes, about three years and seven months ago — when he had invited Frank Sarsfield to confess, and the man had declined, and he had given Frank a piece of advice. Some intuition then had told Father O'Malley that Frank, despite all his repressing of his impulses, despite his accustomed humbling of himself, despite his protestations of having been always 'nonviolent' — well, that Frank Sarsfield potentially was a very dangerous man. A hint of madness, he had noticed then, lingering in Frank's light blue eyes that were forever furtively peeking out of their own corners. And that evening he had said bluntly to Sarsfield, 'Look out you don't turn berserker, Frank.'

Just what impelled this great hulking fellow to confess at last? What had he done — in Detroit, perhaps?

Some bodily form of ill floats on the wind . . .

It wasn't that Sarsfield seemed distraught; on the contrary, that strange giant seemed more easy in manner than ever O'Malley had known him before, more confident, all diffidence gone, as if a tension within him had snapped at last.

Yet how could he refuse Sarsfield's request? Would it have been safe to refuse? Those Detroit priests — what face had they seen in the wee hours?

'Give me a moment to tidy my papers in the study, Frank, and then . . .'

'Now, Father, don't put me off.' That was said with a smile, but Father O'Malley watched Sarsfield narrowly, and did not smile back. 'Let your study tidy itself, and come along into the church with me, while the mood is on me. It was you that told me I ought to confess my sins, and told me ten times over. Here I am for you, Father O'Malley; come straight along, for Christ's sake.'

*   *

Frank at his heels, then, Father O'Malley went downstairs, willy-nilly, and opened the sticky door that gave entrance to the short passage between rectory and church. Why had Sarsfield prevented him from returning to the study? Had he guessed that there was a loaded revolver, never used, in one of the desk drawers?

He led the way along the chilly corridor to the yet colder Church of St. Enoch. Something O'Malley had read in a book about the Mountain Men came into his mind: *Never walk the trail ahead of Hank Williams in starving time.* Frank Sarsfield, potential or actual berserker, was just behind him, silent except for the squeaking of one of his boots.

Father O'Malley reached for the light-switch in the church, but Sarsfield said, 'We know the way, Father; the confessional's just over there; and we don't want any folks wondering what's up in the church at three in the morning.' So they made their way along the aisle of a musty church lighted only by some nocturnal candles in the choir, the wind flinging itself savagely against the tall painted windows, to the antique carved walnut confessional. There the two of them parted momentarily, the priest to his station, the penitent to his stool within the massive box; and then they sat invisible, facing each other, a black curtain between their faces.

'Forgive me, Father, for I have sinned,' said Frank Sarsfield. He was very rusty at this business. He was still for a moment; then, 'How shall I tell you, Father? Do I go through all my life since I was confirmed, or is there some other way?' The huge man was desperately embarrassed, Father O'Malley sensed.

'If you like,' the invisible confessor murmured, 'begin with the greatest sins, the biggest mortal sins, and then go on to the lesser, the venial ones.'

'All right, Father. I've thought about this many a time. Maybe the worst is this: one day or another, one year or another, I robbed seven churches.'

'That is sacrilege. How much money did you take?'

'Altogether, I reckon, three hundred and eighteen dollars and twenty-four cents, Father. And altogether I got fifteen years' imprisonment for it, and more than two times I tried to escape and was caught.'

'Why did you commit such sins?'

'Well, Father, most of those times I was up against it, in big towns where nobody would give me anything, and so I broke open the poor-boxes.'

'What did you do with the money?'

'Oh, I spent it right off for meals, and lodging and some better clothes, Father; and once I bought presents for two little kids with part of the loot.'

This was Sarsfield's greatest sin? He had paid for it ten times over, in prisons. He was an enormous boy, never grown up.

'After these robberies of churches, what was your next greatest sin, my son?'

There came a heavy pause. The deep voice at length murmured, 'Running away from home, I guess, when I was an ungrateful kid. I never saw Mother again, or Dad.'

'Why did you run away?'

'Well, Dad drank a lot — that's why Mother made me promise not to drink, and I never did, except for that one bottle of Mission Bell — and then he'd beat me up. One day he took to licking and kicking me out in the field. I couldn't take it, and I went down on my knees to beg Dad to stop, and I put my arms around his legs, begging, and that made him fall over, and he hurt himself on an old plough. Then I knew that when he got up he'd kill me — really beat me until I was dead, Father, beat me with anything handy, beat me over the head — so I ran for it. As providence would have it, there was a rail line next to that field of ours, and there was a freight passing, and I got aboard before Dad could catch me, and I never went back, not while Dad was alive, not while Mother was alive. My mother was a saint — '

Was the giant sobbing in the dark?

The catalogue of mortal sins ran on; Father O'Malley was astonished at their triviality, though he kept his peace on that point. This man who had passed through some of the worst prisons in the land was almost untouched by such experiences. As if a little child, clearly he was guiltless of sexual offenses. He fought only in self-defense — or for five or ten dollars, against professional pugs at county fairs, where he was beaten invariably. He never had destroyed property wantonly, or stolen without need. He had been arrested for mere vagrancy, on most occasions; and his long sentences had been imposed because he had tried to escape from serving his short sentences. Frank Sarsfield was a fool; a medieval fool that is; one of Shakespeare's half-wise clowns; one of those fools who, the Moslems say, lie under God's especial protection.

They passed on to venial sins, there in the deadly cold of St. Enoch's. Father O'Malley grew weary of the recital, but Sarsfield was so earnest!

317

'And is there anything fairly recent?' the confessor inquired at last, hoping that the ordeal was nearly over.

'Something that may have been recent, Father, though I'm not sure: it might have been last night, or it might have been sixty years ago. Let me tell you, Father, this was a scary thing, and I paid for it. I killed six men in one house.'

'*What was that you said?*'

'I killed six men in one house, Father — almost as good, I guess, as the Brave Little Tailor, "Seven at one blow!"' Here the confessional shook, as if a heavy shudder had run through the man's great body. 'I kept yelling, "All heads off but mine!" and off they came. I used an ax that one of them had tried to use on me.'

Father O'Malley sat stupefied in the dark. Was Sarsfield a maniac? Had he really done this atrocity — and perhaps not in one house only? And having confessed this so fully, would Sarsfield spare the confessor? He managed to gasp, 'You classify this as a *venial* sin?' It sounded absurd — both the offense and the interrogation.

'Oh, the classifying's up to you, Father. I don't know if it was a sin at all. I hadn't much choice about it. Those were the worst men that had broken out of prison, killers and worse than killers, and they were after a young mother and her three little daughters. After I butted in, it was either those six or yours truly. It turned out to be both, Father. It was the only time in my life I didn't behave like a coward, so you know better than I do whether I sinned. Maybe I took Heaven by storm.'

Father O'Malley, trying frantically to form some plan of action, played for time. 'You don't know whether you did this yesterday or sixty years ago?'

'No, Father, it's all mixed up in my head; and usually, as you know, my memory is good — the one thing I was proud of. Probably it's because so much has happened to me since that bloody fight, since I stood in that room like a slaughterhouse.'

The shudder came again.

'What do you mean, *something happened to you?*'

'Why, Father, being shot, and bleeding like a pig on the stairs and in the snow, and then the great long journey — all alone, except for the Watchers. But it turned out better than I deserved, Father. There's a poem by somebody named Blake, William Blake. I can't put into words most of what happened to me after I died, but these lines give you a notion of it:

'I give you the end of a golden string,
Only wind it into a ball,
It will lead you in at Heaven's gate
Built in Jerusalem's wall.'

Justin O'Malley had been a voluble priest, sometimes jocular. But at what Sarsfield had just said, he was struck dumb. The silence grew so intense that Father O'Malley could hear his pocket watch, a good venerable quiet watch, ticking enormously in the empty church; but he dared not draw that watch to find out the time; perhaps this lunatic, this vast overwhelming lunatic Sarsfield, might think he was reaching for something else.

For his part, the madman sat silent also, as if awaiting the imposition of a salutary penance. Father O'Malley shook where he sat. Could Sarsfield detect his dread? Yes, yes, he was supposed to impose a penance now. What penance should a priest impose for the real or imaginary crimes of a homicidal maniac who thinks himself already dead? Father O'Malley could not collect himself. He began to babble hurriedly whatever came into his imperiled head:

'For your grave sins, say ten Hail Marys . . .'

What trivial rubbish was he uttering? Ten Hail Marys for murdering a half-dozen men? Yet the brute on the other side of the curtain was murmuring, like a small boy, 'Yes, Father; I'll do that, Father. . . .'

As if in a nightmare, Father O'Malley dashed from the insufficient penance to the implausible pardon. How much free will had this Frank ever been able to exercise, as boy or as man? Had he ever been perfectly sane? But put that aside, Justin: you've no time just now for casuistry.

'May the almighty and merciful Lord grant you pardon, absolution. . . .' Had he gone mad himself? What impelled him to absolve so casually such a sinner as this? Yet Father O'Malley rushed through the old formula. Then Frank Sarsfield interrupted:

'Father, would you say the rest in Latin, please? They used it all the time when I was a boy. Maybe the words count for more if they're Latin. My mother, rest her, would have said so.'

'If you like,' O'Malley told his monstrous penitent — rather gratified, even in this dreadful moment, to encounter an Old Breed sinner. He hastened on:

'*Passio Domini nostri Iesu Christi, merita beatae Mariae Virginis, et omnium*

Sanctorum . . .' Father O'Malley stumbled a little; it had been long since he had run through the Latin for a penitent; but he finished: *'. . . et praemium vitae aeternae, Amen.'*

'Amen!' Sarsfield responded, his stentorian voice echoing through the high-vaulted church. 'Doesn't that mean *reward of everlasting life?* I heard those Latin words for years and years, Father, and never thought about them.'

O'Malley muttered some banality; he was more immediately concerned at this moment for his own aged mortal envelope, at the mercy of this night visitor. Sarsfield seemed to expect something more, here in the confessional. *'Pax vobiscum!'* Father O'Malley breathed.

'Et cum spiritu tuo,' Sarsfield responded, and then rose, bumping against the wooden wall of the confession-box as he blundered his way out. Father O'Malley wished dearly that he might have remained in the confessional, for his part, until dawn should have come and this grim wanderer should have left St. Enoch's. But that was not to be. He too groped his way to the aisle.

A baker's dozen of votive candles burned near the high altar, the only illumination of the church this fierce night; their flames wavered in the draft.

'Father,' the voice was saying right beside him, 'there's some prayer for somebody dying or dead. Could we go down on our knees and say that together?' He must mean the Recommendation for the Departing Soul.

'Kyrie eleison,' Father O'Malley commenced, kneeling at the nearest bench. To his horror, Sarsfield knelt very close beside him, shoulder to shoulder, in this spreading empty church — as if there were happy contagion in sanctity.

'It will be all right to do this in English, Father,' Sarsfield muttered, 'begging your pardon, because I want to understand all of it.'

'Holy Abel, all ye choirs of the just, Holy Abraham . . .' Father O'Malley rattled through the calendar — John the Baptist, Joseph, patriarchs and prophets, Peter, Paul, Andrew, John, apostles and evangelists, innocents, Stephen, Lawrence, martyrs, Sylvester, Gregory, Augustine, bishops and confessors, Benedict, Francis, Camillus, John of God, monks and hermits, Mary Magdalene, Lucy, virgins and widows, saints. 'From Thy wrath, from the peril of death, from an evil death, from the pains of hell, from all evil, from the power of the devil, through Thy birth, through Thy cross and passion, through Thy death and burial, through Thy glorious resurrection . . .' Where was he? Where was he indeed? 'In the day of judg-ment, we sinners beseech thee, hear us . . . O Lord, deliver him . . . *Libera eum, Domine.*'

'*Libera nos,*' Sarsfield put in, as if responding. 'Lord, have mercy; Christ, have mercy; Lord, have mercy.'

On and on Father O'Malley ran, the killer right against him in the dark, shifting from English to Latin, from Latin to English, as the spirit moved him, Sarsfield now and again responding irregularly or joining the priest in some passage that he seemed to recall. What a memory! Abruptly Sarsfield's voice drowned out O'Malley's:

'Mayest thou never know aught of the terror of darkness, the gnash-ing of teeth in the flames, the agonies of torment. May Satan most foul, with his wicked crew, give way before us; may he tremble at our coming with the Angels that attend us, and flee away into the vast chaos of eternal night. Let God arise, and let His enemies be scattered; and let them that hate Him flee from before His face. As smoke vanisheth, so let them van-ish away; as wax melteth before the fire, so let the wicked perish at the presence of God; and let the just feast and rejoice before God. May, then, all the legions of hell be confounded and put to shame, nor may the minis-ters of Satan dare to hinder our way.'

Then Father O'Malley was permitted to resume. The recommenda-tion seemed to eat up hours, though really only minutes could be elapsing. At length he thought they had finished, and fell silent with a final 'Amen.' Would this killer make an end of him now? But Sarsfield said, 'I think, Fa-ther, there's a prayer to Our Lord Jesus Christ that a dying man says him-self, if he can, and it won't do any harm for the pair of us to say that too.'

With fear and trembling, Father O'Malley began to utter that prayer, and Sarsfield joined him. Sarsfield's voice grew louder and louder as they approached the end:

'Do Thou, O Lord, by these Thy most holy pains, which we, though unworthy, now call to mind, and by Thy holy cross and death, deliver Thy servants praying here from the pains of hell, and vouchsafe to lead us whither Thou didst lead the good Thief who was crucified with Thee.' A few more words, and this second prayer was done.

Father O'Malley could not run away; for Sarsfield sat between him and the aisle, and the other end of their bench ended against the stone wall. To have tried to clamber over the bench-back in front of them would have been too conspicuous, perhaps inviting violence. Sarsfield remained upon his knees, as if sunk in a long silent prayer, but presently sat back on the bench.

'You must have read about those people that claim to have come back from death, Father,' Sarsfield told him, rather hesitantly. Father O'Malley scarcely could make out Sarsfield's face at all. 'You know — there's some woman doctor wrote a book about cases like that, and there's other books too. Most of them tell about some long tunnel, and at the end of it everything's hunky-dory.'

Justin O'Malley murmured acknowledgment. Did this fellow mean to experiment in that fashion with his confessor?

'Well, Father, it isn't like that — not like that at all.' Sarsfield bent to lift up the kneeler, giving more room below for his big boots. 'Once a man's dead, Father O'Malley, he stays dead; he doesn't come back in the flesh and walk around, not unless Jesus Christ does for him what he did for Lazarus. Those tunnel people were *close* to death, that's all: they never went over the edge. Just being close isn't the same condition.

'It's my experience, Father, that when you cross over there's a hesitation and lingering, for a little while. Then you move on out, and that's scary, because you don't know where you're going; you've got no notion whatsoever. It's not that happy little tunnel with light at the end. Why, it's more like a darkling plain, Father. And you're all alone, or seem to be, except where those ignorant armies clash by night. On and on you go. And when you think or feel that at last you've arrived at the strait gate *which leadeth unto life* — well, then you meet the Watchers.'

The Sleepless Ones, the Watchers! Into Father O'Malley's awareness flashed some lines from *Gerontius*:

Like beasts of prey, who, caged within their bars,
In a deep hideous purring have their life,
And an incessant pacing to and fro.

'Understand, Father,' Sarsfield went on, 'I'm trying to put into words for you some experiences that words don't fit. Somebody said, didn't he, that all life is an allegory, and we can understand it only in parable? So when I tell you about the darkling plain, and about the Sleepless Ones, those Watchers, you're not supposed to take me literally, not all the way. I'm just giving you an approximation, in words, of what you feel at your core. That's the best I can do; I'm no philosophist and no poet.

'But sure as hell's a mantrap, it's no Tunnel of Love you find yourself in when you cross over, Father O'Malley. Even if the Watchers don't have claws literally, you sure know they're after you, and they sure know your weakness. I suppose I got past them, almost to the destination, because I'm a fool who took Heaven by storm.'

'But you tell me that you've come back amongst us living, Frank,' Father O'Malley ventured. Just conceivably he might be able to draw this mad Frank Sarsfield, this berserker, back toward some degree of right reason — if he were very cautious in the endeavor. Would that he could recollect his Thomistic syllogisms at this hour! 'So how can that be, Frank, when not long ago you told me that once a man's dead, so far as this world of flesh is concerned, he stays dead?'

From Sarsfield, almost invisible, there came something like a chuckle. 'Ah, I died right enough, Father; they shot me twice and maybe three times. The thing is, I haven't returned to the land of the living. I've come just far enough to meet you in shadow-land.'

Had this thing returned seeking whom he might devour? But Father O'Malley said aloud, 'Why come back at all, Frank?'

'I give you the end of a golden string, Father. I'd gone down the narrow way, as they call it in those old books, until I'd almost forgotten about what I'd left undone. Then I thought of you.

'I can't ever pay you that four hundred and ninety-seven dollars and eleven cents, not now, Father O'Malley. But that doesn't much matter, not where rust doesn't tarnish or moth corrupt. All the same, I might pay you back some of your friendship.

'Father Justin, I couldn't think of any friend but you, as I slowed down there on the narrow way. The Watchers had my scent, but I stood still and thought about you. Nobody else ever gave me a meal without being asked for it, or lent me over a hundred dollars without much chance of getting it back, or — that was best of all, Father — ever talked with me for hours as if I had a mind and was worth passing the time with. So there on the narrow way, when it seemed as if the end would be just around the corner, I turned back toward St. Enoch's and you. I could do it because after I took up that ax in that lonely old house against those six men, I wasn't a coward any longer.

'I came back here, or maybe was sent back here, to lend you a hand on your journey, Father Justin. I know the way to the little gate, so to speak, fool though I am. It's fearsome, Father, groping that way when the Watchers are purring in the dark. But the two of us together . . .'

O'Malley's dread of this madman had diminished a little, though a little only. Sarsfield might mean to take his confessor with him down to dusty death, but his mood of the moment was not hostile. If he could persuade Frank to settle himself down in the bed in the guest room, the poor crazy giant might sleep off his present frantic delusion. Frank must have footed it through the blizzard all the way to Albatross, from God knows where; perhaps extreme weariness had snapped Frank's uncertain grip upon reality. Or if Frank Sarsfield actually had killed six men, only yesterday — why, Justin O'Malley could telephone the sheriff once Frank was abed, and check that out. The sheriff and his boys could take Frank sleeping, without harming him.

'Come back into the rectory, Frank,' Father O'Malley contrived to tell him, 'before I take the end of that golden string of yours. Surely we've time enough to tidy my desk and have a cold chicken sandwich apiece, before we start rolling string into balls.'

'We may blow off like tumbleweeds any moment now, Father,' Frank answered. They returned to the passage between church and rectory.

'Go on ahead, Frank,' his confessor told him, dissimulating. 'You know the way.'

Sarsfield laughed. 'Don't you want me at your back, Father? I always was nonviolent, till the last. It's not Frank Sarsfield you have to worry about: keep an eye peeled for the Watchers. After you, Father.'

So it was Father O'Malley who led the trek back to the rectory, and up the stairs to his study. Every step of the way he had to nerve himself to keep from shuddering. Once, years ago — it came to him now — he had told Frank Sarsfield that some folk work out their Purgatory in this life conceivably; and that he, Frank, might be one such. On another occasion, he had instructed Frank that for the Lord all time is eternally present; and that, knowing the heart, the Lord might have something especial in store for Frank Sarsfield, his failings notwithstanding.

He might as well have preached in Mecca. Indeed the Lord did seem to have reserved something for Frank Sarsfield, heavy vessel for dishonor: the slaying of six men — and now perhaps the murder of the pastor of St. Enoch's. Why was this cup thrust upon Justin O'Malley? This came of leaving doors open to all comers. The Lord had dozed.

*　　　*

The two of them entered the study. Someone was sitting at Father O'Malley's desk — or, rather, had relaxed there with his head resting upon his forearms.

Justin O'Malley started back, pale as a ghost. Frank Sarsfield caught him before he could fall.

'Ah, Father, it gave me such a twist myself, the first moment of awareness. I was looking at myself all blood, head to foot.... Now don't be afraid of what's in that chair, Father. Look at it for the last time. We shall be changed.'

Screwing his courage to the sticking place, Justin O'Malley looked fixedly at that silent old husk. The body slumped there had perished during sleep, without pain, the old heart ceasing to pump. The face had been his own.

'We're off to the gate built in Jerusalem's wall,' Frank was telling him. 'Few there be that find it, they say; but if we humble ourselves, Father, we'll evade those pacing Sleepless Ones. I was sent to be your clown along the narrow way. Here, Father, take hold on yourself: we're going. . . .'

The walls of the rectory fell away, and the winter's landscape disintegrated, and for a moment Father O'Malley knew himself all fractured atoms.

Then the two of them were upon what seemed a darkling plain, and a path led through the marshes. It was all far more real than Albatross, and more perilous, and more promising. There was no pain at O'Malley's heart. Across the fens, drifting in the night breeze, corpse-candles glimmered here and there. But the two of them could make out the high ground far beyond the bogs.

'Let's have no gnashing of teeth now, Father,' Frank was crying, with a wild sort of laugh. 'It's the faint-hearted that the Watchers catch.'

They strode forward as if they wore seven-league boots. At their backs, the sensual world that could be understood only in parable faded to the shadow of a shade.

The Reflex-Man
in Whinnymuir Close

They call this Reflex-Man a coimimeadh *or Co-Walker, every way like
the man, as a Twin-brother and Companion, haunting him as his shadow
and is oft seen and known among men (resembling the Originall) both
befor and after the Originall is dead, and was else often seen of old to enter a
house; by which the people knew that a person of that liknes was to visit
them within a few days. This copy, Eccho, or living picture, goes at last to his
own herd.*

The Reverend Robert Kirk, M.A.
IN THE SECRET COMMONWEALTH

[Editor's Note: The following relation was discovered in a padlocked chest, covered
over by an accumulation of rubbish, at the top of an ancient house in the High
Street of Pittenweem. Together with other papers of less surviving interest, this curious MS was concealed within tied bundles of eighteenth century apparel. The
pages of this memoir, severely damaged by damp and in part illegible, are closely
written upon in a neat but infirm hand, presumably by a person of advanced years.

The MS now is deposited in the library of the University of St. Andrews,
where it may be examined only with the express permission of Drumcarrow Estates, Ltd., and of the Librarian (or, in his absence, of the Vice-Chancellor).

The editor has reason to believe that this peculiar document never reached
the eyes of members of the Fife family of the Inchburns of Drumcarrow, although
it appears to have been written to instruct them. In the end, conceivably, the author of this memoir determined to let the dead bury the dead.

In some instances, the spelling and the punctuation of this narrative, here printed for the first time, have been altered slightly in conformity to present usage. The MS is undated (although internal evidence sufficiently establishes the approximate dates of the events referred to) and is unsigned. — R. K.]

*   *

They have said and they will say: let them be saying. There having circulated among the vulgar and the credulous some perverted tale of what passed within Whinnymuir Close and House when Lord Banford came to his latter end, this veracious record is set down by the palsied hand of one beseeching the Author of our being for mercy. The faggots in the merkat square and the stake at tide-mark on the beach are bygone things now: yet the Lord's vengeance does not sleep.

Commence we with some account of Geoffrey, called of courtesy Lord Banford, being eldest son to Lord Solway (that title today lying dormant, at the decree of Divine Providence). Finding himself deeply indebted to the London usurers, this young lord took up his residence for some months in Edinburgh. The Earls of Solway held neglected properties in the Lowlands as well as their principal estates in Lancashire and Cumberland. Among those Scots properties was Whinnymuir House, the muckle ancient dwelling in the close of that name, betwixt the Cowgate and the High Street. The principal rooms having been plenished tolerably for his coming, Lord Banford lodged himself therein. Young and openhanded, and a pretty man enough, Lord Banford proceeded to spy out the nakedness of his father's Scots estates and of Edinburgh's women.

Now it chanced that there dwelt at a land in the Lawnmarket, that midsummer, a young woman called Janet Kenly, daughter to a clockmaker at Pittenweem. She having been schooled by governesses and tutors beyond her station and her sex, and being puffed up with pride at her father's goods and chattels, did make herself no little of a coquette, though chaste. Her eyes and her ankles, she discovered, were approved by the young gallants of Edinburgh as they had been by the fisher lads of Pittenweem: and thereby came she to her public disgrace and to her soul's peril.

Matthew Kenly, her father, made tall clocks in Pittenweem High Street, and of them some were sold over seas in the Low Countries. Yet his prosperity had more cause than that. His siller notwithstanding, he dwelt still in a small freehold house on the merkat square. The truth of the matter was this: his house lay at the head of a serpentine wynd called the Gylie, winding up from a wee slip or landing-place among the reefs without Pittenweem's harbour. The tide being at flood, boats might run of nights into this narrow haven, and land what the gaugers would have levied duty upon.

In the back wall of Matthew Kenly's dwelling was a round hole, closed by a shutter inwardly; and into this sloping bit tunnel, passing through the thickness of the bieldy wall of rubble, some seaman trotting up the Gylie might slide what he listed. Should the gaugers follow in pursuit, still they might not enter Matthew's dwelling without showing a warrant. When after some hours such a warrant might be issued, no contraband would be found in house, byre, or close.

Thus Matthew Kenly now and anon walked in dark ways, laying up treasure here below. Of his near acquaintance was that Wilson hanged by Captain Porteus in the Grassmarket when Janet Kenly was but sixteen. Had Matthew Kenly been a man of probity, he might not have wedded the wife he did, Agnes Doubtfire: for she, like her mother before her, stood suspect as being a wise woman acquainted with simples and other concerns less simple. Agnes departed this life having not attained thirty years. Matthew then bethought him, out of pride, through which fault fell the angels, to make a lady out of his bit daughter Janet. Upon smuggling were her pretensions founded.

Agnes had borne Matthew a son, Dugald, the year after being brought to bed with Janet. This Dugald, poor lad, was tall and strong but feckless and wild of eye. Some called him loon, dolt, and daft chiel. Brave garments, and his sister, were all his loves. The father spoilt the twain.

Now Matthew Kenly perishing suddenly of a fever from the West Indies, his willful daughter found Pittenweem too petty a stage for her show. In name, her protectress was an aged aunt, Rachel Kenly, with but a moiety of her wits about her. To Edinburgh Janet bore both aunt and brother, taking a floor of a land in the Lawnmarket, its rent no consideration for this impudent baggage.

Once in sight of St. Giles's lantern, brother Dugald, loved by Janet as he loved her, set up for a gentleman of fashion, filling the pockets of tailors and tobacconists and sweetmeats-makers. Aunt and sister grudged him no expense, he being denied by Providence a full portion of prudence. Before a month was out, Dugald fell in with Lord Banford and his Comus' Rout of besotted English and Scottish sprigs. At cards and at dice they fleeced the innocent, night upon night, smirking; and aunt and sister paid his losses.

Yet one uncorrupt acquaintance did Dugald chance to make, and that a grizzled bonnet-laird twice his years and more. Edinburgh wits thought Colonel Ian Inchburn of Drumcarrow near so fey as Dugald himself. Drumcarrow being an ill man to deal with, and sharp of hearing, what they said of him was whispered behind closed doors. There did some of the sprigs, greatly daring, venture to call him the Barbary Ape.

In truth Colonel Inchburn, back from years in East India, was no pretty man. Like his father before him, he was short of leg and long of arm. Over his forehead his thick red hair, shot with grey, descended nigh to his brows, which were huge and beetling as some beast's. He was given to walking with his shoulders inclined somewhat forward, a posture, it was said, become natural to him from bending over his horse's neck while leading the charge of a squadron of sowars. Nearly always he dressed in rusty black, his garments huddled on. For all the roughness of the outer man, his voice was melodious, and his speech that of the universities.

In his youth Ian Inchburn had been sent to St. Mary's College, St. Andrews, to be schooled for a minister — or, failing that, a dominie. At the stony high-lying family property of Drumcarrow, overlooking both the shores of Fife and the howe of Fife, the very roof of the doocot was fallen away: the two farms would not sustain the boy-laird's widowed mother, let alone Ian. His Greek, his Latin, his Bible, he mastered well; he was graduated.

But for this young scholar no parish was found. Like enough the cause was his perilous inclining toward the damnable error denominated by some pillars of the kirk as Gregorianism. Now and again he was overheard chanting in solitude, perhaps in malice — he being wondrous witty when young, when old — some verse or other of a Lyke-Wake Dirge. He would sing out,

'This ae nighte, this ae night,
  — *Every nighte and alle,*
Fire and sleet and candle-lighte,
  And Christe receive thy saule.'

Then anon,

'From Brig o' Dread when thou mayst pass,
— *Every nighte and alle,*
To Purgatory fire thou com'st at last:
And Christe receive thy saule.'

For such hints of Popish inclination was he twice summoned before a kirk session and reproved sternly. Perceiving at length that no parish would have him for minister or even dominie, young Drumcarrow, obtaining the commendation of the Earl of Balcarres and other Fife worthies, was given an East India cadetcy, and out he went to Calcutta.

In later years, intimates would call him in jest Colonel the Reverend Ian Inchburn of Drumcarrow, M.A., nor would he rebuke them. It may be pardoned in Drumcarrow that he wore his learning on his sword-knot, he being given to theological disputation, and not loath to parade his Latin and his Greek. In Bengal he mastered other tongues, and made no slight acquaintance with other faiths than the Reformed. To a brother officer, Drumcarrow confided once that the blackamoor minions of Lucifer were twice or thrice more subtle than Satan's Scots limbs.

This Colonel Inchburn had been lodging for some months in a decayed commodious house in the Cowgate, said once to have been Mary of Guise's. Having come back from Calcutta, men thought, empty of pocket as when he had gone out those many years before, Inchburn of Drumcarrow seemingly had found his fortune at a stay. Despite that, he kept about him in the Cowgate a crew of half-pay captains and lieutenants poorer than himself, sustaining them on watered porridge and thin claret, and regaling them with his tales of Indian marches, fatal encounters, sieges, sacks, and forlorn hopes.

This battered Laird of Drumcarrow was a douce man enough, the thinness of his claret assisting him in that. Many a time he conversed with the professors of the University, hoping always to confute their pedantry. With women he consorted not at all, although knowing her brother, in the streets he would doff his hat to Janet Kenly, sending a keen glance at her from the sea-caves of his een — to which usage from gentlemen and the vulgar she was not unaccustomed.

More than once Colonel Inchburn, M.A., spoke a word of counsel to Dugald Kenly, telling the lad to have an eye to the company he kept. Yet Dugald, pleased though he was by the notable soldier's notice, found the riot and ribaldry of Lord Banford's troop more lively by far, so that the hard siller ran through his fingers like quicksiller. The son of the clockmaking smuggler fancied himself a gentleman, light and debonair, favoured of a peer's son. Just so did his sister Janet, admiring her reflexion in the glass, ask like some princess, Who is the fairest of us all? Perhaps she grew fond enough to think herself fit for some lord's bride, and the portion left to her by her father a grand dowry. She took to rouge and a beauty-patch.

Of afternoons, not infrequently the brother's boon comrades would stroll to the Lawnmarket to drink a dish of tea with the lad's sister. Lord Banford praised her polite learning so rare in a lass, her voice, her hand upon the virginal, and much else beside: not forgetting her black eyes, whose power other young men had remarked. He was infamous in Edinburgh for a rake, but many a chaste woman aspires to entice a rake into the ranks of the godly.

Far from displeased at these kind attentions, Janet Kenly concerted plans for an evening's rout for her brother's friends at her Lawnmarket lodgings, sparing no expense for food, drink, and candles. Doddering Auntie did not demur, while Dugald was pleased as any bairn. The sister, wise after her mother's fashion; the brother, half a man only — these twain never uttered a hard word one to the other, guessing without speech one the other's wishes, as if their souls were entwined. Both were fey somewhat, he in his way, she in hers. Never had they been parted many hours: and when on occasion Dugald gamed long with Banford's set in Whinnymuir House, still Janet might fancy she glimpsed his form in the Lawnmarket kitchen, or heard his tread on the Lawnmarket stair. In her mind's eye, be it said, she beheld him always, as one gifted with the second sight.

On the evening appointed, a score and more of guests clattered up the turnpike stair, five storeys, to Princess Janet's palace. There came but three other ladies, or what passed for ladies, rouged and powdered like Paris hussies, bold of glance and attire, smiling one at another when presented to their hostess.

There came also, half carried up the stair, a gouty old sardonic Scots baronet, Sir Angus Kinkell, who once had commanded a frigate in India waters: he had been at the University with Lord Solway when Solway had been Banford himself, and Solway had asked Sir Angus to keep some rein upon young Lord Banford, otherwise given his head in Edinburgh. What with the fashion the baronet looked upon her, Janet doubted Sir Angus's propriety as a sprig's Mentor.

The saucy Janet sang to her guests, and played upon her virginal; and if they did not harken over keenly, look at her they did, until she blushed crimson. There was playing at whist, and overmuch of drinking of wines and smuggled brandy. Auntie had been bundled into her closet. Poor Dugald, lurching about the whist-tables, was two-thirds bemused by strong spirit. The ladies' voices rose shrill, and the gentlemen's talk was slurred and sprinkled with oaths. Proud Janet well might ask herself if conversations went thus in the salons of Paris.

While she hesitated in the middle of the chief room, perplexed as to whether she should tell the two serving-women to fetch more brandy, there approached her closely Lord Banford, heaping compliments upon her, and begging a word in private. He seemed to restrain as best he might some strong sentiment. Of her own charms Janet doubted not; and even to an English lord, she fancied, the portion her father had bequeathed to her might be not unacceptable. She lowered her lashes demurely.

There being few rooms on a Lawnmarket land's floor, she ushered her noble guest into her own small chamber, nearly filled by the bed her father had bought for her from a Dutch skipper, and the muckle armoire from Brittany that held her gowns, and the shelf with her books. With a slight bow to her, Banford closed the door behind him, his face much flushed. Says he, I've a question to put to you, Madam.

The notion flitted through her foolish head that she might become Lady Banford that very year, and the Countess of Solway in the Lord's good time. Yet that was not the question Banford put to her. She gasped and flared up. Taking her in his grip, Banford poured into her ear words, nay foul fooleries, that never Janet had heard from any man before. He muttered snatches of verse, tugging at her new orange bodice. What was he saying? Was it not Shakespeare?

Then give me leave to stroke thy bubbies,
As they gently rise and fall . . .

Just that, her protests and struggles not availing, Lord Banford proceeded to do. Frantic, she scratched him across his grinning face.

He thrust the silly quean back upon her bed. It came to Janet then that this accomplished rake meant to have her maidenhead instanter. She shrieked so loudly and earnestly as ever she might.

Such was the subtle bond of spirit betwixt sister and brother that

Dugald, for all the brandy he had swallowed, at once heard his sister's cry and was sobered. Banford had latched the door; Dugald flung his weight upon it, burst it open, beheld his sister much disarrayed in his noble friend's clutch, and took hard hold of Banford. In this stramash Lord Banford's wig fell to the floor, disclosing a scalp which, for all its youth, was nigh hairless.

Grasping Banford by the back of his collar, Dugald played Hercules to Banford's Cacus. Him he dragged through the outer rooms, Banford's drunken friends taking the stramash for rough frolic. He thrust the young nobleman out upon the common stair, trundled him downward two or three storeys, and flung him bruised and almost senseless upon the stones. That done, Dugald returned panting and wrathful to his sister's side.

By this time some of Lord Banford's friends had commenced to take a second view of the wrestling on the stair, so that it might have gone hard with Dugald. Yet Sir Angus Kinkell, laughing and puffing, quieted them as best he might. Brawling was sufficiently common at Edinburgh routs, then even more than nowadays. It was not often that a tradesman's son cuffed and buffeted a peer's son, true, and flung him down the stair. Sir Angus, blessed as a peacemaker, nevertheless urged his companions down to the street, picking up Banford in the course of their drunken progress. Lord Banford's curses echoed up to Janet, he yelling like a fiend from the Pit.

Sir Angus limped out last. Says he to Dugald, Have a care of Lord Banford, now, ye brute, ye daft carle. Aye, and take a care for your black-eyed sister.

Sir Angus looked Janet up and down, she endeavouring like some surprised nymph to cover herself. Why, lass, Sir Angus says to her, What else expected ye of my ward? But I do take ye for innocent, sister and brother, more's the wonder. Get ye to a nunnery, lass. Ye'll ne'er make a court lady.

As Sir Angus groped his way heavily down the dark stair, grunting now and again as he bumped his gouty foot, Janet heard her fancied suitor Lord Banford shouting down below. Diana at her bath! screams he, with her bedlam brother for her faithful hound! I'll have that tormenting Scots witch! I'll flog that stubborn prude like a bitch in my kennel!

Then their manservant shot home the bolts in their oaken door, and the words from below could not be made out. Lord Banford's trampled wig lay disconsolate at Janet's feet.

[Here a page of the manuscript is so rotted by damp that no word can be deciphered. We resume with the following page, less damaged. — Ed.]

... as later Sir Angus related it to the Procurator-Fiscal, their talk went much as follows.

Sir Angus: What, call out the daft lad? He'd meet ye, Banford, with joyful alacrity, to cross swords with a peer's son being a patent of gentility. Then ye'd kill him, and find it well to flit to France, or else be hangit in the Grassmarket, earl's son or no. Or should ye but run him through once or twice in parts not vital, ye'd make yourself the town's laughingstock for months on end. What, play at duello with a smuggler's halfwit get because he mislikes your pinching his sister's bubbies? Na, na, Banford: ye'd better paint yourself blue, take cap and bells, and prance naked round Holyrood — 'twould be less absurd.

Lord Banford: Damn you, Kinkell, I'll make that young witch with the black eyes do the prancing. Either her brother will pay me out, or she must.

A.: Why say witch, lad? Did she enchant ye? Have ye knowledge of all they say in Pittenweem? Put not thy trust in witches, Banford, nor know them carnally. In a corner of Pittenweem kirkyard they burnt their witches once, but that fashion's o'er. I knew the tarry wynds of Pittenweem well, and the womenfolk thereof, when I was a beardless midshipman.

B.: What's this of Pittenweem? The burgh's a nest of trulls and witches, you mean?

A.: Not long after I came to my majority, a mob of sailors and fishers there did to death one Janet Cornfoot, accused by a dirty tinker of having sent him into fits. They stoned the old carline, swung her on a rope twixt ship and shore, and at the end pressed the life out of her under a door on the strand. She had gossips.

B.: Curse you, Kinkell, what's all this history to me?

A.: One of her gossips was a Mistress Doubtfire, granddame to your darling Janet. She lay under a cloud for what few more years she spent here below. And her daughter Agnes, too, your light-o'-love's mother, was said to sell simples and be endowed with the second sight.

B.: Then that teasing quean Janet's the devil's dam as well? By God, I'll have her before the magistrates for casting her spell on me!

A.: Time was when you might have done so, my lord. But 'tis late in the day for that. Fourteen years gone, Sheriff Ross burnt an old hag in

Sutherland for a witch: but he'd no jurisdiction, and there was talk of trying him for murder. Na, na, lad, there may be witches still, yet they're burnt nor drowned no longer, in our degenerate age. Ye'll not warm your roving hands at Janet's bonfire.

B.: Mark me, Kinkell, I'll see she's made hot enough, for all that. She'll pay on her bum for the tossing her lump of a brother gave me!

A.: Come now, Banford, your father found willing wenches enough for his pleasure short of vexing clockmakers' witch-daughters . . .

[Here occurs another hiatus in the damaged MS. The narrative then resumes somewhat abruptly. — Ed.]

On the Thursday, a caddie brought to their lodging a line for Dugald from Mr. Robert MacPherson, asking him to whist near the Luckenbooths: and happy was Dugald at that invitation for the next evening, he having been forlorn since parted finally from his old companions at Whinnymuir Close. Not an hour later, another caddie came to the Lawnmarket bearing a card from old Lady Christie, hard by George Heriot's School; and Janet — sequestered since the rout that ended in stramash — found herself asked to hear Lady Christie's niece play upon the spinet, by good fortune at the very hour Dugald would be with MacPherson and his friends. Accordingly on the Friday, as the dark settled upon the town, sister and brother went their separate ways, Janet in a sedan chair: for being now an Edinburgh lady, she would not think of going barefoot on the causeway, as once she had done with the other lasses of Pittenweem. Her shy bit maid trotted behind her chair. The chair-men were stout Highland gillies, not favoured of feature, sparing of speech; she had not seen them before.

On reaching the foot of Candlemakers' Row, Miss Kenly found Lady Christie's lodging quite dark. Pound the door though the Highlandmen did, they roused none within. The old lady, not over strong of intellect, must have set down the wrong night on her card, said the maid to Janet. The Princess of Pittenweem bade the chair-men bear her home again.

Thinking on her brother's bold defence of her, the week gone, Janet did not observe at once that her chair was not being borne directly towards the Lawnmarket. Being jolted as a chair-man stumbled on a stone, she glanced out, to find herself among tombs: for the chair-men had turned in at the yett of Greyfriars kirkyard, passing through which they might gain the Grassmarket and then the Lawnmarket, though it was the longer way and less frequented.

Ere she could ask why they took that gait, a band of men dashed upon her chair and upset it, to send Janet sprawling among the graves. Her chair-men fled into the dark, and the wee maid was bundled off squalling. Scrambling to her feet, Janet found herself captive to six or seven men, some armed, all young, their faces blackened. One laughed low and tore her kirtle clean off her body, and him she knew through his disguise, though he spoke no word: Lord Banford.

Many hands were laid upon her, and one clapped over her mouth. Twist and kick though Janet did, in a few moments they had stripped her bare as any new bairn. Banford showed her a dog-whip that he drew from his belt. Then, flinging her asprawl among the tombstones, he lashed her backsides.

She shrieked like a wounded leopardess in her agony and her shame, but the hour was late and rough sport of common occurrence in kirkyards. When she struggled up, men pulled her down upon her back. Then it seemed worse was to be done to her, for Banford made ready to bestride her, as if he would construprate the lass while his friends looked on. Thus would her pride have a final fall.

As Providence would have it, at that fell moment there passed through the wide kirkyard, coming down from the Grassmarket, a party of strollers. At their head was Colonel Inchburn, unarmed as was his custom in the town, and beside him the Professor of Hebrew at the University, they two hotly disputing over apparitions, Co-Walkers, Purgatory, fixed fate, foreknowledge, and other grave concerns. At the Laird's heels followed a tall sepoy manservant, bearing a muckle staff like to a baton. Behind the blackamoor came two half-pay officers, captain and lieutenant of foot, sharing the Colonel's draughty quarters in the Cowgate. Janet in her humiliation did not make out the others, but the Barbary Ape's stalwart bulk she did discern.

Inchburn of Drumcarrow and his companions drew near at hand. Taking the stramash among the tombs for some squalid brawl of a bully and his trull, Colonel Inchburn turned to pass by on the other side. At night in Greyfriars kirkyard, mutters he to the Professor of Hebrew, *nil admirari*.

Her peril notwithstanding, Janet Kenly had kept her wits about her, though not her garments. Drumcarrow, Janet cries shrill — using the name of his estate to catch his ear, and speaking the broad accents of Fife to the same end. Drumcarrow, Janet shrieks, wull ye no help a neighbour? Breaking free from the hands upon her, she springs up erect.

Of ear and eye, no man was keener than Ian Inchburn. At a glance he makes out Janet, naught of her being hid. Wow! calls out Drumcarrow, and wow! echoes him the Professor of Hebrew. Celerity of decision it was that had given Colonel Inchburn his Indian victories. Your servant, Madam, cries the Barbary Ape.

To the blackamoor Colonel Inchburn flings his rusty cloak, and from him snatches the muckle staff. So armed, he dashes upon the disguised Lord Banford, standing surprised behind his prey. In the dark, the combatants cannot see one the other's face. Banford gives the Ape a stroke of the dog-whip upon his left cheek. Then the Barbary Ape, not to be withstood, tumbles Banford and belabours him unkindly with the staff.

In Banford's party whingers and dirks are drawn, three or four of Banford's friends setting upon the raging Ape. Yet the nimble Ape beats them off, one and all, with his terrible staff: and the captain, the lieutenant, and the sepoy reinforcing Drumcarrow, Banford's minions take to their heels. The bleeding Banford, two teeth stricken out, essays to flee in their company, but the Ape thumps him down again.

Then up trot the Town Guard with their Lochaber axes, summoned by some citizen in the cottages against the kirkyard wall. Colonel Inchburn is well known to the veterans of the Guard, having bestowed upon them many a pot of ale. Friends, says Drumcarrow to the Guard, take in charge this broken bravo, and lodge the ruffian in the Tolbooth.

Meanwhile the sepoy has enveloped poor Janet in Drumcarrow's old cloak, and the Professor of Hebrew has called in another sedan chair from Candlemakers' Row, and the wee maid has been discovered shivering behind a minister's tomb. Janet is borne away to the Lawnmarket, bloody, bruised, and falling into a swoon.

The sergeant of the Guard is fixing manacles upon the felon Banford, who has been rolled in the mud, battered in the face, and thumped without mercy by the muckle staff in the Ape's muckle hands. Unhand me, loons, gasps he, for I'm Lord Banford.

Drumcarrow laughs loud in his face. This lump of filth an English lord? says Drumcarrow to the sergeant. Aye, put him down as an impostor forby, sergeant. To the Tolbooth's cage Lord Banford is dragged, and he passes some wretched hours therein ere Sir Angus Kinkell persuades the Provost that this groaning hulk indeed is a peer's son.

[Of the following page of the MS, only some words and phrases are plain. In substance, it tells how Janet's aunt and brother comforted her, and how Colonel Inchburn, Scots Samaritan, was left with the weal from Banford's whip on his cheek. One gathers that Janet refuses to proceed against Banford, dreading more public shame. Out of delicacy of sentiment, it appears, Drumcarrow refrains from calling upon Miss Kenly, though she has his cloak. When the MS becomes sufficiently legible once more, one encounters a second report of a conversation between Lord Banford and Sir Angus Kinkell. — Ed.]

Further, Sir Angus Kinkell made deposition to the magistrates that he apprehended imperfectly the drift of Lord Banford's discourse, else he would have dissuaded him from his purpose or sought some act of interdict to restrain him. It was thus that they had talked together, three days after Lord Banford's discharge from the Tolbooth.

Sir Angus: My lord, having been drubbed first by a half-witted lad, and second by an Ancient Pistol with sinews like unto an ape's, all for the sake of leaving a stripe or two upon a maiden's bum, ye'd be well advised to withdraw to Cumberland for the time, before some third Scot extracts the remainder of your teeth. Or if ye fear your father's wrath, take ship to the Continent for three months, a safe remove from Pittenweem enchantments.

Lord Banford: To Hell with your coward devices, Kinkell. You'll have the goodness, gout or no gout, to carry my challenge to Inchburn.

A.: Do ye tire of life, lad, young though ye are? Think what he did to ye with a stick, as to some schoolboy. What would he do to ye with a sword? I was acquainted with Drumcarrow at Calcutta, though I ne'er cared for the canting dominie-colonel. Mind ye, he ne'er lost a battle nor a duel. Think on those ape-long arms of his: he'd spit thee like a suckling pig. They say he's made his bargain with some Indian devil, taking not gold in exchange for his soul, but martial triumph. Ye've been tutored by a French fencing-master, aye. What's that to Drumcarrow? Na, na, Banford: standing *in loco parentis* to thee, I'd send ye back to the rats of the Tolbooth rather than have ye carved by the Ape.

B.: Faith, Kinkell, I confess you do dissuade me. Yet what of this: there's many a dark wynd in this town.

A.: D'ye fancy we're in Venice, with bravos for hire? Mind the ragged regiment that Drumcarrow keeps about him in the Cowgate: they and their patron would make mince pies o' any smilers with the knife. More, ye rascal, I'll tolerate no dastard ambuscade, though I've pardoned many a scrape o' thine: I'd bear witness against ye myself, as a gentleman and one that has borne the King's commission.

B.: Go to, old Bobadil. I'll spare the Ape: he's beneath me. Yet I know how to make the Janet-witch repent, weeping her black eyes out.

A.: What mean ye? Forget the bonnie jut o' the Kenly's bum. The Watch will watch ye henceforth, and Drumcarrow has set his sepoy to dog her chair, friends tell me, when the jade begins to venture out again. Would ye relish another night in the Tolbooth, and worse than that? Why, I think our Pittenweem enchantress has addled your wits. I'm none o' the unco' guid, lad, but I say to ye, stick to drinking and wenching, putting out of your head flogging and stabbing. Your lordship must confine yourself to the genial vices . . .

[Here again the MS is illegible, a full two pages not only damp-damaged, but in part crossed and hatched out, perhaps by the author. When the narrative resumes, it is set down in a hand spidery, hasty, and often scrawled, as if written in recollected passion. — Ed.]

Dugald came not home to the Lawnmarket that night. In dread, she sent a caddie with word of this to Drumcarrow, who dispatched back to her a letter sprinkled with Latin tags, in substance saying that a young man consorting with bad companions soon or late takes to all the pleasures of the flesh; and that like enough Dugald, if she would forgive the phrase, had bedded with some wench in Leith, and would return a sadder and a wiser man. He presented his compliments, adding that he would call for his cloak when assured that Miss Kenly had recovered her composure.

Yet another night passed, and Dugald came not. Then was Janet Kenly distraught. Once she fancied she glimpsed her brother peering out from the pantry, but flinging open the door, found no man. Thrice she heard his tread upon the common stair, and scampered down to meet him, yet encountered only empty air. Again, from the corner of her eye, she beheld his form seated in a chair, gazing upon her: she sprang towards him, but clasped nothing.

Hope ebbing, she did then what must put her soul in jeopardy. Those things her mother had taught her in secret she recollected well, though never before had she practiced them. Into a trance she cast herself, invoking the power of second sight. In vision verily she beheld her brother where he lay. For some hours thereafter was she senseless. Rising at length, she looked into the book of the learned divine Robert Kirk, whom the Subterraneans carried off for his knowing overmuch of them; and into certain writings at the bottom of a chest that her mother had bequeathed to her.

Not every man or woman has a Co-Walker, but they only who are fey in some degree, and even of the fey not all. Yet Janet long had sensed beyond the senses that sometimes there walked an Image or Echo of her brother Dugald, a simulacrum, mayhap the missing half of the terrestrial Dugald.

Steeling herself, Janet Kenly then did what must be done to raise the Co-Walker, or Reflex-Man, and to send it on its way. For the living Dugald she would not see again here below: the Reflex-Man must serve her turn.

[At this point in the MS, ink appears to have been spilled or poured upon some few pages. Close examination discloses that on these pages probably were set down spells of formulas. When these blotted pages are submitted to recent specialized technologies, conceivably it may be possible to decipher this writing, seemingly in a dog-Latin. The page following the formulas is headed by a verse from Job, below, after which the narration shifts to Whinnymuir Close. — Ed.]

> Then a spirit passed before my face,
> the hair of my flesh stood up.
> It stood still, but I could not
> discern the form thereof: an image
> was before mine eyes.

Among his serving-men at Whinnymuir House, Lord Banford kept one Tam Alloway, ill-visaged and sly, said to have been a pirate in the West Indies. This Alloway served his master as pander and ruffler. Together with four other servants, Alloway was lounging by the house door, after nightfall, when the porter at the pend of the close cries out sharp, Stand, stand ye! Thereupon, his challenge being unheeded, the porter runs incontinent from the pend towards his fellows, his face ashen, wailing as he runs.

There comes into the close one that shimmers as he strides towards the house. In his right hand the shape holds a naked sword. Though the clothes upon him are fine, with silver lace, they are all besmirched and bespattered. This shape is tall and broad of shoulder, and grim of countenance. As it comes upon them, the serving-men about the doorway gasp and shake, and the porter goes down upon his knees.

Now the boldest of Banford's men, Tam Alloway, sets himself in the path of this shimmering one with the drawn sword. What would ye? begins Alloway. Then the shape stares him full in the face.

O God! cries Alloway, Dugald Kenly, ye're dirked and sunk! This Alloway tumbles down in a fit, kicking and frothing upon the stones, a thing mindless.

Speaking no word, the shimmering shape passes through the doorway into Whinnymuir House, without let or hindrance, the men shrinking together with a grue, none venturing to withstand the intruder. He mounts the stair within: and as he goes up, one or two of the serving-men perceive that in the back of his fine coat is a sore rent, with stains all about it.

It is nigh to midnight. Lord Banford has been with a woman in the Canongate, but just now returns to his house, finding no porter at the pend and Alloway writhing like a stricken serpent at his house's threshold.

What's this riot? says Banford, thick of speech from overmuch brandy. He glares upon his men's pallid faces.

The under-steward answers him, My lord, 'tis Master Dugald Kenly has gone up the stair, with his hanger in his hand, and mud upon his clothes.

Lord Banford shakes as if an ague were upon him, and he strikes the under-steward upon the face with his gloved hand. You lie, cries Banford, confess to me that you lie. Who's paid you for this lie?

Na, na, my lord, say the other serving-men, that daft Dugald, or else his twin brother, passed us by and went up the stair, and he was all besmirched, with a rent in his back.

Banford curses them for fools and cravens, but leans most pallid against the wall. Then 'twas Tam Alloway lied to me, says he, and kicks Alloway where he lies writhing. Alloway, Tam Alloway, roars Lord Banford, say that Dugald lives, and that you lied to me, man. Yet Alloway does no more than gabble like some bird.

Banford turns upon his serving-men, saying, Get you in the house and take him or cut him down, he being mere man. Yet the under-steward, with blood upon his lips where his master has struck him, says softly, bowing, Lead on, my lord.

Lord Banford toys with his sword-hilt, yet does not stir, as one lost in horrid thought. Of a sudden, he commands the under-steward, Nay, run and fetch me Colonel Inchburn of Drumcarrow.

Drumcarrow, my lord? asks the under-steward, not believing his ears.

Speak him soft, man, says Banford, his breath coming hard. And as if to himself, They say the Ape's made his pact with the Devil, and the Devil protects his own. And Dugald was the Ape's friend. None but damned Drumcarrow might coax the tyke out.

The porter sings out shrill, Some face at that window — pointing to the third storey of the house. What face, what face? screeches Lord Banford. But it has gone.

The young witch has sent the thing, Banford says low, conjuring it out from Hell or the loch. Then more loud, Aye, man, run to Drumcarrow in the Cowgate, speaking him fair. Say that Lord Banford craves his mercy, being in dire need, and will repay his kindness in whatsoever form Colonel Inchburn of Drumcarrow desires.

So while Banford and his men linger craven at the stair-foot, the under-steward hies him to the Cowgate with all expedition. By chance Drumcarrow is alone in his lodging, save for a pensioned major with one leg and an old maid-servant. The under-steward stammers out his message.

What, Lord Banford begging my service? says Drumcarrow. Then he bethinks him, poor Dugald, an he have wandered into Whinnymuir House, stands imperilled in that vipers' den. Aye, we must have him out of there. Where has the lad been these two nights?

Go not alone to an enemy, Colonel Inchburn, says to him the one-legged major. Needs must, lest they dirk the lad, Drumcarrow answers.

He glances about for some weapon. Hanging on the wall is a jewelled sword with a hilt of carved ivory that a Ranee had bestowed upon Colonel Inchburn when he commanded her horse. He snatches the court tulwar from the wall and runs, the under-steward at his heels, the short distance to Whinnymuir Close.

There stands Banford at the door, sword in hand. Colonel Inchburn, says he, letting bygones be bygones, will you come with me and take this Dugald out of my house? For doubtless he means me a mischief.

And you mean no mischief to him? Drumcarrow asks. An you swear, my lord, to fetch him out whole and scatheless, I'll adventure with you.

At that, Banford's words stick in his craw: but presently he gasps out, If he go, I'll touch him not.

Then Drumcarrow and Banford ascend the stair, Drumcarrow leading, for Banford hung back to let him pass.

Whinnymuir House, ere by chance or Providence it was burnt in late years, was within like unto a Cretan labyrinth, being of much age and added to, within and without, at divers times. A candlestick in his left hand, Drumcarrow makes his way along a narrow passage, calling out, Dugald! Dugald Kenly! Dugald, lad! 'Tis Drumcarrow, come to take you to your sister! Looking behind him presently, he finds that Banford is not at his back, having taken another turn somewhere in the house-maze.

Drumcarrow gropes on alone, turning a corner. He draws in his breath: for some paces distant he sees a shimmering shape, man-high, fronting him; the face he cannot discern. Dugald, says Drumcarrow, if that be you, come to me, lad.

Yet the shape recedes and vanishes, perhaps into a chamber. Drumcarrow presses on, though tempted to turn tail.

Of a sudden, there comes from behind him an eldritch scream, so loud and wild that the candlestick falls from Drumcarrow's left hand and he is left in blackness. There follows the sound of running feet, Drumcarrow turning round to confront whatever rushes upon him, his court sword in his right hand.

In that darkness, a shrieking thing hurls itself against Drumcarrow. He is flung against the wall in the strait place; and one hacks at him with a whinger, taking clean off the wee finger of Drumcarrow's left hand.

Drumcarrow thrusts against his adversary like bull or ape, his blood up. With his Indian tulwar he runs the thing through: and it yet standing against the passage wall, wailing fearsomely, Drumcarrow runs it through again, and it falls, and is still.

Blood from his left hand pouring out fast, Drumcarrow feels about the floor for his candle; most coolly takes out flint and steel, and lights it again; peers into the dead face at his feet. It is the face of Lord Banford, much contorted.

Here's a pickle! Drumcarrow tears a bit of linen from the dead man's shirt to bind up his hand. He wipes his sword on Banford's coat, and sheathes it. Looking about him, Dugald he calls, five times: yet no answer comes. Dugald was not in this house, thinks Drumcarrow, not this night: the shimmering one was not canny. Good Lord deliver us!

So Drumcarrow goes back down the stair, and finds the craven servingmen still clustered round the doorway. Having heard the shrieks within, they shake every man of them. Look to your master, says Drumcarrow to them, but no more. They stand out of his way, and he makes straight for the Provost's lodging, though all over blood, to tell of Lord Banford's strange end: the sooner and more fully told, the less the odds for a hanging.

Two days later, fishers in the Nor Loch came upon the corpse of Dugald Kenly, stabbed in the back and weighted down with lead. When Tam Alloway, gibbering, was searched in the Tolbooth, there was found in his pocket a gold locket that had been Dugald's, with the miniature portrait of Janet Kenly therein. Alloway they hanged in the Grassmarket. When they had put him to the question in the Tolbooth, he had said he had done the stabbing at his master's command; but Alloway had gone mad, so that his evidence was tainted; and beside, Lord Banford was dead and gone to his reward.

[There follow in the MS three pages of prayers, evidently copies from a prayer-book; also copied comminations. These are omitted from this published version. The MS passes over what difficulties Colonel Inchburn may have encountered with Scottish authorities in consequence of the slaying. From another source, it is known that Colonel Inchburn of Drumcarrow enjoyed the intimacy of the Procurator-Fiscal — who, indeed, was cousin to Drumcarrow; that friendship may have been of assistance to the redoubtable Colonel. The narrative is resumed several days later, it appears, after Janet Kenly had given up her Lawnmarket lodging and returned to her house on the square at Pittenweem. Some scrawled sheets of accounts, inserted in the MS at this point, suggest that Janet found herself nearly a bankrupt, after her brother's extravagance and her own at Edinburgh. — Ed.]

Having had her brother's coffin brought over the Forth from Leith to Pittenweem, Janet Kenly buried Dugald by the massy tower of Pittenweem kirk, and upon his stone was graven Blessed are the pure in heart: for they shall see God. It might be well, said she to dying Auntie, to have Janet Kenly's stone graven too, for she felt not long for this world. Yet upon Janet's stone it would be impudence to grave a Beatitude.

She dwelt deep in the valley of humiliation, weeping long for Dugald and for herself. Her fine gowns she bestowed upon Pittenweem lasses, attiring herself in black only; her shoes too she gave to the poor, going about the house with naked feet, as becoming a clockmaker's daughter. She had done with rouge and the beauty-patch.

Words of her disgrace had made its way to Pittenweem: therefore she scarce left the house on the square, lest the fisher lads mock her. Their money was spent, nearly all; she had drawn the last of the siller from the Royal Bank of Scotland. When Auntie should die, the house must be sold or let, and Janet must go into service, if any mistress would take a maidservant called a wanton and a witch.

One debt there remained to pay: that to the valiant Laird of Drumcarrow. His cloak she had with her in Pittenweem: she had washed it well, and now she embellished it with silver lace, for Colonel Inchburn had written to her in the Lawnmarket that he would come for it. He had served her twice, still better the second time than the first.

On a bright afternoon a fisherman came up from the harbour to hand her a letter sent from the Cowgate by Drumcarrow, saying that if Miss Kenly was not otherwise engaged, he would call on the Friday for his cloak. He would be on his way inland to Drumcarrow Tower, the Colonel added, where masons and slaters were setting the doocot to rights, and pointing the Tower, for he meant to dwell there as a laird should. It should be his Sabine Farm for his declining years. He expressed his hope that her anguish might have abated somewhat. There was no word of his as to what had passed in Whinnymuir House.

She dared not wait on Pittenweem pier that Friday, but sat with her hands in her lap that morning and much of the afternoon, in her chamber on the upper floor, which served her as parlour and bedroom.

As the bonnie tall clock struck four, somebody tirled at the pin on the High Street door: and peering down undetected, she beheld Drumcarrow. His sepoy stood sentry on the opposite side of the square. It was an altered Drumcarrow, for he wore a saffron cloak of some gorgeous Indian stuff, and a new beaver upon his head, and at his hip swung a court sword in a scabbard with silver mountings.

His nose is noble, thought she, and his mouth and chin: never mind the missing right ear, and now the missing wee finger of the left hand: never mind, least of all, the whip-welt, taken for her, on his cheek. See the valiant soldier's breadth of shoulder and depth of chest! Knowing she would not look upon Ian Inchburn, her saviour, after this hour, she strove to fix his image in her mind so that it might linger there to her dying day. An ape indeed! Nay, Drumcarrow is a kingly lion, the Scots lion.

Her shy maid has shown him in, and now his boots clatter on the stair. She composes herself, Janet does, as best she may: she must not greet in his presence, nor haver. For all his civility, Inchburn of Drumcarrow will not linger long with such as she.

Colonel Inchburn enters, sweeping off his beaver: bows somewhat stiffly: surprising her, he takes her hand to kiss it lightly, as if he had been Paris bred. Your servant, Madam, says Drumcarrow.

That salutation brought to her mind his same words when he had rescued her at Greyfriars, so that she says to him, Laird, does the cut on your cheek heal well?

Tolerably well, Madam, answers he. And yours?

Janet went scarlet in shame. Then did Drumcarrow's face flush as well, so that she knew he had meant no innuendo by his words, but had spoken innocently enough. His blunder seemed now to tie his tongue.

She motioned him to her best chair, but he paced instead to the window that looked from the gable towards the kirk tower. He's eager to be gone, thought she. Taking the garment from a table, she says, Laird, I have made ready your cloak for you; but now you require it not, for you wear some Rajah's robe.

He took the old black cloak into his hands. Why, Madam, he tells her, this is brave work your fingers have done upon it! Nay, I'm grateful; I'll give the Indian thing to my sepoy, and wrap myself in what has wrapped you also.

Here again her colour flamed up, and next his as well.

Nay, Madam, forgive me, he says after a stillness in the chamber, for I am no squire of dames, and my rude tongue betrays my folly. I meant naught amiss.

Why, says she to herself, the Laird is ill at ease. Something he means to say that must pain me: he cannot bring out his words.

Now in that tower, Drumcarrow says, nodding towards the kirk at the other end of the High Street, time was when the kirk session kept accused witches in a little room, and questioned them.

I know it too well, she answers, with fear at her heart.

Drumcarrow: Let me question then, Madam. In a passage at Whinnymuir House, before my finger was taken off, I seemed to see a shimmering shape, and I called it by your brother's name. I'll be blunt, Madam: was it true what Banford's men said, that the ghost of your brother entered into the house?

Janet: Nay, not Dugald's ghost, Laird, but his semblance. The thing was a Reflex-Man. D'ye ken my meaning?

D.: Well enough, Madam: such shapes walk in India also.

J.: And yet, Laird, in some sense it may have been Dugald's spirit: for but half of him ever was in this world, and mayhap the other half, lingering, affrighted Lord Banford's men.

D.: Aye, and sent Banford mad beside, so that he flew upon me and made me his executioner. Like enough the thing caught him at some turning and peered into his face, as it looked in Alloway's. Sent you that Reflex-Man, Madam, and saw you it?

J.: Laird, I sent it, but ne'er beheld it.

D.: And did some power out of you, lass, send me from the Cowgate to Whinnymuir Close? For as I buckled on this sword that night, the vision of your fair — of your fair face came into my mind, and hastened my steps.

J.: Na, na, Laird, I ne'er would have sent you to confront that shape in that house, for already I owed you more than mortal woman may pay. That sword — is it at your side now?

Drumcarrow drew the sharp pretty thing. Its ivory hilt was carved as a leopard's head, with rubies for eyes: a weapon of great price. The blade was a trifle bent, from pinning Banford like some butterfly to the wall.

Taking the keen tulwar into her hands, she kissed its blade most ardently with her red lips.

Drumcarrow: Well done! You're a brave lass, Janet Kenly. Aye, that blade evened Dugald's score with Banford.

Janet: Nightly, Laird, I pray for Banford's damnation.

Drumcarrow: Och, Janet lass, you lay waste your time. Such a one's Hell-bent by nature. Purgatory's not for him. On Purgatory, I hold, against our Scots doctors of divinity. . . . But lass, I'll weary you: more of doctrine another day.

J.: They say, Ian Inchburn, that a Reflex-Man goes at last to his own herd — below, Drumcarrow, below. Then what of Dugald?

D.: Above, Janet, above. He was a little child, and of such is the Kingdom. The semblance sinks, the soul rises. Corruption shall put on incorruption, and we shall be changed, lass, in the twinkling of an eye.

Now, to her shame, the tears ran freely down her cheeks. She seated herself, for she could not stand longer. On a table lay a neat embroidered purse, her handiwork, and her last gift to Drumcarrow, as the restored and embellished cloak had been her first.

She put the purse into his hand, saying, Drumcarrow, my brother and I give you this for token of our gratitude unto you.

Your needlework, Janet Kenly? asks Drumcarrow. Gladly I'll keep it by me. But what's this within? He jingles the purse in his broad palm, and scowls fearsomely, so that Janet quivers in her chair.

The day being warm, the window by Janet stands open. Out that window Drumcarrow tosses the purse, and Janet hears it clink upon the paving of the close.

D'ye take me for some Venice bravo, lass? cries Drumcarrow. Man of blood I may be, but on the field of honour: I take no pay for stabbing damned men in black passages.

She is sobbing hard now. Laird, she tells him, it was all the siller left to us, to the last baubee. Tomorrow Auntie and I must sell my father's plenishings, even this tall clock, the last he made. And I'd heard tell that you'd returned from India with empty pockets, and my brother and I loved you, and I thought . . .

Colonel Inchburn goes down on his knees beside her chair, and takes her hand. Janet, says he, Janet my bonnie dear, I'm not so poor as some be. With that, he draws from a pocket a wee leathern bag, and empties its contents into Janet's lap: threescore precious gems and more, some of them great ones. Not being yet wholly purged of the vanities of this world, she runs her fingers through them.

Janet, in wonder: How came you by these, Laird?

Drumcarrow: Not by sack or theft, but as a gift from my Ranee.

J.: And why gave she them to you, Ian Inchburn?

D.: For that I had laid her enemies in heaps. Lass, my Ranee had seen more than eighty withering summers.

J.: You must not carry them about like cairngorms, Drumcarrow: put them into a strongbox in the Royal Bank of Scotland.

D.: Nay, put them there yourself, Janet, an you like. The baubles are yours, lass, to adorn your loveliness.

She went first crimson and then white, ghost-white. Yet the soldier deserved his reward: after what he had done, in justice she could deny him nothing. If he would make her his light-of-love — why, her pride had gone before her fall. If a leman he would take, she would give him who had slain Lord Banford what pleasure she might. He would keep her in Edinburgh, like enough, secure at least from the taunts and the stones of fisherfolk. She cast down her eyes, saying to him, Laird, there's no need to buy me: take back your stones, for I submit without them.

Drumcarrow: What's this, Janet? D'ye ken, lass? The Barbary Ape, poor fool, asks your hand in wedlock: poor fool, because you are young and he is old; you beautiful, he hideous. Yet there's this, Janet Kenly: the Ape does not fear you, while any other man might come to shiver at your gifts. If we are wed, there must be no more raisings and sendings; nay, even no simples, Janet. Now d'ye scorn me?

The gems fell from her lap to the floor; neither heeded them. He had clasped her about her knees, and was now speechless, as if he feared she was about to pronounce his doom. She ran her fingers through his unruly red hair, lifted his head, fixed him with her black eyes, and kissed the Ape. Then Janet wept harder than before, knowing her unworthiness, marvelling that Drumcarrow did not abominate her, and fearing still her soul's damnation. And she swore to her betrothed that she would call nothing from the vasty deep.

As they were picking up the jewels from the floor, some time later, Janet whispered to him of her mother's and her grandmother's powers of second sight, that they had hidden under a bushel — as she must hide hers. Then, hand in hand, they ran down the stair, cannily, to retrieve the purse tossed into the close.

[At this point are inserted in the MS several pages of drawings, executed with some skill, of the extensive additions to Drumcarrow Tower commenced about 1740. It is possible, though not certain, that some pages of the narrative are missing: at any rate, we are given no account of the events of nearly a decade. The concluding pages of the extant MS (written, conjecturably, not long after 1784, when most of the forfeited Jacobite estates were restored to the descendants of proprietors out in the Forty-five) touch upon events during 1744, 1745, and 1746. — Ed.]

Much to his satisfaction, and even more to hers, Janet had borne to Colonel Inchburn four sons and one daughter. The sons inherited their father's valour and strength; the daughter, her mother's eyes and ankles, yet not her mother's secret talents. He had sought Janet's hand somewhat abruptly, Drumcarrow told his wife during the first year of their marriage, as much for her fortitude as for her beauty: he had foreseen that she would make a Roman mother. As for her charms, having viewed those extensively in Greyfriars kirkyard, he could not put them out of his head, for all the austere celibate life he had led.

That enchantment, Laird, was unintended, says Janet to him.

To the pledge she had made him at their betrothal, that she would raise no semblances nor send them to do her bidding, Janet was faithful so long as her husband lived.

Yet in the fatal year of 1746, she imperilled her soul once more. During 1744, Drumcarrow's sight commenced to fail him, and he suffered from time to time pangs about his heart. Janet, says he, you and the bairns are well provided for by our East India Company stocks. I would not linger a blind hirpled creature, to burden you.

His wife, clinging to him, implored Drumcarrow to abide with her so long as the Lord left breath in his body. Yet when the Claimant landed in the West, Drumcarrow resolved to aid the Prince's cause with his sword, in despite of the years that lay upon him. To her he repeated the lines of Lovelace:

I could not love thee, Dear, so much
Lov'd I not Honour more.

Having embraced her ardently for the last time, Colonel Inchburn rode off alone to join his Jacobite friend the Earl of Balmerino, in whose Horse Guards he served without commission.

Wise in war, Drumcarrow entertained scant hope of victory for the Prince. He therefore prudently entered upon the muster-roll another name than his own when he joined Lord Balmerino by the merkat cross at Cupar. Under that chosen name, Donald Auchtermuchty, he rode throughout the course of the Rising. By the time the Prince's army had withdrawn to Inverness, Drumcarrow was one of the few in Balmerino's broken troop still possessed of a good horse.

On the sixteenth day of April, 1746, the second sight came upon Janet Inchburn once more, about two of the afternoon. Giddy, she sank upon the floor, and there beheld in her mind's eye a broad moor, and upon it a furious battle. Up galloped some two score Jacobite horse, to fall upon a cloud of red dragoons. Foremost among the Prince's troopers was an old man with grey hair, leaning over the neck of his horse. The saddles about him were emptied by shot or sabre, yet he rode on slashing the dragoons, as if invisibly protected. Clean through the dragoons he burst; and then, when he might have dashed away scatheless, he wheeled to charge the enemy solitary. Soon a ball struck him: flinging up his long arms, he toppled from the saddle, and the dragoons rode over him, hacking at his head.

Some few days later, full report of the defeat at Culloden Moor was brought to Mrs. Inchburn of Drumcarrow. She did not cry out, for at the very day and hour of the battle she had known of her husband's death.

There had been found on the field, a yard or two from Lord Strathallen's corpse, the crushed body of an old man trampled upon by Cobham's Dragoons. The face was ruined beyond recognition. In the trooper's pockets were papers that gave his name as Donald Auchtermuchty. What with the long arms of this corpse that lacked a face, it was said to the Duke of Cumberland by one or two officers that the old dead trooper might be Drumcarrow, the Barbary Ape; moreover, the one called Auchtermuchty had been gallant and fearless as Drumcarrow.

Yet it was not proven that Inchburn of Drumcarrow had been at Culloden; nor that, supposing him there, he had fought for the Pretender. As for the old man's corpse, it was flung into a pit along with those of many other Jacobite fallen.

Ian Inchburn was not seen again by any man, and his eldest son, Roy, succeeded him at Drumcarrow. Some attempt was made to have the estate forfeited to the Crown, yet the heir's men of law baffled that endeavour. Wise in his last hour, as throughout his earthly life, the Barbary Ape had preserved the lands for his posterity. Had he been taken living, or recognized dead, the lands of Drumcarrow would have fallen forfeit until this year at best.

Nay, no man saw Colonel Inchburn after Culloden. Yet I the witch saw him.

Not Reflex-Men only did my mother teach me to summon up. As the woman of Endor raised Samuel, so out of my passion I conjured my Ian. Be he above, or with the herd below, or in the Purgatory of which he had talked, I must look upon him once more. It might be that I would behold but a broken cadaver on Culloden Moor, even as I had seen dear stabbed Dugald beneath the Nor Loch before I worked my vengeance upon Banford. Yet such knowledge would be better than weary ignorance.

The conjugation went otherwise. For one moment, Ian Inchburn stood before me. From out of his glorified body shone his goodness and his generosity. He had been raised in incorruption: he it was, though transfigured. He had been purged of dross and defect, and yet he was Ian Inchburn, loved by his witch-wife.

This visible flesh, says Augustine, we must without doubting believe will rise again. I learnt the truth of that.

Mightily I dreaded my husband's wrath for summoning him against his command. Though he spoke not, he smiled: and then winked at me; and was gone. He was no Semblance, no Simulacrum, no Reflex-Man, but Ian Inchburn, quick beyond Time's confines.

Now I do entreat the Almighty's forgiveness for my saucy flouting of my Ian's command; and for exercising that last time those arts forbidden. *Adjuvante Deo resurgam.* I have sinned, O Lord, but let my cry come unto thee. Let me with Ian be forever not semblance, but substance. I have survived the hero these forty years: now let thy faithless servant depart in peace, awaiting the Last Trump. I have put away my vanity: let him who reads this do likewise.

> When thou from hence away art past,
> — *Every nighte and alle,*
> To Whinny-muir thou com'st at last;
> *And Christe receive thy saule.*

The Invasion of the Church of the Holy Ghost

Some say no evil thing that walks by night
In fog, or fire, by lake, or moorish fen,
Blew meager Hag, or stubborn unlaid ghost,
No Goblin, or swart Faery of the mine,
Hath hurtful power o'er true virginity.

Comus

What occurred in my church last night must be committed to writing without delay. Having discovered my own feebleness, I do not know how long I might resist, should some other presence enter the church. Fork cast out the night-walkers, and the girl too has gone, but there is no discharge in this war.

Perhaps the one devil who stared me in the face may gather seven other spirits more wicked than himself, so that my last state should be worse than my first. If such ruin comes to pass, at least I will have set down these happenings. Knowledge of them might preserve my successor at this Church of the Holy Ghost.

Successor? No likely prospect. Were I to depart, the bishop would lock the bronze doors — and soon demolish the hulking church, supposing him able to pay the wreckers' bills. Our bishop, saints forgive him, spends his days comminating the president of the United States and ordaining lesbians. The Right Reverend Soronson Hickey regards me as a disagreeable, if exotic, eccentric who fancies that he has a cure of souls —

353

when every right-thinking cleric in this diocese has been instructed that the notion of souls is a fable. Had I been born white, the bishop would have thrust me out of the Church of the Holy Ghost months ago.

Whoever you are, reading these scribbled pages — why, I may be dead or vanished, and the dear bishop may be my reader — I must first set down my name and station. I am Raymond Thomas Montrose, doctor of divinity, rector of the Church of the Holy Ghost in the parish of Hawkhill. This parish and the neighboring districts make up the roughest quarter of what is called the 'inner city.' I am an Episcopalian priest, the only reasonably orthodox clergyman remaining in Hawkhill, which Satan claims for his own.

Thomas is my confirmation name, and my patron is Saint Thomas of Canterbury. Like my patron, I stand six feet four in my armor. Yes, armor; but my mail is black leather, and I sleep with a pistol hanging from my bedhead.

A sergeant's son, I was born in Spanish Town, Jamaica, and I am shiny black: nobody excels me in negritude. The barmaids of Pentecost Road say I have a 'cute British accent.' I believe in the Father, the Son, and the Holy Ghost; the resurrection of the dead; and the life everlasting. I am celibate, not quite forty years of age, and since my ordination chaste of body. I have survived in Hawkhill a whole year.

My rectory is a safe-house, after a fashion. Occasionally I lodge behind its thick walls and barred windows — the builders of a century gone builded more wisely than they knew — girls off Pentecost Road, fugitive from their pimps. The bishop admonishes me that this unseemly hospitality may give rise to scandal. I have replied that I do not desire carnal knowledge of these young women. It is their souls I am after. At such superstitious discourse the bishop scowls. Were I a pathic, he would not reprove me.

My Church of the Holy Ghost is Richardsonian Romanesque in style, erected more than a century ago, when red sandstone and Hawkhill were fashionable. The bishop has exiled me to the furthest frontier of his diocese, no other clergyman applying for my present rectorship. I accepted cheerfully enough a cure of souls in what the humorists of our daily press call the Demilitarized Zone of our city. Would that it really had been demilitarized! I did not obtain a permit for a pistol out of mere bravado.

The Church of the Holy Ghost, Protestant Episcopal, looms handsomely though grimly over Merrymont Avenue, three blocks east of the junction with Pentecost Road. (In the believing early years of our city, those names were not thought absurd.) Some fine old houses still stand on Merrymont; many more have been burnt by arsonists (often hired arsonists) or have fallen into hopeless ruin. Where once our upper classes gloried and drank deep, the owl and bat their revel keep — or, more literally, the poorest of our poor get drunk and disorderly whenever they can.

I make no claim to have cured many souls near the junction of Pentecost and Merrymont. Occasionally my Sunday services are attended by perhaps seventy persons (in a building that might seat seven hundred), most of them immigrants (chiefly illegal) from the Caribbean like myself. There is a peppering of quiet little people from southeastern Asia, and a salting of old white folk stranded in Hawkhill by the pace of change in our city. One of the last group, Mrs. Simmons, still has some money, which enables me to keep the church doors open. The bishop doles me out next to nothing for any purpose.

The sheltered broad steps ascending to the magnificent doors of my church are carpeted wall to wall, on clement days, by the Old Soldiers, winos, and other derelicts; some bums sleep on those steps all night in summer, although not at this season. (Were I to let them lodge inside, they'd have the church befouled, looted, and desecrated within an hour.) A brace of policemen clear the Old Soldiers off the steps for my Sunday morning service. Some few of these Ancient Pistols even join my congregation, to escape snow or wind. I have made Anglo-Catholics of two or three.

Although less poverty-racked than Merrymont Avenue, Pentecost Road is more dreadful. For Pentecost Road has become the heart of the domain of the pushers and the pimps. Young women and female children of several colors parade the Pentecost in hope of custom; so do a number of boys, also for general hire. 'If you want it, we've got it,' is the legend painted above the entrance to the best-patronized bar on Pentecost Road. At the devil's booth all things are sold.

Besides believing earnestly in the doctrine of the soul, I believe with all my heart in Satan, whose territories are daily enlarged. I know myself for a castellan of Castle Perilous — my Church of the Holy Ghost looking like a mighty fortress — beset every hour by Satan's minions.

Reader, whoever you are, you might call me an educated Salvation Nigger. I am called worse than that, frequently, on Pentecost Road. Few of Satan's minions on that street know me for a man of the cloth; they are not numbered among my communicants. In vestments, and with my hair brushed, I look quite unlike myself when in my Pentecost Road armor. Touring the Pentecost bars, I wear a greasy broad-brimmed hat, and under my leather jacket a very loud suit. Somehow the word has been passed round that I am an unsuccessful chiropractor who likes his rum drinks.

I frequent Pentecost Road to snatch from the burning what brands I may. In this thankless labor I found an improbable coadjutor in the person of Fork Causland.

A source of the rumor that I am a chiropractor is Fork Causland's custom of addressing me as Doc. But I am in his debt for much more than that.

The first time I saw Fork, he was descending nimbly from a bus — nimbly for a blind man, that is. Under his left arm he gripped a sheaf of placards announcing a wrestling match; these he was posting in the windows of barber shops and other small businesses. This bill-posting was one of the several means by which Causland supported himself, accepting no welfare payments.

I watched him while he clanked his brass-shod stick upon the sidewalk and cried out to the world, in jovial defiance, 'North-west corner of Beryl and Clemens! Don't tell me I don't know where I am!'

Fork wore black goggles that fitted tight to his broad half-Indian face. Quite as invariably he wore, indoors and out, a black derby hat — what would have been called a bowler, down where I was born. Although not tall, Fork was formidably constructed and in prime condition. His facemask was the hardest visage that ever I have looked upon: 'tough as nails,' they say. Also it was a face humorously stoical.

On that street corner I merely stared at Fork, who brushed past me to enter a cafeteria. It was a week later that I first conversed with him, in the Mustang Bar, Pentecost Road.

I was sipping a daiquiri — 'pansy drink,' a mugger type at the bar had growled, but I had stared him down — when somebody outside shouted, 'The old Mustang! Wahoo!' Something rang upon concrete, and there bounced into view Fork Causland. I write 'bounced': that is what he did. The burly blind man flung himself into the air, his left hand clutching the head of his stick; and he seemed to hold himself suspended in the air for half a minute, miraculously, his soles a foot or more above the pavement. Either Causland had a marvelously strong left wrist, or there was something preternatural about this blind man who could set at defiance the law of gravity.

Nobody else happened to be watching Fork's performance at that moment, but later I inquired among barflies about him. Some thought that Causland had been a circus performer in his youth, and had fallen from a high wire, destroying his eyes. Others said that he had been a sergeant of military police, blinded in line of duty. (If so, where was his pension?) Yet others suggested that acid had been thrown in his eyes when he was a strikebreaker, or perhaps a striker. Fork kept his own counsel. Surely that levitation-performance was odd, extremely odd; so were other feats of his, I was to learn.

'That old Mustang!' Fork announced again, very loudly, to an uncaring Pentecost Road. He passed through the open doorway of the Mustang to seat himself at the blond piano in the middle of the smoky room. (The Mustang reeks with marijuana.) 'The regular, Ozzie,' Fork called to the barman. A waitress fetched him a tumbler of cheap whiskey. Having tossed off half his drink, Fork began to play that battered piano.

I remember that he played 'Redwing' — the taste of the elder spirits among the Mustang's patrons being oldfangled and sentimental; and he sang the lyrics in a melodious deep voice. 'The breeze is sighing, the night birds crying . . .' He elevated the lyrics from bathos to pathos. He was not a piano-player merely, but a pianist, this blind chap.

I asked the waitress the man's name. 'Homer Causland, but for the last two years they've called him Fork.' She added, *sotto voce,* 'Don't give him no cause to take offense.'

I shifted to a table beside the piano. 'Mr. Causland,' I said to him, 'have you ever played the organ?'

'You're from Jamaica?' he responded, without hesitation. His head turned in my direction, the hard taut face inscrutable.

'Not Long Island,' I answered. 'You've a good ear for speech, friend.'

'That's part of my survival strategy. You a doctor, maybe?'

'Of divinity, Mr. Causland. I'm rector of Holy Ghost Church.'

'If you need somebody to play the organ there, Doc, you could look further than me and do worse. What do you pay?'

We settled on five dollars a Sunday, all I could manage, but a substantial augmenting of Fork's income. I found that he could play Mendelssohn and Bach tolerably well from memory. Where Fork learned piano and organ, he never confided to me.

Pentecost Road took it for granted that Fork had 'blown his lid' on some narcotic, so accepting his eccentricity. I found him neither mad nor half-mad, odd though he was. He was quick-witted, shrewd, and capable of serious reflection. From listening to records and tapes for the blind he had picked up a miscellany of literary and philosophical knowledge. The recurrent extreme oddity of his public conduct — his acrobatic tricks (if such they were) and his shouting — I judged to be part of a general pose or blind (not to pun). Yet for what purpose this concealment of his real nature?

In the course of a month, I extracted from Fork and from others the explanation of his soubriquet 'Fork.' That account, set down below, may seem a digression; but it is bound up with the unnerving things that occurred during the past week at my church.

*   *

Pentecost Road respects one thing chiefly: successful violence, better even than riches. From such an act Fork Causland had obtained his familiar name and his high repute on Pentecost Road.

Occasionally fragments of conversation of a sinister bent may be overheard by a sharp-eared man who for drinks and tips plays the piano in rough saloons. In the Mustang, Homer Causland happened to gather enough of one tipsy dialogue to recognize it as a conspiracy to murder. He informed the police.

It was a gruesome, interesting case, that conspiracy to murder: but I am trying to be succinct. Despite Causland's warning, the murder in question actually was perpetrated — while the police were trying to fit Causland's testimony into the jigsaw puzzle of the suspected conspiracy. It was the killing, the prolonged and hideous slaughter, of a disobedient young prostitute.

Although Causland's evidence did not prevent the crime, it did enable the police to identify the three principal criminals, leaders of a 'vice ring.' They had been often arrested, yet scarcely ever convicted. Now the charge was homicide in the first degree. With his accustomed stoic courage, Causland testified fully in open court; the police rarely had been able to produce so convincing a witness. Nevertheless, an intimidated jury and a judge who disgraced the bench found the three accused not guilty.

One of the accused was a Big Man on Pentecost Road: big in narcotics, big in prostitution. Generally he was called Sherm; sometimes Sherm the Screamer, from his accustomed mode of addressing young women under his control; also, perhaps, because of his talent for compelling other people to scream. He had been tried under the name (doubtless an alias, his original name being unknown in our city) of Sherman Stanton. He was a youngish man, lean, curly-haired, even handsome except for the persistent sneer on his face. Nobody knew where Sherm had come from before he began to dominate Pentecost Road's traffic in drugs and flesh.

Such talented and aggressive criminals build up a following of young men and women, moved by the emulatory passion, in such districts as Hawkhill. Sherm, despite his nasty manners and ways, obtained a large and devoted band of disciples. What was less usual, he riveted his grip upon his dupes by posing as an occult prophet of sorts. Oh, he was clever!

We have a sufficient number of queer creeds in Jamaica, but Sherm's pseudoreligion was worse than any of those. In some ways his rubbish — cribbed from paperback novels, possibly — resembled the cult of Thuggee. How much of his own mystagogy about Kali and Ishtar did Sherm the Screamer actually believe? He was after domination of minds and bodies — especially bodies; but he seems to have subscribed to some of his own devilish dogmas. He claimed to be able to project his essence out of the body, and to travel as pure kinetic energy through space and time. Also he declared that he could not perish.

The pretense of exotic religiosity was of some utility to him. I am told that he tried to obtain exemption from property taxes for the storefront 'church' that was his ring's headquarters; and he hired a lawyer to plead the first clause of the First Amendment when police asked for a warrant to search that 'church.' One detective remarked unguardedly to a reporter, 'Hell, that "Church of Ishtar and Kali" is just a kinky bawdy-house.'

When I write that some of us are engaged in a holy war, I mean that literally. We are a scant rearguard, and we are losing, here below, in this fallen age. Like the Celts of the Twilight, we go forth often to battle, but rarely to victory.

Satan is come among us as a raging lion, having great wrath. Sherm was a limb of Satan: that too I mean literally. He corrupted and peddled young girls for the pleasure of seeing them destroyed. He laughed whenever he had persuaded some fool to burn out his own brains with hard drugs. In our day the Sherms multiply and prosper. You have only to spend a year in the neighborhood of Pentecost Road to understand that Satan is a person and a conscious force, no figure of myth merely. He takes possession of empty vessels.

On Pentecost Road I learned that the time is out of joint — and that though I could not set it right, still might I set my face against temptation, as did my patron Thomas à Becket. I digress: I must keep to the point, for the night cometh when no man shall work.

But at my back in a cold blast I hear
The rattle of the bones, and chuckle spread from ear to ear.

Yes, Sherm and his friends were set at liberty. This enabled them to deal with Causland, whose testimony had come near to getting them life sentences. Sherm the Screamer did not tolerate informers on Pentecost Road. Blind Homer Causland knew what to expect.

Prosecutor and police conveniently forgot Causland when the trial had ended in acquittal; they had plenty of fish to fry. Had he gone to the prosecutor's office, perhaps some nominal protection might have been extended to him; but Causland, a lone wolf, didn't bother. He hadn't the money, or perhaps the will, to leave the city altogether. Once upon a time Causland may have been good with a gun, possibly in line of duty; but a blind man has no use for such toys. All Causland could do was to wait upon the event, which might lie in the hand of God or in the hand of Satan.

On his way home from bill-posting one afternoon, Causland halted at a tumbledown secondhand shop. He had a speaking acquaintance with the proprietress, an alcoholic crone.

'What you rummagin' for today, Homer?'

'Garden tools, Mrs. Mattheson.'

'Pardon me sayin' so, but I didn't never hear of no blind man growin' no garden.' Mrs. Mattheson tittered at her own wit.

'Why, Mrs. Mattheson, a blind beggar can make a compost heap. Do you have in stock such a thing as a pitchfork?'

She did: an old rusty one, the upper part of its hickory shaft somewhat split. Causland fingered the crack, asked for a small saw, and skillfully sawed off the upper portion of the shaft, shortening the tool by a foot. He paid Mrs. Mattheson sixty-five cents for this purchase, and a quarter more for a little old greasy whetstone.

Causland lived in a tall brick house that had seen better days — much better. So had his ancient Christian Science landlady. A battered cast-iron fence still surrounded the yard. The several tenants, whatever their moral attributes, were tolerably clean and quiet. Three effeminate young men occupied most of the ground floor. Causland had one room on the top floor; a narrow staircase was the only normal means of access. But Causland's room was one of three in which the Christian Science landlady, Mrs. Bauer, took a peculiar pride. Those three had, or could have had, dumbwaiter service. The dumbwaiter was a forgotten token of genteel living on Merrymont Avenue. Though nothing much had gone up or down the dumbwaiter for years, its electric controls remained operable.

Causland's room had been furnished by the landlady. It was an old-fashioned widow's room, actually, with austere straight-backed chairs, cane-seated, bought cheaply about 1900; a vast heavy venerable wardrobe; an old chest; a pine table; a narrow iron bedstead. Everything was desiccated, and the lace curtains seemed ready to disintegrate. Yet the room was clean. Blind men, I suppose, are indifferent to furniture styles and the hues of wallpaper.

The one feature of that room to relieve the eye was the glossy-varnished oaken door to the dumbwaiter. It was a large dumbwaiter — possibly it had been used for carrying firewood and coals, before the house's fireplaces had been bricked up and papered over — so that a slim man might open the door and climb into the contraption, if he chose.

Causland's lodging-house stood on Merrymont, only three blocks east of my church. Here, in point of continuity, I digress again. By chance, one midnight I found myself strolling a few yards to Fork Causland's rear as he proceeded home. He was accompanied by boon companions, Old Soldiers, one on either side of him. It was a slippery winter night. The Old Soldiers reeled and staggered alarmingly, but Causland swaggered confidently between them, striking the sidewalk with his stick as he went, his derby roofed with snow.

'Where you livin' now, Fork?' one of those Old Soldiers ventured. 'Same place where — where you give it to 'em?'

'Same place, my friend: old Mother Bauer's, top floor, hot as a fry-pan in summer and cold as James Bay these winter months.'

'You don't have no bad feelin' about stayin' on there, Mr. Causland?' the other Old Soldier inquired. (This latter comrade was a white-bearded character known on Pentecost Road as The Ambassador from Poland.) 'I don't mean a troubled conscience, like they say. I mean — well, like sumpthin' might jump out an' grab you?'

'Ambassador,' Fork Causland said to his second henchman, 'keep on that way, and you'll earn yourself a split lip. Wahoo! Take me to old Mother Bauer's, boys, or I'll jump out and grab *you!* Wahoo!'

Then Fork performed another of those astonishing tricks of his. He took his stick between his teeth; flung himself straight upward with a muscular jump; as he descended, he thrust his rigid forefingers upon the arms of his tipsy companions. Then he rode along as if those two were his native bearers, his feet well clear of the ground, he seemingly supported only by those strong forefingers of his resting on the Old Soldiers' forearms.

His companions did not seem oppressed by his weight, though they kept their forearms extended and parallel with the ground, as if they had done Fork like service before. On they reeled for another block, Fork riding between them, chanting some old tune I did not recognize. When they were about to cross Thistle Street, Fork dropped back to the sidewalk to swagger along as before.

I have never seen such a thing done by anybody else. I do not know if this may have been some sort of acrobatic play. Surely the two Old Soldiers were not acrobats. I don't know how to convey the wonder that I felt at that moment. Was I wandering in a world of *maya*, of illusion? Could any man make himself weightless when he chose?

At some distance I followed the three companions to the walk that led up to Mrs. Bauer's house with the cast-iron railings. Causland slapped his comrades on the back, roared goodnight, and positively trotted all by himself up the steep steps of the porch, to vanish behind a handsome antique door. The Old Soldiers reeled onward, probably toward some dosshouse or the Salvation Army hostel; I retreated to my citadel of a rectory.

But I am running ahead of my proper narrative. Of course the above nocturnal mystery occurred long after the battle at Mrs. Bauer's lodginghouse, which converted Homer Causland into Fork Causland. I turn back to the dumbwaiter and the compost fork. Causland had whetted well the prongs' points. I surmise that there must have been a faint smile on his hard-as-nails sightless face as he fingered the tines.

*   *

No police patrol-cars rove Hawkhill at three of the morning. As Sergeant Shaugnessy said to me the other day, when I was imploring him for some effective help in rescuing girls, 'What's all the world to a man when his wife's a widdy?' At that hour especially, Hawkhill belongs to Satan's limbs like Sherm the Screamer.

Sherm brought with him to Mrs. Bauer's house, at three of the morning, nine of his boys. As matters turned out, it would have been more prudent to have fetched fewer helpers; but *hubris* now afflicted Sherm the Screamer. Having special plans for the informing blind piano-player, he prepared to fend off any interference. Probably the original design was to snatch Causland, lock him into the trunk of one of the cars, and transport him elsewhere, to be tormented at leisure — perhaps in Sherm's 'church.' Sherm left the drivers in both of the cars, with the motors running quietly.

A merciful providence had sent Mrs. Bauer crosstown that weekend to visit a niece. Sherm's boys had successfully jimmied the front door when one of the three limp-wristed young men living on the ground floor happened to open the door of their apartment, intending to put out a milk-bottle.

'What do you guys want?' he demanded. Eight men were filing into the corridor, all of them high on something costly. The tenant made out their faces. 'O God! Billie, call the cops!' he screeched back to one of his friends.

They sapped him the next moment, and burst over his body into the ground-floor apartment. This taste of blood broke the invaders' fragile control over themselves. Roaring, they worked over the other two young men with blackjacks and bars. (One of those unfortunates was crippled lifelong, after that night.) The victims' screams roused the tenant at the top of the house. Causland always had been a light sleeper.

Instantly he understood what must be occurring below. In no way could he assist the ground-floor trio. The diversion downstairs gave him three or four minutes' grace, and for such an event he had made some preparation. Being a very strong man, he was able to thrust the huge wardrobe hard against his door. Back of the wardrobe he forced the iron bedstead. Thus he filled completely the space between the doorway and the outer wall of his room. His door opening inward, this defensive strategy made it impossible for the door to be opened by his enemies, no matter how numerous and frantic they were: they might have to chop their way through with axes, or else use explosives. Either method would require time and noise. He was well aware of the possibility that, so baffled, they might instead burn down the whole house with him inside.

There was no salvation for him through a window — not three flights up, with no fire-escape, and he blind. With admirable presence of mind, Causland took his whole cash reserve, seventy dollars, from his moneybelt. The bills and some private papers he concealed under the carpet. Then he took up his pitchfork.

Now the gang came roaring up the stairs and burst against his barricaded door. He recognized some of the voices: they were careless in their howling, which signified that they did not mean him to come alive out of this, to bear witness against them. In particular he knew the torturer's voice of Sherm the Screamer.

'Come on, open up, Causland!' they were shouting, surprised at not being able to budge his door. 'We're just going to ask you some questions.' Causland said nothing in reply. He had no telephone in his room; and though he might shriek from a window, no one would rush to his assistance in this neighborhood, at this hour. No neighbor would venture so much involvement as to call the police, for that matter — not unless the tumult at Mrs. Bauer's house should threaten to spread to the adjacent houses.

Those smashing at his door were up to their eyes in cocaine, he guessed. Somebody out there was clearheaded enough to grunt, 'Get the door off the hinges!' But their superfluity of numbers hampered the assailants in that narrow corridor. Then someone screamed — oh, he knew that voice — 'There's another way!' Causland heard three or four men pounding back down the stairs. Meanwhile the savage smashing at the door continued.

Yes, there was another way: Sherm's men must have learned about Mrs. Bauer's dumbwaiter. That device was no escape-route for Homer Causland, for its mechanism could not be operated from within the dumbwaiter itself, and besides, what figure would a blind man make, emerging below, helpless before his enemies? Therefore Causland took his stand in a shadowy convenient corner, as he had planned, awaiting the event.

The clanking of the dumbwaiter's chain and the growling of its motor, like Hallowe'en sound-effects, gave Causland plenty of notice of his enemy's approach. The car in the shaft halted opposite the aperture of Causland's room now; the man within knew what he was doing. It still might have been possible for Causland to press the 'down' button by the dumbwaiter door, in hope of returning the car to the ground floor. But Causland preferred tactics more decisive.

'Hold it, Ralph!' the man in the car shouted to his helper below. 'I'm getting out.' It was the Screamer's dreadful voice.

Sherm had risen by audacity. And after all, how much resistance could be offered by a blind piano-player, twice Sherm's years?

Sherm banged open the dumbwaiter door and began to scramble through the narrow opening, into the total darkness of Causland's room. He cracked his head against the oaken door-frame, trying to emerge quickly, and cursed. Happily for Fork, as matters turned out, Sherm was carrying a sawed-off shotgun. 'Homer Causland, you old stoolie,' the Screamer screamed, 'get down on your knees and start begging!'

'Hi!' said Causland softly, from the shadows. 'I've got something here for you, Screamer.' As Sherm swung toward him, raising the shotgun, Causland lunged. He contrived to drive the prongs of the fork straight through Sherm's lean belly. The force of Causland's rush bowled Sherm over, and Causland fell upon him. 'Goodbye, Sherm,' Causland panted.

Then Sherm the Screamer screamed his loudest ever. Causland heard the shotgun crash to the floor of his room. Groping about, he encountered the shaft of the fork; he tried to extract it from the belly of his enemy, whose heels were drumming on the floor. But this was an awkward undertaking, and Causland feared that meanwhile the door of his room might be taken off behind him.

So, panting, he managed in the darkness to thrust the dying Sherm, head first, back into the dumbwaiter. Blind Homer pressed the 'down' button, sending the fatal car on its return journey to bear back to his disciples the Screamer, perforated, with the fork still in him. Like the beasts, the Prophet Sherm could perish, after all.

Disposing of Sherm had required about one minute. Yes, the door had been lifted off its hinges now; Causland's ears informed him that his adversaries were trying to kick their way through the second barrier, the sturdy back of the enormous wardrobe.

From the bottom of the stairs, a member of the gang shouted up, desperate, '*Christ, guys, he's gutted Sherm!* Get through that door and smash him!'

Causland had the shotgun in his hands: a double-barrelled repeater. His fingers checked its triggers and magazine. This gun would do very well.

Shifting his station to the foot of the iron bedstead, seven feet from the tottering wardrobe, he pointed the barrels carefully. There was mighty confusion beyond that blocked doorway, some men running upstairs and others downstairs. Sherm's screams from below seemed less vigorous; Causland had angled his fork somewhat upward when he had made that dread thrust.

Now the carved doors of the wardrobe splintered into fragments, and a big body became entangled with the bedhead, struggling to enter the room. Causland gave this intruder one barrel.

In the little bedroom that reverberation was exquisitely painful to Causland's sensitive auditory nerves; but the result of his discharge was exquisitely gratifying. A body crashed backward. Later Causland learned that he had aimed a trifle high, so taking off the man's face.

Now Causland must carry the war into Africa. Risky strategy, that; yet not so risky as to wait for the gang to set the house afire. Gun at the ready, Causland clambered over some bloody bulky thing, through the demolished wardrobe. To clear the way, he fired the second barrel at a venture into the corridor beyond.

Someone else shrieked, fell, lay groaning hideously. Causland heard the whole crowd of them tumbling back down the stairs. Kneeling to thrust his weapon between the wooden balusters, the blind champion fired downward, both barrels. To judge by the anguished complaints, he had severely damaged one or two of the enemy.

Somebody fired back — a pistol, Causland thought — but missed him. Vexed, Causland gave them both barrels a second time: more screaming. It was like old times overseas.

At that moment, the horn of one car waiting at the curb began to honk furiously; then the horn of the second car. Later he was told that the drivers, on edge, had heard the siren of an ambulance on Pentecost Road and had taken that for a patrol-car.

Causland struggled back into his room. A small window looked toward Merrymont Avenue. Flinging up the sash, Causland fired into the blackness toward the honking. He heard the cars begin to pull away; again Causland fired in their direction. To his pleased surprise, there came a loud resounding bang, but not a gunshot: he must have hit a tire. A moment later a crash followed, for the car with a blown front tire, in fact, had careered across the street and struck a tree.

The other car roared away. Causland heard the running feet of the members of the gang abandoned by the driver. Then the house fell silent except for the horrid moaning of the man whom Causland had shot in the third-floor corridor.

Having made his way down to Mrs. Bauer's telephone, Causland called the police. After five or six minutes, some of the bolder spirits in the neighborhood actually ventured out of their lairs and began to converse, in hushed tones, before Mrs. Bauer's house. But nobody dared ascend the steps until the police arrived.

Sergeant Shaugnessy and his men found one man dead, three dying, one shot in the legs and unable to walk, one stunned in a car that had rammed a tree, and gouts of blood on the sidewalk from one or two others who had escaped. Sherm the Screamer gave up the ghost in the ambulance bearing him to the hospital.

In Causland's phrase, 'Sergeant Shaugnessy was flabbergasted but appreciative. They didn't indict me for anything.'

After that he was 'Fork' to boon companions and 'Mr. Causland' to the less privileged. Nobody gave him trouble thereafter. He had attained the equivocal distinction of general recognition as Hawkhill's most accomplished resident. It is said in the Mustang that Fork sent a basket of poison ivy to Sherm's funeral; but that report I doubt. Wondrous to relate, all but two of the survivors of the attempt on Fork Causland were convicted on charges of attempted murder, criminal assault, unlicensed possession of a deadly weapon, or breaking and entering.

Fork Causland's fearsome reputation enabled him to walk the streets of Hawkhill at any hour, unmugged. There arose a popular belief that in reality he was not blind at all, but had especially keen sight behind those dark goggles. Some took him for an undercover detective. Who could have killed Sherm and his boys without seeing them? Or conceivably — this suggestion occurring particularly among Hawkhill's West Indian element — Causland was a conjure-man, invulnerable and deadly.

Yes, he swaggered along the nocturnal streets. Yet the Screamer's band was not extinct; and those two who had survived the encounter at Mrs. Bauer's, and had not been imprisoned, would not forget. Fearsomeness wears thin with time, and the disciples of Sherm might take heart again. But Fork said no word of that.

*   *

No one could enter my church without my knowledge. I must make that point wholly clear. Were it not so, there might be some quasi-rational explanation of last night's events.

What is rare in American churches of the Romanesque revival, the Church of the Holy Ghost has a narthex, or galilee. (I prefer the latter term.) Above the broad steps frequented by the Old Soldiers of Merrymont Avenue, the great doors open upon this galilee, which traditionally is less sacred than the body of the church.

Within this interior porch, or galilee, I conduct most of my business with comers to the church — particularly with the street girls. In a vaulted chamber off the galilee I maintain a desk, some chairs, and a typewriter; this chamber has a functioning fireplace. I frequent this sentry-post (so to speak) of the Holy Ghost because it is situated near the grand entrance to the church's west front. Only at this point may the whole church complex be entered nowadays.

For I have sealed the several other entrances, even that to the 'service' regions of the complex, although closing the other doors has made it necessary for Lin, the Cambodian man whom I have appointed verger (janitor, in reality), to transport rubbish in a barrow to the west front. When I write 'sealed,' I mean bricked up. No doubt I have violated fire inspectors' rules; but the public authorities, winking at worse offenses in Hawkhill, have not troubled me concerning my precautions.

The small roundheaded windows of the church, on the northern side, are set too high for burglars to operate without ladders; also they are narrow, with a stone pillar fixed in the middle of each window-arch. The rector who preceded me in this living (!) had a heavy wire screen attached to the outer side of every window, to protect the painted glass from boys' stones. The southern windows face upon the cloister, not upon a street, and in effect are protected by the tall rectory.

A benefaction from old Mrs. Simmons enabled me to secure the windows of the adjoining rectory with interior steel shutters. I have sealed the rectory's street doors, now reaching my rooms there by passing through the galilee and the cloister on the church's south side. Need I remark that no building is entirely secure against intruders who possess special tools for burglary? However that may be, on the nights to which I refer below these defenses of the Holy Ghost were undisturbed, and no alarm sounded on the electronic warning system purchased out of the Simmons benefaction. I am satisfied that no one could have entered the church except through the galilee.

In one of the massive bronze doors (opened only on great feast days) of the west front is set a kind of postern door, also of bronze, so narrow as to admit only one person at a time. It is this small door through which everybody and everything pass ordinarily. Only the verger and I possess keys to this door, which moreover is secured within, when I am there, by a police-lock and other devices. My small vaulted reception-chamber or office is situated close to this postern, so that when I am at my desk I may see who enters and leaves the church. I am as much porter as rector. Thus all of my parishioners, and other callers, must pound the enormous bronze knocker or ring the electric bell, if they would see me.

The sacred vessels, the tapestries, and other furnishings of the Church of the Holy Ghost being highly valuable, efficient robbers might be attracted — were it not for the smoke-grimed exterior of the building, which suggests impoverishment and dereliction. I had provided as best I might against casual thieves, and for the safety of the complex's temporary or permanent inmates. Yet all these precautions seemed futile last night.

It should be understood that during daylight hours I make the nave accessible for private devotions (not that many take advantage of the opportunity) or for the rare visitor interested in the architecture of the Holy Ghost Church. I do try to make sure that either the verger or his Cambodian wife (who does our mopping and the like) is present in nave or galilee during the hours when the postern door is unlocked. So it is barely conceivable that some person might have crept into the church and concealed himself until yesterday night, perhaps in the blindstory. Yet such an explanation is even more improbable than the supposition I will imply toward the close of this document.

When Fork Causland became our church organist, I offered him a key to the church, but he refused it, saying that he could ring for the verger or myself. From the first I was confident of his honesty. In corrupted Hawkhill, he appeared to have no corrupt habits. Though fond of whiskey, Fork never was drunken. He paid little or no attention to the girls hanging about the bars where he played the piano. The pushers feared him. His conversation was always decent and sometimes amusing. Considerably to my surprise, I found that he was familiar with our liturgy and that he prayed in church.

From asides in his talk, I gathered that he had been a wanderer, a beggar, a peddler, an acrobat, a carnival hand, a soldier — not in that order, presumably, but at one time or another. Was his proficiency at killing derived from military experience only? Two or three times I entered the church to hear the *Dies Irae* pouring from the organ: Fork at practice in his grim humorous fashion. 'Doc,' he would say, descending from his bench, 'it will be with this city as with the cities of the plain.' He was apt at biblical quotations and curious applications of them.

Yet I cannot say that we grew intimate. My situation is lonely; I have no Hawkhill friends; I would have been glad if Fork had accepted my offer of a room in the rectory, that echoing habitation not being less homelike than his room at Mrs. Bauer's. He thanked me, but said, 'I'm not a comfortable neighbor, Doc.'

I do not think that he held my color against me — not that he could discern it literally. And aside from chance drinking-companions, clearly he had no friends of his own. He seemed armored by a self-sufficient stoicism. I envied him that.

I inquired discreetly about Fork among my parishioners and among the denizens of Pentecost Road. Nobody seemed to know how long Causland had lived in Hawkhill. Some said, 'Always, I guess'; others, 'Three years, maybe'; yet others, 'Never noticed him till this past winter.' So far as I could ascertain, nobody ever had conversed seriously with Fork longer than I had. His oddity had tended to deter familiarities even before his bloody amazing victory at Mrs. Bauer's house. After Fork had killed Sherm and his chums, a certain deadliness seemed to hang about the piano-player. (I did not sense it myself, I refer to a discernible reverent uneasiness among the habitués of the Pentecost bars.) Despite Fork's isolation, somehow I fancied that of all the grotesques of Pentecost Road, he alone was permanent, the rest evanescent.

Occasionally, after he had practiced at the creaky old vast organ, Causland and I talked in a parlor of the rectory, over tea brewed by the Cambodian woman. (Both of us took rum in our tea, in that damp stone building.) Fork could converse sensibly; also somewhat mystically. He knew all of Hawkhill's secrets, and sometimes hinted at mysteries of the world beyond the world, as if he were Tiresias, or Homer, or some other blind seer. Now and again he deferred, during these talks, to my theological learning — or what he took for my erudition.

'Doc,' he inquired at the session I best recollect, 'what's possession? Being possessed by a spirit, I mean.'

I endeavored to explain the church's doctrine concerning this, but that was not what he wished to know.

'I mean, Doc, how does it *feel*? Can something get inside you, and yet leave room enough for yourself? Can you be comfortable with it? Can you live with it as if it were your brother? Can it help you?'

Naturally I was startled by this. 'Are you talking about yourself, Fork?'

He nodded. 'I think there's been somebody else with me for years now. Once, Doc, you said something about "levitation" and that jumping I do — but then you beat around the bush. Well, it's not St. Vitus's dance, Doc. Something that's got into me does the jumping — not that I object much. And when I was in real need, it lent me its sight.'

I drew a long breath. 'You're talking about the time Sherm came for you?'

'That's it. I know the Old Soldiers say I can really see whenever I want to. But that's a lie.' He tapped his goggles. 'I could take these off to show you what's underneath my eyelids, Doc; but that would give you a turn. All the same, somebody or something lent me sight that rough time.'

Fork's one indulgence, not counting the free whiskies, was Brazilian cigars. He unwrapped one now, and I lit it for him.

He puffed on the black wrinkled thing. 'I've told this to nobody but you, Doc. Let me tell you, it came as a blessed shock to me. I'd made my preparations blinder than any bat, and I didn't expect miracles. But when it happened, everything was coming at me so quick that I just accepted the sight, no questions asked at the moment. It didn't come upon me until the last chance. You better believe me, Doc.' He blew smoke from his nostrils.

'I kept this quiet because anybody that dared would have called me a damned liar. The moment Sherm pushed open that dumbwaiter door, sight came to me.

'Or maybe I shouldn't say "sight": well, "perception" — that's more the word. I seemed to see outlines. There was a twenty-watt bulb dangling in the dumbwaiter, and Sherm was outlined against it. That was no time for musing on miracles. I knew he couldn't make out hide nor hair of me. His outline, sort of like a paper doll, turned toward me, blindlike, when I spoke to him, and the outline of a shotgun went up to his shoulder. That cleared the way for me to dive under the gun and run him through the belly.'

Deftly he relit his cigar.

'Mind you, Doc, I could make out only movement. So once I sent the elevator back down to the ground floor, I was blind as before. But when one of the gang broke through the wardrobe, I made out the shape of him plain, and blew the face off him. Then when I pushed into the corridor my-

371

self, I could — well, perceive, I guess — perceive the lot of Sherm's boys running back downstairs, and I fired into the midst of them. And when I gave both barrels to that car outside the house, I could see the thing moving away from the curb. After that, right after that last shot, whatever lent the perception to me took it back again. Is there a name for what happened to me, Doc?'

'Not a medical term, Fork,' I said to him. 'There's a psychological term: extrasensory perception. Lord knows what that means.'

'You half believe me, don't you, Doc? Nobody else would. Well, what about the possession? Do you half believe that, too?'

Now the sun had sunk beneath the level of the barred windows of my rectory; we had no light but the glow from the coals in my fireplace. I shivered. 'What could it be that's got into you? May it be a devil, do you think?'

'I'm asking you, Doc. How the hell should I know?' Fork sprang up and performed a little song-and-dance routine in my parlor, chanting:

'He's a devil, he's a devil,
He's a devil in his hometown.
On the level, he's a devil . . .'

Then Fork sat down as abruptly as he had risen.

'Look out, Doc: that was it, the thing in me, just now. He hears you. But no, I don't think it's a demon. It's a killer, though, and not pretty.'

The parlor door swung open; we both jumped at the sound and the draught of cold air. But it was only the verger's wife, my housekeeper, come to carry off the tea things. Evidently Fork thought that he had uttered too much already, for he clapped his derby on his large head and went out, back toward Pentecost Road.

We never had opportunity to resume that chilling conversation about the possessed and the possessor. I suspect that Fork may have been capable of elaborate hoaxes, for the fun of them — but not on that dark subject.

*　　　*

How often, my gun under my jacket, have I strolled almost the length of Pentecost Road, praying as I ambled! Desperate though the neighborhood is, some franchise eating-houses make a good profit there, at high nocturnal risk to their cashiers. Much of the Road is brightly lit by neon. 'Twenty Gorgeous Bottomless Dancers, Stark Naked or Your Money Back,' one sign blinks on and off. I pass four or five massage parlors.

Shoddy little theaters for X-rated films (their marquees promising more than they can deliver, in competition with the living flesh next door or down the road); 'adult' bookshops for retarded adolescents and middle-aged illiterates; scantly stocked tiny 'notion' shops that are fronts for narcotics-peddling — these are the thriving enterprises of Pentecost Road, in this year of our Lord. The hideousness of it hurts as much as the depravity.

Now I have to write about Julie Tilton.

There is no coincidence: everything that occurs is part of a most intricate design.

The Mustang, where the daiquiris are good (though nothing else there has any admixture of good in it), is situated at the intersection of Pentecost and Merrymont. A great deal of money changes hands, more or less surreptitiously, at those corners. For that reason the sidewalk outside the Mustang is frequented by mendicants. I usually give something to the old man with no legs, selling pencils, who rides a board to which four roller-skates are fixed; he is there on the bitterest days. Another begging habitué is the idiot woman shaped like an interrogation point. Also 'religious' freaks are to be seen, especially an Indian fakir in nothing but a loincloth.

The beggars and the madmen are outnumbered by the street girls, some promenading, some lounging against the wall, awaiting custom. Few are birds of paradise. I labor under no delusion about harlots. With very rare exceptions, the kindly prostitute is a creation of novelists and playwrights. As a class, such women are psychopathic, devouring, and treacherous. They have their uses, particularly to the police: in the hope of reward, or out of unblemished malice, they betray their bullies and lovers. I have discovered among them, on Pentecost Road, no heroic repentant Magdalene. All that I can accomplish among them, pastorally, is to persuade a few of the young ones, strutting down Pentecost under compulsion, to go back to their parents or to whoever in the hometown might receive them. I have facilitated a number of such escapes, after conversations at my office in the galilee. The first stage on my underground railway is a lodging for a night in that safe-house, my rectory. They do not tempt me. Ever since my ordination, I have kept myself under a most strict discipline; and even had I not vowed myself to celibacy and chastity, still I would be no fool — though sensual, more sensual than most, by nature.

On Monday evening, as I approached the Mustang, the girls were particularly numerous and importunate. I shouldered my way among them — black hat, black face, black leather jacket — in my role of hard-drinking impecunious chiropractor. Just outside the door of the Mustang someone gripped me by the arm — but not with the customary unimaginative 'Want to have some fun, honey?' This person was saying, 'Brother, have you been washed in the blood of the Lamb?'

I swung round. It was a young black man, fantastically dressed, a street preacher, wild-eyed. He had a companion.

This colleague, seated in a sort of primitive wheelchair, was paler than death. He did not move a muscle, not even of lips or eyes. At first I took him for a paralytic, trundled about for a holy show by his preacher-captor. Then the thought flashed through my mind that this white boy, bare-headed, neatly dressed, might be a corpse: things not much less shocking are seen from time to time at Pentecost and Merrymont.

'Brother, have you been saved?' the mad preacher was demanding of me. 'Have you been washed in the blood of the Lamb?'

I unfixed his hand from my arm. 'Nobody can answer that question with full knowledge, brother,' I told him.

But already he had turned from me and was addressing the passing streams of tarts, procurers, pushers, drunkards, and males of various ages 'out for a little fun.' 'Brothers and sisters,' he was crying, 'where'll you spend eternity? Wine is a mocker, strong drink is raging, and whoever is deceived thereby is not wise.'

He then plucked the white boy out of his chair and exhibited him at arm's length to the street-people. Praise be, the pallid thing was an inanimate manikin, marvelously realistic, after all. I wouldn't have to telephone Shaugnessy.

''Cept you take the Lord Jesus for your personal saviour, you're no better'n this here dummy!' the wild-eyed preacher was shouting. 'Where you goin' to spend eternity? You want to spend it with the Whore o' Babylon and the Beast, whose number is six six six? The wages of sin is death. You want to be like this here dummy, no brains in your head? You want to be cast into the fire eternal? Brothers and sisters, death is all around us. Old Mister Death, he comes here, he comes there. Old Mister Death, he grabs you when you're on a high, when you're drinkin' and fornicatin', and he takes the breath out o' your body, leavin' you no better than this here dummy! He takes you where the worm never dieth and the fire is not quenched. 'Cept you follow the Lord Jesus, Ol' Man Death put his bony hands on you, and you curl up like a worm. . . .'

Two mighty hands took me by the shoulders, from behind. Their clutch was terribly painful; a shock like electricity ran through me. 'Gottcha, Doc!' said Fork. 'You come along with me into this hell on earth they call the Mustang. Wahoo!'

His ears had singled me out in the crowd by my few words in retort to the street-preacher.

'In a minute, Fork, you Beast from the Abyss,' I muttered.

With his stick tucked under his arm, the blind man stood beside me, listening to the crazy preacher. 'It always was a scandal, that faith, eh, Doc?' He poked me in the ribs with the head of his stick. 'That there raving and ranting fellow — sort of like a caricature of you, eh, Doc?'

'Go to hell, Fork,' I told him.

'All in good time, Doc; all in God's own good time.' He chuckled harshly.

''Cept you repent, brothers and sisters, you gonna die the body of this death,' the crazy preacher was exhorting some tarts and three beggars. He brandished the manikin. 'No brains, jes' like this here dummy; no heart, no guts, no nothin'. If you don't have no immortal soul washed in the blood of the Lamb, you got nothin'. Old Mister Death, he got your 'pointed day writ down on his calendar, you poor dummies. . . .'

'You've got some competition in the soul business, Doc,' said Fork, half-needling me, half-serious. We were entering the Mustang. 'You ever repent of taking up this line of work? Feel sorry about not marrying, and taking up the cross in Hawkhill?'

'It's a calling, Mr. Homer Causland; I wouldn't have it any other way. What's your calling? Speaking of Old Man Death, killing seems to be your talent.'

'In the line of duty, Doc: add that qualification. You're welcome to call me a rat, Reverend Doc. On one of those records for no-eyes, once, I heard a poem by some Scotchman about a rat's prayer:

> 'God grant me that
> I carrion find,
> And may it stink;

O Father, kind,
  Permit me drink
Of blood ensoured . . .
  There is no waste
Where rats are fed,
  And, for all haste,
Grace shall be said.'

Fork had astounded me once again. 'In what corner of hell did you hear that, you blind devil?'

'Devil? Not quite that, Doc; devil's cousin, maybe. Wahoo!'

He sat down at his piano, called for his whiskey, and began to play. I took a table near him. The Mustang was two-thirds full, that night, of the lost. The blind devil played for them like an angel. Even to acid rock he imparted a sombre pathos; or so it sounded to my priestly ears.

I was roused out of a reverie brought on by Fork's 'not marrying' when a girl's voice, a sweet one, said, 'Excuse me, sir.' She withdrew a chair from my table, turned it in Fork's direction, and sat waiting for him to pause in his playing. I saw her in profile.

She was beautiful, but more than beautiful: lovely. She wore her blonde hair long, very long. Nose, lips, and chin all were delicate and perfect; so was her figure. She was six feet tall at least. Her blue eyes were impossibly innocent. I judged her to be sixteen or seventeen years old. This was nobody off Pentecost Road. Face aside, she was dressed too decently for that.

When Fork had stopped playing, she said to him, 'Excuse me, sir. Maybe you can help me. Have you seen Alexander Tilton?'

Fork turned toward her his poker face with its black goggles, taking the cigar from his mouth. He removed his derby. 'Why do you ask a blind man a question like that, lady?'

I watched her blush. Her fair skin was suffused with a soft delicious pink. 'Oh, I'm sorry; I didn't know. I thought you looked like a man who might have met a good many people in this part of town.'

'I do, lady, but I never met anybody by that name. Doc, could you check at the bar?'

I rose. Who wouldn't do anything for this young lady? Indeed, I bowed the first bow ever executed in the Mustang.

'Meet the Reverend Raymond Montrose, rector of Holy Ghost Church, lady, even if he doesn't look it.'

'I don't want to disturb you, Reverend Montrose,' the beauty said. She blushed again.

'It's a pleasure, young lady,' I assured her, stuttering a little. 'But not "Reverend Montrose," if you please. Father Montrose, or Dr. Montrose, or even Mr. Montrose; but never Reverend Montrose. I'm a stickler for forms, being an Anglo-Catholic.'

'Oh, I'm a Methodist, I'm afraid, Father.'

'Don't be afraid, not even in this bar. Excuse me, Miss . . .'

'I'm Julie Tilton, and Alexander Tilton is my brother, twelve years older. The last letter he sent us was on the stationery of the Tangiers Motel, Pentecost Road, and so I got a room there, half an hour ago, but they hadn't heard of him and said somebody at the Mustang Bar might know him. I took a taxi straight here.' She was genuine!

'You better check out of the Tangiers Motel, lady; they got something worse than the veterans' disease there. Doc, stop your bowing and scraping, and ask after one Alexander Tilton at the bar. I'll keep an eye on this Miss Tilton, in a manner of speaking.' Fork resumed his derby.

The bartender and the waitresses hadn't ever heard of an Alexander Tilton, they informed me. When I returned to the piano, I found three unpleasant young toughs standing by Fork and the girl, flies drawn to honey.

'How about a dance, baby?' said the biggest of them.

'Move on, brothers,' I told them. They stared at me.

'You heard Doc,' Fork growled. 'Scoot, boys.'

They went, swearing, but softly.

'Pay them no mind, lady,' said Fork. 'They'll get their comeuppance before long, I promise you. Now this brother of yours — what did he look like?'

'My grandmother and I haven't seen him for nearly ten years, but he must still be very good-looking. He's about as tall as I am, and slim. The girls back home were wild about him. He got one — but that doesn't matter now.' Another blush.

'He used to write about once a year,' she went on; 'then, better than two years ago, he stopped writing. I thought that everybody around here must know him, because he did so well in this city. He sent lots and lots of money for us to keep for him. "Bury it in the cellar in tight cans," he wrote to us. Some people don't trust banks, I guess, and he's one of them. He even sent the cash in little sealed boxes, by special messengers! Except for letting us know his money was on its way, Sherm never told us much in his letters.'

'*Sherm?*' said Fork, drawing out the name.

'Here in Hawkhill, Miss Tilton,' I put in, 'a good many people get lost — and not found. I thought you said your brother's name was Alexander.'

'Oh, it is, Father Montrose: Alexander Sherman Tilton. But we've called him Sherm in the family ever since I can remember.'

Fork, silent, relit his cigar.

'Possibly there are other ways you might identify your brother, Miss Tilton,' I continued. 'His voice, for instance: was it soft as yours?'

She smiled angelically. 'Oh, no. Sherm always spoke very loudly — loud enough to hurt some people's ears. When he was angry, could he ever yell!'

'Ummm,' from Fork. 'Now this brother Sherm, lady: did he ever use other names?'

'Not that I know of. Why should he? But perhaps he used the "Alexander" in this town, because he always signed his letters to us that way, as if he had gotten more formal. It was just "Alexander," not signing his last name. We mailed back letters to Alexander Tilton, at the post office box number he gave us; but he never answered until he decided to send more money home.'

I presented to her my engraved card, in the hope of achieving in Miss Tilton's admirable eyes a respectability that my beard and my fancy boots would not convey to her. Or might she, untraveled, fancy that all doctors of divinity went about so attired? 'Did you have some particular reason,' I inquired, 'for coming all this distance to look for your brother?'

'No, Father; it's just that he's my only brother, and I haven't any sisters, and Dad and Mom died five years ago. In his last letter, Sherm told me that I ought to come to the big city and live with him; that I'd really go places here. He practically ordered me to come. I wrote back that I would, whenever he wanted me to. He didn't answer me, though, so I waited until after graduation, and at last I decided that the thing for me to do was simply to come here and look him up. Here I am!'

Yes, here she was, Iphigenia in Aulis, come unwitting to the sacrifice. Here she was, a brand for me to snatch pastorally before she had been even singed!

'This gentleman at the piano is our church organist, Mr. Fork Causland,' I informed her. I gave Fork a gentle stealthy dig in his ribs. 'He and I will do what we can to help you.'

'Sure, lady,' Fork said. 'I wouldn't go asking around this here bar, if I was you.'

378

The three unpleasant young men had not scooted very far: I noticed them standing at the bar, scowling at us. I recollected, or thought I recollected, that two of them had been surreptitiously pointed out to me, months ago, as survivors of the Screamer's gang. It wouldn't do to linger. I put my hand on Fork's shoulder.

'The two of us had best take Miss Tilton back in a taxi to the Tangiers Motel, Fork, and get her bags now. I can put her up at the rectory, if she doesn't mind.'

'Right, Doc — I guess. There's too many vermin at the Tangiers, lady. Just one more question, before we go.' Fork swallowed the remnant of his whiskey. 'Brother Sherm — in his last letter, better than two years ago, did he give you any idea of what he was going to have you doing in this town?'

'I'm quite a good typist, Mr. Fork, but Sherm didn't mention that. All he suggested was that he knew a lot of interesting boys to take me out.' Here she colored more furiously than before.

We made our way to the door, I running interference. All the men in the Mustang were staring, and three or four whistled loudly. 'Where you takin' that kid, Fork?' somebody called out. Somebody else muttered, 'For Christsake, don't rile him.'

A taxi was at the curb, letting out a drunken fare. Julie Tilton got in with us two strangers, ingenuously. Possibly my 'cute British accent' was reassurance of sorts. With no other two men from the Mustang would she have been able to check out of the Tangiers uninsulted — or worse than that. Coincidence again? I think not.

'I fancy you come from a rather small town, Miss Tilton,' I said on our way to the motel.

'How did you know, Father? Titus isn't much more than a church, a general store, and a dozen houses. Sherm used to call it Hicksville or Endsville.'

'How you gonna keep 'em down on the farm, after they've seen Hawkhill?' Fork had been humming. He ceased, saying, 'Julie, pardon my asking, but was this brother Sherm in more sorts of trouble than one, when he left Titus nearly ten years ago?'

'He got himself into a peck of troubles, Mr. Fork. But he must have straightened himself up, or he couldn't have earned all that money to send home.'

At the flashy Tangiers, I thought it prudent to go with Julie to her room for her suitcase. I was pleased and somewhat surprised to find the bag still there; they had not given her a key for her room. While Julie and I were down the hall, the desk clerk tried to make trouble about this guest being taken away by two men, but Fork gave him the rough side of his tongue. Undoubtedly the desk clerk had plans for the lady guest. He asked her to come back any time; he meant it.

'How you goin' to keep 'em away from Pentecost, jazzin' around, paintin' the town?' Fork was humming as we drew up before the Church of the Holy Ghost.

The lovely big girl was overwhelmed by the scale of my church.

'This must be a very religious town, Father Montrose! I hope I'm not causing your wife too much trouble.'

'Once upon a time, it was. I'm celibate, Miss Tilton. Our housekeeper, the verger's wife, will get your room in order and bring you tea — and a sandwich, if you'd care for one.' Providentially, no fugitive street-girl was lodged in the rectory that night. I unlocked the postern door, and we three entered.

The galilee of my church had taken the galilee of Durham Cathedral for its model, in part. The rows of pillars, and the roundheaded arches with their chevron moldings, took Julie's breath away. From my office, I rang a bell connected with the verger's rooms at the top of the rectory, summoning the little Cambodian woman, whose English was tolerable.

We had our ingenue safe out of the Mustang, safe out of the Tangiers Motel. What next?

'Will it be all right for me to stay here until I find my brother?' Julie asked, as the verger's wife waited to lead her across the cloister. 'I don't know how to repay you, Father. I'm sure that Sherm's somewhere very close; I just simply feel it.'

*　　　*

'We could have ridden on to Mrs. Simmons's, Doc. She'd have taken the girl in if you'd asked her. It wouldn't have been like imposing a street-walker on the old lady.'

'She's safer in the rectory, Fork.'

We two sat in my office off the galilee. It was midnight, and Miss Tilton doubtless was sleeping the sleep of the guiltless — a few rods distant from me.

'Maybe,' said Fork. 'Probably they're looking for her right now.'

'Who in particular?'

'Those three that wanted to dance with her at the Mustang. The guy that spoke to her and gave us some lip — I knew his voice. He was one of the two acquitted after my fracas at Mrs. Bauer's. His name's Franchetti. He was Sherm's number one enforcer. He's getting his nerve back, two years after the treatment I gave his pals. Sherm's sister would be worth plenty to him.'

'Is she actually Sherm's sister?'

'Why not? It all fits together. I bet Franchetti saw they were two peas in a pod. Sherm must have told his boys she'd be along. What does the girl look like?'

'A rose in bloom.' I had not been able to keep my eyes off young Miss Tilton; I supplied particulars, perhaps too enthusiastically.

'That's enough detail, Doc. Sherm was a good-looking goon, except for the smirk, they tell me. He was her height, her coloring, and "Sherman Stanton" is close enough to "Sherman Tilton."'

'But her coming straight to the man who executed her brother? That's too much of a coincidence, Fork.'

'There's wheels within wheels, Doc. She was sent, God knows why. It did give me a jolt when she said "Sherm," let me tell you.'

We fell silent for a minute or two.

'We can't let Julie know what her brother was, nor how he ended,' I said then.

Fork nodded. 'She's got to go back to Titus, pronto.'

'It won't be simple to persuade her of that, at least for a few days. She says her intuition tells her that Sherm's near at hand. Girls and their notions!'

'She may not be so far wrong, Doc. That's been my intuition, too.'

'Don't be a fool, Fork.'

'I never would have lasted this long if I'd been a fool, not with the life I've led. Now look: in this here Middle Ages church of yours, you've talked to me more than once about death and judgment. You're a Middle Ages parson, Doc, and I'm with you. What's the teaching about what you've called "the interval"?'

He had cornered me with my own doctrine. 'I know what you're thinking, Fork. Once upon a time, everybody believed it. When a man dies, that's not the end of his personality — not until the Last Judgment. There may be a kind of half-life, though the body has perished. After all, in the twentieth century we know that what we call "matter" is a collection of electrical particles, held in an arrangement by a power we don't understand. That arrangement falls apart when a body disintegrates; but the particles, the energy . . . ah, there's the rub, Fork. Even a consciousness may survive, Fork, in a twilight realm of which we receive glimpses, sometimes, that startle us, the living. Until the Last Judgment, what we call ghosts . . .'

'All right, Doc: that's your teaching. You believe it?'

'Yes.'

'And you believe in possession?'

'Yes.'

'Sherm was possessed, Doc, if ever a man was. Maybe I am, though not in the same way. Something might possess you. Watch your step.'

'What do you mean?'

'You ought to know, Doc.'

I shrugged that off. Another interval of silence followed. Then I said, 'Why did Sherm tell Julie to come to Hawkhill?'

'Unnatural affection, Doc. After he'd taken his pleasure with her, he'd have peddled her on Pentecost Road.'

I crossed myself. 'Lord! And this girl!'

'Sherm drove out any goodness that had been in him, leaving himself empty. A demon entered in. You better believe me, Doc.'

I let my friend out of the church then, and he went his way into the darkness intrepidly; standing at the postern, I heard his stick striking the sidewalk occasionally as he made his way toward that desiccated room at Mrs. Bauer's.

Having secured the door, I passed through nave and choir to the apse. Tall archaic carvings of saints loomed above me. For half an hour I knelt in prayer. 'Pray for us sinners now and at the hour of our death.' I prayed even for Sherm, unlikely creature. As I passed back through the nave, my eye somehow was drawn upward to the blindstory along the north wall. But if there had been any slight movement, it must have been a rat's: the vermin plagued us; I had extirpated them from the rectory, but they continued, a few of them, to haunt the church itself.

In my rectory, I paused at Julie's door. The keys to the rectory's interior doors had been lost years ago. Should I knock? Should I simply look in upon her, silently, to make sure she was all right — and for a moment's glimpse of that perfect face in sleep? But restraining myself, I went on to my own whitewashed room (ascetic as any monk's cell), three doors farther on.

The rectory was so well built, and fitted with such heavy doors and draperies, that the Cambodians on the top floor could hear nothing of noise on this ground floor, I reflected.

*   *

On Tuesday morning, the housekeeper served a decent breakfast to Julie and me in the dining-room, so seldom used, musty and sepulchral. I found the young lady surprisingly perceptive; and she could converse animatedly. She was interested in my Church of the Holy Ghost; I, in her charms. Her face helped me somewhat to drive out gross images from my thoughts: its purity was foreign to Hawkhill. The delicate flare of the tall beauty's nostrils! I thought of her dead brother, so like, so different.

She insisted upon combing the city for her brother. It would have been perilous to have taken her walking on the streets of Hawkhill, especially if the remnants of her brother's gang were looking for her. Having persuaded her to visit officialdom instead, I called a taxi and took the darling on a tour of police headquarters, city hall, the central post office, the county coroner's office. Nobody had heard of a youngish man called Alexander Tilton. Of course I did not inquire after a person called Sherman Stanton. Only four Tiltons were listed in the telephone directory, and from downtown we rang up all of those, unavailing.

Sergeant Shaugnessy, Vice and Homicide Squad, gave us half an hour of his time. That visit was risky; but though Shaugnessy stared at Julie fixedly, apparently he could not place the resemblance between this lovely innocent and the worst man in Hawkhill. He told us that if we would come back another day, he would try to go through his 'morgue' of photographs with us. I did not mention that I intended to ship the girl back to Titus before that might occur. Happily Julie did not reveal to the sergeant that her brother's middle name was Sherman — though it is unlikely that he would have been quick-witted enough to make that improbable connection. Also she said nothing about the money he had sent home.

I took her to dinner at a cafeteria downtown, and then we returned to the rectory. Fork stopped by a few minutes after we had got back; we reported to him our failure.

'For all you know, Julie,' said Fork, 'your brother may have moved on east, or west. There's an Amtrak train tomorrow noon that could take you within ten miles of Titus; I stopped by the station. Oh, you know about that? Take it, girl, take it.'

It entered my mind that I did not wish to let her go so soon. She was protesting to Fork that she was ready to stay here a week, if there were any chance of finding brother Sherm.

'There'll be other trains, Fork,' I said. 'Or she could fly back, about the end of this week.'

'And you'll comfort Julie spiritually until then?' Fork inquired, in his most sardonic way. But the girl appeared to catch no imputation. I could have struck Fork.

'Father Montrose already has given me such good advice!' she told the old blind devil. 'He's taken me to see everybody who might know something about Sherm. I don't know what I can ever do to make it up to him for all his trouble.'

I almost said at that point, 'I do know.'

'If you're going to hang on here, Julie,' Fork was telling her, 'don't go outdoors by yourself. Any girl's in danger on these streets, even in daylight — and you in particular, sweet girl graduate of Titus Rural High.'

'Why especially?' Her eyes widened.

Fork ignored that question. 'And if anything should happen to the reverend ecclesiastic here, call a taxi and go to Mrs. Simmons's house. Doc will write down the address for you.'

She was startled and concerned. 'Why, whatever could happen to Father Montrose?'

'Some of the boys at the Mustang Bar have it in for him now, and I'm told they've learned where he lives. That's one thing possible; there are other possibilities. Doc, take out your notepad and give her Mrs. Simmons's address right now.'

I did that.

Julie was puzzled and shaken. 'Ah, well,' I told her, 'that's merely for emergencies which don't happen. But I'll telephone Mrs. Simmons to tell her about you.'

'I'll be off,' Fork said, 'and back tomorrow evening.' Wednesday was his night for prolonged practice on the organ. 'Keep her indoors, Doc. Tell her about Ol' Mister Death putting his bony hands on you here in Hawkhill. And, Doc, exert your will, as you're given to saying in your sermons: don't let anything occupy you.'

384

He sauntered away down Merrymont, tapping past its boarded-up storefronts, its derelict gasoline stations, its fire-gutted mansions, its wastelands of unprofitable parking-lots, a deadly kind man. At the moment I hated him: he surmised too much. Now I most bitterly repent that malign emotion.

It being nearly time for evensong, I must put on my vestments. I conscientiously perform my daily offices, although no one attends my services except on Sundays. Somehow I did not wish to have Julie at my vespers: I suppose now that I sensed, given my growing desire for her, how Julie for a congregation might have made evensong a mockery.

'What shall we do with you while I'm in the church, Julie?' (The phrase itself sounded erotic to me.) 'Possibly you need to write a letter home? Do you play dominoes? Perhaps we'll have a match when I come back.'

Or perhaps we'll have a match of something else, I added for my own delectation, silently. I had begun to lose control of my fancies about this Miss Julie Tilton, kid sister of the pillar of unrighteousness. Othello, Desdemona, and the beast with two backs were only the beginning.

That she was so innocent, and I under a vow, made these prospects yet more attractive. Abelard and Heloise! Or, from *Notre Dame*, the lascivious archdeacon and virginal Esmeralda. I would laugh, toying with her in the beginning, tugging at her long hair. . . .

Fork, the homicidal old devil, damn him, must have sensed my change of mood — my change of character, almost. What had he meant by his 'don't let anything occupy you'? But Fork would not return until tomorrow evening. Meanwhile, Julie and I could have a very lively time. Perhaps. There were risks. . . .

While sinking into these amorous reveries, I had put on my vestments. I was about to enter the church, to celebrate evensong at the apsidal chapel of Saint Thomas of Canterbury, when the electric bell rang at the great doors. The Cambodian couple were out for the evening, at the cinema — a thoughtful suggestion of mine, that. Damn the bell: let it ring! But then, Julie might hear it and foolishly open the postern; Lord knows who might enter. No, I had best respond myself.

I endeavored, while passing through the galilee, to put Julie out of my mind. Her body had become an obsession, all six feet of her young inexperience. My amorous images were turning toward violent acts, in my mind's eye. It was as if the appetites of someone else . . .

Releasing the several locks, I swung open the postern door. A big man stood there. By the light of the small bulb that burns above the door, I made out his face. It was Franchetti, once Sherm's chief enforcer, the man who had accosted Julie in the Mustang the previous night.

Though not so massive as I am, Franchetti was tall and tough: that pleased me. Rather than slamming the door in his face, I said to him, 'Good evening, Mr. Franchetti. You've come to evensong?'

He seemed taken aback at my knowing his name, and he did not understand my invitation. Also he may have been confused as to my identity: as I mentioned earlier, I look different in cassock and surplice.

'Hi, Doc — I mean, Rev,' he began. 'You're the chief honcho here, right? I got a deal to make with you.'

'Do come in, Franchetti.' I stood back to admit him.

The spectacle of the dimly lit galilee obviously bewildered my visitor. To him this splendid Romanesque porch, with its shadows and mysterious columns and many arches, must have seemed like the setting for a horror movie — not that any mere film could be more horrid than Franchetti's own mode of existence. Locking automatically, the door closed behind him.

'You've come to divine worship, Franchetti?'

He snorted. 'Some joker! Rev, we could do you a lot of damage.'

'I'm aware of that, Brother Franchetti. You might even murder me — or try to. It could turn out like your attempt on Causland.'

He stared at me; decided on a new tack. 'Okay, Rev, let's drop that line. I come here to give you money, real money.'

'How much?'

'A thousand bucks, right now, Rev.'

'For the succor of the poor?'

He snorted again. 'If that's the way you like to kid, Rev.'

'Possibly you expect something in exchange?'

'We sure do. You're goin' to give us that young blonde you been amusin' yourself with. You got no claim on her.'

'You have?'

'Sure. Sherm promised her to the boys two years ago, and he took it in the guts, but now we're goin' to collect her.'

'You take her to be Sherm's sister?'

'Sure, Rev. Sherm was goin' to have his kinky fun with her, and then turn her over to us to be eddicated for the street, understand? You didn't never meet Sherm? Well, her and Sherm coulda been identical twins, see, 'cept for differences in the right places. She's our stuff. You already had your pleasure, Rev, with what she's got.'

I sucked in my breath: he had shot near the mark. My adrenalin could not be restrained much longer. Yet I contrived to prolong our conversation for a few moments.

'What makes you say that, dear Brother Franchetti?'

'Hell, Rev, we found out you took in four or five kids, two of 'em our property, for your private use in this here crazyhouse of yours. None of 'em ever showed up on Pentecost again. What'd you do with 'em, Rev? Got 'em chained in the cellar? Buried in the cellar? I hate to think of what you done with them girls, Rev — and one of 'em a gold-mine. Why, you're a public menace. Somebody ought to turn you in to the pigs.'

At this point in our dialogue I burst into laughter, hearty if hysterical. The sound echoed through the crepuscular galilee. Franchetti joined somewhat uneasily in the dismal mirth.

If we poor feeble sinners — of whom I am the chief — are engaged in a holy war against the forces of Satan, we ought to ensure that not all the casualties fall on our side.

'Franchetti,' I said, 'I have been unfair to you. Before you entered this place, I ought to have informed you that from the age of four upward, I was trained in the manly and martial arts by my sergeant-father, at Spanish Town. The door is locked. Do you think you can contrive to get out of this place alive?'

Being an old hand at such encounters, Franchetti reached very swiftly for what he carried within his jacket. Yet I, strung up for this contest, was swifter. I gave him a left in the belly, a right to the jaw, took him by the throat, and pounded his head against the sandstone wall. He collapsed without being able to draw, and I disarmed him. He slumped down to the flags.

'You mistook me for a Creeping Jesus, perhaps,' I remarked. I dragged him up and knocked him down again. Then I proceeded to kick and trample my victim, with truly hellish fury.

I have been in many fights, principally before I was ordained, but never before had I treated a fallen adversary in that fashion. What was it Fork had said? 'Watch out — something might get inside you, Doc'? I didn't care now.

Having unlocked the door, I took the broken man by his ankles and dragged him outside, face down. I pulled him some distance, round the corner to the lane that runs alongside the north wall of the church. A large trash-bin is chained there. In the chill rain, no witnesses passed. Having administered several more kicks to Franchetti, I heaved him into the bin, head down. The garbage truck would find him in the morning, if no one noticed the wreck before then. One more of the mugged would rouse no great sensation in Hawkhill. What Franchetti had done to others, now had been done to him.

On my way back to the postern, I noticed that Franchetti's billfold had fallen on the sidewalk. In it I found nearly two thousand dollars in hundred-dollar bills. The wallet and Franchetti's gun I flung down the opening of a convenient storm-sewer. The bills I stuffed into our poor-box within the galilee, so laying up treasure in heaven for Franchetti.

I felt like Hercules or Thomas à Becket. Should I swagger down to Pentecost Road, seeking out Franchetti's two particular chums, to give them a dose of the same medicine? But I was weary: it was as if abruptly the destructive energy were being drained out of me. Instead I went back into the church, forgetting evensong for the first time, and strode through the cloister to my rectory.

Libido dominandi, for the time being, had driven out a different lust. Besides, exhaustion and disgust had begun to set in. I passed Julie's door, reeled into my own room, and slept in my vestments.

*   *

Before breakfast, Sergeant Shaugnessy telephoned me to report that a man named Franchetti, who had a long criminal record, had been found badly damaged near my church, and now lay in critical condition in Receiving Hospital. He wondered if I had heard anything outside in the street, during the night. I informed him that no sounds penetrated through our great bronze doors. This seemed to satisfy the sergeant, not solicitous for Franchetti's well-being. 'Franchetti's got the d.t.'s,' he informed me. 'He keeps groaning that a nigger preacher who breaks bones took his money and beat his brains out.'

I contrived to be urbane with Julie at breakfast. My ambition to conquer somehow was diminished in the morning; I felt affection more than appetite. We spent the day visiting, by taxi, the city office of the FBI, the state police headquarters, and the hospitals: no discoveries about any Tilton.

But as evening approached, images of concupiscence rose strong again in my head. I arranged for the verger and his wife, to their surprise, a second expedition to the flicks, in a suburb. They protested that the taxis would cost too much; I brushed that aside, handing them forty dollars. I would have Julie at my undisturbed disposal for at least three hours. Miss Tilton would be worth two twenties.

Yet there was Fork to be reckoned with: I had almost forgotten that he would arrive about nine or nine-thirty to practice on the organ. Well, he had no key to the church: let him ring in vain for admittance. I would not be diverted from what Julie had to offer.

I took the trouble to book a taxi, for precisely eight-thirty, to come to the church door and take the Cambodian couple to the suburban movie house. I would take Julie into the church itself, the moment they left: a piquant setting for what I intended. Tuesday night I had enjoyed battering Franchetti in the galilee; this night I would have the relish of sacrilege with Julie in the sanctuary.

I knew what I was doing and just how I would go about everything, rejoicing in outrage. Yet something else in me still protested against this wildness.

About seven o'clock, I went into the church, took some kneeler-cushions from pews, and laid them conveniently before the little altar in the apse-chapel of Thomas of Canterbury. Here I meant to celebrate my peculiar evensong with Julie Tilton.

An interesting architectural feature of my Church of the Holy Ghost is a large entrance, at the crossing, to the crypt. The stair downward, and the balustrades that guard it, are of splendid marble. I am told that this construction closely resembles the approach to the tombs at a church in Padua, which I have not visited.

As I returned from the apse toward the nave, I thought for a moment that I heard a voice down the sepulchral stair. Could it be the verger? My impression of a voice was so strong that I descended into the large low-vaulted crypt. I found everything in order, and no man or woman. My conflict of emotions must be affecting my perceptions. Julie would have to pay for that, in precisely an hour and a half.

The two of us ate a simple dinner in the rectory; I told the Cambodian housekeeper not to bother with the dishes until she came back from the cinema. Julie must have thought my manner odd: I talked confusedly of everything under the sun and the moon — theology, Jamaica, low life in Hawkhill, the bishop, Fork (but there I checked my tongue), Mrs. Simmons, the lonely existence of a celibate. I stared hard at her all the while. Though presumably a little disturbed by my eccentricity, Julie remained pleasant, now and again asking a sensible question, and occasionally a naive one. I must have her.

'I don't suppose you've ever been present at a liturgy of the sort we celebrate in this church, Julie.'

'Oh, no, Father Montrose, I haven't; but I'd just love to.'

'It happens that I have arranged a special evensong liturgy for you alone, Julie. You'll be my whole congregation, a few minutes from now, at our Chapel of Saint Thomas of Canterbury.'

Her assent was delicious. What was to follow might be rather rough on Miss Tilton, but delicious for me. Let the consequences be damned.

I took my prize by the hand and led her to the galilee. My grasp did not startle her; quite possibly she thought it part of the liturgy.

It was nearly half-past eight. The old Cambodian verger was unlocking the postern door.

'Taxi honk, Father,' he told me. 'My wife, she come down in minute.'

I had held open the carved wooden doors to the nave, but Julie hung back. 'Just a minute, Father: I'll say "Have a good time" to the housekeeper when she comes down.'

Gripping her slender hand so that she winced a trifle, I tugged Julie through the entrance to the nave. 'Come on, kid,' I heard myself saying harshly, 'we've got no time to waste.'

'Oh!' she cried.

'What's wrong, Julie, you little fool?'

'It's funny: you sounded just like Sherm then. It could have been his own voice, Father Montrose.'

*   *

We stood at the foot of the central aisle. The Norman pillars of the nave interrupted the beams of dim religious light from such concealed fixtures as I had chosen to switch on. Far ahead of us, a huge ornate sanctuary-lamp shone upon the high altar; and smaller sanctuary-lamps glimmered from the side-chapels.

I squeezed her hand. 'This is going to be a totally new experience for you, Julie. Perhaps you'll not enjoy all of it so much as I intend to.'

'Father, I just know it's going to be marvellous!'

I had begun to lead her down the broad aisle.

Then for the second time I heard a harsh incoherent voice from the crypt-stair near the crossing.

I stopped dead. Julie almost tripped.

'What's wrong, Father?'

'I don't know. . . . What can have spoken?'

'Spoken, Father? I didn't hear anyone at all.'

Then came the first scream, so terrible that I reeled against a bench-end. Ah, the ghastly echoes of it in nave, in aisles, in the choir, back from the blindstory!

'Oh, Father, are you all right? What's happening?'

'My God, Julie, didn't you hear that howl?' I could do no more than whisper the inquiry to her.

'I don't know what you mean. For just the littlest fraction of a second, though, I thought I heard my brother whispering in my ear.'

At that moment, in the dim sanctuary-light, a head emerged above the balustrade of the crypt-stair. Other heads followed it. They seemed like jelly, glistening.

In the horror of that moment, I broke free from the spirit that had entered into me. I knew of a sudden that I had been occupied and made an agent. Whether from shock or from grace, I was enabled to regain my will. Through me, these things from below had schemed to take Julie.

Swinging round, I snatched up Julie and ran with her, bursting through the doors into the galilee. The verger and his wife were going out the door to take the taxi. Upon them I thrust my Julie.

'Drive her to Mrs. Simmons, quick!' I ordered them. It seemed to me as if I were grunting like a hog. 'Quick!' And to Julie, 'Goodbye, my darling. Don't ever come back here!'

Before I slammed the door behind them, I had one last glimpse of her astounded pallid lovely face, forbidden to me ever after.

Then I ran back into the nave, to impede the damned invaders.

*   *

Having emerged from the stair, the things were wavering slowly up the aisle toward me. In their insubstantiality they seemed to shimmer. There came four of them, inexpressibly loathsome. I knew they must be the men who had died on Causland's fork or by his gun.

391

As they drew nearer, I could make out the face of the first only. Lips and nostrils were hideously contorted; yet the resemblance to Julie could not be denied. From four wounds, gouts of blood had run down the thing's middle.

In my extremity I tried to stammer out the Third Collect:

Lighten our darkness, we beseech thee, O Lord, and by Thy great mercy defend us from all perils and dangers of this night, for the love of Thine only Son, our Saviour Jesus Christ.

Yet the words, inaudible, stuck in my craw. Then came the Screamer's second tremendous howl, surely from the Pit. This thing had told his disciples that his essence could transcend space and time.

I clutched a pillar. These 'beasts with the souls of damned men' would overcome me, for too much of them had entered into me already. We were sib.

That second screech was followed by an unbearable silence. The Sherm-thing's tormented face drew nearer mine. He would enter. We would be one.

In that silence rang out the sound of brass upon stone. Fork thrust himself between me and the Screamer. 'Wahoo!'

It seemed to my eyes that Fork leaped twenty feet into the air; lingered suspended there; then returned, laughing as a hyaena laughs.

The four dead things shrank from him. They seemed gelatinous, deliquescent; no words might express the ghastliness of them.

But Fork was all compact, glowing with energy, transfigured and yet in semblance himself, that hard taut face invincible.

'So must you ever be,' said Fork, pointing at the four his blind-man's stick. 'This place and this man are too much for you. Into the fire, Sherm and all!'

They receded. Screaming, they were swept into nothingness. I fell.

* *

If it was consciousness I regained, that was an awareness of the world beyond the world. Incapable of speech or movement, I seemed to be lying in some shadowy cold enclosed unknown place. Was it a sepulchre? The form of Fork Causland — derby, stick, cigar, and all — seemed to stand before me.

'In the hour of need, you were a man, Doc,' he said to me, 'a man in the mold of your friend Thomas à Becket. It was the old Adam in you that admitted those four spirits from below, but the better part in you withstood them. I take off my hat to you' — and so he did, sweepingly, in Fork's sardonic way.

'You'll not see the girl again, Doc, here below, nor Fork Causland. His time came; it would have come more terribly two years ago, had I not occupied him then and thereafter. The end arrived in a moment of grace while he was on his way to reinforce you; and it will be well with poor Fork.'

Though I strove to speak, I failed; the semblance of Fork shook its head. 'Listen. That you should see me without your blood freezing, I have come to you in the mask of your friend Fork. I shall come to you once more, Thomas Montrose — no, priest, I'll not specify the year, the day, the hour, humankind not being able to stand much reality — and then as a friend, civilly inviting you to enter upon eternity. Why, I'll stand then hat in hand before you, Doc, as I stand now. Shall I come in the semblance of Fork Causland, on that occasion too? I would please you.'

Lying rigid with fright, I could not reply to this being. He smiled Fork's stoical humorous smile.

'Do you take me for a demon, Doc? No, I'm not what possessed Sherm, or what came close to possessing you. Through Fork's lips I told you that I was only cousin to devils. I'm a messenger, penetrating Time, taking such shapes as I am commanded: sometimes merciful, sometimes retributory.

'The old Greeks called me Thanatos. The Muslim call me Azrael. You may as well call me — why, Fork will do as well as any other name. Fast and pray, Doc. You have been tried, but not found wanting. In the fullness of time, as our blind friend Fork would have put it, "I'll be seeing you."'

Then he was gone, taking everything with him.

*   *

The ringing telephone on my bedside table woke me. Somehow the returned Cambodian church-mice, taking me to be drunken merely, had contrived to drag me to my bed.

'Reverend Montrose?' the efficient voice of a woman inquired from the receiver. 'Do you know somebody named Homer Causland? We found your name and number in one of his pockets.'

'Yes. Something happened?'

'Mr. Causland was struck by a hit-and-run driver shortly after eight-thirty last night. His body was taken to Receiving Hospital, but there wasn't anything we could do for him here. He didn't suffer. The police have got the driver and booked him for murder. Can you make the arrangements — that is, was Mr. Causland a friend of yours?'

'My only one,' I told her. '*Requiescat in pace.*'

I have sent Julie Tilton's bag by taxi to Mrs. Simmons's big house, and Mrs. Simmons will see that Julie flies home, however bewildered, this evening.

If an energumen from below may penetrate even to the fastness of the church, how shall we prevail? Yet I fast and pray as one should who has been in the company of the dead damned, and has heard the speech of the Death Angel.

In all of us sinners the flesh is weak; and the future, unknowable, has its many contrived corridors and issues. Lord, I am a miserable thing, and I am afraid.

Puffed up with pride of spirit, by which fault fell the angels, I came near to serving the Prince of the Air. From the ravenous powers of darkness, O Lord, let me be preserved; and I entreat thee, do cast the lurking spirits instead, into the swine of Gadara.

For hours I have sat here, meditating, now and again scribbling these pages at my table in the galilee. The coals having expired in the grate, I am cold now.

The race is not to the swift, nor the battle to the strong.

Winter is coming on, this is a night of sleet. What is tapping now, so faintly, at the great knocker on the bronze door? It never can be she. Has the order of release been sent? 'Watch ye, stand fast in the faith, quit you like men, be strong.' I'll unbar the little door. Pray for us sinners now and at the hour of our death.

An Encounter by Mortstone Pond

We die with the dying:
See, they depart, and we go with them.
We are born with the dead:
See, they return, and bring us with them.
The moment of the rose and the moment of the yew-tree
Are of equal duration.

"Little Gidding"

To the north, the little town of Mortstone, in Michigan, is bounded by the old millpond. A long earth-dyke, great willows rooted in it, runs out to the dam of rubble. On a November morning in the year 1919, with thick white mist upon pond and dyke, Gerard Peirce was walking slowly back from the tumult of waters at the dam, toward Sloat's store and the old miller's house on the knoll above the pond.

From the dyke he could see the mellow brick walls of the tall store, star-shaped braces of iron set in those red walls to secure the iron rods that reinforced the brick. A little farther down the winding millpond road stood the white handsome old house that some forgotten purse-proud miller had built in the Greek Revival years: a warm house with recessed porch and pilasters at its entrance, and at the rear a labyrinth of storerooms and rat-plagued woodsheds, clapboard wing appended to clapboard wing.

This had been Gerard's house ever since he had been born. Now he was ten years old, and wishing he were dead.

His father had been killed in France, a year ago; they had buried his mother last week. The lovely house was to be sold, and in a few days he would be sent to San Francisco to live with an aunt. Mr. and Mrs. Sloat had moved into his house to keep him company until then, and he hated the pair. They meant to buy the house, though not the derelict mill.

Two hundred yards to the east of the house began the black cast-iron fence of the old Mortstone graveyard, where Gerard and his mother every spring had swept clean the stones of the early settlers. On the far side of the cemetery stood the tall granite monument to his soldier-father; and now beside that was put the new small blank stone under which his mother lay.

Since his mother's funeral, Gerard had spent his days stubbornly walking first out the dyke to the dam's raging sluices, and then back along the millpond road to the cemetery, where he would sit for hours under a yew close to the Peirce shaft. Mrs. Sloat said reproachfully that such conduct was 'morbid'; but having taken the boy out of school in preparation for the trip to San Francisco, they could think of nothing better for him to do.

Had he loved his mother as she deserved to be loved? How might he have loved her enough, within himself? He could do nothing at all about that, now.

He stared at the classical lines of his house as he idled along the dyke, trying to fix every detail in his memory. Great masses of maple leaves lay upon the lawns. They too were dead. His mother and he would light no more bonfires on Hallowe'en.

He was wholly and forever alone. There could come no relief, ever, from his misery. He had prayed by his mother's bedside in her pretty room for a month, as she lay dying, and in her agony comforting her little son so far as she could. 'You must grow up, my darling, to be the sort of man your father was,' she had told him. Tears began to run down his face again; he did not trouble to brush them away. The thing to do — he had felt this impulse before — was to dash back along the dyke and go over the dam.

Then, most abruptly, a chill ran all through him. In horror, Gerard became aware that he was not alone. Someone who could not be seen now walked beside him on the dyke. He could have hugged his mother's ghost, he had thought, should *she* have come to him; but now he was ice.

He could hear no footsteps, and could see only faint drifting curls of pond mist; yet he was aware of a dread pacing presence, not palpable. Gerard forced himself to walk stiffly onward: perhaps if he paid the thing no heed, it would drift away. Nevertheless, the presence continued to accompany him. He could not cry out, shriek for help, though he wished to.

It was not his mother: no, this was a man, this presence, or something like a man. An angel, a devil?

Now certain words from without were impressed upon his consciousness — although no voice sounded in his ears, as speech is heard. Amidst the terror and the wonder of this encounter, somehow he contrived to grasp the meaning of what was being communicated to him.

The silent words ran to this effect: 'The pain will end, boy, or nearly end. This too shall pass. You will grow to be a man. They will love you always, being made for eternity.'

No more words penetrated to his consciousness. Yet he felt, or thought he felt, the faintest pressure upon his right hand, for the tiniest moment. Though no voice had sounded without, in some manner the words had possessed a tone, a timbre, grave and heartening. That tone and timbre had not been his father's, so far as he could recall his father's voice.

The dreadful cold ebbed out of the boy's mind and body, but awe remained. On he walked, the presence accompanying him to the slope where the dyke merged into the knoll. There, abruptly as it had come, the presence departed — although how he knew this, he never could explain to himself in later years.

Gerard was weak in his knees; yet in his daze he began to run, so fast as he was able, past the store, the miller's house, the white pines that lined the way to the graveyard. Gasping, he knelt by his mother's blank tombstone and prayed as his mother had taught him to pray.

His father's shaft cast its long shadow upon him. He had spelled out the words of its inscription a half-dozen times; now he did so again.

SACRED TO THE MEMORY OF JEROME PEIRCE
1889-1918
CAPTAIN OF INFANTRY

Still seems it strange, that thou shouldst live forever?
Is it less strange, that thou shouldst live at all?
This is a miracle; and that no more.

Gerard puzzled over the lines; he would puzzle over them from time to time in the course of an eventful and violent life, long after the little uncanny episode on the dyke had been forgotten — or had settled into a most remote corner of his memory.

The boy kissed his mother's headstone, pulled his shoulders back as his father had done, and left the graveyard. The communication on the dyke had nerved him. Three days later, commended to a conductor, he was put on the train to Chicago; relatives there kept him overnight and saw him aboard the train to San Francisco. 'The pain will end, or nearly end,' he kept repeating silently, across plains, mountains, deserts. And as he grew up, self-reliant and quiet, the pain of parting indeed was deadened — or locked away and forgotten, for the sake of survival.

*   *

On a November morning in the year 1969, Major General Gerard Peirce, or what was left of him, walked stiffly along the dyke leading to the dam at Mortstone pond. The huge willow trees were dying of extreme old age; fog shrouded them mercifully. His artificial leg troubled the General somewhat this morning, as it did many mornings. He had been a year in hospital.

He had lost the leg at Hué, and much more damage had been done to his body there. When he was released from the hospital, the doctors had told him, with such tact as they possessed, that he ought to put his affairs in order.

His wife had learned to live without him during those unending years in Indo-China; he had been with her only twice, on brief furloughs, all that long while. His return to her at last, he all appliances and scars, must have been to Sally the rising of a phantom. In his long absence, their children had been reared, schooled, married. Perhaps in eternity this wife and this husband would know one the other as in some remote past they had loved; but it was otherwise here below.

Discontent in San Francisco, he had thought of the town he had not seen since he was ten years old. Had anyone ever cut an inscription upon his mother's stone? Sally had raised no objection to his flying to Michigan merely a fortnight after their reunion; she had not inquired as to when, precisely, he would come back to her. At the San Francisco airport, he had detected in her eyes some pity and some terror.

Mortstone, like nearly all the world, had been altered mightily in half a century, and not for the better. The heart of the town had been urban-renewed nearly out of existence; a tremendous interstate highway cut off the Lower Town from the rest of the place.

Yet his boyhood's Lower Town, near the millpond, had been spared, to his surprised pleasure. The mill had been demolished, and the willows were senile, but otherwise Time had been kindly. Sloat's tall store still remained, though vacant. What mattered most was the miller's house. It stood in neat repair, occupied by somebody or other, praise be — even if the nethermost woodshed had been swept away and a brown brick chimney, erected to the south side, marred the symmetry of the temple-house.

Descending the slope with some difficulty, Gerard Peirce had limped all the way out to the dam. There he had rested for a quarter of an hour, dreamily watching the river spout and gurgle through the sluices; he might have been Heraclitus, musing there. But why reproach the river of Time? He had loved, fought, gloried in his victories, endured with some fortitude his defeats. Life is for action, some philosopher had written; well, Gerard Peirce had known plenty of action. He had succeeded in life, in that he had done what his dying mother had instructed him to do: to become such a man as his father had been.

Now for the graveyard — a *double entente*, that. The General rose from the damp bench and turned back down the dyke-path toward his old house and the little-visited cemetery beyond it. He would walk the whole way, ache or no ache. 'It's a question of who's to be master, that's all' — his broken body, or his will.

He had trudged nearly halfway to the knoll when there ran through him a thrill far stronger than the pain in his stump. For someone unseen was walking beside him. He very nearly cried out.

Did the mist suggest some small form? No sound came to him but the rushing and splashing from the dam. His hearing and his eyesight had suffered at Hué. Yet he did not require keenness of eye and ear to know that he was accompanied.

What walked beside him, a sense beyond the senses informed the General, was a being intensely miserable, abandoned to despair. The General, long familiar with death in many forms, steeled himself to respond to a dumb appeal. After what he had seen and done in other lands, no bodiless companion could affright him — or so the General endeavored to assure himself.

The thing beside him was like one of his own men ripped up by automatic fire, or like a broken adversary begging for mercy. It was — was it a boy of ten, in agony of spirit?

Words came into the General's head, and after some choking in his throat he managed to utter them.

'The pain will end, boy, or nearly end. This too shall pass. You will grow to be a man. They will love you always, being made for eternity.'

He reached out with his good left hand. Was it an illusion that for the briefest possible moment, flesh encountered flesh?

No intelligible response came — no word, no touch, unless that faintest of hand-sensations was the ghost of a touch — but a kind of sympathetic warmth crept through the General's infirm chilled body. The invisible boy continued by his side until the foot of the knoll was reached. And then what had been little despairing Gerard Peirce, perhaps heartened, was swept away by the current of Time.

* *

General Peirce found himself now within the neglected graveyard, scarcely able to account for having made his heavy painful way so far.

The marvels of time, of consciousness, of personality, nearly undid him. He sank down before his father's granite shaft.

We are essences, the General thought, essences that flow like mercury. Each of us is a myriad of particles of energy, held temporarily in combination by purposes or forces we understand no better than did Lucretius.

We are essences — but insubstantial really, such stuff as dreams are made of, not understanding death because we do not know what life is. Across the gulf of years, had the boy who was to be a man and the man who had been a boy met in some fashion? Had a conscience spoken briefly to a conscience?

Personality is a mask; the soul seems indefinable. What gives coherence to our essences? In erring reason's spite, the General wondered, am I a part of that once-venerated Mystical Body?

He looked up at his father's shaft. Fleshly life is a miracle, Young's lines told him in the deep-cut inscription; so is the life eternal. The encounter beside the millpond of two aspects of a self had been miraculous — and numbing, as is the way with miracles.

Did those few words of assurance my older self gave to my younger

400

self really issue from *me?* Or were they put into my consciousness by a tender Other?

Gerard Peirce of the later years limped the few feet to his mother's grave, and went down on his knees to pray, as he had done half a century before. Someone — surely not those Sloats — had graven an inscription upon her stone! Perhaps those Detroit cousins on the distaff side? They had taken her epitaph from a twentieth-century poet:

REQUIESCAT IN PACE
MARJORIE JOHNSON PEIRCE
1890-1919

And what the dead had no speech for, when living,
They can tell you, being dead: the communication
Of the dead is tongued with fire
Beyond the language of the living.

RESURGAM

A Cautionary Note
on the Ghostly Tale

Elaborated from certain encounters of mine with life and death, these stories were not written for children. Some of my perceptions, impressions, or experiences occurred three or four decades ago — which dusty fact accounts for the very modest prices and wages incidentally mentioned in a number of my yarns. Worse, a few of my stage-settings and backgrounds — from Los Angeles to Stari Bar, from Pittenweem to Marrakesh — have been knocked about, since I wrote, by urban renewers and other misguided evangels of progress.

Such nostalgic archaism (though unintended when I wrote these stories) has its literary advantages. As M. R. James remarked while praising Sheridan Le Fanu, 'The ghost story is in itself a slightly old-fashioned form; it needs some deliberateness in the telling; we listen to it the more readily if the narrator poses as elderly, or throws back his experience to "some thirty years ago."'

Alarming though (I hope) readers may find these tales, I did not write them to impose meaningless terror upon the innocent. The political ferocity of our age is sufficiently dismaying: men of letters need not conjure up horrors worse than those suffered during the past decades by Cambodians and Ugandans, Afghans and Ethiopians.

What I have attempted, rather, are experiments in the moral imagination. Readers will encounter elements of parable and fable. Gerald Heard said to me once that the good ghost story must have for its kernel some clear premise about the character of human existence — some theological premise, if you will. Literary naturalism is not the only path to apprehension of reality. All important literature has some ethical end; and the tale of the preternatural — as written by George Macdonald, C. S. Lewis, Charles Williams, and other masters — can be an instrument for the recovery of moral order.

The better uncanny stories are underlain by a healthy concept of the character of evil. Defying nature, the necromancer conjures up what ought not to rise again this side of Judgment Day. But these dark powers do not rule the universe: by bell, book, and candle, symbolically at least, we can push them down under.

Because the limbo of the occult has no defined boundaries, remaining *terra incognita* interiorly, the imaginative writer's fancy can wander there unburdened by the impedimenta of twentieth-century naturalism. For symbol and allegory, the shadow-world is a better realm than the mechanized empire of science fiction. The story of the supernatural or the mystical can disclose aspects of human conduct and human longing to which the positivistic psychologist has blinded himself. The more talented fabulists of the occult and the crepuscular — among these Mircea Eliade and Robert Aickman, in their different fashions — piece together into a pattern those hints and glimpses offered fragmentarily by mystical vision, second sight, hauntings, dreams, wondrous coincidences.

As a literary form, then, the uncanny tale can be a means for expressing truths enchantingly. But I do not ask the artist of the fantastic to turn didactic moralist; and I trust that he will not fall into the error that the shapes and voices half-glimpsed and half-heard are symbols *merely*. For the sake of his art, the teller of ghostly narrations ought never to enjoy the freedom from fear. As Samuel Johnson lived in dread of real torment beyond the grave — not mere 'mental anguish' — so the 'invisible prince,' Le Fanu, archetype of the literary men of this genre, is believed to have died literally of fright. He knew that his creations were not his inventions merely, but glimpses of the abyss.

In an era of the decay of religious belief, can fiction of the supernatural or preternatural, with its roots in myth and transcendent perception, succeed in being anything better than playful or absurd? The lingering domination of yesteryear's materialistic and mechanistic theories in natural science persuades most people that if they have encountered inexplicable phenomena — why, they must have been mistaken. How is it possible to perceive a *revenant* if there cannot possibly be *revenants* to perceive?

Take George Orwell. In 1931 he wrote to a friend 'about a ghost I saw in Walberswick cemetery.' He described his encounter in considerable detail, including a plan of church and graveyard. But he concluded, 'Presumably an hallucination.' Ghosts did not square with Orwell's rather belligerent denial of the possibility of the life eternal. Yet he would have liked to believe. And what is an hallucination? On reading Orwell's letter, I was reminded of an acquaintance of mine who accounted for several astounding simultaneous occurrences in a house as 'entropy.' What is entropy? I inquired. 'Oh, things like that.' A scientific term sufficed him.

Most people nowadays continue to share Orwell's uneasy rejection of 'psychic' phenomena. An English *aficionada* of the ghostly tale instructs us at considerable length that the ghost story has died: Sigmund Freud slew the poor thing. Wisdom began and ended with Freud.

But did it? C. G. Jung's theories about psychic phenomena differed radically from Freud's. Startling personal experience converted Jung from his previous belief that such phenomena were subjective 'unconscious projections' to his later conviction that 'an exclusively psychological approach' cannot suffice for study of psychic phenomena of the ghostly variety. And no wonder! For while Jung was staying in an English country house, there abruptly appeared on his pillow 'the head of an old woman whose right eye, wide open, was staring at me. The left half of her face, including the eye, was missing. I leapt out of bed and lit a candle' — at which point the head vanished.

Although a vulgarized Freudianism remains popular today, as an intellectual force Freudianism is nearly spent. The philosophical and ideological currents of a period necessarily affecting its imaginative literature, the supernatural in fiction has seemed ridiculous to most, nearly all this century. Yet as the rising generation regains the awareness that 'nature' is something more than mere fleshly sensation, and that something may lie above human nature, and something below it — why, the divine and the diabolical rise up again in serious literature. In this renewal of imagination, fiction of the preternatural and the occult may have a part. *Tenebrae* are woven into human nature, despite all that meliorists declare.

'We have heard a whole chorus of Nobel Laureates in physics informing us that matter is dead, causality is dead, determinism is dead,' Arthur Koestler wrote in 1972. 'If that is so, let us give them a decent burial, with a requiem of electronic music. It is time for us to draw the lessons from twentieth century post-mechanistic science, and to get out of the straitjacket which nineteenth century materialism imposed on our philosophical outlook.'

Amen to that. Our literary assumptions and modes, like our philosophical outlook, were oppressed by the heavy hand of 'scientific' materialism and mechanism, which regime in effect denied the existence of souls. It becomes possible to admit once more the reality of a realm of spirit. It does not follow necessarily that we will acquire a great deal more knowledge about shadowland. 'The limitations of our biological equipment may condemn us to the role of Peeping Toms at the keyhole of eternity,' Koestler concludes his slim book *The Roots of Coincidence*. 'But at least let us take the stuffing out of the keyhole, which blocks even our limited view.'

A reason why I write stories like those in this present collection — aside from the fun of the process, which scandalizes — is that I aspire to help extract the stuffing from the keyhole. The tales in this volume have retributive ghosts, malign magicians, blind angels, beneficent phantoms, conjuring witches, demonic possession, creatures of the twilight, divided selves. I present them to you unabashed. They may impart some arcane truths about good and evil: as Chesterton put it, all life is an allegory, and we can understand it only in parable.

But let me say also that my bogles are not to be taken lightly. I could offer you True Relations — my own experiences, or those of friends — quite as startling as my fictional narratives, though more fragmentary and inconclusive. I do tell such 'true ghost stories' aloud to audiences; but the True Relation, a sudden puzzling phenomenon, does not make by itself a polished piece of humane letters; it must be embroidered and enlarged by literary art, to be worth printing.

No one ever has satisfactorily supported by evidence a general theory accounting for ghostly apparitions and similar phenomena. Yet a mass of testimony from all countries and all ages exists to inform us that strange happenings beyond the ordinary course of life and matter have occurred at irregular intervals and in widely varied circumstances.

Possibly we never will understand the character of such phenomena better than we do already. Suppose, suggests C. E. M. Joad, that we appoint a sober committee of three to sit in the haunted room at midnight and take notes of the appearance of the reputed ghost. But suppose also that one of the conditions essential for the occurrence of this particular phenomenon is that there *not* be present a sober committee of three: well, then, the very scientific method has precluded the possibility of reaching a scientific determination. Our human faculties may not suffice to extract the stuffing from the keyhole. If so, our mere inadequacy does not prove that nothing lies beyond the keyhole. From behind that locked door still may come thumps and moans, which some of us hear better than others do. It is well to be skeptical in such concerns — skeptical of the 'light at the end of the tunnel' enthusiasts, but equally skeptical of the old-fogy doctrinaire mechanists.

Enough: I do not intend to let this preface to grimly amusing tales become a didactic treatise on a shrouded huge subject. I am merely a humble follower in the steps of Defoe, Scott, Coleridge, Stevenson, Kipling, the Sitwells; of Hawthorne, Poe, Henry James, Edith Wharton — and many other writers of high talent who did not blush to fancy that something may lurk on the other side of the keyhole. If I bring discredit upon their genre, I will deserve to be hounded to my doom by James Thurber's monster the Todal (who, in *The Thirteen Clocks*, smells like long-unopened rooms, and gleeps), 'an agent of the Devil, sent to punish evildoers for having done less evil than they should.'

Nearly all these tales were published in periodicals or anthologies, over the years: *Fantasy and Science Fiction, London Mystery Magazine, The Critic, World Review, Frights, Dark Forces, Whispers, New Terrors*. They were written in haunted St. Andrews, in the Isle of Eigg, at Kellie Castle, at Balcarres House, at Durie House (which has the most persistent of all country-house spectres), and at my ancestral spooky house at Mecosta, Michigan — this last house totally destroyed by fire on Ash Wednesday, 1975; also nocturnally in my silent library (once a factory) at Mecosta.

These lines are written at the hour of three, the witching hour, when most men's energies are at ebb, 'in the silent croaking night,' a cricket for company. 'The small creatures chirp thinly through the dust, through the night.' Pray for us scribbling sinners now and at the hour of our death.

RUSSELL KIRK
Piety Hill
Mecosta, Michigan

406